CREDIBLE
THREAT

ALSO BY J.A. JANCE

ALI REYNOLDS MYSTERIES

Edge of Evil
Web of Evil
Hand of Evil
Cruel Intent
Trial by Fire
Fatal Error
Left for Dead
Deadly Stakes
Moving Target
A Last Goodbye (**A Novella**)
Cold Betrayal
No Honor Among Thieves (**A Novella**)
Clawback
Random Acts (**A Novella**)
Man Overboard
Duel to the Death
The A List

JOANNA BRADY MYSTERIES

Desert Heat
Tombstone Courage
Shoot/Don't Shoot
Dead to Rights
Skeleton Canyon
Rattlesnake Crossing
Outlaw Mountain
Devil's Claw
Paradise Lost
Partner in Crime
Exit Wounds
Dead Wrong
Damage Control
Fire and Ice
Judgment Call
The Old Blue Line (**A Novella**)
Remains of Innocence
No Honor Among Thieves (**A Novella**)
Random Acts (**A Novella**)
Downfall
Field of Bones

J.P. BEAUMONT MYSTERIES

Until Proven Guilty
Injustice for All
Trial by Fury
Taking the Fifth
Improbable Cause
A More Perfect Union
Dismissed with Prejudice
Minor in Possession
Payment in Kind
Without Due Process
Failure to Appear
Lying in Wait
Name Withheld
Breach of Duty
Birds of Prey
Partner in Crime
Long Time Gone
Justice Denied
Fire and Ice
Betrayal of Trust
*Ring in the Dead (**A Novella**)*
Second Watch
*Stand Down (**A Novella**)*
Dance of the Bones
*Still Dead (**A Novella**)*
Proof of Life
Sins of the Fathers

WALKER FAMILY MYSTERIES

Hour of the Hunter
Kiss of the Bees
Day of the Dead
Queen of the Night
Dance of the Bones

POETRY

After the Fire

CREDIBLE THREAT

AN ALI REYNOLDS MYSTERY

J.A. JANCE

Gallery Books

New York London Toronto Sydney New Delhi

Gallery Books
An Imprint of Simon & Schuster, Inc.
1230 Avenue of the Americas
New York, NY 10020

GALLERY BOOKS and colophon are registered trademarks of Simon & Schuster, Inc.

Design by Erika Genova

Manufactured in the United States of America

ISBN 978-1-9821-3107-4

For Joe and Kathy K.,
make new friends

CREDIBLE
THREAT

|PROLOGUE|

On a mid-March afternoon as the sun drifted down over Piestewa Peak, seventy-year-old Rachel Higgins wrapped her sweater more tightly around her body and took another sip of her vodka tonic. Snowbirds might be running around dressed in Bermuda shorts, Hawaiian shirts, flip-flops, and sandals, but for Rachel—a Phoenix native and true desert dweller—mid-March still counted as winter.

Even so, she wasn't ready to go inside, not just yet. For one thing there was nothing to go in for other than another evening of mindlessly viewing whatever empty-headed crap happened to be on TV. No, she was better off staying outside, savoring the luscious perfume of orange blossoms from the trees in the yard next door and appreciating the fact that her neighbors' dim-bulb Chihuahua wasn't outside barking his head off.

Rachel had long since become immune to the rumble of rush-hour traffic on State Route 51 and Highway 101 in the near distance. Back in the eighties, at the time Rachel and her husband, Rich, had bought the place on Menadota Drive, the nearby mountain, formerly known as Squaw Peak, had not yet been renamed Piestewa Peak in honor of Lori Piestewa, a young Hopi woman who during the Gulf War had become the first Native American woman ever to die while serving in the U.S. military.

When Rachel and Rich first moved to the neighborhood, both the 101 and the 51 had barely been a gleam in the eye of some crazed highway engineer. Now the name Squaw Peak was no more, and what had once been a serenely quiet desert landscape was perpetually overwhelmed by the unrelenting roar of 24/7 traffic.

This had been their dream home back then—one of the first houses to be built in a newly created subdivision. The house was a far cry from the modest bungalow off Seventh Avenue and Indian School that had been their first home. No, this one was spacious inside and out. Rich had told her at the time that a lot at the end of the cul-de-sac would be plenty big enough to accommodate a pool, and five years later they had one. At the time it had seemed as though their family life was coming to order at last. Rich had just earned an amazing promotion as an engineer at the Salt River Project, one that had made their purchase of the new place financially feasible. As for Rachel? At age thirty-six, after years of trying, a miracle had happened and she managed to get pregnant. On the day they moved into their new house, her precious son, David, was a babe in arms.

Rachel had been ecstatic with the way things were turning out. Although she'd taught school to pay the bills while Rich finished his degree, she'd never wanted to be anything but a housewife and mother. That's why she'd majored in home ec in college. *Was that major even an option these days?* she wondered. Rachel didn't know, but that's exactly what Rich had wanted back then, too—a stay-at-home mother and housewife—and Rachel had settled into her chosen profession with enthusiasm.

Rachel's father, Max, had been an accountant as well as a mousy little man with a propensity for letting people walk all over him. Her mother had been glad to spend his CPA earnings, all the while calling him a milquetoast behind his back. Naturally Rachel had gone looking for a different family dynamic, and Rich Higgins had turned out to be her father's polar opposite. Even though he was five years younger than she, Rich had taken charge of their marriage, calling the shots in a "my way or the highway" fashion. That had worked fine in the beginning, but what happens when the guy calling the shots loses his bearings? What are you supposed to do then?

Once Rich got his degree in civil engineering, he became the sole breadwinner. He handled all the finances, most of the time without con-sulting Rachel. Since he'd been making good money, his running the financial show hadn't been an issue—until it was. At age sixty, when given a choice between retiring early or being fired, he had opted for the former and hadn't said a word to Rachel about it until after it was a done deal. It was several years before Rachel figured out that his having started his pension so young meant their retirement income amounted to far less than expected.

When things began getting tight, Rachel had offered to try going back to work, but Rich nixed the idea. No wife of his was going to work outside the home. They would survive on the money he brought home come hell or high water. It was what they'd agreed on to begin with, and that was the way it would be.

And what had Rachel done about that? Absolutely nothing. In her sixties she had somehow morphed into a female version of her father. She'd let Rich have his way and gone along with the program. Besides, when it came to entering the workforce after an almost forty-year absence, what could she do? Go back to teaching school? Hardly. Schools were a mess these days. Office work? Not likely. She could manage her laptop well enough to find information and send the occasional e-mail. But she was far from computer-literate, and her typing skills were limited to the hunt-and-peck variety. She could have looked for a job as a salesclerk, she supposed, but she couldn't imagine standing behind a cash register for eight hours a day scanning other people's groceries at Safeway or AJ's Fine Foods.

In the end it had been easier for her to be complicit and go with the flow. She and Rich had made their bed together, and they were lying in it together as well. Except that wasn't entirely true. They slept in separate bedrooms now. Rachel had the master, and Rich slept down the hall in the room that had once been David's. They woke at different times and went to sleep at different times. The meals they ate together were generally consumed in silence. They were more like roommates than husband and wife. Was Rich as unhappy as Rachel was? Maybe, but it wasn't something they discussed, because they mostly didn't talk.

At this point Rachel was bored. She'd had a few flirtations here and there, but her outside relationships had never gone beyond that. Dealing with one man was quite enough, thank you very much! Had she thought about getting a divorce? Not really. For one thing they couldn't afford it. For another, despite the fact that neither she nor Rich had attended Mass in years, she still regarded herself as a Catholic, meaning that divorce was out of the question. She would do the same thing her mother had done and stick it out to the bitter end.

Once Rich's Social Security checks started coming in, those, too, were lower than they would have been had he started collecting benefits later. While Rich was still working, they'd spent (Rich said squandered) big chunks of their retirement savings sending David off to one useless rehab outfit after another. Now, though, all that missing money loomed large. As the reality of their financial situation came into focus and they were forced to cut one corner after another, Rachel didn't dare complain, because she'd been the one who had insisted on investing so much cash in David's drug issue. Instead she stuck to her part of what was now an increasingly bad bargain. She looked after the house, read the books she dragged home from the library each week, perused her online newspapers, watched TV, and otherwise lived the life of a hermit—or at least the life of a hermit's wife.

The shabby cars they drove—her aging Mercedes and his Cadillac Escalade—were ten and fifteen years old respectively—but at least they still worked. Years of being parked in direct sunlight in the driveway meant that their exterior paint jobs had faded to powder, and the interiors were ragged with drooping headliners and sun-damaged upholstery. However, at this point the idea of buying a new car was totally out of the question.

As their mandatory belt-tightening continued, the social life Rachel had always taken for granted simply disappeared—restaurant meals, golf outings, casual gatherings with friends, going to movies, standing appointments at her favorite nail salon. It came as a real blow when Rachel had been forced to let her longtime cleaning lady go. They still had a yard man and a pool guy, but only because the homeowners' association would have come after them if they'd let those slide, and Rich adamantly refused to do the work himself. He was too busy—making birdhouses!

With mourning doves cooing in the background, Rachel thought about how things had been when they'd first moved here as opposed to how things were now. The lot their house was on had been one of the first to be carved out of open desert. Shortly after moving in, Rachel had discovered that the lot's original inhabitants were none too happy about ceding their long-held territory to a bunch of annoying interlopers.

As a toddler, David had never been allowed to play outside alone without his eagle-eyed mother watching over him. On more than one occasion, Rachel had wielded a hoe to dispatch rattlesnakes that had somehow slithered into the yard. In addition to snakes, there'd been a plethora of centipedes and scorpions, but Rachel had signed on to protect her child from all comers, and that's exactly what she did.

When it came time for David to go to school, she had cheerfully donned her chauffeur's hat and driven him back and forth to a small, newly established parochial school at St. Bartholomew's Church on Shea Boulevard several miles to the south. She'd been responsible for taking him everywhere he needed to go—Boy Scout meetings, Little League games, and swim lessons—because that's what she'd signed up for, to raise her son, to take care of him and see that he thrived. But then . . . She shook her head. How on earth could it all have gone so terribly wrong?

The slider was open, so when the doorbell rang inside, she could hear it out in the yard. Later Rachel would think of that sound as something her high school drama coach, Miss Reavis, would have called a "knocking within" when, at a critical juncture in a play, an offstage character announces his arrival with some kind of racket and brings with him an important piece of compelling information that will propel the story to its final conclusion. Over the next several months, Rachel finally came to realize that's exactly what the ringing doorbell had been that day—the crucial tipping point that had turned everything in her life upside down. At the time, however, it was nothing more than an unwelcome infringement on her solitary afternoon cocktail.

There was no question about Rich emerging from his workshop long enough to answer the door. Even if he'd heard the bell, he wouldn't have bothered bestirring himself from behind his workbench. And that was Rachel's initial reaction, too—that she would simply ignore the ringing bell until whoever this unwelcome visitor was would finally give up and go away. After all, how important could it be?

In the old days, a caller this late in the afternoon might have been a paperboy out collecting from customers on his route, but Rich had stopped subscribing to paper-and-ink newspapers long ago. Since this was March, it might be one of the Brownies from up the street out peddling Girl Scout cookies. Or it might even be some political hack out canvassing the neighborhood, looking for votes in an upcoming municipal election.

The doorbell rang again, but still Rachel didn't move. After a minute or so, it rang a third time. Obviously whoever was at the door wasn't giving up or going away. They probably assumed that, with two cars parked out front, someone had to be home. Only then did Rachel finally get up to go to the door. In the front entry, she paused long enough to peer through the peephole. What she saw on the front porch was a heavily tattooed young woman wearing jeans and a T-shirt and holding a banker's box. She was a twenty-something from the looks of it, so she was most definitely not out hawking Girl Scout cookies.

Once Rachel unlatched the dead bolt and security chain, she swung the door open. "Yes?"

"Are you Mrs. Higgins?"

"I am," Rachel responded.

"David Higgins's mother?"

"Yes," Rachel replied. "I'm David's mother. Who are you, and what do you want?"

"My name's Tonya Bounds," the young woman said. "My dad was Jake Bounds, and I came to give you this."

She held out the box, but Rachel made no move to accept it.

"Who's Jake Bounds?" she asked.

"After my folks divorced, my father took in boarders for a while," Tonya answered. "I'm guessing your son must have rented a room from him at one time or another. My father died a couple of months ago. My boyfriend and I have been helping Mom get the house ready to sell. The place was a mess. We found this box in a corner of the garage with your son's name on it. Inside was a copy of his obituary. I found your address, but when I tried calling, the phone had been disconnected."

"Yes," Rachel said, "we gave up having a landline years ago."

"I didn't know if you still lived at the same address, but since it's on my way home, I decided to take a chance and try dropping by."

"What's in the box?" Rachel asked.

Tonya shrugged. "Not much, just a few things David left behind. I'm not sure why my dad bothered saving it. There's a comb and brush, some clothing, and a pair of shoes, along with some other odds and ends—a class ring, a picture from Disneyland, and a school yearbook. Just random stuff, I guess."

Relenting, Rachel reached out and took the box. When she did so, she found it to be far lighter than she'd expected.

"Thank you for going to the trouble of tracking us down to deliver it."

"You're welcome," Tonya said with a smile. "Like I said. Your address is on my way. I live just south of the Scottsdale city limits in Tempe."

"If you don't mind my asking, what did your father die of?"

Tonya's smile faded and she shrugged. "An overdose," she answered bleakly. "What else? That's what caused Mom and Dad to split up in the first place. Dad was in and out of rehab time and again. He lasted longer than anyone thought he would, but still . . ." She paused for a moment before adding, "But then I'm guessing you know that drill."

Rachel nodded. "I guess I do," she agreed, "and it's no fun. So sorry for your loss."

Tonya turned to go. Rachel remained on the front porch long enough to watch the young woman drive off before going back inside, closing and latching the door behind her. Initially she started toward the kitchen with the box before changing her mind and heading for her bedroom instead.

David's untimely death was what had plunged Rich into his pit of despair in the first place. To this day even the mention of their son's name was enough to provoke a quarrel. Rather than leaving the box out in the open, Rachel tucked it into the back corner of her closet and shut the door. When she returned to the kitchen, she was surprised to find Rich there, making himself a bologna sandwich.

The way things were these days, Rachel no longer bothered with cooking nutritious meals. Chances were, Rich wouldn't be interested in eating them in any case. Instead they subsisted on a steady diet of cold cereal and sandwiches. Rachel's natural metabolism still served her in good stead. Rich's didn't. In the past seven years, he'd gained at least fifty pounds, probably more. She hadn't said anything about it, though. If he didn't care, why should she?

"Who was that at the door?" he asked.

She wanted to say, *Why didn't you answer the damned door yourself?*—but she didn't. "Magazine salesman," she replied, lying to him without the slightest hesitation. "I told him we didn't want any."

"Good," he said. "We don't."

With that, Rich collected his sandwich along with a bottle of Bud Light and returned to the garage without bothering to clean up his mess. Rachel did so because that's what she always did—clean up after him. Then, rather than making herself a sandwich, she poured another vodka tonic. Before she would be able to face the contents of David's box, she'd need some of what her mother had always referred to as "Dutch courage."

It wasn't until much later that night, after Rich had retreated to his room without a word to Rachel and after his TV set was blaring behind his closed door, that Rachel, more than slightly drunk, finally meandered down the hall to her own room, where she closed the door, pulled the banker's box out of the closet, and moved it to her bed.

When she lifted the lid, the first thing she saw, of course, was the obituary and the printed program from the funeral home—the one that had been handed out to people attending the service. That meant Tonya's father had been enough of a friend that he'd actually gone to the funeral, but Rachel had been in so much pain at the time that she had no real recollection of that day—not of the service itself or of the small number of people who'd bothered showing up. Jake Bounds might have lived and died a druggie, but he'd been kind enough to preserve David's paltry collection of belongings, and Rachel was grateful for that.

Just under the yellowed newspaper clipping and funeral program was David's moth-eaten letterman's jacket from Scottsdale's St. Francis High School. David had been an outstanding athlete. He'd lettered in basketball and swimming all four years. He'd played point guard on both the JV and varsity basketball teams and had been captain of the swim team his senior year when St. Francis had walked away with the state championship. He'd been smart, too. He should have gone on to college, but he hadn't. Rachel had never understood why David had simply turned his back on the idea of continuing his education, although Rich claimed it was because he was too much of a "mama's boy." The night David had told them once and for all that he was done with school, father and son had gotten into a terrible row.

"Do you have any idea what you're doing?" a livid Rich had demanded. "Don't you care anything about your future?"

"No," David had replied. "I don't."

He packed up his things that very night and moved out of the house. As far as Rachel knew, he'd never again stepped inside a classroom. He'd held a series of menial jobs, but mostly he'd hung out and done drugs, drifting deeper and deeper into that world until there was no coming back. A heartbroken Rachel had tried reaching out to him from time to time, insisting that they help with rehab. Rich had stayed clear. Once David was dead, Rachel had the advantage of having already processed some of her grief. Rich, on the other hand, had been utterly broken. Paralyzed with guilt and unable to cope at work or at home, he'd fallen into an endless downward spiral and had been stuck there ever since.

Rachel unfolded the jacket and held it up to her face, hoping that some trace of David's scent might linger in the fabric. It did not. All she smelled was dust with just a hint of motor oil in the background. Laying the jacket aside, she returned to the box. Next up were a few shirts, two worn pairs of Levi's, and a broken-down pair of Nikes. At the bottom of the box, she found the odds and ends Tonya had mentioned.

The first of those was the photo from Disneyland. Rachel picked it up and studied it for a long while. David had been seven at the time—the perfect age to go to Disneyland—and the trip really had been one of their best ever. The photo featured David and Rachel standing together, posed in front of the iconic entrance to the Magic Kingdom. All these years later, Rachel was struck by the fact that his happy grin was marred by his missing front teeth.

Her eyes filling with tears, Rachel returned to the box. All that remained were the class ring and a copy of the 2001 St. Francis High School yearbook, *The Clarion*.

Two thousand one had been David's senior year, and the swim team had been the center of his existence. Since St. Francis had won the state swimming competition title that year, it was hardly surprising that when Rachel held the book in her hand, it opened almost of its own accord to a page featuring the swim team in the sports section near the back of the book. The shock of what she saw there took Rachel's breath away. There was a full-page photo of the ten members of the team along with their coach, Father Paul Needham. The boys, grinning for the camera, all wore their swim trunks. As for the priest? He was fully dressed, but above his white dog collar every feature of his face had been blacked out with a Sharpie.

In that instant and despite all the vodka Rachel had consumed, she found herself stone-cold sober, because for the first time in so many years she finally had some inkling of the reality of what had happened to her beloved son. And that's when the tears came.

She and Rich had always wanted only the best for their David. That was why he had attended parochial schools. That's why they had coughed up the tuition to let him attend St. Francis High, and yet all their good intentions had backfired on them. In wanting to give David everything, they'd given him worse than nothing. Rich and Rachel had failed their son, and the Catholic Church had failed the whole family. In 2010, nine years after graduating from high school, a drug-addicted David Higgins was declared dead at age twenty-six. Ever since, Rachel had agonized over wondering why.

Years after David's death, there'd been a huge scandal when Needham was arrested as a pedophile. She had recognized Father Needham's name, of course, and remembered that he'd been David's swim-team coach, but not once had it ever occurred to her that David might have been one of Needham's victims. If he had been, wouldn't he have mentioned it to his own mother?

She'd been mystified when, during his last two years in high school, her once happy-go-lucky son had pulled away from her and turned into a difficult, brooding teenager who hid out in his room in much the same way his father currently hung out in his garage. David had shut her out, and now she knew why.

The storm of fury that followed rocked Rachel to her core. At last, spent with weeping, she dried her tears, repacked the banker's box with David's things, and then steeled herself for the grim task ahead. One way or another, she would have her revenge. Someone needed to be held responsible for David's death, and if God wouldn't smite them, she would.

|CHAPTER 1|

On a bright Monday morning in late June, Ali Reynolds and her husband, B. Simpson, sat drinking coffee on the patio outside the master bedroom of their Sedona home.

"Okay," he said. "The party's over, so time's up. Are you coming to London with me or not?"

The party in question had been a garden-party homecoming event for current and past recipients of Amelia Dougherty Askins scholarships, aimed specifically at students attending Verde Valley schools. When Ali had been a senior at Cottonwood High, she was among the first students to be awarded one of those, thus enabling her to attend college, something that would otherwise have been beyond her reach. She'd gotten a degree in journalism that had allowed her to pursue an award-winning career as a television newscaster. When that had fallen apart, she returned home to Sedona, Arizona, to regroup. Sometime later she found herself in charge of the scholarship program from which she herself had once benefited.

Yesterday's afternoon tea had been in the works long before Alexandra Munsey, one of Ali's good friends from her L.A. news-anchor days, had been brutally murdered in her home outside San Bernardino. In the aftermath of Alex's death, Ali, along with several members of B.'s cyber-security firm, High Noon Enterprises, had been sucked into the vortex of a homicide investigation.

Alex and Ali had both led complicated past lives. Maybe that's part of what had created such a strong bond between them. Their lives had crashed and burned at about the same time, and they'd both reinvented themselves afterward. At the time of her death, Alex had been on the cusp of a blossoming literary career. The novel that had been published within days of her death was a huge success and had made the *New York Times* list several weeks in a row. Maybe that was one of the reasons Alex's homicide had hit Ali so hard. Death had forever denied Alex the critical and literary accolades she so richly deserved.

As for Alex's killers? Hannah Gilchrist, one of the people responsible, was dead of natural causes. The other conspirators were either already incarcerated on other charges or in jail awaiting trial, but Ali knew that it would take years of court proceedings before justice was finally served—if ever. Even so, there would be no eye for an eye here. No matter what the final outcome was in some California courtroom, nothing would ever bring Alex Munsey back. She would never live to see her precious grandson grow up, graduate from high school, go off to college, marry, or have a child of his own. She would never have the opportunity to write and publish another book. No, her untimely death had destroyed all those potential outcomes, and the unbearable finality of that was wearing Ali down.

Weeks earlier she had risen to the challenge, traveled to L.A., and stood up to speak at Alex's funeral, but back home it had been all she could do to go through with the party. The food had been catered by one of the scholarship fund's food-science graduates, and B. and Ali's new majordomo, Alonzo Rivera, had sorted out most of the physical details. Still, it had taken real effort on Ali's part to simply dress up, put on a happy face, and go forth to welcome her guests. Once the party had ended, late in the afternoon, she'd been on the verge of collapse.

B. was due to attend an international cybersecurity conference in London at the end of the week. Days earlier he'd invited Ali to come along, with the added incentive that they'd be able to see a play or two in the West End and maybe spend a couple of days hiking in the Cotswolds once the conference ended.

"Come on," he'd said. "It'll be good for what ails you. We've got a full team on board to look after things in your absence."

If B. had expected an enthusiastic affirmative, it wasn't forthcoming. "Maybe," she'd told him back then. "Let me get through the garden party first."

"I just checked with BA," he added. "There are still a couple of first-class seats on my flight. Shall I book one for you?"

Ali had stalled him on the subject earlier, but now, with the party in the rearview mirror, it was time for her to give him a final answer.

"All right," she agreed reluctantly. "I'll come along, but I'm not sure I'll be very good company. When do we leave?"

"Wednesday," he replied. "Wednesday afternoon."

"Sorry," she said after a thoughtful pause. "I guess I'm acting like an ungrateful, spoiled brat."

"You are," B. agreed with a smile while reaching across the table to take her hand. "But at least you're *my* spoiled brat, and you've been through one hell of an ordeal."

"Thank you," Ali replied. "Maybe a change of scenery is just what the doctor ordered."

|CHAPTER 2|

On a Monday morning in late June, Francis Gillespie, archbishop of the Phoenix Archdiocese, fled the air-conditioned chill of his study for the welcome warmth of his shaded outdoor patio. An eight-foot-tall stuccoed wall surrounded the residence itself, while a chain-link fence augmented by an impenetrable hedge of twenty-foot-tall oleanders lined the perimeter of the entire property. Looking over the back hedge, the archbishop could see the craggy red expanse of Camelback Mountain looming large against a hazy blue sky. To the front, the wall and hedges combined to shield the property from the rush of city traffic speeding past on East Lincoln Drive. Inside that green barrier, however, the manicured grounds of the archbishop's residence constituted a whole other world.

The archbishop loved sitting here on his quiet patio, surveying his lush domain. Because the residence had its own private well, water was not an issue. There was grass, plenty of hardy, thick-bladed St. Augustine. There were raised beds scattered here and there, all of them alive with riots of vivid color from blooming petunias and snapdragons. Most of the palm trees on neighboring properties had been stripped bare of their skirts, but that wasn't the case here. Every year the gardener came to the archbishop begging to be allowed to whack off the palm trees' masses of hanging dead limbs, and each year he was overruled. Those dead palm fronds provided habitats for any number of flying creatures—a flicker or two, a woodpecker, and whole squadrons of bats. Several rock doves resided there, along with a pair of house finches who migrated back and forth between the trees and the bubbling fountain at the foot of the patio.

The archbishop had moved his old bones out of the air-conditioned residence to warm them in the welcome heat of the outdoors, but he'd brought his work with him. His Holiness at the Vatican might have taken exceedingly strong positions on things like climate change and reducing carbon footprints, but Archbishop Gillespie had seen no reduction in the amount of tree-based paperwork that flowed like a gigantic river in and out of the Holy See. After being sidelined by ill health for the better part of two months, the archbishop regarded the incoming missives as more of a flood than a river.

In late March something the archbishop had tried to pass off as a minor cold had soon morphed into a full-blown case of bronchial pneumonia. He had spent close to three weeks in the ICU at the Mayo Clinic Hospital south of the 101 Loop and another four weeks confined to their rehab facility. The exceedingly young doctors had warned him that at his age—eighty-six, going on eighty-seven—he was lucky to still be "on the right side of the grass" and that his recovery would be a "long, slow process."

That was certainly proving to be true. To his dismay, Francis still had to rely on a walker to get around, and the previous night, while trying to push his way through another stack of paperwork, he'd fallen asleep at his desk and had awakened a full three hours later. He was making better progress in the paperwork department now, but with a noontime appointment looming he wasn't going to come close to reaching the bottom of the pile.

At that moment the patio slider opened and Father Daniel McCray, Archbishop Gillespie's private secretary, stepped outside.

"Excuse me, Your Grace, but one of your luncheon guests has arrived early and would like a word."

Father Daniel and Archbishop Gillespie had worked together on a daily basis for a decade and a half. Although the archbishop might have welcomed a bit of informality between them on occasion, Father Daniel always maintained the proper amount of distance and decorum.

Archbishop Gillespie removed his reading glasses and set his paperwork aside. Back when he'd been a parish priest, his flock had been his parishioners. Once he was appointed archbishop of the Phoenix Archdiocese, his flock had become the priests and nuns who do the hands-on work of spreading the Gospel. Some archbishops tended to isolate themselves and stay far above the fray. That was not Archbishop Gillespie's modus operandi.

He understood the essential loneliness of living the godly life. A shepherd is there to guide and protect his sheep, not to befriend them. As a result priests were always set apart from their parishioners. While serving as both bishop and archbishop, Francis Gillespie had loved the camaraderie of meeting with others of his own ilk—men who knew the joys and burdens of doing God's holy work. While still a young priest, he had formed long-lasting friendships with several of the men he'd met at those early church gatherings, one of whom was now a cardinal.

Francis wasn't a political animal. At the time of his appointment, there'd been two warring factions inside the Phoenix Archdiocese. Considered to be a natural outsider, he had been promoted from within for that exact reason—because he wasn't a member of either clique. He had risen through the priesthood by dint of being both smart and direct. If he saw a problem, he didn't care to sit around endlessly jawing about it; he wanted to fix it. As a consequence, early in his tenure as archbishop, he'd made himself available to his flock by hosting monthly luncheons for the priests in his charge. The gatherings, held in his residence, were certainly not mandatory, but they were always widely attended, as much for the delicious food provided by Father Andrew, the archbishop's cook, as for the fellowship engendered by simply being together.

The archbishop's luncheons were customarily held on the last Monday of the month—Mondays being the one day of the week when priests might reasonably take a day off. The luncheons allowed his far-flung clerics to socialize and come to know one another. For Francis Gillespie the gatherings allowed him to keep his finger on the pulse of his flock. Since the previous two luncheons had been scrapped due to his illness, the expectation was that this one would be especially well attended, and Father Andrew had been cooking up a storm for days.

"Which priest?" Archbishop Gillespie asked.

"Father Winston from Prescott," Father Daniel replied.

Father Jonathan Winston was one of the newer priests in Archbishop Gillespie's fold. He was a Gulf War veteran who had gone to seminary and joined the priesthood after three separate deployments to the Middle

East. In addition to serving as the priest at St. Mary's in Prescott, Father Winston did a good deal of chaplaincy work at his local VA hospital. He and the archbishop had carried on many long conversations about how best to serve veterans dealing with cases of PTSD.

"Have Father Winston come out here, then," Francis told Father Daniel. "Once I've had a chance to hear what's on his mind, the two of us will go in to the luncheon together."

"Very well," Father Daniel replied, nodding his assent. He disappeared through the slider and returned a few moments later with Father Winston in tow. Once he had delivered the guest into Archbishop Gillespie's presence, Father Daniel disappeared inside.

With the exception of his white collar, Father Winston was dressed all in black, and it occurred to the archbishop that perhaps the younger man wouldn't find the outside heat nearly as comfortable as Francis did.

"Your Grace," Father Winston said, holding out his hand. "It's good to see that you're on the mend."

"Mending, but not altogether one hundred percent," the archbishop replied, waving in the general direction of his much-despised walker. "I'm still having to use that confounded thing."

"We've missed you," Father Winston said.

"Thank you," the archbishop said. "I've missed you, too. Have a seat," he added, "and tell me what's on your mind."

Seating himself at the round patio table, Father Winston withdrew something from his pocket and handed it over. Looking down, Father Gillespie saw a standard offertory envelope. There were designated spaces where parishioners could write in their name, address, and phone number along with the amount of their offering. All those lines had been left blank.

"What's this?" Archbishop Gillespie asked.

"It showed up in the collection plate yesterday when the deacon in charge was sorting the banking deposit. Take a look inside."

Archbishop Gillespie opened the envelope and pulled out a folded three-by-five card. On it, handwritten in ink, was the following message:

HEY, HEY, HO, HO.
ARCHBISHOP GILLESPIE HAS TO GO!

Looking up from the message, the archbishop smiled. "I'm sure this reflects the feelings of any number of folks around here who are of the opinion that I'm well past my pull-by date."

Father Winston didn't smile in return. "It sounds like a threat to me," he said. "And the fact that it was anonymous . . ."

"I doubt it's as serious as all that," Archbishop Gillespie advised. "What is it they call people like that—the ones who post all kinds of awful things on the Internet under the mask of anonymity?"

"You mean trolls?" Father Winston asked.

"That's it exactly—trolls. Trolls used to hide out under bridges and cause trouble for passersby. Now they hide out behind computer screens or—as in this case—inside an unlabeled offertory envelope, where they can be totally anonymous and feel perfectly free to say any number of appalling things. Hidden behind a curtain like that, they can spit out all kinds of nonsense that they'd never have gumption enough to say directly to someone's face. If I were you, Father Winston, I wouldn't give this message another moment's thought."

With that the archbishop returned the card to the envelope and slipped it into his pocket. Then he gathered his papers and rose to his feet. "It's getting hot out here. What say we go inside and see what Father Andrew has been up to? He told me at breakfast that he's outdone himself today."

For the remainder of the day, Archbishop Gillespie followed his own advice and didn't give the handwritten missive another thought. In fact, it wasn't until much later that evening, as he was emptying his pockets in preparation for going to bed, that he came across the envelope again. He studied it for a moment before slipping it, unopened, into the top drawer of his dresser.

Father Winston was a priest who'd had firsthand experience with war. He'd been in combat. He'd done tough things and seen worse. No wonder he was suspicious and maybe even a bit paranoid. But that wasn't Francis Gillespie's worldview.

"It's nothing," he said aloud, closing the dresser drawer with a thump. "It's nothing at all."

Unfortunately, he was wrong about that. The message that had been dropped into the collection plate at St. Mary's in Prescott was anything but. It might have been the first threat Archbishop Gillespie received, but it was certainly not the last. Although the wording was somewhat different, each of the subsequent notes would be similar in nature and dropped off in collection plates in churches scattered all over the archdiocese. And each time Francis Gillespie added a new one to the growing collection first in his dresser drawer and later in his Bible, he was forced to come to one simple conclusion. Someone was after him, and whoever it was wouldn't quit until he was gone.

|CHAPTER 3|

That Monday morning, a few miles almost due north of the archbishop's residence, Rachel Higgins, like everyone else, had taken to the outdoors. She was sitting there in the shade of the back patio, drinking a glass of iced tea and feeling enormously pleased with herself. Yesterday, finally, after months of research and internal debate, she had done what needed to be done—she had made her formal declaration of war.

In the months since Tonya had handed Rachel the banker's box containing David's belongings, that treasured collection had become her deepest, darkest secret. She'd ditched the container itself early on out of fear that if Rich stumbled across it, he might ask too many questions.

Long ago Rachel had routinely worn hats to church, and in the process she had amassed a variety of hatboxes. When hats fell out of fashion at church, she'd held on to some of the boxes for storing her selection of sun hats—some straw, some cloth. With her golfing days apparently over, she had divested herself of most of the remaining hats and all but one of the hatboxes—an especially pretty one—that she kept on the top shelf of her walk-in closet.

That first night after seeing the blacked-out pictures in the yearbook, she had dragged the hatbox down from the shelf and exchanged her two remaining hats for David's sad collection of personal effects. The hatbox was returned to her closet shelf while the banker's box containing the hats went straight to Goodwill the next day. Ever since, the hatbox now containing David's paltry possessions had been hidden in plain sight on the top shelf of her closet. And all the while the hurt that Rachel had felt that first night had continued to fester like an infected wound, morphing first into anger that had, over time, expanded exponentially into single-minded fury.

Had the people at David's school been totally unaware of what was going on under their very noses, or, worse, had they known and simply turned a blind eye? She remembered the head of the school, Father Dorian, speaking at David's commencement, talking about how he expected that year's graduates to go out into the world and raise their families using the values and principles they had learned during their time at St. Francis. Had Father Dorian believed a single word that came out of his mouth that night, or was he like so many politicians these days, talking a good "family values" game while violating the laws of God and screwing everything in skirts? Or even not in skirts, for that matter.

And who was ultimately responsible for all this? The pope, of course, the head of the Catholic Church, because, if you believed what you saw on the news, there were problems with pedophile priests everywhere. Even if the pope *was* responsible for what had happened to David, he was also out of reach. What about finding someone else, someone closer to hand? What about the pope's duly appointed representative, the archbishop of the Phoenix Archdiocese? What if Rachel focused all her energy and anger on him?

An Internet search of the Phoenix Archdiocese eventually brought Rachel to the Facebook page for Archbishop Francis Gillespie. His face was there, smiling broadly into the camera, and his blog post for that week was all about shepherds guarding their flocks and being responsible for the well-being of each and every sheep.

"What about the well-being of my son?" she'd demanded aloud of the smiling face on the screen of her laptop. "What about my poor David?"

Without even thinking, she fired off a blog comment: "How dare you call yourself a shepherd?" Wanting to remain anonymous, she had posted the comment under her grandmother's name, Susannah, but she'd had to use the real e-mail address she shared with Rich, randr@gmail.com. From that point on, however, that was the only direct electronic communication she had allowed herself. Once Rachel had set her sights on a definite course of action and a real target, those kinds of Internet exchanges seemed too risky, because they could be so easily traced.

Within days of knowing at least part of the truth about David, Rachel set herself on the trail of Father Paul M. Needham. Unfortunately, it was a very short trail, one she found by simply running his name through local newspaper archives. In 2005 Father Needham had been arrested and charged with seven counts of sexual misconduct with minors under the age of eighteen. When Needham was found guilty on all charges, the judge had stacked his assortment of felony convictions, resulting in a twenty-six-years-to-life sentence at the Arizona State Prison in Florence, where, in 2008, he died of what the media reported to be "natural causes."

Once Rachel discovered that Needham was dead, it had taken some sleuthing on her part to track down the exact nature of those "natural causes." Eventually she managed to turn up a copy of his death certificate. Surprise, surprise. Paul Needham had died of AIDS. At the time of David's death, Rachel was the only one who had insisted upon looking at the autopsy report. Rich had been offended by the very idea of having an autopsy performed and refused to have any part of it. Rachel had studied the document in detail and knew from that moment on that David had been HIV-positive at the time of his death.

She was grateful that Rich hadn't seen the telling detail. At the time she had attributed the presence of the virus in David's system to dirty needles and to his intravenous drug use rather than to any kind of homosexual encounter. But Rich? He would have seen the term "HIV" and simply freaked. As far as he was concerned, AIDS was God's divine way of punishing those who engaged in the mortal sin of homosexuality. It was bad enough having a son who was "too damned lazy to go to school," but Rachel had no doubt that Rich would rather have a dead son than a gay one. She had kept the HIV issue a secret over the years while the disconnect between Rachel and her husband grew from a crack to a chasm. Now she kept the Father Needham issue a secret as well.

For Rachel, seeing Father Needham's blacked-out photos in the yearbook was proof enough of the priest's victimization of her son and of the shame that might well have been what led David into the world of drugs in the first place. But now, with the AIDS issue front and center in Rachel's mind, the whole situation crystallized as never before. Now she could see that not only was David's former swim coach the source of her son's HIV, he was also ultimately responsible for his suicide, because in her heart the two went hand in hand.

Rachel knew that over the years there had been huge improvements in the treatments for patients suffering from both HIV and AIDS, but in the dark world of drug addiction had David seen any glimmer of hope? Probably not. It was more likely that he had peered into his future and was able to glimpse only the grim prospect of dying of AIDS. How hopeless he must have felt, how lost, alone, and isolated! David's death might have been ruled accidental by the powers-that-be, but for Rachel it hadn't been an accident. Forced to choose between what he must have anticipated as a slow, painful end or a swift one, David had opted for the latter. Rachel no longer blamed him for that. It had been his choice to make, and he had done so.

As March sped by, Rachel continued to delve into every detail of what had happened between David's demise and now. In 2013, fourteen of his victims had filed a class-action suit against the Phoenix Archdiocese, a lawsuit that was settled in 2015 for "unspecified damages" without ever going to trial.

Rachel couldn't help but ask herself: If David had been alive at the time, would he have joined the class-action suit? Would he even have known about it? Once he graduated, Rachel couldn't recall him ever chumming around with any of his old pals from St. Francis High. She had always wondered about that, chalking it up to the increasing moodiness and isolation she'd witnessed at home, but she had also attributed it to the fact that almost all the others had gone on to college while David had not.

As for Rachel herself? Denial is powerful. At the time she'd remained totally oblivious, refusing to even consider the possibility that what had happened to those other boys might have happened to her son as well. She had recognized some of the names mentioned in the news. She had known some of the parents involved, but she hadn't reached out to them to offer her support, and neither had Rich. Interactions with those other families would have forced him to admit in public that, rather than going on to live a successful life, his son had turned into a drug-addicted bum who'd died of an overdose next to a downtown dumpster. Copping to his son's failed life would have forced Rich to acknowledge that his sole attempt at fatherhood had failed as well.

So although Rachel had avoided following all the details of either the criminal or the civil proceedings at the time they were occurring, now she devoured every word, up until the story vanished from the media.

While Rich remained closeted in his garage-based workshop, Rachel had tied herself to her computer keyboard, doing countless Internet searches on any number of related topics. Whenever she took the hatbox down from the shelf, she opened the tattered yearbook to the swim-team page so she could study the faces she found there—her son's face as well as those of the other boys.

How many of them had been victimized right along with David? At the time had any of them come forward and revealed what was going on to a trusted adult or even to one another? Wasn't that what kids in those situations were advised to do—to tell someone, to confide in and seek help from a trusted adult? But what if the predator—the faceless priest in the team photo in this case—happened to be your coach? What were you supposed to do then? If he couldn't be trusted, who could?

Time and again Rachel paged through the yearbook from beginning to end, searching for an image of Father Needham's face. In each instance, however, she found that his likeness had been carefully obliterated by pen and ink. From the captions she learned that in addition to coaching the swim team he'd also been the debate team sponsor—another position, Rachel realized, that might well have called for team travel events that would have allowed the man unfettered access to even more kids and even more victims.

It was one of Rachel's relentless Internet searches that finally delivered her first clear view of the monster's face. It was in a mug shot taken on the day of his arrest. By now Rachel's hatbox had become the repository of printouts of all her search results. A copy of the mug shot went straight into the hatbox. A few days later, she stumbled across newspaper coverage of the state swim competition from 1996. One of those featured the winning team—the swimmers along with their coach. When she finally saw a contemporaneous photo of Father Needham, she was shocked. He was younger than she'd expected—probably only fifteen years or so older than the boys in the photo, but already a monster.

The final photo to be added to Rachel's growing collection had been taken as Needham was being led from the courtroom after his conviction. The caption under that photo referred to him as Paul M. Needham, as opposed to Father Needham. Had the church officially divested him of the title "Father," Rachel wondered, or had he abandoned it on his own?

After she found that particular photo, she had sat for a long time, studying it. At this point Needham was dead and beyond the reach of the law. So who was responsible for the crime? Who was there to be held accountable for the immeasurable damage done to Rachel's son?

It was the article under the photo that gave her the final answer. It came in the form of a quote from Francis Gillespie, the archbishop of the Phoenix Archdiocese: "The jury has spoken. It is with profound regret that I acknowledge that someone we in the church once thought of as a trusted colleague could have inflicted such irreparable harm on the innocent young lives entrusted to our care."

As far as Rachel was concerned, with those few words Francis Gillespie had sealed his fate. Back in her snake-killing days, Rachel had learned that the best way to dispatch a snake was to whack off its head with a hoe. The Phoenix Archdiocese had accepted responsibility for what had happened to the other boys, and to her son as well. Since Francis Gillespie was the head of the archdiocese, he was the snake upon whom she would wreak her revenge. And now, weeks after that crystallizing realization, she put her plan in motion.

The day before, she told Rich that she was driving to Prescott with a friend so she could visit her friend's dad at the VA hospital up there. Of course there was no friend, and no friend's father either. Rachel had driven back and forth to Prescott entirely on her own, but Rich hadn't questioned the trip. He'd barely looked up when she told him she was going.

Between March and now, Rachel had watched several episodes of *How to Get Away with Murder*, looking for ideas, but what she saw there wasn't at all helpful. A crash study of shows on Investigation Discovery had convinced her that if she was going to send a personal message to Francis Gillespie, she couldn't risk leaving behind DNA or latent fingerprints.

After thinking long and hard about how to avoid mistakes in those areas, she had gone to Walgreens and bought two necessary items—a package of latex gloves and a packet of three-by-five cards still in a cellophane wrapper. She had used the gloves to remove one of the cards from the packaging and also to pen the note she wrote on it. Creating an appropriate message took several tries. When she finally settled on what she wanted to say, she wrote it out in her very best penmanship with no effort to disguise her handwriting. Why should she? No one was ever going to trace the note back to her.

Once the note was written, she dropped it into a plastic sandwich bag for safekeeping. On Sunday morning she had arrived for Mass at St. Mary's early enough that she was able to choose between a number of empty pews near the back. She had entered the church wearing a pair of gloves. After finding a seat, she collected several offertory envelopes from the pew in front of her and stowed all but one of those inside one of the unending supply of sandwich bags she now carried inside her purse. Before anyone joined her in the pew, she slipped the prewritten note card into the remaining offertory envelope before dropping that back into the original sandwich bag.

Had anyone objected to her not removing the gloves, Rachel would have told them that she was dealing with a suppressed immune system, but no one raised so much as an eyebrow. Later in the service, when the collection plate came around, she was able to deposit her envelope with all the others, confident that she had left behind no smidgen of trace evidence that might come back to haunt her.

When Mass ended and it was time to leave, the young priest bidding good-bye to his departing parishioners in the narthex reminded her so much of Father Paul Needham that Rachel had to summon her last reserve of self-possession in order to accept and return his proffered handshake. What she wanted to do instead was slap the priest's welcoming smile right off his smug face.

"I don't believe I've seen you here before," he said pleasantly.

"No," she replied. "This was my first time."

"I hope you'll be joining us again."

"I doubt it," she said. "I'm just here visiting my cousin."

Rachel walked back to her car with her knees knocking and her breath coming in short, quick gasps. Afraid she might pass out, she dropped into the SEL's driver's seat and turned on the ignition. Once the car cooled off, she sat there for several minutes longer, letting the blowing air from the A/C revive her.

"Buck up, girl," Rachel told herself aloud when she finally put the car in gear and drove out of the church parking lot. "As for you, Archbishop Gillespie? This is only the beginning."

|CHAPTER 4|

When the first of October came around that year, the last thing on Ali Reynolds's mind—the very last thing—was the idea of having a Halloween costume party. She wasn't in a partying mood and hadn't been for some time. Even B.'s treating her with a trip to the UK earlier in the summer hadn't been enough to pull her out of the doldrums left behind by Alex Munsey's death. Ali hadn't been over it then, and she still wasn't.

Back home in Sedona, Ali had spent the remainder of the summer coping as well as she could. Every morning she'd put on her best imitation of a happy face and gone to work, but rather than functioning as the easygoing calmer of troubled waters, she'd tended to be impatient and short tempered. She snapped at people, and not just at work either.

One Saturday in early September, just after school started, her grand-kids, the twins, Colin and Colleen, had been spending the day with B. and Ali. When Colin bumped a glass of milk and splattered it across the kitchen floor, Ali jumped all over him, leaving the poor kid in tears.

"Why are you so mad, Gran?" Colleen had asked. "It's just milk, and Bella is cleaning it up."

That was indeed the case. Bella, their miniature long-haired dachs-hund, had most of the mess cleaned up before Ali managed to grab a paper towel.

"I don't think she's mad," B. had observed from behind his copy of the *Wall Street Journal* at the far end of the kitchen table. "I think she's just having a bad day. Why don't we all go outside for a while and give her some space?"

Ali didn't think she needed "space," and his remark didn't exactly improve her frame of mind. Left alone, she found herself still fuming. *Is it asking too much to expect a kid to pay attention to what he's doing once in a while?*

Word of the incident eventually got back to Ali's folks, Bob and Edie Larson. A few days later, when Ali and her mother went out for lunch, Edie had tackled the issue head-on.

"Have you ever considered looking into grief counseling?" Edie had asked. "It seems to me that Alex's death has really knocked the pins out from under you."

"Why would you say that?" Ali demanded.

"Because of the way you've been acting," Edie replied. "You're not yourself at all."

"Not myself? What do you mean?"

"Think about the way you climbed all over Colin's frame the other day when he spilled his milk."

"Come on, Mom," Ali objected. "He was being careless and not paying attention. Besides, it wasn't that big a deal."

"Maybe it wasn't a big deal for you, but it was for Colin," Edie replied. "He just wants his gran back, and I don't blame him a bit. I want my daughter back, too."

Ali's thought at the time was that her mother was being entirely unreasonable, but the truth is, Edie's direct, wake-up-call approach had succeeded in getting Ali's attention. Through the course of the next several days, as she mulled the conversation in her head, it occurred to her that maybe her mother wasn't that far off base, but needing grief counseling due to the loss of a friend seemed a bit much. Still, ever since Alex's funeral it seemed as though a dark cloud had settled over Ali's life. As she thought about it, she could see the similarities between this emotional black hole and ones she'd endured before. After all, Ali had lost spouses—twice, in fact.

The first time had been in her twenties when her first husband, Dean, had succumbed after a brief but terrible battle with glioblastoma. Left as a very young widow with a newborn son, Ali wouldn't have made it through had it not been for her mother's patient help and wise counsel.

The second time she'd fallen into an emotional tar pit had been the result of two devastating blows that had landed almost simultaneously—the abrupt ending of her career as a newscaster combined with the equally abrupt ending of her second marriage to TV executive Paul Grayson. It had been the initial shock of their separation that had brought Ali back home to Sedona, arriving there as an emotional wreck. Later, when Paul turned up murdered, she'd been forced to confront the full extent of his philandering betrayals, and that had fixed her grief problem on the spot, because she'd been too pissed off to be depressed. Maybe that's what was missing here. She needed to be mad as hell at someone, and not at poor Colin for spilling his milk.

Now that Ali's mother had shone a light on the problem, however, that didn't mean Ali was going to march right out and go looking for the nearest grief-counseling clinic either. Instead she simply vowed that she'd do better.

A couple of weeks later, when Camille Lee, Cami for short, had come into Ali's office and broached the subject of having a company Halloween party, Ali should have seen her mother's fingerprints all over that game plan, but she didn't. With the idea of self-improvement in mind, and even though she hadn't really wanted to, Ali had gone along with the idea, saying yes when her every instinct was to say a definitive "No way!"

"Why not?" she'd replied, making an effort to appear more agreeable than she felt. "It sounds like fun."

Much to Ali's surprise, however, as she got caught up in the planning process, she discovered she really was having fun. The party quickly expanded from being a company-only event to being an inclusive, come-one-come-all bash. The initial idea had been to schedule the party for Halloween night itself, but once family members were included on the guest list, Colin and Colleen's plans to go trick-or-treating had to be taken into consideration. Ultimately things got moved up to Sunday afternoon, two days before Halloween itself.

Cami had insisted that this would be an honest-to-goodness Halloween party, complete with costumes, bobbing for apples, and a pumpkin-carving contest. Her intention to have a potluck went sideways when Ali's mother got involved and organized food assignments to make sure no one would go away hungry.

At the last minute, B. and Ali made a quick trip to a costume-supply shop in Phoenix. When Ali emerged from a dressing room decked out head to toe in a Wonder Woman costume that included a short red skirt, a knockout pair of red leather boots, and a flowing black wig, B. had whistled admiringly.

"Nice legs," he said. "If you've got 'em, flaunt 'em, but with you dressed like that, what the hell am I supposed to wear?"

In the end B. had opted for a vintage World War II army officer's uniform so he could masquerade as Wonder Woman's longtime beau, Steve Trevor. And that was how B. and Ali were dressed late Sunday afternoon as they welcomed people into their home. Their super-hero duds elicited plenty of oohs and aahs from their elaborately costumed guests, and the reverse was also true.

Betsy Peterson, the twins' maternal great-grandmother, had shown up as a daunting 1930s Miss Marple, accompanied by Colin and Colleen. Since the twins' father was a longtime *Star Wars* fan, it was hardly surprising that Colleen came dressed as a lovely Princess Leia in contrast to Colin's scary Darth Vader. Betsy had somehow managed to use a cheap wig to craft a reasonable facsimile of Princess Leia's distinctive double buns.

Pressed for time for their own costumes, Chris and Athena, the twins' parents, had arrived in ordinary street clothing but wearing hand-printed placards that read THE SIX MILLION DOLLAR MAN and THE BIONIC WOMAN. Considering Athena's two prosthetic limbs, compliments of a National Guard deployment to the Middle East and the doctors at Walter Reed Medical Center, calling her a bionic woman wasn't far from the truth. Ali's parents showed up—Edie in overalls and a painted-on beard, pretending to be a train engineer, while Bob came dressed as a Harvey Girl, complete with a frilly white apron and a long blond wig.

As for High Noon's employees? To the twins' delight, Stuart Ramey, B. Simpson's second-in-command, turned out to be a very large and hairy Chewbacca. In honor of the occasion, Lance Tucker, High Noon's latest hire, left his prosthetic leg at home and showed up with one empty pant leg tied off at the knee. Making do on a wooden crutch, he wore a fake sword, a black eye patch, and a red bandanna on his head. The stuffed green parrot pinned to his shoulder completed his transformation into a swashbuckling Long John Silver. Cami came dressed as a ninja warrior, while Shirley Malone, their receptionist, showed up in a witch's outfit, complete with bright green face. Alonzo Rivera, Ali and B.'s majordomo, was typecast as a chef, including a towering toque. Since his responsibilities included being in charge of both the pumpkin-carving project and arranging the buffet, that was all to the good.

While Steve Trevor greeted arriving guests at the door, Wonder Woman passed around beverages and hors d'oeuvres. When she approached her daughter-in-law with a glass of her favorite merlot, Athena waved it aside.

"I'm off the sauce for the duration," she said with a sly grin. "I believe I'll have some of the kids' Hawaiian Punch."

"For the duration?" Ali repeated with a frown, not quite getting it.

"About the next six months, I'd say," Athena added.

It took a beat for Ali to make the connection. "Wait, you mean you're expecting?"

"Yes, we are," Athena said, smiling in return. "We wanted to wait a couple of months before letting the cat out of the bag."

"Twins?" Ali asked faintly.

"Nope, not this time around," Athena answered. "I don't think I could survive another set of twins."

"Congrats," Ali said, "and one glass of Hawaiian Punch coming up."

She had just delivered it to Athena when the last two guests arrived, Ali's longtime friend and Sister of Providence, Sister Anselm Becker, and her recently appointed assistant and driver, Sister Cecelia Groppa.

Ali hurried over to the front door to join B. in welcoming the new arrivals.

"I'm afraid the cupboard at the convent was bare as far as costumes are concerned," Sister Anselm murmured after first shooting Ali's costume an appraising glance and then looking around at the other guests.

"Not to worry," Ali said quickly, giving the older woman a hug. "I'm delighted you could both come. Welcome."

Because bobbing for apples wasn't as easy as people thought it would be, that part of the party wasn't a huge success, but the pumpkin carving was. With Alonzo's able assistance and supervision, the front porch was lined with a set of handsomely carved jack-o'-lanterns glowing in the approaching darkness as dinner was served.

In the course of the afternoon and evening, Ali had more fun than she'd had in a very long time. There were too many people for everyone to find seating in the dining room, so some had to be diverted to places in the kitchen. Dinner was over and guests were tucking in to slices of Edie Larson's homemade pumpkin pies when the doorbell rang.

Usually arriving visitors had to press a buzzer at the bottom of the driveway to come up to the house, but today, with so many people coming and going, Ali and B. had decided to leave the gate open. Still, looking around the room, it was hard to imagine there was anyone else who might stop by. Since Ali's end of the table was closest to the front door, she waved to B., letting him know she would handle the new arrival. Expecting a door-to-door sales pitch, she was fully prepared to tell whoever it was to buzz off when she switched on the light and opened the door.

With the aid of a walker, Archbishop Francis Gillespie stood on the front porch, staring at her. "Obviously I'm interrupting something," he said quickly. "Please forgive my showing up without any advance warning."

For a moment Ali had forgotten she was dressed in her Wonder Woman costume, and the last person she expected to encounter on her doorstep was the archbishop of the Phoenix Archdiocese. Between the two, it was difficult to tell who was more surprised.

"So sorry," he continued. "This will only take a moment. My driver is waiting. We're on our way back from a conference in Las Vegas. On a whim I decided to stop by, but since you're clearly busy . . ."

"It's just friends and family," Ali interjected, stepping aside. "Please come in. You're not interrupting. You and your driver are both welcome. Believe me, there's more than enough food to go around."

"No, thank you," the archbishop said. "I'd rather not advertise my presence here to anyone, including Sister Anselm. I believe I noticed her Mini Cooper among the cars I saw parked in the drive. I have a matter of some concern and was hoping to discuss it with Mr. Simpson—and with you, of course. The situation requires some delicacy, and if the two of you could stop by my residence in Phoenix at your earliest convenience, I'd be most appreciative."

There was no mistaking the anxiety in the archbishop's voice.

"This sounds serious," Ali murmured.

"It is," Archbishop Gillespie agreed, "quite serious."

"B. is due to fly out again on Wednesday afternoon, but Monday is relatively open. Would tomorrow afternoon work for you?"

"Tomorrow would be fine," the relieved archbishop replied. "How about you show up midafternoon. We can talk and then have a bite of supper."

Ali smiled at that. The archbishop's calling the evening meal supper rather than dinner showed his midwestern roots.

"Supper sounds great," Ali said.

Archbishop Gillespie started to walk to his car, but then he turned back. "By the way," he said, "you make a very fetching Wonder Woman. I loved those comic books when I was a boy, but I had to sneak them in and out of the house. My mother never read comic books. She only saw the covers, and she thought Wonder Woman's short skirt was scandalous."

Moments later, as the archbishop let himself out through the front gate, Ali was still blushing.

|CHAPTER 5|

"I guess you didn't feel like going to Mass this morning," Rich muttered. He was standing at the kitchen counter making yet another bologna sandwich. That was his go-to meal these days.

For a moment Rachel was too startled to respond. That casual, out-of-the-blue remark meant that he was paying attention to her comings and goings. After years of his barely acknowledging her presence, a sudden surge of interest wasn't what she wanted—certainly not now, not with her planned D-Day attack only two days away. She had mentioned a few times over the course of the last several months that she was going to church, but her announcements had been met with so little response that she sometimes doubted that Rich had heard them. Now, with a sinking feeling, she realized that not only had he been listening, he must have been paying attention. What else might he have noticed?

"Just didn't feel up to it today," she answered quickly. "It seemed like too much trouble."

The truth is, she'd delivered the last of her collection-plate messages a week earlier when she ran out of envelopes. She was done with issuing warnings; now it was time to deliver on those threats.

For a moment Rachel worried that Rich might question her—that he'd ask for more details—but fortunately he didn't. Instead he took his sandwich and beer and retreated to the safety of his garage, allowing Rachel to breathe a sigh of relief. She didn't even mind that once again he'd left the counter a mess. Cleaning up after him gave her something to do with her hands, something that helped reduce her agitation.

In the aftermath of David's death, Rich had gone into a slump that eventually resulted in his being forced to take early retirement. As Rachel gradually became aware of the reality of their financial situation, even with their mortgage paid off, she had halfheartedly suggested going back to work herself. That idea had been a nonstarter. Then she suggested maybe Rich could try doing some consulting work, and that might have worked if his older brother, Peter, hadn't died.

Pete was fifteen years Rich's senior. He and his wife, Lucille, had already spent a number of years living in a fifty-five-plus community outside Casa Grande. He'd died quite suddenly, shortly after a diagnosis of pancreatic cancer, leaving behind a widow who was also in ill health. When Lucille decided to check herself into an assisted-living facility, she sold off their retirement home along with everything inside it. Since none of their kids were interested in inheriting their father's woodworking tools, she'd offered them to Rich instead.

And that, Rachel realized now, had been the end of a number of things—not the least of which included being able to store cars in the garage. It had been the end of Rich looking for any other kind of work. Consulting jobs that could have been quite lucrative went away in favor of his building birdhouses, a hobby that, as far as Rachel was concerned, was nothing but a waste of time.

Rich's newfound and complete focus on woodworking had also marked the end of their marriage in any ordinary sense. Theirs was now a union of necessity. They stayed in the house together because they couldn't afford to live apart, living as roommates rather than spouses, with only the roof over their heads in common.

At first Rachel had missed Rich's bossy and sometimes overbearing presence in her life, but eventually she'd grown accustomed to living without it. And now that she'd found her own focus and purpose in life, she had no interest in changing the dynamics of their relationship.

If Rich had paid attention to the fact that she'd returned to church after years of backsliding, had he also noticed her sudden interest in physical fitness and the fact that she'd become addicted to daily walks? Did he ever question why she always walked elsewhere rather than strolling around in their own neighborhood?

"I'm off to meet up with Maggie and Yvonne for a walking session," she would tell him. "I'll be back later."

Maggie and Yvonne were as much figments of her imagination as was the friend whose equally fictitious father was supposedly confined to the VA hospital in Prescott. Rich never asked how and where she'd met any of these people, thus sparing her the trouble of having to create any kind of detailed backstories for her imaginary pals. So where did she do most of her solitary walking? Let's see. That would be on Lincoln Drive, right outside the oleander-lined perimeter of her target's private residence.

If you had told Rachel Higgins on the morning of her seventieth birthday that she would spend much of the following year planning to commit a homicide, she would have said you were nuts. But that's exactly what she'd been doing. That's what she *was* doing.

When it came to food, Rachel wasn't one of those pinch-of-this and dash-of-that kind of cooks. Similarly, when she traveled, she did so with a map and a clearly laid-out itinerary in hand. The major problem with becoming a first-time killer at age seventy was that there *were* no road maps. She had to figure it out as she went along. She also had to figure out how to pay for it. You'd think that killing someone would be pretty much cost-free, but that turned out not to be the case, not if you wanted to get away with it.

Rachel's first idea—hiring a hit man—came with an immediate drawback—money. Supposing she managed to find someone willing to do the job, if the going price happened to be five thousand dollars, where was she supposed to come up with that kind of money? Tell Rich she needed an advance on the next several months' worth of the household budget? If you were trying to kill someone and you had an insurance policy on the victim, you might be able to negotiate with your killer to defer paying him until the insurance settlement came in. Unfortunately, there was no such policy, because Rachel Higgins had zero insurable interest in the life of Archbishop Francis Gillespie.

So not only did hit men cost money, they also came with another serious risk. A separate series of online searches revealed that all too often those supposed hit men turned out to be undercover cops or confidential informants. In those instances the hits didn't happen and the person doing the hiring ended up in jail.

Since neither of those was an acceptable outcome, Rachel had been forced to seek out an alternative strategy. She needed a way to get close to her target. She needed to study him and understand his comings and goings. And that's where those daily walks on Lincoln Drive came in. She was there almost every day, right in his neighborhood. Rachel even caught sight of Francis Gillespie on occasion, but she was quite sure he never saw her, and that was just how she liked it.

|CHAPTER 6|

O n Monday morning when Ali opened her eyes, the world was somehow a brighter place. B. and Bella had both departed the bedroom.
In the air she sniffed the beckoning aroma of both brewing coffee and
baking waffles. When Ali ventured into the kitchen a few minutes later,
B. was already there, chowing down.

"Good morning," he said, greeting Ali with a smile. "How's my hostess
with the mostest? You sure know how to put on one heck of a party."

"It was fun, wasn't it?" she agreed.

"And congrats on your upcoming grandson," B. added. "I'll bet Colin
is over the moon at the idea of having a baby brother."

So B. knew that Chris and Athena were expecting a boy while she
didn't? What kind of deal was that?

Alonzo handed her a cup of coffee and a plate with a steaming waffle
already in place. "Thank you," Ali said, accepting both.

After breakfast Ali and B. drove over to Cottonwood and stopped by
the office for a time, but by two o'clock that afternoon they were tucked
into B.'s Audi R8 and headed south on I-17. The Audi was several years
old now. B. occasionally mentioned getting a new car, but as little as he
actually drove these days, that seemed like a waste.

With the party over, their costumes were in their proper bags and
ready to be returned to the costume shop on their way to the archbishop's
residence. As they motored southward, it was hardly surprising that Ali
was thinking back on the previous evening.

"As Mom and Dad were leaving last night, Mom admitted that she was the one who suggested our having a party in the first place."

"That figures," B. said with a grin. "If Edie had broached the idea to you directly, you probably would have either turned it down cold or dragged your heels every step of the way. Regardless of whose idea it was, it was a great evening. Everybody had a good time, from the twins right up to and including Sister Anselm."

"I had fun, too," Ali admitted, "but speaking of the twins, I was astonished when Athena told me that she and Chris are expecting."

"I wasn't," B. said.

Ali gave her husband a questioning look. "You weren't?"

"I knew that they'd been trying," B. said. "Chris had mentioned that to me months ago. I'm glad it's coming together for them."

Ali chewed on that for a time. Chris had let his stepfather know he and Athena were trying to get pregnant, but he hadn't mentioned a word about it to his own mother? In terms of bonding between the two men in Ali's life, that was probably a good thing, but she couldn't help feeling a little hurt that she'd been left out of the loop.

"You haven't exactly been yourself the last few months," B. suggested when she said nothing more. "Maybe neither one of them thought you were in a place where you were ready to hear about members of your own family dealing with possible fertility issues."

Alex Munsey's death had come about as a direct result of her long-ago involvement with a fertility clinic. After a moment's reflection, Ali nodded. "They were probably right," she said.

B. chuckled. "The only thing about the party that I regret is missing out on seeing the expression on Archbishop Gillespie's face when you answered the door in full Wonder Woman mode."

"Let's just say we were both surprised," Ali said. "I was expecting some kind of political canvasser handing out leaflets. I most definitely was not expecting to come face-to-face with Archbishop Gillespie."

"You mentioned he seemed worried," B. said. "I believe 'anxious' is the exact word you used. What do you suppose this is all about?"

Ali shook her head. "I have no idea. He said it was serious and delicate, and he most definitely didn't want Sister Anselm to know he was out on our doorstep asking for help."

"He's familiar with what we do," B. said. "It's probably some kind of security breach inside the archdiocese."

"Probably," Ali agreed. "But isn't it a little weird that he's inviting us to have a meal with him rather than setting up a regular appointment? And why us?"

"Why not us?"

"For one thing," Ali replied, "I'm guessing there are plenty of cyber-security companies out there that are run by practicing Catholics. I'm a fallen-away Lutheran, and you're a self-described agnostic, but here we are going to the archbishop's residence for dinner."

"Francis knows us, Ali," B. assured her. "Don't forget we've had deal-ings with the man in the past. He understands how we operate, and there's a good deal of trust running in both directions. I haven't forgotten that he was the one who sent in reinforcements when we were in deep caca with Lance Tucker's situation down in Texas. We still owe him big for that timely assistance. Besides, if Francis is dealing with a problem inside the church, maybe that's exactly what he needs—an outsider's opinion."

"Well, he certainly called that shot," Ali replied. "We're definitely out-siders."

The costume store was located near Metrocenter, just off I-17. The clerk, overwhelmed with last-minute Halloween shoppers, was a bit mystified as to why they were returning costumes prior to October 31 rather than after. She examined the clothing for damage before refund-ing their deposits and sending them on their way.

They drove east on Glendale Avenue just as afternoon traffic was picking up and arrived at the archbishop's residence at the stroke of four o'clock. When B. rolled down the car window to press the inter-com buzzer at the gated entrance, Francis Gillespie's voice boomed out through a speaker as the iron-barred gate opened for them.

"Just park out front under the portico," he directed. "It's shady there."

B. parked where he'd been told. The shade was fine, but in late Octo-ber that wasn't nearly as critical as it would have been in the summer with the thermometer hovering around 110 degrees.

The heavy mahogany door swung open before they managed to punch the doorbell. Ali fully expected a minion of some kind to be standing just inside. Instead the archbishop himself, hunkered over a wheeled walker, waited to greet them.

"Welcome, welcome," he said heartily. "Please come in. I hope traffic wasn't too terrible."

"Not bad," B. said. "We're ahead of the worst of it."

"You're probably worn out after your big shindig last night," he said, glancing in Ali's direction.

"It was fun," she said, "and believe me, I had lots of help."

"We had a get-together here at the residence today, too," Archbishop Gillespie said. "Not a costume party, of course," he added with a smile in Ali's direction. "It was our monthly priestly meeting. Once that was over, I gave everyone the afternoon off, including Father Andrew, who runs the kitchen. I've ordered a pizza delivery for our dinner—thin-crust pepperoni with jalapeños. I hope that's okay."

Ali blinked at that one. They would be dining on pizza with the archbishop? That seemed downright weird. What she said aloud was, "Pepperoni with jalapeños is perfect."

"You're looking better than I expected," B. commented as the archbishop led the way through the public spaces in the residence and toward his personal quarters.

"Don't patronize me," Francis Gillespie grumbled back at him. "I know exactly how I look—like an old man who coded twice on his way to the ER and who very nearly didn't make it. Some people may see a bright light under those kinds of trying circumstances. Apparently I'm not one of them, but I'm pretty sure I felt that second jolt when they zapped me with the paddles. Hurt like crazy. I knew I wasn't dead about then, but I wished I were."

At the end of the hallway the archbishop stood to one side and motioned them into his apartment. Ali had been in the bookshelf-lined study that served as the archbishop's front office on several occasions. Like the other public parts of the residence, his official study came equipped with all the accoutrements befitting a man of his elevated station. A hand-knotted Oriental rug covered a marble-tiled floor. Leather-bound volumes graced the bookshelves, and the ornate antique furnishings, including a hand-carved desk, looked as though they might have arrived in this part of the world after sailing around Cape Horn.

The contrast between the archbishop's public office and his private domain couldn't have been more striking. Entering his apartment was like stepping into an unpretentious middle-class home from forty or fifty years earlier. A polished cherry dining table set for three and awaiting the pizza delivery occupied the near end of the room, next to a doorway that led off into a small kitchenette. At the other end, four worn leather armchairs and a collection of reading lamps were grouped around an old-fashioned butler's table. One of the chairs seemed to be more butt-sprung than the others. A haphazard stack of books on the side table next to it suggested that to be Francis Gillespie's chair of choice. The top book on the pile was a shabby, much-used Bible with what appeared to be multiple bookmarks peeking out from among the pages.

"I take it this is where you do your devotional reading?" Ali inquired.

"Guilty as charged," Francis said with a grin, "and my recreational reading as well. Won't you have a seat?"

Ali found herself in a chair facing the far wall, the centerpiece of which was an unlit wood-burning fireplace. Above the mantel, on an expanse of smooth white plaster, hung a distinctive piece of artwork—an immense oil painting of a Madonna and Child on what appeared to be a jagged slab of driftwood. Ali's eyes widened as she recognized the vivid colors and the distinct style.

"Is that an original DeGrazia?" she gasped.

Francis nodded. "Yes, it is," he replied. "Ted and I became friends when I first came to Arizona back in the early seventies. I called him Teddy, and he called me Father Frankie. He gave me the painting as a gift shortly before he got into that big uproar with the IRS and set fire to many of his works. It's been with me ever since, but my plan is to leave it here for the next archbishop to enjoy once I'm gone—which could be soon, by the way, and that's why *you're* here." With that Francis parked the walker and settled into his preferred chair.

"You're retiring?" B. asked.

"Not exactly," Francis said, "but close. What would you care to drink? Since I'm stuck with this dratted walker, you'll have to help yourselves, but I have a full selection of sodas in the fridge. Before Father Andrew left for the day, he brought over a pitcher of freshly made lemonade. We have orange, lemon, and grapefruit trees just outside the kitchen. They're not in season right now, but when they are, you can't beat citrus fruit fresh off the tree."

"I'm for lemonade," Ali said, standing up, "and I'll be happy to go get it."

In the small kitchenette just off the living room, Ali found a crystal pitcher full of lemonade in the fridge. A silver tray with a loaded ice bucket and three empty glasses waited on the counter. When she returned to the seating area and placed the tray on the butler's table, B. and the archbishop were busily chatting about the ups and downs of the stock market. As she poured glasses all around, Ali recognized the stock-market discussion for what it was—a delaying tactic. Francis was busy discussing what wasn't important in order to keep from discussing what was.

"You said last night that this is serious," she prompted once all three of them had glasses in hand. "So why don't you tell us what's going on?"

"Do you believe in heaven and hell?" the archbishop asked after a thoughtful pause.

A theological discussion with a Catholic archbishop over lemonade and pizza? Ali wondered. In terms of life planning, those were things that had never been on her bucket list.

"I guess so," she replied at last, not so much because she really believed one way or the other but because, under the circumstances, that seemed to be the only acceptable answer.

B.'s response was a bit more honest. "I'm not so sure," he said.

"Well, I do," Archbishop Gillespie countered. "If you're in hell, you're forever separated from God's healing grace." He paused. "I suppose you've both heard the term 'mortal sin'?"

Ali and B. nodded in unison.

"If you commit a mortal sin and die without repenting and receiving absolution, that's what happens. You're forever separated from God's love. You've lost your immortal soul. I've spent decades trying to save people's immortal souls, and I'd like to do so in this instance as well."

"In what instance?" Ali pressed.

Archbishop Gillespie paused. "I believe someone is planning on murdering me," he answered at last. "If the killer succeeds and dies without receiving absolution, he or she will be going to hell."

A drop of Ali's lemonade went down the wrong pipe. "You think someone is trying to murder you—seriously?" she managed once her coughing fit subsided.

Francis Gillespie nodded. "I do."

"You said 'he or she,'" B. cut in. "Does that mean you think the person targeting you might be a woman?"

Francis smiled in response. "Well," he replied with a twinkle, "I'd say the odds are pretty much fifty-fifty. Wouldn't you?"

"Touché," B. replied, raising his glass.

"In any event, my best bet for keeping that person from going to hell would be preventing my murder in the first place. That's why I came to see you. I'd like High Noon Enterprises to keep my potential killer from reaching his goal."

"How is it you're aware someone's out to get you?" B. asked. "Have there been threats?"

Rather than reply aloud, Archbishop Gillespie picked up the Bible, pulled out what Ali had assumed to be bookmarks, and passed them around. She found herself holding a collection of small envelopes that were seemingly all alike. Printed on the outside were lines calling for a first and last name, an address, and a phone number, along with an additional line with a dollar sign preceding it. None of the lines had been filled in.

"Offering envelopes?" B. asked.

Archbishop Gillespie nodded. "All the churches in the archdiocese use the same envelope from the same manufacturer. We get a better deal by ordering in bulk. What's problematic, however, is what you'll find inside."

For the next several minutes, Ali and B. silently opened the collection of envelopes and perused what was inside. Each contained a folded three-by-five card containing a note. In the upper-right-hand corner of each card, in different handwriting, was a notation listing the date as well as the name and location of a particular church. As for the notes themselves? The handwriting was the same in each instance, and the messages, although slightly different, spelled out more or less the same message.

Archbishop Gillespie must be cast out.

Hey, hey, ho, ho
Archbishop Gillespie has to go.

Soon Archbishop Gillespie shall cease from troubling,
And all will be well.

To slay the serpent one must cut off its head.
Archbishop Gillespie is the serpent.

Archbishop Gillespie is Satan personified.
Get thee behind me, Satan.

"So these are all aimed at you," Ali concluded, looking up after reading the last one.

"Presumably," Archbishop Gillespie agreed.

"And where did they come from?" B. asked.

"Who knows?" the archbishop answered with a shrug. "They've been dropped into collection plates at services throughout the archdiocese, coming in at a rate of two or three per month. That's why I put the dates and locations on each of them. I was trying to establish if there was any particular pattern."

"Did you?"

"No."

"Have you notified law enforcement?" B. asked.

The archbishop nodded. "Someone from Phoenix PD looked into it. According to him I'm a relatively public figure and open to a certain amount of public criticism. These notes are anonymous and nonspecific. As such they're not considered credible threats."

"And nothing can be done about them until something bad happens," Ali suggested. "Except by then it will be too late."

"Precisely," the archbishop agreed.

"What about fingerprints or DNA?" B. asked.

"None of the flaps were sealed shut," the archbishop replied, "so there's no chance of finding usable DNA there. The contents of the collection plates are handled by any number of people in each of the parishes, and there's no way to obtain elimination prints on all those folks without causing a complete panic inside each affected congregation. Creating panic is something I'd like to avoid if at all possible."

"But there was no definitive distribution pattern, correct?" B. asked.

"That's true," the archbishop said. "The first one showed up at St. Mary's Parish in Prescott in early summer. Since then they've come in from various churches, and never the same one twice."

"Do the churches have guest books?" Ali asked.

"They do," Francis said, "but just because someone attends Mass at a different church doesn't mean they'd necessarily sign a guest book."

"Especially if they were going around making death threats," B. muttered.

"This started when?" Ali asked.

"This past June," Francis replied, "and they're still coming in. The last one arrived a week ago."

"Did you show all of them to Phoenix PD?" B. asked.

"Not the last few," Francis replied. "There didn't seem to be any point."

"And nobody there asked you to leave the messages with them?"

"No."

"If they're done with them, may we take them?" B. asked.

"To what purpose?"

"I'd like to have the handwriting analyzed as well as the messages themselves," B. replied. "The phraseology used may give us some hints about the identity of the person who wrote them and where he or she may be from."

"You can tell that from handwriting?"

"I'm not sure," B. replied, "but it doesn't hurt to try."

"Does that mean you're willing to help?"

B. nodded. "I suppose." He sounded less than thrilled.

"Feel free to take them, then," Francis said. "Help yourselves."

A cell phone rang, and the archbishop plucked a phone out of his hip pocket. "Oh, good, you're here. I'll buzz you in. And if you don't mind, please bring it around to the usual place on the back patio. I'll meet you there."

He stood up and reached for his walker.

"Do you want someone to come along to help?" Ali asked, rising to her feet.

"Oh, no," the archbishop replied, waving her offer aside. "Don't bother. The driver will bring the pizza inside. I'm something of a regular customer, you see. Other people give up chocolate for Lent. I give up pizza. That was the worst part of being in the hospital. What they claimed was pizza didn't pass muster."

As he stomped away, Ali gathered up the collection of envelopes and shoved them into her purse. She wished she'd had an evidence bag at hand, but considering the number of people who had already touched the envelopes, it didn't seem to matter. The archbishop returned, followed by the delivery guy, who was lugging an insulated pizza bag. At the archbishop's direction, the driver removed the pizza box and set it in the middle of the table before showing himself out the way he had come.

"Soup's on," the archbishop announced. "I happen to have some excellent wines. I'd be happy to open a bottle."

"No, thanks," B. said, replying for both Ali and himself. "We have to drive back to Sedona tonight, so wine is probably a bad idea. We'll stick with lemonade."

Their host, Archbishop Gillespie, served pizza to his guests, speaking as he did so. "Coming from Chicago, you'd think I'd lean more to the thick-crust side of things, but I'm team thin crust all the way." After filling his own plate, he added, "So where do we start?"

"We should probably start at the beginning," Ali answered. "Who hates you enough to want to kill you?"

|CHAPTER 7|

"To that end, the first question would have to be, do you have any enemies?" B. asked.

Archbishop Gillespie smiled. "Apparently," he responded. "I don't suppose you get to this stage of life without collecting a few enemies along the way, starting with my older brother, Anthony, of course. He's five years older than I am. Tony had a good thing going as what was essentially an only child until I showed up several years later and spoiled his whole game plan. According to our mother, he hated me from the moment she brought me home from the hospital. Although we haven't spoken in decades, his daughter, my niece Marcella, tells me he still does—hate me, that is."

"And he's still alive?" Ali asked.

Francis nodded again. "Very much so. He's confined to an old folks' home in Green Bay, Wisconsin, and probably isn't destined to live much longer. Lung problems, I believe. He was a smoker early on and didn't quit until a few years ago."

"The two of you didn't get along?"

"Never," Francis said with a sad shake of his head. "When our parents weren't around, he beat me up with astounding regularity, so once we were grown, there wasn't a lot of love lost. He came home for our mother's funeral but not for our father's. There was bad blood between the two of them as well."

"You hear from your niece regularly?"

Francis nodded. "Marcella sees herself as the family historian. She sought me out several years ago when she started doing genealogical research on our family tree. We've stayed in touch ever since."

"If Anthony is confined to an assisted-living facility of some sort," Ali offered, "it seems unlikely that he'd be responsible for a series of threats turning up in collection plates scattered all over central Arizona. And since that's how the threats were delivered—in collection plates—doesn't it seem likely that our bad guy is someone connected to the church?"

B. nodded his approval to that line of questioning. "Maybe a rival of some kind," he said. "How about whoever else was in the running when you were appointed archbishop?"

Francis considered the question for a moment before he answered. "Of the four possibilities, I was by far the youngest and was considered a dark horse. I had worked out on the reservation rather than in one of the larger parishes, and people thought I wouldn't be up to the task. But there were other considerations happening back then—a potential schism within the archdiocese—that made bringing in an outsider a good idea.

"Priests are human, of course," he continued, "and I'm sure there were some hard feelings at the time. As far as the other candidates were concerned, I had jumped the line, but two of the other three are deceased now, and the third one is currently in an Alzheimer's care facility. That's what happens when you get to be my age," the archbishop added with a sad smile. "You tend to outlast both your friends and your enemies."

"What about your staff?" Ali asked. "Any dissension or hard feelings there?"

Francis shook his head. "There are a number of people who work for me, on both a part-time and a full-time basis. The two who are closest to me are the household staff, and they both live on-site. Father Andrew O'Toole is our chief cook and bottle washer. He's the youngest of the bunch, and when driving is called for, he's usually the one behind the wheel. Father Daniel McCray is my private secretary. Father Andrew has been with me for ten years and Father Daniel for fifteen or more. We're a team. In all that time, I don't believe a cross word has ever passed among us."

"What about the priests out in the various parishes?" Ali asked. "Any ambitious up-and-comers who might be looking for advancement?"

"The church believes in promoting from within wherever possible.

There are two or three priests in the archdiocese who would make out-standing candidates, but that's not up to me. Archbishops aren't allowed to choose their own successors—that's considered to be above our pay grade. Father Benjamin, the man who was appointed to be my coadjutor and who would have succeeded me automatically in the event of my death or retirement, passed away himself a number of months ago. So far no one has been named to fill his position."

"Are there any priests in the archdiocese you would consider to be bad actors?" B. asked.

"Every barrel has a few rotten apples," Archbishop Gillespie responded. "So there are people I keep a close watch on, but I wouldn't categorize any of them as actual enemies."

"What about predatory priests?" Ali asked. "There's a lot of coverage about that in the news these days."

"Yes, but not here, thankfully," Francis said, "at least not now. That was one of the things I tackled head-on when I first came on board, and the archdiocese was required to pay damages in a number of civil lawsuits. My no-nonsense stance on that issue may well have been the primary reason I was appointed in the first place. As archbishop I've maintained a zero-tolerance policy toward predatory priests. The four who were brought to my attention have, in each instance, been reported to the proper civil authorities and dealt with by law enforcement and the justice system. In the past those kinds of behaviors were often swept under the rug and the offending priests were shipped off to other unsus-pecting parishes, where they could victimize even more children."

"Names and outcomes?" Ali asked.

"An arrest warrant was issued for Father James Hatfield, but he committed suicide before he could be taken into custody. Fathers Gregory Powell, Paul Needham, and John Haynes were all arrested, tried, convicted, and sent to prison. Two of them—Powell and Haynes are still there. Needham died of natural causes in 2008, two years after his conviction."

"You're sure this Father Needham wasn't shanked by some other inmate?" Ali asked.

"Not so far as I know."

Ali pulled out her phone and made a note of the offending priests' names, verifying the spelling in each case.

"Have you had contact with any of the defrocked priests since they went to prison?" Ali asked.

"Excuse me, Ali," Archbishop Gillespie interjected, "but the whole notion of defrocking priests sounds a bit too much like a case of religious strip poker. The priests in question have simply been removed from the clerical state. That means they can no longer refer to themselves as priests. They can't celebrate Mass or hear confessions, except in cases of dire emergency where someone who is in danger of dying requests the sacraments and no other priest is available. As to your question, once arrests were made, I've had no contact with any of them. If one of them were to ask me to come hear his confession, I would do that, of course, but so far nothing like that has happened. And I don't foresee it happening in the near future."

"In other words," Ali concluded, "you don't know of any individual who wishes you harm?"

"That is correct," the archbishop agreed. "I have no idea."

"What kind of security arrangements do you have around here?" B. asked.

"The residence is gated, as you well know. The property is totally surrounded by an eight-foot chain-link fence augmented by a formidable oleander hedge. We have anti-intrusion devices scattered here and there throughout the lawns, as well as surveillance cameras that provide full coverage of the grounds. We have intruder alarms on all the doors and windows. That might seem excessive, but our precautions aren't that different from other households in the neighborhood."

"What kind of transportation do you use?" B. asked.

"We have a rather ancient Lincoln Town Car," the archbishop replied. "Not quite as much of a relic as I am, but getting there. Several people have mentioned that we're due for an upgrade in the vehicle department. But I'm rather fond of the old crate, and I'm not ready to give it up. Father Andrew sees to its maintenance. When it comes to automobiles, he and I are on the same page—why trade it in?"

"When you're out and about, who does the driving?"

"As I said earlier, Father Andrew is my designated driver. For one thing, he's thirty-plus years younger than I am. That means his vision and reflexes are also thirty years younger. When I hit eighty and found night-time driving to be challenging, I stopped renewing my driver's license."

"But we're still no closer to figuring out who might wish you harm," B. said.

"No, we're not," Francis agreed. "The culprit must be someone I've offended along the way, most likely without my even being aware of it."

A short silence ensued, and Ali was the one who broke it. "Last night you specifically asked that I not let Sister Anselm know about your visit. Is there any particular reason for that?"

"She's a friend, and I should have told her, I suppose," the archbishop replied, "but the truth is, I haven't exactly been forthcoming about the situation with anyone inside the church. I went so far as to let people know they should inform me about anything unusual surfacing in their collection plates, but I didn't go into specifics because I didn't want to create a sea of suspicion. I expect congregations to welcome strangers into their midst rather than regarding every newcomer as a would-be assassin."

"But one of them just might be," Ali objected.

"I suppose so," the archbishop admitted reluctantly, "but still . . ."

"How public is your schedule?" B. asked him.

"It's posted on social media, if that's what you mean. I'm on Facebook, of course, and there's a Twitter account and most likely an Instagram one as well."

"Who maintains those?"

"My secretary," Francis responded, "Father Daniel. When it comes to computers and programs, he's far more adept than I."

"For the time being, you might want to suspend those," B. suggested.

"But I'm a public person," Archbishop Gillespie protested, "and the people of the archdiocese need to know where I am, where I'll be, and when they can see me. It's my job to be available to them."

"Phoenix PD may not regard your offering-plate messages as credible threats, but until we know otherwise, Ali and I do," B. advised him. "And we're going to need you to act accordingly."

"You expect me to lock myself up in the residence here and bury my head in the sand until all this blows over?"

"I think you need to exercise a certain amount of caution and be a little less forthcoming," B. replied.

Francis thought about that for a moment. "I didn't become a priest or an archbishop in order to hide my light under a bushel basket," he said at last. "And as I said, my primary interest isn't so much about saving my own life as it is about saving my potential killer's immortal soul. I have no intention of letting these threats keep me from doing my job."

"Have it your way," B. responded dubiously. "In the meantime, though, Ali and I will see what we can do. But isn't there something in the Bible about God helping those who help themselves?"

Archbishop Gillespie smiled at that. "You might think so," he said. "However, I believe that quote actually originated in Aesop's Fables."

Francis might have expected to impress his audience with that bit of trivia, but Ali forged ahead without comment. "Now that we know about those social-media accounts, we'll need to have complete access to what's there," she said firmly. "That includes administrative records where any names, home addresses, and IP addresses are kept. The person behind this might be hiding in plain sight among the regular followers on one of your various media platforms."

Francis issued a resigned sigh. "All right, then," he agreed finally. "Tomorrow morning, first thing, I'll have Father Daniel send you all applicable information, but only the ones from my public accounts," he added. "You won't be allowed anywhere near my private ones."

Ali nodded. "We understand that," she said, "but please tell Father Daniel we'll need his administrative passwords."

Archbishop Gillespie shook his head. "I really don't see how tracking down my various Twitter followers is going to be of any use."

"You'd be surprised," Ali told him. "In homicide cases there's usually a personal connection of some kind—often a close connection—between victim and killer. Whoever's behind this may be delivering his message by using the collection plates, but that doesn't mean he isn't lurking out in the online world somewhere, keeping an eye on your comings and goings."

Ali and B. left shortly after that. It was well after eight when they turned right onto Lincoln and headed for the 51.

"He's one stubborn old guy," B. muttered as they motored north. "He wants our help, but I'm not sure he'll take our advice."

"Right," Ali agreed. "When you suggested suspending his social-media accounts, I thought he was going to fire us on the spot."

"But he didn't," B. said. "So where do we start?"

"The offering envelopes weren't sealed. That suggests that whoever is behind this understands that DNA profiling might lead us back to him."

"Or maybe he just watches *Forensic Files*," B. suggested.

Ali gave him an exasperated shrug. "Maybe," she agreed. "On the other hand, he doesn't need to worry much about fingerprints. There might be prints on the notes themselves, but as for the envelopes? As Archbishop Gillespie told us, the fingerprints of everyone involved in handling offering plates would be on the envelopes, and tracking down elimination prints on all those folks would be a monumental job. On the other hand, there's always the possibility that our potential killer used gloves, so maybe his fingerprints weren't there to begin with."

"Why exercise that kind of caution?" B. asked.

"Our suspect might be someone with prior convictions, so his prints and DNA would already be in the system."

"That would be true for cops as well," B. said. "Their prints and DNA profiles are also in the system."

"So we might be looking for a crook, a cop, or even a crooked cop," B. mused.

"Or, as you said, maybe just a devoted fan of *Forensic Files*," Ali added with a small smile. "But about those messages. I can't quote them chapter and verse, but they all seemed vaguely biblical. So maybe whoever's behind this is connected to the Church."

"I know someone who might be able to sort out all those chapter-and-verse issues," B. said after a pause. "In order to keep Frigg on the straight and narrow, I believe Stu has set his juvenile-delinquent AI off on a Bible-study course."

From High Noon's inception, Stu Ramey had been B.'s right-hand man. As for Frigg? That was the name given to an artificial-intelligence program that, in the aftermath of a solved homicide investigation, had inadvertently fallen into Stuart's hands. Frigg's creator, a brilliant but fatally flawed computer scientist named Owen Hansen, aka Odin, had built the AI to serve as his partner in crime in Owen's grand scheme of becoming a serial killer. As Odin's assistant, Frigg's primary responsibilities had been to do risk assessment and to provide strategic planning.

When Stu had launched an effort to rescue one of Owen's intended victims from certain death, his timely interference had caused the would-be serial killer to become not only more frustrated but also more unhinged. At some point Owen became so distracted that he began disregarding his AI's strategic advice. Somehow the deep learning that Owen had used to instill criminal behavior into his cyberassistant's algorithms had also introduced her to the concept of self-preservation. With Owen clearly veering into self-destruct mode, Frigg had set out to save herself by entrusting both her programs and Owen's vast fortune to the man who eventually succeeded in bringing the killer to ground— namely Stuart Ramey.

Stu had been anything but overjoyed to have a criminally minded computer program placed in his care and keeping. His initial intent had been to take Frigg off-line the moment he'd worked his way out of the web of financial transactions she'd used to ensnare him. Before that could happen, however, Frigg had proved herself invaluable in several lifesaving instances. Her incredible hacking skills were, by and large, totally illegal, but they were also remarkably effective.

After Frigg's hacking had been instrumental in saving Ali's life the previous summer, the people at High Noon had put the question of Frigg's continued existence to a vote, and the result was unanimous. It had been determined, however, that it would be best to keep Frigg's functions entirely separate from those of High Noon Enterprises. The AI operated out of Stu's home in Oak Creek Village on the outskirts of Sedona, thirty miles away from company headquarters in Cottonwood.

Teaching Frigg to color inside the lines and play well with others had turned out to be far more challenging than anyone had anticipated. The current focus on Bible study was only one of the techniques Stu was using to counter Frigg's criminally based algorithms and instill an understanding of right and wrong.

"Good thinking," Ali said, after a very long pause. As B. steered the Audi northbound on I-17, she added, "We can ask him to put her on the case first thing in the morning."

That was the idea of course, but it turns out things didn't quite go as planned.

|CHAPTER 8|

Long after his guests departed, as Archbishop Gillespie prepared for bed, he parked his walker and knelt on the prie-dieu at the end of his narrow cot. Having to resort to using a prayer desk had been a far more private humiliation than having to use the walker, but his aging limbs had finally betrayed him. One night after evening prayers, he'd had to summon Father Andrew to come help him regain his feet.

Unlike his wobbly legs, Francis Gillespie's simple faith was as abiding as it was strong. As a boy he had walked his mother to and from Mass every morning before school, and the lessons he'd learned in those early-morning services had lasted a lifetime.

Now he said his prayers, ending as he always did with a recitation of the Lord's Prayer. When he reached the part that said "lead us not into temptation, but deliver us from evil," he really meant the word "us." He meant it for himself, of course, but even more so he meant it for the unknown person who was intent on killing him.

Later, lying in bed and waiting for sleep to come, he thought back over his long conversation with B. Simpson and Ali Reynolds. B. was correct, of course. The archbishop couldn't help but recall that old Greek legend about the drowning man who asked the goddess Athena for help, only to be advised that he should try swimming first. No, Francis Gillespie decided, he would be neither that stubborn nor that stupid.

Tomorrow, after early-morning prayers and breakfast, he would speak to Father Daniel and suggest that for the time being it might be a good idea for the archbishop of the Phoenix Archdiocese to take a hiatus from social media. After all, there'd been archbishops out in the world for millennia, doing their jobs effectively without the use of either Facebook or Twitter. If generations of archbishops before him had done it, so could Francis Gillespie.

Having put the matter to bed, he should have been able to go to sleep, but he wasn't. Instead he lay awake, staring up at the ceiling and thinking about his brother—about Tony. Their enmity had been plain for all to see from the beginning. It was chronicled clearly in a family portrait taken by a professional photographer in 1931 on the occasion of Francis's baptism. At the time of the photo, Francis's three much older siblings, two sisters and a brother—Katherine, Irene, and Jeffrey—had all been in their teens. Wearing fixed smiles, they stood in the back row, dressed in their Sunday finest while their parents, Gertrude and Frank, staring directly into the camera lens, were seated in front of them. His mother held Francis, still dolled up in his baptismal gown. Five-year-old Anthony, on their father's right, stood just far enough away to be out of reach. He glared at his father rather than at the camera, with his arms folded defiantly across his chest. Baby Francis was the only one of the bunch who seemed remotely happy.

A small framed copy of that portrait was still displayed on the archbishop's desk in his public office. He looked at it on an almost daily basis, remembering as he did so that other than Francis and Anthony, all the people pictured there were gone now. A much larger copy of the family portrait had been the centerpiece of his parents' living room, hanging in a place of honor over the fireplace. Francis had a clear memory of his paternal grandmother, Grandma Gillespie, stopping in front of the photo one day, staring up at it, shaking her head, and muttering under her breath, "That boy was born with a chip on his shoulder." And Francis had known exactly who she meant.

From the time of Francis's earliest memories, Tony had been his tormentor-in-chief. He had shoved the younger boy into countless snowbanks and mud puddles and peppered him with snowballs. Whenever Francis went crying to their mother over something that had happened, Tony goaded him about being a crybaby.

An indifferent student, Tony dropped out of school his sophomore year and went to work as a bag boy at a local grocery store. He didn't make enough to live on his own, so he stayed at home, making small contributions to the family coffers, taking his sullen place at the dinner table each night, and torturing Francis whenever the opportunity presented itself.

The year Francis turned twelve, Grandpa Gillespie had a stroke. Francis had spent that summer on the family farm outside Elgin, Illinois, helping Grandma Gillespie with the chores, and those months of doing hard physical labor had made all the difference. When Francis came home that fall, a growth spurt meant he was now far closer in height to his older brother. The next time Tony lit into Francis, the younger kid had come out fighting and used his work-hardened muscles to blacken both his brother's eyes. At the time it happened, no one had been more surprised than seventeen-year-old Tony.

That night at dinner, Tony was unaccountably absent. "Where's Tony?" Gertrude asked.

Francis shrugged his shoulders.

"And what happened to your eyes?" she asked, examining her son's damaged face.

"A guy hit me," Francis answered. He wasn't about to be accused of being a tattletale.

"Haven't you ever heard about turning the other cheek?" Gertrude asked reprovingly.

"I did," Francis said, "but when he hit me again, I got up and bloodied his nose."

Later that night, as Francis was getting ready for bed, his father tapped on his bedroom door.

Frank opened the door but didn't step inside. "Was it Tony?" he asked.

Francis simply nodded.

"All right, then," his father said. "I'll handle it."

The next night there were only three places set at the table, and his mother was in tears.

"What's wrong?" Francis asked.

"Ask your father," she said.

Francis looked askance in his father's direction. "Your brother decided to join the navy," Frank said.

"Because your father gave permission for him to go," Gertrude muttered accusingly. "How could you do such a thing, Frank? Tony's only seventeen, little more than a baby. We're at war. What if he dies at sea? What if we never see him again?"

"Don't worry," Frank assured her. "Tony's like that bad penny. He'll be back."

Gertrude had fled the table in tears, while Francis and his father finished the rest of the meal in silence. It wasn't until they were clearing up that Frank spoke again. "Your brother's always had a mean streak. He won't bother you anymore."

Francis had simply nodded. That week he went to church and confessed his sin, admitting to the priest that his first thought upon hearing the news about Tony going to war had been, *Good, maybe he won't come back.*

The priest had told him to say twenty Hail Marys and granted him absolution. Tony had survived World War II with his mean streak still very much intact and with a soul that was wounded to the core. He'd married a girl from Wisconsin. He had stayed on in the navy for the next twenty years and then gone to live, work, and finally retire in his wife's hometown, and all the while the unresolved feud between the two brothers remained a thorn in Francis Gillespie's soul.

And although the church might have absolved Francis of committing that long-ago sin of wishing his brother ill, the archbishop himself had not.

|CHAPTER 9|

Much to Rachel Higgins's dismay, waging war against Archbishop Gillespie had turned out to be an expensive proposition. Initially the high price of gas had come close to being her undoing. She had needed to spread her collection-plate messages over as wide an area as possible. That often called for driving fifty to a hundred miles round-trip from her home in north Phoenix, and those trips cost money. It wasn't as though Rich went out to the driveway to check the mileage on her car—he wasn't that interested in her comings and goings—but he did keep an eagle eye on her credit-card usage, and that first telltale upswing in her Visa balance happened right after her trip to Prescott.

Needing cash to cover any additional expenses that might have aroused Rich's suspicions, Rachel had turned to a friendly pawnbroker, one who was clearly nowhere near her own neighborhood. Rachel didn't have a lot of jewelry, but what she did own was quality stuff. By pawning various items, she was able to bring in enough money to keep her unauthorized gasoline expenditures off her credit card and invisible to Rich's prying eyes.

As what she referred to as D-Day approached, Rachel needed to find a weapon. She wanted a gun—a relatively small one, preferably something she'd be able to carry in a purse without anyone being the wiser. When she went cyber-window-shopping, she was shocked to discover how much new ones cost and how much paperwork was involved.

She priced used ones at the weapons counter in the pawnshop, too.

Even there the cost was more than she could handle without selling her last piece of jewelry—her damned wedding ring. Rich hadn't noticed the other items gradually disappearing, but the wedding ring? He might well pay attention to that. And a weapon she personally purchased, whether online or in a brick-and-mortar store, would inevitably lead back to her once a homicide investigation was launched in the aftermath of the archbishop's death. Her plan was to do this and not get caught.

Eventually Rachel realized that she already had exactly what she needed, right there in the house—in her walk-in closet. Rich's dad had given him a .22 revolver in honor of his sixteenth birthday. Rachel remembered going out into the desert with Rich and doing some target practice together—shooting at beer bottles—back when they were first married and before they had David. Once their son arrived on the scene, she'd insisted that Rich make arrangements for a suitable place to keep it, and that's how a pistol safe had come to be installed in their master bedroom.

The weapon had remained there untouched for so long that Rachel had completely forgotten about it, but once she remembered, she knew it was exactly what she needed—a lethal weapon that was probably unregistered and wouldn't lead back to anyone at all. As for the combination to the safe? It would have to be something Rich wouldn't forget. Under the dark of night, on her very first attempt to unlock the safe, Rachel had keyed in her son's birth date and the door clicked open. The safe contained three items—the weapon itself, the gun-cleaning kit she'd given Rich as a Christmas gift the first year they were married, and a partially used box of ammunition.

That time she had simply closed the safe without touching a thing. But tonight was different. With Rich shut up in his room, his television set booming away, she donned a pair of latex gloves, opened the safe, and emptied it completely.

When Rachel hefted the weapon in her hand, she was dismayed by how big it was. And it was far heavier than she remembered. There was no way it would fit in a pocket. Fortunately, she still had a few purses and bags that might fill the bill.

As far as firearms were concerned, Rachel had done her homework. She understood that if you wanted a weapon to work when it came time to use it, the gun had to be clean. She wasn't about to go to all this trouble and end up with a gun that wouldn't fire when she pulled the trigger. So that was her assignment for tonight—cleaning and loading Rich's .22. There were plenty of videos online explaining exactly how to do it. Even though she'd never cleaned a gun of any kind before, following directions was Rachel's long suit.

It had been years since Rich had ventured into the master bath, but tonight, just in case, she locked the door behind her. Shoving aside the makeup on her vanity counter, she laid out everything she needed just the way the videos directed. As soon as she opened the bottle of cleaning fluid, she worried that the pungent odor might permeate the rest of the house, so she stopped what she was doing and ran a bath, filling the tub with hot water and half a bottle of heavily perfumed bubble bath. Then, donning a pair of latex gloves, Rachel went to work. She started by checking to be sure the weapon wasn't loaded, then took it apart a piece at a time, thinking about the way her mother had taught her to break down a whole chicken years earlier.

An hour later the tub was drained, the makeup on her counter was back where it belonged, and the gun? Now clean and loaded, the .22 was in a clear plastic zip bag in the bottom of her oldest, largest purse. There were probably all kinds of traces of Rachel's DNA on the inside of the purse, and she didn't want any of that to be transferred to her intended murder weapon.

As for Rich? If he ever noticed the weapon was missing, she'd remind him that they'd agreed to get rid of the gun years ago, back when David was in junior high. Since the conversation had never happened, he wouldn't be able to remember it, but Rachel would make him think it had, because if push came to shove, she'd be able to convince him she was right and he was wrong. Rich Higgins was good at keeping an eye on the checkbook and credit-card balances, but remembering long-ago conversations wasn't in his wheelhouse.

When Rachel went to bed that night, she did so with the full knowledge that not only was she armed and dangerous, she was literally locked and loaded as well. It was time for her to go to war, and she was ready.

|CHAPTER 10|

B.'s cell phone rang at 1:00 a.m. When they first married, Ali had resented being jarred awake by middle-of-the-night phone calls, but she'd since accepted the reality that calls like that came with the territory.

High Noon's customer base was spread across several continents and numerous time zones. The hard-driven executives B. dealt with on a daily basis were often narcissists, egocentrics who seldom, if ever, glimpsed the world through anyone else's point of view. When making phone calls, they tended not to worry if the recipient happened to be on the far side of the continent or even on the far side of the international date line. Since *they* were at work, they expected everyone else to be at work, too.

Given all that, Ali had learned to disregard the disruption, roll over, and go back to sleep. She started to do that this time as well, but then she heard the concern in B.'s voice.

"Yes, Dieter," he said. "Please calm down. What seems to be the problem?"

Without having to be told, Ali knew that Dieter Gunther was the D. half of one of High Noon's major international customers, A&D Pharmaceuticals, based in Zurich, Switzerland. The company had been started by Dieter and his brother, Albert, each of whom was a brilliant chemist in his own right. Under their leadership the company had flourished, establishing a research-friendly environment that resulted in the creation of several cutting-edge drugs.

Ali knew from long experience that the eight-hour time difference between Sedona and Zurich meant that Dieter had most likely just arrived at the office for the beginning of his workday.

"Why, no," Ali heard B. say. "As you know, we've gone to incredible lengths to make your network cyber-resilient, with multiple firewalls protecting your most sensitive data. We've had no intrusion alerts on our end, and I doubt this is anything you need to worry about, but let me check with my people—"

Cut off in midsentence, B. fell quiet. Ali couldn't make out any of the words, but when B. held the phone away from his ear, she could hear jagged shards of Dieter's one-sided rant. She could also hear the very real worry in her husband's voice when he responded.

By then Ali was sitting up in bed and had switched on her bedside lamp. If there'd been a data breach at A&D, it had the potential of posing a very serious problem for High Noon Enterprises.

"How exactly did this so-called ransomware demand come in?" B. was asking.

There was a long pause on his end as another torrent of unintelligible words tumbled out of the phone.

"By drone?" B. asked. "Are you kidding me? The note was delivered to your personal residence by drone? How much are they asking?"

Dieter answered, but Ali couldn't make it out.

"The first thing you should do is notify law enforcement. Have you done that?" B.'s question was followed by another very long pause. "All right, then," he said at last, "we can talk about that when I get there. I'll start my people checking on this right away. What time is the car due here?" Another pause followed. "Okay, I'll be ready. See you as soon as I get there."

The call ended, but without even turning to look at Ali, B. dialed another number. "Hey, Cami," he said a moment later. "Any alarms on your end? . . . Nothing at all? Well, I've just had a panicked call from Dieter Gunther at A&D in Zurich. He says they've been hit with a multimillion-dollar ransom demand by someone who claims they can take down the company's entire network. The fact that the crooks are asking for dollars makes me think the demand might have originated on this side of the Atlantic. If it had come from Switzerland, it would be for either Swiss francs or euros. They claim to have installed a data-destroying trojan that can be unleashed at any time. A&D's IT people have looked and aren't seeing any signs of a breach. If there aren't alarms on this end, neither are we."

There was a pause. "You're right, Cami. It may be bogus, but we can't take any chances. Call in the troops and run scans like crazy. See if you can find anything. You might also check to see if any of our other customers are dealing with similar issues. Where there's one, there may be more."

He paused long enough for Cami to reply. "No, I won't be coming in. Dieter needs some serious handholding, and he's chartering a Gulfstream to pick me up at Sky Harbor. A car will be here for me in a little over an hour. Any communications about this will need to be encrypted. . . . Right. Good luck on this, Cami. We need to get it sorted."

B. put down the phone and got out of bed. "You're going to Zurich tonight?" Ali asked.

"So it would seem," B. said. "You got the drift of all that?"

"Pretty much. You think Dieter is just pushing panic buttons?"

"I do, but I'm not the one who woke up to find a ransomware demand sitting on my doorstep."

B. went into the closet and emerged with suitcases in hand. "We built layers of security into A&D's system," he continued, putting the bag on the bed and zipping open the lid. "Just because hackers penetrate one level, that doesn't mean they'll have access to any of the others."

"So if you think the ransomware thing is mostly an empty threat, why are you on your way to Zurich in the middle of the night?"

"Because the customer is always right," B. answered, "even when he's wrong."

B. kept a partially packed go bag at the ready at all times, so he was able to finish the job while carrying on a sensible conversation. When he was almost done, Ali climbed out of bed and extracted Bella from the cozy spot under the covers where she'd buried herself.

"Come on, girl," Ali urged, slipping into her robe and tying the belt. "Let's go to the kitchen, make some coffee, and leave Daddy to shower and dress in peace."

Out in the kitchen, Ali opened the gate at the bottom of the drive so the car-service driver would be able to come up without having to use the intercom. After making a pot of coffee, she took that and two mugs into the library and turned on the gas-log fireplace. She was sitting in front of the fire with a coffee mug in hand when B. emerged dragging not one but two Rollaboard suitcases. Ali knew that once he put out the fires with Dieter Gunther in Zurich, he was due at a conference in Munich.

"The problem with A&D is serious, isn't it?" she asked.

B. nodded. "If someone has managed to penetrate their network, we're in big trouble. The difficulty is, there's a chance Dieter may knuckle under and pay the ransom prematurely. Either way it'll be our problem."

"You're afraid he might pay up without waiting around long enough to discover if the threat is real or not."

"I am," B. said, "and that would be a lose-lose for us all the way around. I have it on good authority that Dieter's the kind of guy who would make our lives a living hell."

"It sounds as though Dieter Gunther isn't a very nice person," Ali observed over the rim of her cup.

"He's not," B. agreed, "but working with guys like him is what pays the bills."

"And you've gotta do what you've gotta do," Ali added.

"So I will," B. agreed. "In the meantime, though, I feel like I'm leaving you in the lurch. I'm the one who more or less committed to helping Francis Gillespie with his problem, and now I'm flying off and leaving you high and dry."

"Not to worry," she assured him. "You take care of things on your end, and I'll look after Archbishop Gillespie. If he really is being targeted and if there's any kind of digital trail, I'm pretty sure Frigg and Stu will help sort it out."

Once the car showed up, Ali saw B. off, then returned to the bedroom, but she didn't have much hope of going back to sleep. Yes, it was barely after two in the morning, but she'd had far too much coffee for that. Instead she settled into bed with a book propped in front of her, but she didn't read either. She sat there and fumed, angry that a displeased customer on the other side of the ocean could disrupt their daily life and maybe even their entire business. Who was Dieter Gunther anyway? What gave him the right to demand B. drop everything and come to Switzerland?

When she finally calmed down some, Ali turned her attention to her book. At some point after that, she must have fallen asleep. She awakened to the smell of coffee brewing. It was seven in the morning, and

Alonzo Rivera was up and on the job. The book she'd been trying to read had fallen off the bed and onto the floor. The bedroom door was ajar a telltale dachshund's width, letting her know that Bella had already decamped for the kitchen in search of breakfast. Dressed in her night-gown and robe, Ali followed suit.

When Ali's original aide-de-camp, Leland Brooks, had retired and returned to the UK, B. and Ali had gone in search of a replacement. Alonzo, a retired naval submariner, had ably stepped into Leland's shoes. He'd spent his entire naval career as a culinary specialist on board various submarines, and so he'd been pleasantly surprised by the spaciousness in B. and Ali's kitchen.

"Good morning," he said when she entered the room. "Who came and went in the middle of the night?"

Dieter's hired car would have driven past Alonzo's sleeping quarters in a fifth-wheel trailer parked next to the garage. Over Ali's first cup of coffee, she told Alonzo the story behind B.'s abrupt departure.

"You're telling me that everyone in Cottonwood has been up and on the job since one a.m.?" he asked when she finished.

"Most likely," she said.

"Are you going in to work?"

"As soon as I get showered and dressed," she answered.

"All right, then," Alonzo said. "Why don't I whip up a frittata and maybe a batch of biscuits, too? When you're dealing with a full-blown crisis, you've got to feed your crew."

With Alonzo busy rattling his pots and pans, Ali hurried off to get ready.

|CHAPTER 11|

Francis Gillespie awakened feeling fully rested for a change. Once he'd finally fallen asleep, he slept well. Rather than wrestling with the threats on his own, he'd turned the problem over to B. and Ali, and he felt sure he had placed the issue in good hands.

After getting out of bed, it took time for his feeble limbs to be up to the task of making himself presentable. He was grateful to have a stool in the shower to sit on and a bar to grab to help raise and lower his frail body as needed. Getting old was a pain, yes, he decided, but at least he was still alive and more or less kicking.

When he went out into the other room, everything was in order. The debris from his evening pizza party had been cleared away. The silver tray that had held the lemonade pitcher and ice bucket the night before was now loaded with a carafe of coffee, a single cup and saucer, a glass of freshly squeezed OJ, and an eggcup containing the archbishop's morning collection of pills. Next to the carafe was a printed card, prepared by Father Daniel, containing a listing of that day's scheduled calls and appointments. Two priests new to the archdiocese were coming by for audiences this morning, one at ten and another at eleven. Francis made it a point to personally welcome each new arrival. He wanted to meet them, greet them, shake their hands, look them in the eye, and attempt to assess the kinds of men they were.

According to the schedule, however, this day would be a mixture of in with the new and out with the old. That evening the archbishop was scheduled to attend a farewell celebration for Father George McKinley, who was retiring from St. Augustine Church in Peoria. Father George had served the parish for more than twenty-five years—longer than Francis Gillespie had been archbishop. It was bound to be a big celebration—a potluck in the parish hall followed by a roast. Francis had already begged off on attending the potluck. The round of spoken tributes would probably last later into the night than Francis liked, but he would be there nonetheless with a suitable comment teed up and ready to deliver.

Years earlier he and Father George had been partnered in a fund-raising golf tournament. Father George had resorted to utilizing his "Florsheim wedge" to extract his ball from a particularly difficult bit of rough. Unfortunately for him, the archbishop had caught him red-footed, as it were, and had never let the man forget it. Tonight reliving that awkward moment would be good for a laugh, and Archbishop Gillespie would be there to do his bit.

Boosted by the orange juice and a few sips of coffee, the archbishop and his walker made their slow way to the chapel for morning prayers. Later at breakfast he grabbed the social-media bull by the horns and broached the subject of suspending his accounts without necessarily mentioning why he was doing so.

"I've decided to go dark on social media for a bit," he told Father Daniel. "People spend far too much time on their devices these days. Maybe I should take a step back from that for a while."

"You want me to shut down everything?" Father Daniel asked, sounding somewhat dismayed.

The archbishop nodded. "Facebook, Instagram, the blog—all of it."

"But I've already posted this week's public events," Father Daniel objected. "They're already out there."

"That's fine," Archbishop Gillespie told him. "Next week will be plenty of time for us to back away."

"But how will people know where you're going to be and when?"

"I guess they'll have to do it the old-fashioned way," Francis said with a smile. "They'll have to resort to reading their printed programs when they come to Mass. While you're at it, I'll need a listing of the administrative passwords on each account."

Father Daniel frowned. "Is this about the threats?" he asked.

Since the archbishop's incoming correspondence went through

Father Daniel, he alone, other than the archbishop, was aware of what was going on. In fact, Father Daniel was the one who had urged Archbishop Gillespie to go to Phoenix PD with the threats. When the authorities had declined to do anything about it, Father Daniel was ready to bring in a squad of armed security guards. Only a stern talking-to from the archbishop had dissuaded him from that course of action.

"I've been speaking to my friend B. Simpson from that cybersecurity firm up in Sedona. If there's some kind of digital connection to the threats, High Noon may be able to find it."

"Is that why you're shutting down the social media—on Mr. Simpson's advice?"

"Yes," Archbishop Gillespie replied, "on B.'s advice."

The expression on Father Daniel's face spoke volumes of disapproval, but the words that came out of his mouth were quite different.

"Very well, Your Grace," he said evenly. "I'll cancel all further postings and bring you the administrative information as soon as I can assemble it."

"Thank you," Archbishop Gillespie said, pushing away from the table and collecting his walker. "I guess I'd best get busy. I'm assuming my collection of correspondence and morning briefings are all awaiting me?"

"They are," Father Daniel replied. "The folder is on your patio table, and I turned on the outdoor heater—unless you'd rather work in your office."

"Thank you," the archbishop told him. "I'd much rather work outdoors for now, but when it comes to visiting with the new priests, my office would probably be best. What are their names again?"

"Father Manuel Martinez will arrive first," the secretary supplied without having to consult any kind of appointment book. "He's due at ten. Father Bartholomew Mayer should be here an hour or so after that."

"All right, then. Please check on me around nine thirty to be sure time hasn't gotten away from me. I don't want to be late."

With that the archbishop limped off down the hallway. As promised, the daily folder awaited him on his patio table, and an outdoor infrared heater took the morning chill out of the air.

At the top of the pile was the daily correspondence, followed by a sheaf of printed pages of that day's briefings from Rome. As far as Francis Gillespie was concerned, those could stay at the bottom of the heap for as long as possible. Later in the afternoon, he would have plenty of time to see the news of the day from the Vatican. He doubted there'd be anything good. There hardly ever was.

For official routine correspondence, Francis dictated letters to Father Daniel, signed the typed documents, and sent them off without a thought. But for the personal letters that came to him—from people dealing with health issues or grieving the death of a loved one and from priests facing some personal crisis or another—he felt constrained to answer each one individually. It wasn't his style to dash something off on a keyboard and then scrawl his name at the bottom of a typed sheet. No, Archbishop Gillespie replied to each of those missives on his personally embossed stationery, using the Montblanc fountain pen that had been given to him decades earlier by the archbishop of Chicago.

Fresh out of seminary and as a young priest working for the Archdiocese of Chicago, Francis had managed to head off a feud between two sets of warring priests that would have caused a major embarrassment had the dispute become public. Only four years into the priesthood, he had made a huge impression on the then-archbishop, Ronald Moser, with that piece of deft diplomacy, and the senior cleric had given the young priest the pen as a token of his gratitude.

Archbishop Moser had served as Francis Gillespie's mentor from then on. Eventually Archbishop Moser became Cardinal Moser and went to Rome to serve in the Vatican. It had been through Cardinal Moser's intervention that Francis Gillespie had been asked to serve as a special emissary to Vatican II.

During those years the fact that the young priest had garnered such favoritism from a cardinal had not gone unnoticed by Father Gillespie's fellow priests. Once he returned from Rome, and without his mentor's proximity and protection, the long knives in Chicago's upper clergy had come looking for him. Eventually he'd been shipped off to what was intended to be suitable exile on a remote Indian reservation in Arizona. He had fooled them, however. Like Br'er Rabbit in his briar patch, Francis Gillespie had not only thrived in Arizona, he had also managed to rise to the top.

All that was water long under the bridge. Cardinal Moser had been deceased for more than twenty years now, but the pen remained one of Francis Gillespie's most treasured possessions. This morning, as he wrote to a grieving father who'd lost his wife and children to a drunk driver, he felt as though the comforting words spooling out of his pen and onto the paper came not only from him but also from the Vatican itself. It was also his hope that his handwritten note, despite the somewhat shaky penmanship, would serve as a blessing to the recipient long after Archbishop Gillespie had disappeared from the scene.

Done with his correspondence, Francis had launched off on the briefings when Father Daniel entered the patio with a reminder that his appointment with Father Martinez was fast approaching. Before Father Daniel left, he handed over a printout containing the social-media information the archbishop had requested.

"All the accounts are on hiatus now?" Francis asked.

"Yes, Your Grace," Father Daniel replied stiffly, "all of them. They'll be turned off as of tomorrow morning."

In terms of their working relationship, this wasn't exactly an exchange of cross words, but it came very close.

Francis Gillespie paused long enough to write one last note, and then he slipped that, along with Father Daniel's printout, into an envelope, which he addressed to B. Simpson at High Noon Enterprises.

Finally, with a regretful sigh, he left the bright autumn sunshine behind and went inside to greet the first of his incoming priests.

|CHAPTER 12|

There was enough food that Ali needed Shirley's help to shuttle her collection of Alonzo-prepared dishes into the office and bring it to their recently remodeled break room, which was equipped with a stove, a microwave, and a dishwasher along with a well-stocked fridge. A Formica-topped conference table provided a more-than-adequate eating surface. Behind a partition was what they called "the quiet room," a cozy sitting room complete with a massive sofa where people could grab quick naps as needed.

Alonzo had packed the food into thermal bags, so both biscuits and frittata emerged from the bags still hot from the oven, despite the thirty miles separating Sedona from Cottonwood. As Ali set out food and dishes and Shirley brewed new coffee, a bleary-eyed Cami appeared from behind the partition.

"I managed to sleep for a couple of hours," she said, hand-combing her hair as she came, "but do I smell food?"

"Yes you do," Ali replied. "Breakfast is served."

Summoned by Cami, Stu and Lance appeared in the break room, carrying with them a palpable sense of weariness.

"Find anything?" Ali asked as they gathered at the counter and dished food onto paper plates.

Stu shook his head. "Nada," he said. "There's no sign of an intrusion of any kind. I'm beginning to think this whole deal is some sort of hoax."

"What does B. have to say about that?" Ali asked.

"He's maintaining radio silence at the moment," Lance replied. "Probably grabbing some sleep on the plane. The last message he sent said for us to keep looking, so that's what we're doing."

Ali had arrived at the same conclusion, which was why she hadn't bothered trying to call.

"Before you go back to your battle station, Stu, I need to ask a favor."

"Sure," Stu said. "What's up?"

"I'd like to borrow some computer power from Frigg. A situation has arisen with Archbishop Gillespie down in Phoenix, and B. has asked me to look into it while he's out of town."

"What do you need?"

"Can Frigg do handwriting analysis?" Ali asked.

"Probably," Stu replied.

"I have some of that for her, then," Ali replied. "I'd also like her to assemble dossiers on several people from Archbishop Gillespie's past."

"I'll be glad to have her look into doing those for you, too, but not right now. At the moment Frigg's resources are totally focused on the A&D ransomware situation. Once she's finished with that, I'll have her send you a text."

Ali was thunderstruck. "Wait, are you saying you granted Frigg access to High Noon's files?"

"I granted her limited access to A&D's files for the sole purpose of tracking down the ransomware," Stu corrected, "and I did so on B.'s express instructions. We were coming up empty on this end, and we needed answers faster than Cami, Lance, or I could produce them."

"But is that even safe . . . ?" Ali began.

For months now there had been a concerted effort to keep Frigg far away from any and all High Noon files.

"I've created some backdoor procedures and safeguards that will allow me to monitor Frigg's behavior," Stu told Ali. "I've also served notice that if she steps out of line, she'll be terminated."

"All right, then," Ali said dubiously. "I'll be here in the office. Have Frigg text me when she's available."

Regardless of what was going on with Frigg or in High Noon's computer lab, it was Ali's job to keep the lights on and the bills paid. As a consequence she spent the rest of the morning glued to her desk and playing accountant. It was almost the first of the month, so there was more than enough to do. She wrote a check to cover that month's Amex bill. She read through the printout from the company that handled their online billing and made sure all the finances were in order. One of their office-complex tenants was more than thirty days past due on his rent, so she typed out a warning and had Shirley walk it over and deliver it by hand. Fortunately, she came back wearing a smile and holding a check. That was for the October rent, however, so Ali knew they still weren't entirely square.

Math and bookkeeping had never been Ali's strong suit, and the work required complete concentration. She was so caught up in the task at hand that she lost track of time. In midafternoon, when her cell phone buzzed in her pocket, she reached for the device thinking that it was probably announcing an arriving text from B. Instead it was the low-battery alarm. She'd forgotten to charge her phone overnight, and the battery power was now down to less than 10 percent.

Reaching into her purse to locate the extra charger she kept there, she encountered Archbishop Gillespie's collection of threatening notes. With everything else going on, they'd been virtually forgotten. She laid them out on the desk and was examining them one by one when Cami popped her head in the door.

"How are things back in the lab?" Ali asked.

"We haven't found anything in A&D's network so far, but B. came up with a brainstorm and sent us a text."

He could have sent me one, too, Ali thought but didn't say. "What kind of brainstorm?"

"He's wondering if the threat came from someone inside the company rather than outside it."

"An inside job, then?" Ali repeated.

"Exactly," Cami replied. "B. had A&D's head of security send us a complete list of current and former home-office employees and staff, including dates and places of birth. Frigg is in the process of doing detailed background checks on all of them."

"How many employees are we talking about?"

Cami consulted one of her computer screens. "That would be three thousand five hundred and sixty-four," she replied.

"Won't that take forever?" Ali asked. "I was hoping to have Frigg's help on another project."

"Not nearly as long as it would without Frigg on the job," Cami answered, "but what do you need? Is there something I can do?"

Ali glanced down at the collection of note cards scattered across her desk. Archbishop Gillespie had asked for High Noon's help, not just Ali and B.'s, and Cami Lee was part and parcel of High Noon.

"Maybe you could help me with these," Ali said. "I was hoping Frigg could do a forensic analysis of both the handwriting and verbiage and tell me if they give us any clues about the person who wrote them."

Cami picked up first one and then another, reading each in turn. "These are threats," she said, stating the obvious.

Ali nodded. "That's what we think, too."

"What about calling the cops?"

"Already done, but Phoenix PD gave them a pass, saying they're not credible. The archbishop asked us to look into them to see if we can find any clues about their origins."

"These were sent directly to Archbishop Gillespie?"

"Indirectly," Ali replied. "Between early June and now, they've been placed in unsealed envelopes and dropped, one at a time, into offering plates at churches located throughout the archdiocese."

"You're saying no DNA and no prints."

"Most likely."

"Why don't I scan them into a file?" Cami offered. "That way I can send them to Frigg and put them in the queue so they'll be next up whenever she finishes the background checks. Anything else?"

Before Frigg appeared on the scene, Cami had been High Noon's primo expert when it came to background checks.

"Maybe there is," Ali replied. Her phone was still charging, but she opened it to the Notes app. "I need any information you can gather on the following people: Anthony Gillespie, the archbishop's older brother, who lives in Green Bay, Wisconsin, in some kind of assisted-living facility. His daughter, Marcella, evidently looks after him. In addition, over the years there've been a number of disgraced priests inside the archdiocese. One suspected pedophile committed suicide before he could be arrested. Three others were convicted and sent to prison. One of those died in prison, while the last two are still incarcerated."

"Names?" Cami asked.

"Fathers James Hatfield, Gregory Powell, Paul Needham, and John Haynes," Ali answered. "Hatfield and Needham are deceased."

"Got it," Cami said. "Do you want me to print out whatever I find and bring it to you?"

Ali glanced at the clock on the wall and was surprised to see that it was almost four. "How are you guys all doing in the sleep department?" she asked.

"We're good," Cami answered. "We've been able to take turns grabbing naps."

"You may have had naps," Ali said, "but I haven't. After being up half the night getting B. off to Sky Harbor, I'm beat. I'm giving myself the rest of the day off and hitting the hay early. Whatever you learn, just e-mail it to me."

Cami came back a few minutes later and laid the cards back down on Ali's desk. "I made copies for Frigg," Cami explained, "but I thought you might like to have the originals."

"Thank you," Ali said, slipping them into her purse. "That was very thoughtful."

Later, as Ali packed up to leave, she checked the time on both her watch and her cell phone. With B. out of the country, she used the phone to keep track of local time while the watch on her arm was already set to Swiss time. It might have been almost quitting time for her, but it was just after midnight in Zurich. If B. had been texting back and forth to the crew during his flight, obviously he was preoccupied with the business at hand. Rather than bothering him with a text of her own, she decided to go home and wait to hear from him.

|CHAPTER 13|

On D-Day, Rachel awakened much later than she had intended. The gun-cleaning process had taken longer than anticipated, so she'd gone to bed late and then hadn't been able to sleep. Nerves, she supposed, and pre-battle jitters. Soldiers probably had those kinds of sleepless nights, too.

The first thing she did was open her iPad and log on to the archdiocese Web site. She emitted a sigh of relief when she saw that the archbishop's public schedule remained just as it had been listed the day before. This evening he was due to appear at a farewell gathering for the priest at St. Augustine's in Peoria with the timing of his arrival listed as 8:00 p.m.

In her months of both tracking and analyzing Francis Gillespie's comings and goings, she noticed that whenever there was a church supper preceding an appearance, his scheduled arrival was always after the conclusion of the dinner. Once aware of that anomaly, she had wondered if he suffered from food allergies of some kind. In any event it didn't matter. If things worked the way Rachel planned, the archbishop was destined to miss the evening's festivities at St. Augustine's altogether.

Rachel pulled on her robe and went to the kitchen to make coffee. Rich had made some earlier. The dregs from that were still warm in the pot but bitter beyond drinking. When she went to make a new pot, she discovered that Rich had taken it upon himself to make hot cereal that morning, leaving a dirty saucepan crusted with dry oatmeal still on the stovetop and an equally crusted, unrinsed cereal bowl sitting in the sink.

While the coffee brewed, a furious Rachel scrubbed both the pot and the bowl before slamming them into the dishwasher. Rich kept his workshop spotless. He never quit for the day without having vacuumed up every speck of lingering sawdust. But the house itself? If it were left to him, the house would have been the same kind of disaster as his room. And without Rachel, the kitchen would have deteriorated into an unsanitary, filthy mess, with dirty dishes stacked sky-high in the sink and on the countertops.

As she thought about it, the irony of her situation almost made her laugh. On the day she planned to murder Archbishop Francis Gillespie, the first thing she had to do was clean the kitchen. Did this happen to other people in her position? For instance, on November 22, 1963, did Lee Harvey Oswald have to clean up his wife's dirty kitchen before he went out to murder John F. Kennedy?

By the time the kitchen was back in order, Rachel was close to being late for her morning walk, but because she wanted today to seem normal in every way, she put on some speed and was in her usual spot in an office parking lot on Lincoln Drive a few minutes before 11:00 a.m. She had walked here almost every morning for months now, getting the lay of the land around the archbishop's residence. She didn't worry about being recognized there, because she didn't look the least bit like Rachel Higgins on those morning walks. Her appearance was such that even Rich, she suspected, would walk right past her without a second glance.

In real life Rachel Higgins never went anywhere without having her makeup in impeccable order. For her morning walking excursions, however, the makeup stayed home. She dabbed on sunscreen, but that was it. She didn't even wear lipstick, and the truth was, without a bit of help from Max Factor she looked her age and then some. For her walks Rachel hobbled along using a fold-up cane that she kept stowed under her car seat without ever taking it into the house. The jogging outfits she wore didn't make her fashion-plate material either. Most of her face was hidden behind a pair of enormous sunglasses, the kind usually worn by post-cataract-surgery patients. They were big and bulky and available for purchase for a song at the nearest Walgreens.

But the crowning glory of her disguise was the pink scarf. When David was little, his preschool teacher at St. Bart's, Miss Ginger, had been diagnosed with breast cancer. Both the school and the church as a whole had united behind her and devoted a year's worth of outreach to the scourge of breast cancer. They had participated in walks, donated hair, and canvassed for the American Cancer Society. Rachel had even spent time volunteering at a cancer support group where she'd helped fit patients with needed bras, wigs, and scarves.

Much to her surprise, Rachel had been a whiz at tying those scarves. Once postsurgical patients were able to raise their arms high enough, she'd taught them to tie their own. It was a talent that had worked for her as a cancer volunteer and was still working for her now as a would-be assassin. As she prepared to launch her campaign against Francis Gillespie, she had gone to a cancer support organization—one where people didn't know her—and purchased both scarves and a pair of affordable wigs. She didn't feel any particular guilt about the idea of taking Francis Gillespie's life, but walking around wearing a phony scarf bothered her.

Years earlier she'd gone to Scottsdale Fashion Square with a friend. Both women had been in their forties at the time and perfectly healthy, but the friend had hauled out her mother's handicapped sticker to score a prime parking place next to the mall entrance. Rachel had never quite forgiven her now-former friend for that bit of handicapped appropriation. Wearing a cancer-survivor scarf was every bit as unacceptable, but guilt-ridden or not, wear it Rachel did.

The combined effect of the cane, the glasses, and the scarf gave people she met on the street a completely different idea of who Rachel was. Those who encountered her on those Lincoln Drive walks regarded her as a frail and harmless little old lady. They admired her. After all, despite serious health issues, she still managed to show up each day and make a game effort to stay fit. And although she never exchanged a word with most of them, they had all become nodding acquaintances.

She strolled along at a leisurely pace commensurate with her age and physical capabilities, making no effort to imitate the brisk pace of all those people she dismissed as step-counting zealots. For the most part, those folks didn't bother nodding. They stormed past without acknowledging anyone around them, often completely absorbed in whatever was being beamed into their heads through seemingly permanently attached earphones.

As a rule the dog walkers were more relaxed and friendly, smiling in acknowledgment as they passed. The smartly dressed guy with a matched pair of well-behaved poodles never failed to tip his straw hat in her direction whenever they met. There was a red-haired lady about Rachel's age whose three noisy dachshunds were always a tangled knot of leashes, tumbling down the sidewalk and forcing everyone else out of the way. There was a twenty-something who was evidently a professional dog walker. She seemed to specialize in big dogs and was accompanied by an ever-changing cast of characters. There was a couple with a pair of elderly golden retrievers and an increasingly pregnant young woman whose walks included a little boy in a stroller and a honey-colored cocker spaniel who didn't seem the least bit fazed by the fact that his leash was attached to the handle of a toddler's stroller. The last three were absent today, causing Rachel to wonder if the new baby had arrived. In that case how would the woman manage to walk everyone at once?

As Rachel approached the archbishop's residence, she worried that her favorite regular—her future fall guy, the one she really needed to be on the scene today—was missing, but then the break in the oleander hedge parted and the homeless guy with his sign and kitchen stool emerged from the greenery. Once on the sidewalk, he unfurled an enormous golf umbrella and set up shop in the shade of his bumbershoot. He smiled and waved when he caught sight of her, and those welcoming gestures caused Rachel to feel the tiniest stab of guilt.

Over time Rachel had learned that the guy's name was Jack Stoneman. She wasn't sure of his age. He walked with a pronounced limp and wore a ball cap that identified him as a veteran of Desert Storm. He was on-site every day, seven days a week, working a shift that stretched from midmorning into the early afternoon. He always came equipped with a kitchen stool for seating along with a collection of hand-lettered signs that varied from day to day—WILL WORK FOR FOOD; HOMELESS PLEASE HELP; GOD BLESS. He always placed his stool just to the left of the driveway leading into the residence, making sure that he was in full view and within reach of anyone stopping to use the intercom button that operated the electronic gate blocking the entrance.

Rachel had befriended Jack early on by bringing him iced lattes from Starbucks, which she continued to do, even today. Considering her limited budget, those lattes were expensive, but the information Jack provided in exchange was priceless.

"Wouldn't you be better off stationed by a traffic light somewhere?" she'd asked the very first morning after she handed him his drink.

"No ma'am," he replied. "A church bigwig of some kind lives just up that driveway. The people who go in and out visiting him all act like it's their Christian duty to help out those less fortunate—especially if they think someone higher up might be watching."

"Watching?" Rachel repeated.

Jack had taken a sip of his latte before jerking his head in the direction of the gate. "There's a camera up on that post. I don't know if it's on or off, but it keeps everyone on their best behavior."

Rachel had glanced surreptitiously in that direction, too, and spotted a telltale box mounted on the gatepost. From that moment on, she realized that in doing her planning she would need to take that camera's presence into consideration.

"How do you get here every day?" she'd asked. "With all this stuff to carry around, someone must have to drop you off and pick you up."

"No, ma'am," Jack replied. "I bunk with some friends in a place off East Washington. I don't have a car, but I do have a bus pass. I ride back and forth on buses."

"With a kitchen stool and an umbrella in hand?" she'd asked in disbelief.

Grinning, he jerked his head in the opposite direction. "I've got me a little hidey-hole tucked away inside that hedge. I stow my things there overnight without anyone being the wiser. Except for when it rains," he added. "I used to have to take the signs with me when it rains because the ink would run. Now I have a cooler, and I can store them in that overnight."

A few nights later, under the cover of darkness and with the aid of a flashlight, Rachel had checked out Jack's so-called hidey-hole. The outside of the oleander hedge was lush and green, but inside there was a small area of shade-covered clearing backed by a chain-link fence that was invisible from the street. The interior of the hedge was gloomy and dusty. Paper debris from various fast-food establishments and numerous empty pint-size tequila bottles were scattered around the area. The trash indicated that Jack Stoneman often did his eating and drinking there. An unmistakable odor suggested that he sometimes relieved himself there as well. But that night, other than the stool, umbrella, and cooler, there was nothing that counted as furnishings. There was no tent or cot to indicate he sometimes stayed overnight.

On this cool autumn morning, he was just settling onto the stool with the GOD BLESS sign in hand when Rachel walked up to deliver his morning latte.

"Happy Halloween," she announced cheerily, handing it over. "I hope you like pumpkin spice."

"Love it," he said. "Thanks."

"How are things?"

"Yesterday was real busy," he said, "but it's pretty quiet today."

"And how are your new shoes working out?" she asked.

In reply he held up one foot, showing off what was clearly a brand-new shoe. She had given him a pair of Skechers the day before—size ten, medium—presenting them to him in an open box. He'd pulled out the shoes, tissue paper and all. Rachel kept the box. The box most likely had her DNA on it; the shoes did not.

"They're great," he said admiringly. "I gave my old pair to one of my roommates who needed shoes worse than I did."

She didn't mention that she had a second pair just like this one squirreled away at home. She had purchased two identical pairs at Walmart two days earlier, paying cash. Size ten would be several sizes too large on her, but stuffing the toes with tissue would make them work for as long as she needed them to work.

"Thank you," he added. "I told the guys I live with that you're like my guardian angel or something."

That wasn't quite how Rachel saw herself, but she smiled in return. "You're more than welcome," she said. "It's my small way of saying thank you for your service."

A car that was clearly a ride-share vehicle pulled up to the gate and stopped within reach of the intercom. There were two people inside, the driver and a passenger in the backseat who appeared to be a priest. Jack did his best to catch the passenger's eye, but once the gate rolled open, the car pulled through the opening with no donation forthcoming.

"You can't win 'em all," Jack told Rachel with a grin, "but at least I have my Halloween latte. Thanks again for that," he added.

"Glad you like it," she said. "I'd best be on my way."

She walked on feeling lighter than air. That's what she'd been hoping—

that Jack would be wearing his new shoes today. She knew exactly what was coming. Jack Stoneman had no idea.

She nodded a greeting at an approaching jogger and smiled at the young woman walking her German shepherd. Both knew her, and both smiled back, but they would have been surprised had they been able to read her mind. She was totally preoccupied with the idea of DNA, specifically trace DNA and what was the best way to put it in a place where it was sure to be found. In the end, rather than doing her customary route and coming back on the far side of Lincoln, she turned around a short time later and returned the same way she'd come.

By the time she reached the driveway of the archbishop's residence, the empty Starbucks latte cup was sitting on the sidewalk next to Jack's stool.

"You're back early," he observed as she approached.

"Just not feeling quite up to doing a whole lap today," she explained.

"Are you gonna be okay?" he asked with obvious concern.

"I think so," she replied. "Just a little tired is all. I believe I'll go home and have a lie-down." She glanced at the empty cup. "Are you done with that?"

"To the very last drop."

"Why don't I take it with me, then?" she asked, picking it up. "No sense in being a litterbug."

She was pretty sure there wouldn't be enough DNA on the tip of the straw to dose the handle of the .22, but she hoped there would be enough to salt at least one of the bullets. As far as cops were concerned, finding someone's DNA on a bullet casing from inside a murder weapon should be nothing short of a slam dunk.

|CHAPTER 14|

The introductory meetings with Fathers Martinez and Mayer had gone well. When the priests had arrived in Francis Gillespie's office, one after the other, the archbishop had risen to greet each of them with an outstretched hand, and they responded with satisfactorily firm hand-shakes of their own and reassuringly direct eye contact.

Francis's father had taught all his children that was the only way to take an accurate measure of someone you'd just met—judging them by both the quality of their grip and how they held your eye during that first face-to-face meeting. A too-limp handshake might indicate someone who wasn't entirely trustworthy. One that left you with days of aching fingers meant you were most likely dealing with a bully.

That was exactly what fifteen-year-old Anthony had done to Francis in the course of their father's handshake lesson. Tony had ground Francis's fingers together so hard that his knuckles were sore for a week. At the time Francis had managed to fight back his tears, refusing to give Anthony the satisfaction and something else to crow about later on. That experience was most likely why the lesson had stuck with the archbishop as it had, and it was something that had served him well from then on, both in the church and out of it. Anthony had most certainly been a bully, and so had some of the priests and parishioners Francis had met through the years. Today he was relieved that both incoming priests had passed his initial meet-and-greet litmus tests with flying colors.

These introductory visits were designed to be brief and cordial. After only a few minutes of conversation, the archbishop was confident that both of the newcomers would be good fits in their respective parishes. Father Martinez would be going to the Church of the Holy Virgin, a small and underserved parish in South Phoenix, where his youthful enthusiasm and energy were bound to serve his new parishioners well.

Before meeting the man, the archbishop hadn't been quite so sure about Father Mayer's placement. From New York City originally, the new priest was in his mid-forties and had spent years working on both the Wind River and Pine Ridge Reservations. Now he was being posted to the St. Thomas Mission on the Gila River Reservation south of Phoenix.

Francis Gillespie knew a bit about missionaries on reservations. He'd been around the same age as Father Mayer when he was posted to the Tohono O'odham. Francis had been sent there as a form of punishment, as a way for an incoming archbishop to take him down a peg after the favoritism shown him by the archbishop's predecessor. In truth, Indian reservations were often considered dumping grounds for failing clergy members from any number of denominations. As a consequence Archbishop Gillespie wondered if Father Mayer was coming to this new post of his own volition or because he'd messed up somewhere else and was being shipped off to the Gila as a way of getting rid of him.

"Why Gila River?" he asked. "What made you apply for the posting at St. Thomas?"

"The weather." Father Mayer's reply was disarmingly simple. "Last winter in Wyoming was brutal. I'm ready for warm."

"That's easy to say on a warm, sunny day in late October," the archbishop countered with a smile, "but when it gets to be the middle of July, it's a hundred and eighteen in the shade and you're living in a double-wide—"

"I've been told it's a dry heat," Father Mayer replied, brushing off the concern. "As for mobile homes? I've lived in a few of them before. Generally speaking, they qualify as tin cans in which you either bake or freeze. Between baking and freezing, I think I'll prefer baking."

The archbishop found the humor in Father Mayer's remarks both refreshing and reassuring.

"I felt the same when I left Chicago and ended up on the Tohono O'odham west of Tucson, so welcome to Arizona. By the way," he added, "my best friend on the reservation turned out to be the local medicine man. After I left there, we corresponded for years. I've been assured that the mission will be holding a welcoming feast in your honor. The women will serve popovers and chili. The chili will look lethal, but it's usually far milder than you expect. In addition to the food, my guess is that the local medicine man will be on hand to do the invocation. Having him in your corner will make all the difference. I suggest that you try to sit with him if at all possible. Turning him into a friend and ally will make your life on the reservation much easier."

"Good advice," Father Mayer replied, "and I plan on taking it to heart."

He departed a short time later, leaving the archbishop alone in his office. In his casual discussion of feasts, Archbishop Gillespie had somehow failed to mention how difficult it had been for a youthful Father Gillespie to attend those tribal feasts and dances when he'd first come to the reservation. Standing in line at feast houses had been too much like attending the church potlucks that had been the bane of his existence growing up.

His mother had been a dreadful cook. Countless times she left eggs boiling on the stove for so long that they exploded, leaving behind clouds of vile smoke and an assortment of wrecked WearEver aluminum pots and pans too charred to be usable. Other kids' mothers did canning. Gertrude did not. Other kids' mothers made cookies and cakes. Gertrude's baked goods always came out burned on the bottom. There were a few items in her limited cooking repertoire that were more or less acceptable, but the casseroles she created and offered up for church potlucks were generally inedible. Most of the time, the ladies in the kitchen simply dumped the contents without letting Gertrude's dish make it as far as the serving table.

Francis was ten and helping out in the church kitchen when he overheard one of the ladies say to another, "Just toss Gertrude's dish in the trash. Her food's so awful I don't know why she even bothers."

That year for Christmas, Francis had saved up enough money to buy his mother a cookbook. She never even opened it, and it wasn't until years later that Francis understood why. After his father's death and while settling Frank Gillespie's affairs, Francis learned that his mother had been left with a small pension as well as a ten-thousand-dollar life-insurance policy. When Francis tried to encourage Gertrude to open a checking account, she told him flat out that she didn't need one of those.

"I'll be fine with a savings account," she said. "I don't need anything more than that."

At the time Francis had simply accepted that decree as one of his mother's many odd idiosyncrasies. Later, after discovering that the title to his father's aging DeSoto was in Frank's name alone, Francis had wanted to put his mother's name on the title.

"Since I can't drive, there's no reason for me to own a car," she told her son. "Just sell it and give me the money."

That Gertrude didn't drive had long been a fact of life in their family. Her husband had done all the driving. It was why Francis had walked his mother back and forth to Mass every weekday morning for years. It was why Gertrude patronized only stores that were within walking distance. The L was just a few blocks away from their apartment, but Gertrude absolutely refused to use it on her own. Tony had stayed in the navy after the war ended. With him away at sea and with the older kids married and gone, in the aftermath of his father's death Francis worried that his mother would be left stranded.

"There's no reason you couldn't learn to drive," he'd said reasonably. "I could give you some lessons this summer when I'm home. After that, all you'd have to do is take the test."

"No," his mother had said.

"Why not?"

"I just can't."

"Why not?"

For the first time in his life, Francis's mother had turned on him in utter rage. "Because I can't read!" she'd railed at him. "I never learned how because I was too stupid!"

Francis was older and wiser now. His mother had been anything but stupid, and he'd come to realize that not only had she been dyslexic, but she'd probably also suffered from attention deficit disorder, which might well have accounted for all those exploding eggs and burned meat patties. Less than five years after Frank died of a heart attack at age fifty, Gertrude was gone, too, also age fifty. The death certificate listed an ulcer as the cause of her death, but Francis always suspected that she'd died of a broken heart.

Sitting there in his office, alone and lost in thought, the archbishop looked at the clock on the wall and was startled to see how much time had passed. It was time to go back to the patio and finish reading through that day's collection of documents. Just then there was a tap on the door, and Father Andrew entered carrying a tray of freshly made sandwiches and a pitcher of iced tea.

"I brought you a little something to hold you until the dessert line," Father Andrew said.

Archbishop Gillespie's antipathy toward church potlucks was a well-established fact of life inside the residence, but he usually allowed himself a brief trip to the dessert table so as not to appear snobbish.

"What time do we need to head out?" he asked.

"It'll be after rush hour," Father Andrew said. "If we leave at seven, that should give us plenty of time to get there, have dessert, and socialize a little before the program starts."

"Fair enough," Francis said. "I'll be ready at the stroke of seven."

|CHAPTER 15|

With B. out of the country, Ali had told Alonzo to take the day off and not worry about cooking, so he'd set aside plenty of leftovers from the party for her to eat. Her plan had been to have some dinner and go to bed early. That didn't happen. She was still at the kitchen table when the first of Cami's background check e-mails arrived. Once Ali opened the links, what she found there wasn't exactly light reading.

Cami had gathered most of the material from standard news sources—newspaper archives and public records. Although the articles were written in journalistic prose, they focused on the essential facts of the various abuse cases. Ali had done enough advocacy work over the years to understand the awful realities lurking behind the deliberately bland and inoffensive words. She was combing through the newspaper coverage of the class-action suit when her phone buzzed. Expecting either a text or a call from B., Ali was surprised to find that Frigg was the sender.

> Good evening, Ms. Reynolds, I
> do hope you're having a pleasant
> evening. Ms. Lee told me the
> general parameters of your
> project, and I have a few items
> ready to send. Do you wish to
> have the material sent to your
> phone, iPad, or computer screen?

My iPad will be fine.

My initial analysis of the
handwritten messages is that the
author is female and at least fifty
years of age. Individuals younger
than age fifty no longer learn this
style of penmanship.

That was hardly news to Ali. These days kids used computers to do
their homework. Ali had waged a personal crusade to make sure both
Colin and Colleen were proficient at writing and reading cursive.

You believe the writer to be
female?

That's not definitive. Some
elements in the formation of
the letters suggest that the
author is female. Also, there
was additional pressure applied
to the pen in the passage
concerning the snake that would
suggest a personal connection
of some kind.

The idea that Frigg would somehow conjure up the ability to perform handwriting analysis shouldn't have come as a surprise to Ali, but
it did.

A woman at least fifty years of age, but she could be older than that, too,
Ali mused to herself as she studied the words. On Archbishop Gillespie's
list of possible enemies, who would that be? His niece, maybe? If her
father was incapacitated, could Anthony's daughter be intent on doing
his bidding?

> What about Anthony Gillespie's
> daughter?

> That would be Marcella
> Gillespie Hosfield. I compared
> handwriting from her banking
> records to the threat messages.
> In my opinion Marcella is not the
> author.

Ali didn't want to think about how many laws Frigg had broken in obtaining that handwriting sample. Thankfully, this wasn't a case involving law enforcement. Frigg's usual strategy was to create detailed dossiers on every name associated with any investigation. Explaining her methods to a visiting cop wouldn't be good for anyone, most especially for the owners and operators of High Noon Enterprises.

Fortunately, an artifact from Frigg's days as Owen Hansen's serial-killer sidekick still remained as part of the AI's software repertoire. Using Frigg's TD or Total Delete option, it was possible for recipients to scrub all of Frigg's incoming and outgoing messages, leaving behind no cybertrace that the material had ever existed. In addition, Stu had installed guidelines in Frigg's operating system that meant all her interactions with High Noon personnel—whether via text, voice, or e-mail—unless otherwise specified, were automatically deleted using the same TD protocol sixty seconds after being read.

This exchange was a good case in point. Information that was clearly available on an open-source basis could be retained with no problem, but from Ali's point of view anything else—including Marcella Hosfield's illegally obtained penmanship sample—needed to vanish sooner rather than later.

Ali took a deep breath before sending the next text:

> Handwritten threats aside,
> are you making any progress
> on doing a general threat

assessment for Archbishop
Gillespie?

My research reveals that his
area of greatest strength is
also the source of his greatest
vulnerability.

What does that mean?

Internal communications
indicate his appointment to
archbishop was in large part
due to his stance on pedophile
priests. Other candidates
favored a "more measured"
approach while his was
described as unflinching. That
is defined as not shrinking or
yielding, resolute.

Frigg continued to have difficulty with bits of English language phrase-ology. Ali did not. She understood exactly what was meant. Francis Gilles-pie had been intent on tackling the problem of predatory priests head-on regardless of the consequences to the wayward priests themselves or even to the church as a whole. A "measured" approach would have meant sweeping the mess under the rug. But, Ali realized, if Frigg had developed this assessment based on internal documents from inside the Catholic Church, this was another conversation that needed to disappear.

When it comes to child abuse,
being unflinching seems like a
good idea.

Sources inside the church hierarchy have been outspoken concerning the "exorbitant amounts in damages" the archdiocese has paid out due to several class-action lawsuits.

Are you suggesting that someone inside the church may be the source of the threats?

Not of the threats per se, but there have been some pointed calls for him to retire due to health concerns.

Then where are we?

Back to the lawsuits. The most publicized of these concerns Father Paul M. Needham and fourteen of his former students. That suit was settled for unspecified damages. Church records reveal the actual amount to be $14 million plus attorneys' fees.

A million dollars apiece? That's a sizable settlement!

> Please take a look at the
> attached document from the
> Pinal County Office of the
> Medical Examiner.

When Ali clicked on the link, she found herself looking at a copy of an autopsy report for Paul M. Needham. There were no wounds showing on the diagram. His manner of death was listed as "natural." His cause of death was listed as "complications of AIDS."

Ali was aghast—a predatory priest with AIDS? Before she could comment, Frigg's next text appeared on the screen.

> So far I have determined that
> two of the fourteen plaintiffs
> died of complications due to
> AIDS.

Ali found herself staring at her iPad screen and shaking her head. In the face of a catastrophic illness like AIDS, a million-dollar settlement that sounded huge on the surface wouldn't have stretched very far. The men who were already dead had died at a young age. Ali thought back to what Frigg had already told her about the author of the collection-plate threats being female. What were the chances that some grieving relative—a mother or a sister—might lash out against Francis Gillespie, the very person who'd been responsible for bringing Father Paul Needham's exploitation to light and turning him over to the justice system?

> Do we have any direct
> testimony about all this?

> Because there were no actual
> court proceedings in the civil
> case, I'm unable to provide
> actual transcripts of that. So
> far I have failed to obtain

transcripts of any depositions.
However, I have been able to
locate the names of all plaintiffs
involved and am in the process
of creating dossiers on each
of them. Individual interviews
with survivors or with surviving
relatives may provide additional
information.

And maybe even unearth a few suspects, Ali thought.

I'm also compiling information
on the other three cases. The
next link will be to a copy of the
James Hatfield autopsy.

A quick glance at that told Ali that Father Hatfield's manner of death
was suicide and the cause of death was asphyxiation.

Was there a class-action lawsuit
for Hatfield's victims as well?

Yes, ten plaintiffs in all. Again
settled out of court for an
undisclosed amount. Church
documents reveal the actual
number to be $1.5 million,
including attorneys' fees.

The Hatfield case had preceded the Needham one. In that instance
each plaintiff had come away with something well under a hundred
thousand dollars, leaving Ali to conclude that the difference in amounts
payable was most likely due to the absence of the AIDS virus in the
Hatfield case.

Reading transcripts of witness testimony in Paul Needham's criminal trial was far different from reading the media's accounts of what had happened. These were the real words of real victims, sitting on the witness stand and recounting in excruciating detail the indignities to which they'd been subjected as adolescents. The questions asked by the prosecutors involved were bad enough, but the probing questions asked by the defense attorneys filled Ali's heart with outrage. Often the defense's line of questioning was shut down by objections from the other side of the courtroom, but many of them were clearly intended to make the victims themselves seem culpable—as if they'd somehow asked for or even encouraged whatever had happened to them.

As Frigg continued sending one report after another, Ali got caught up in her reading and lost all track of time. The more she read, the more appalled she was by the evils perpetrated on these innocent young men by people who should have been their trusted educators and spiritual advisers. And the more she read, the more she appreciated Archbishop Francis Gillespie. He had taken a stand against the evildoers, and the ones who'd come to his attention had been brought to justice.

By the time Ali finished reading the trial transcripts, Frigg had sent another stack of dossiers. With the weariness Ali had felt earlier vanished, she forgot about her plan for an early bedtime and kept right on reading.

|CHAPTER 16|

Rachel Higgins stood in front of the bathroom mirror and applied the last of her makeup—a layer of bright red lipstick. She would take tissues along so she could wipe it off later, but for leaving the house tonight lipstick was a must, and the brighter the better.

Turning away from the mirror, she glanced at her watch. Time seemed to have slowed to a crawl, and it was still too early to leave. Back in the bedroom, she opened her laptop and called up the schedule page on Archbishop Gillespie's Web site. How many times had she checked it this afternoon? Ten times at least. In months of keeping track of the archbishop's comings and goings, she had noticed that last-minute schedule changes were sometimes posted. Thankfully, the schedule for today remained just as it had been the first time she'd checked that morning: "7:30 p.m., Retirement Celebration for the Reverend George McKinley, Parish Hall, St. Augustine's Catholic Church, Peoria, Arizona."

A nervous Rachel allowed herself to breathe a small sigh of relief. A few minutes later, that same case of nerves drove her to go back through her kit one more time. She was intent on committing the perfect crime. In order for that to happen, nothing could be left to chance.

For this occasion she had chosen one of her old beach bags, because beach bags were roomier than any of her remaining purses. Besides, the cheery yellow-and-white one didn't look the least bit threatening. Plus, she had purchased it on a trip to San Diego to watch David swim in competition. That very real link to her lost son made the bag's part of the operation all the more appropriate.

Rachel had packed the whole thing earlier. First she'd used latex gloves and the tip of the straw from Jack Stoneman's pumpkin-spice latte to apply what she hoped would be traces of his DNA to the shell casing on one of the bullets inside the .22 revolver.

It had been years since Rich had entered the master bedroom, but before dumping the contents of the bag out onto her bed for a final check, Rachel locked the door. One by one, she examined each of the several items before returning them to the bag. First off came the revolver, confined to a gallon-size Ziploc bag. She held it for a moment, studying it. Feeling confident that the weapon was clean and in good working order, she placed it at the very bottom of the bag. Next up was the now-almost-depleted box of latex gloves. Tonight she'd want to have gloves on hand for sure. Third came the second pair of size-ten Ske-chers—carbon copies of the shoes she'd given Jack Stoneman the day before. These were already pre-stuffed with enough toilet paper to keep them from flopping on her much smaller feet. Yes, the shoes were ter-ribly uncomfortable, but she wasn't planning on running a marathon or doing a ten-mile hike in them. They would be perfectly fine for as long as Rachel needed to wear them, and that was all that mattered.

Next into the bag was the extra clothing required, including a worn pair of Rich's baggy sweatpants and one of his old hooded rain jackets, which would be topped by the Desert Storm ball cap she'd scored from a Salvation Army thrift store weeks earlier. Once Rachel returned home tonight, she intended to launder everything, shoes included, thus rid-ding them of any possible gunshot residue before dropping them off at a Goodwill collection center bright and early tomorrow morning. The shoes, sweats, and jacket would go to one Goodwill location. The beach bag and Desert Storm cap would go to another. None of the clothing would be remotely traceable back to her.

The last item placed in the bag was her favorite bright red St. John sweater, one she'd purchased years earlier, which would now have to be done away with along with all the other crime-scene clothing. For Rachel, being able to go out and buy a replacement was no longer finan-cially feasible. With winter coming on, she knew she would miss the sweater terribly, but she didn't have a choice. Yes, the sweater was her favorite—that's why she still had it—but red had been David's favorite color. In the end the symbolism of being able to wear something directly connected to her son was what ruled the day.

With the bag now fully loaded and sitting on her bed, Rachel stood there staring at it for a time, studying her handiwork. This wasn't simply premeditated murder—it was meticulously premeditated. Rachel knew, for example, that forensics people often identified individual shoe imprints based on wear patterns. These two pairs were so new that wear patterns on any shoe imprints left under the oleanders would be virtually identical. Surely no one would ever tumble to the fact that they came from two different pairs of shoes—good for her and too damned bad for Jack Stoneman.

Before leaving the room, she removed her phone, switched the ringer to silent, and slid the device under her pillow. Leaving it here in the house would give her a plausible alibi. Rachel's few remaining friends would be more than happy to tell any inquiring detectives that she never went anywhere without her phone. None of them knew about the prepaid phone she kept fully charged and hidden under the driver's seat of her aging Mercedes.

The doorbell rang just as she picked up the bag and slung it over her shoulder. Rachel jumped as though she'd been caught doing something bad, which indeed she had, but she didn't hurry out to the front entryway to answer the door—and for good reason. She knew all too well what day this was and exactly what would be waiting for her on the front porch.

When David was young, he'd always been more excited about Halloween than he was about Christmas. He and Rachel would spend weeks in advance designing and creating his trick-or-treat costume, and it was always Rachel rather than Rich who followed in the boy's footsteps, hovering in the background as he walked up sidewalks and onto front porches to collect his goodies. And now each year when Halloween came around, it reminded her of those long-vanished days of innocence.

So she didn't go to the door. She had left a dish filled with miniature candy bars on the front porch with a handwritten Post-it on the lid saying HELP YOURSELF. That was fine, she supposed, but only if the kids ringing the bell were old enough to read.

Rachel waited in the bedroom for another five minutes, giving the trick-or-treaters a chance to move a few houses down the street before she headed for her car. Force of habit meant she left through the kitchen, stopping at the door to the garage to tell Rich good-bye.

She stood in the open doorway for a long moment considering the man hunkered over his pristinely clean workspace and mentally comparing the neatness of his garage surroundings to his pigpen of a room. It was such a mess that Rachel refused to set foot in it anymore. She washed and folded his clothes when he brought them to the laundry room, but that was it.

Rich's workshop, on the other hand, resembled a surgical theater, with every tool clean and in its proper place. He stood there frowning in concentration, painstakingly brushing some kind of stain onto the exterior of his most recent creation. Made from scraps of lumber scavenged from a high-end cabinet manufacturer, Rich's hand-crafted birdhouses were all pieces of woodworking art, mortised together without the use of nails or any other hardware. Rachel sometimes wondered if any of the birds using those one-of-a-kind creations were impressed by the craftsmanship in their custom-made homes.

The Rich she saw standing there now was a mere shadow of the person she'd once loved. Falling apart was the last thing she would have expected him to do after David's death. She had wanted Rich to get up off the mat and fight back. She had wanted him to do something that would make David's death meaningful to both of them. Instead he'd simply collapsed in on himself, leaving Rachel as the only person alive who cared enough to hold the responsible party accountable. Rich sure as hell wasn't going to do it.

As she stood there, the only sound in the garage was the sharp-edged voice of Judge Judy, blaring from the small-screen TV positioned on the worktable next to Rich's elbow. She was busily haranguing some poor miscreant or another who'd been dumb enough to venture into her courtroom in search of justice. Good luck with that.

"Who was at the door?" Rich asked.

So he'd heard the doorbell but hadn't bothered to answer. Typical.

"Trick-or-treaters," she replied.

"It's Halloween already?"

She sighed. No surprises there. Rich barely bothered looking at the calendar anymore. The seasons came and went almost without his noticing.

"Yes, it's Halloween," she answered. "I left candy in a dish on the front porch. If the doorbell rings again, you can just ignore it. I'm going to be out for a while."

As if he would bother doing anything but *ignore people at the door.*

"Okay," he said. "See you later."

That was it. He didn't ask where she was going or when she'd be back because he simply didn't care and hadn't cared for a very long time.

Without another word Rachel closed the door to the garage and then left the house via the front door. The candy bars in the dish were somewhat depleted, leaving her to hope there would be enough left to get through the remainder of the night. These days most of the kids she knew in the neighborhood were well beyond trick-or-treating age.

Once in the driveway with the engine running, Rachel had to wait with the car idling while a group that included two princesses and a Spider-Man made its way past her back bumper and up the sidewalk to the house. Pulling out into the street, she stopped next to the two adults accompanying the kids and buzzed down her window.

"The candy's on the front porch," she told them. "I have an appointment, and I can't be late."

And that was the truth. She did have an appointment—with vengeance. The Catholic Church she had once loved had cost her both her son and her husband, and Archbishop Gillespie was the one who would pay the price for her losses. She had set herself on this path with every intention of carrying it out, and she had never once wavered. She might have lain awake worrying about *how* she would do it, but she'd never strayed from the idea that she *would* do it. Now it was time.

After merging onto the 51 at Shea, Rachel drove south to the second exit, where she turned left onto Lincoln Drive. Heading eastbound, she drove past the entrance to the archbishop's residence. At six thirty on the dot, she pulled in to her customary spot in the office complex parking lot. Once parked, she changed out of her loafers into the oversize Skechers. Then she headed out on foot.

It was dark and well after close of the workday, but there was still plenty of traffic rushing by. As she neared Jack Stoneman's sheltered spot in the oleander hedge, she slowed her pace enough to find a pause in passing traffic before slipping through the virtually invisible opening and into the darkened interior.

All day long she'd worried about the possibility that the archbishop might change his mind and not attend the St. Augustine event. She had also worried that Jack might have changed his mind as well and ended up camping out inside the hedge overnight rather than going home to wherever he lived. As a result, as Rachel entered the clearing, she literally held her breath, but as her eyes adjusted to the darkness, she was relieved to find that she was alone.

Sitting on Jack's stool, she pulled Rich's capacious sweats on over her own jeans, using the tie string to keep them from falling down. Next she donned the jacket. After raising the hood, she topped that with the ball cap. Only when her disguise was complete did she remove the revolver from the beach bag. Sitting on Jack's stool, she placed the weapon, still encased in plastic, on her lap. Then, with a new pair of latex gloves on her hands, she settled in to wait.

At that point her eyes had fully adjusted to the intermittent darkness left in the wake of passing headlights. She didn't worry about knowing when it would be time for her to take action. She had heard the gate roll open enough times to recognize the sound. When the archbishop's Town Car emerged from the residence, she would be ready.

|CHAPTER 17|

Archbishop Gillespie was a great believer in that old adage "Ad-libbing is for amateurs." He was always prepared, so he spent the late afternoon working on his speech, which would be partially a roast and partially a heartfelt tribute to the much-beloved Father George.

St. Augustine's associate priest, Father Donovan, who would be stepping into Father George's shoes, was in charge of the evening's festivities, including serving as emcee for the roast. He had assured the archbishop that the program wouldn't start before eight. A seven thirty arrival would give the archbishop a brief shot at the dessert selection before the tables in the parish hall were to be collapsed and put away and the chairs rearranged.

Since it was well past rush hour, Father Andrew estimated that the trip across town to St. Augustine's wouldn't take more than thirty minutes. When the archbishop came outside at 7:00 p.m. exactly, Father Andrew had the venerable black Town Car shined up, ready to go, and waiting in the porte cochere. Father Andrew helped the archbishop into the backseat and then loaded his bulky walker into the trunk. It was the deluxe rolling kind that took up more room in the spacious trunk than one would have expected.

The archbishop was religious, all right, but not when it came to wearing seat belts. Long experience had told him that the shoulder belt in the backseat of the Lincoln hit him in just the wrong spot on his clavicle.

Father Andrew had installed a sheepskin pad that was supposed to ease the pressure. It helped a little, but not nearly enough. When they were out on some highway, speeding along at seventy-five miles per hour, the archbishop minded his manners and wore the belt as required. As for driving in town? Well, maybe not so much. Unfortunately, that night just happened to be one of those times.

It's dark, Archbishop Gillespie thought, letting the belt silently retract into its holder. *What Father Andrew doesn't know won't hurt him.*

Father Andrew climbed into the driver's seat, fastened his own belt, and started the engine. "Traffic's supposed to be light," he announced. "The GPS says we'll arrive at seven twenty-six."

"Perfect," the archbishop replied.

With that, Father Andrew steered the vehicle out onto the curving driveway. There were streetlights beyond the intervening oleander hedge and small solar-powered yard lights lining their path, but most of the grounds surrounding the residence were bathed in darkness. At the end of the drive, Father Andrew waited while the automatic gate rolled open. After passing through, he eased the car toward the roadway.

Although the posted limit on Lincoln was somewhat lower, most vehicles sped past at forty-five to fifty miles an hour. Approaching the roadway with some caution, Father Andrew had paused to check for traffic when a black-clad figure emerged from the shadows of the hedge and tapped lightly on the driver's-side window.

"Looks like somebody with car trouble," Father Andrew muttered over his shoulder as he buzzed down the window. "Can I help you?"

Francis Gillespie had no warning that anything was amiss, but "Can I help you?" were Father Andrew's last words. A blast of gunfire exploded inside the car as a bullet slammed into his forehead, killing him instantly. The Town Car had still been in gear when Father Andrew paused to survey traffic. Now, as the deadweight of his foot slipped off the brake pedal and landed full on the accelerator, the vehicle shot into traffic.

Plunging forward across Lincoln, the out-of-control vehicle first slammed into a westbound Hyundai Sonata and sent it spinning. It then crashed into an eastbound Dodge minivan. Finally it smashed head-on into the soundproofing wall on the far side of the street. The speeding Town Car's glancing blow to the driver's fender of the minivan had been powerful enough to shove it into the curb, where it toppled over onto its side. Once the shriek of rending metal came to an end, the only sound remaining was the ungodly howl from the Lincoln's back tires, smoking and spinning furiously on the sidewalk because Father Andrew's foot was still glued to the gas pedal.

———

Several passing motorists stopped their vehicles and hurried to help. One of them, a man named Sidney White, approached the Town Car, reached into the open window, and pawed through the layer of deflated air bags until he managed to locate the ignition and shut down the racing engine. Once the screeching of the spinning tires finally ceased, the night was filled with terrified cries for help from occupants still trapped in the overturned minivan.

The Good Samaritan turned his attention to the motionless figure of the driver. "Hey man," he said, "are you all right?"

When there was no response, he pulled out his phone and activated his flashlight app, realizing at once that the man behind the wheel was a priest. Groping for the driver's wrist in hopes of finding a pulse, he caught sight of the entry wound and understood that the gray substance his flashlight had illuminated on the headrest behind the driver was actually a gory spray of brain matter.

Sickened by the sight, Sid grabbed the window frame and used that to support himself while he emptied his guts into the dirt. Only when he stopped heaving did he hear his wife calling.

"Sid," she said, "is everybody all right? Are they okay?"

Right then Sid was incapable of speech. Wiping his mouth on his sleeve and shaking his head, he stared unseeing at the wreckage. Just then the glow from his flashlight revealed something moving under the morass of deployed air bags covering the backseat. Someone was still inside? He moved to the passenger door directly behind the driver's seat and attempted to wrench it open. Naturally, that didn't work.

Only then did Sid find his voice. "Someone's trapped inside!" he croaked over his shoulder. "Call 911. I think the driver's dead, but there's a person in the backseat who's still alive!"

By then some other onlooker must have made the call, because in the distance Sid already heard the distinctive wail of approaching sirens. Reluctantly, he turned back to the open driver's window, but before he leaned into the vehicle, he turned off his flashlight to avoid seeing the awful gore he already knew was there.

"Hang in there," he called to the invisible person struggling desperately to escape from under the layer of air bags. "Help is on the way."

|CHAPTER 18|

During Rachel's months of preparation and after she had determined Rich's .22 to be her weapon of choice, she had read up on guns. Articles about handguns used for self-defense all said the same thing—you needed to practice to be proficient and to keep from having your own weapon used against you. Unfortunately, Rachel hadn't followed that sage advice.

For one thing, she hadn't wanted to remove Rich's handgun from the safe until the last possible moment, in case, for some strange reason, he happened to go looking for it. And she had zero interest in going to a gun range for practice, where her likeness might well end up recorded for all posterity on some video surveillance system.

Waiting in the gloom of that dusty clearing with the cocked revolver in her hand, Rachel Higgins felt fairly confident as far as her gun-handling skills were concerned, but she found herself regretting not having gone out into the desert at least once to plink away at a few beer bottles. Had she done so, however, shattering beer bottles wasn't nearly the same thing as shooting a living, breathing human being, even if he was your sworn enemy and even if you'd planned for months to end the man's life.

But then, after what seemed an eternity, she heard the rumble of the gate as it rolled open. At last it was time, but when she stood up, she was shocked to find that her knees nearly buckled under her weight. Stumbling toward the almost invisible opening in the hedge, her legs wobbled and her breathing quickened. As for her hands? Both of them were suddenly shaking uncontrollably, the same way her mother's hands had quivered in the final stages of Parkinson's, when she could no longer hold anything—not a spoon or a pencil or even a book. Rachel had prepared for every contingency, she thought, but she had not prepared for this, not for her hands to betray her and suddenly go berserk.

By the time she managed to lurch out of the darkness of the hedge and onto the sidewalk, the Town Car was paused, waiting for a break in traffic before turning right onto Lincoln. Rachel's legs were still being uncooperative as she staggered up to the driver's side of the vehicle. The gun out of sight in her right hand, she tapped on the driver's window with her left. As the glass slid down, a passing car's headlights flashed across the scene. In that sudden strobe of illumination, Rachel realized that the man behind the wheel wasn't Francis Gillespie. She leaned forward, trying to see if he was in the backseat. At that same time, she raised her right hand in order to bring the .22 into a firing position. That was when her quaking body betrayed her. Without meaning to and without taking aim, she pulled the trigger. In the split second that followed, she had no time to cock the weapon and fire off a second shot. The Town Car's V-8 engine roared to life, and the archbishop's car rocketed into the street, plowing directly into the path of oncoming traffic.

As cars crashed into one another, Rachel didn't stay to watch. Instead, turning away from the mayhem, she slipped back into the shelter of the oleander hedge. Had her bullet found its mark? She had no way of knowing.

She stopped just inside the clearing and stood there for the better part of a minute, waiting for her body to stop quaking and for her breathing to return to normal. That pause gave her enough time to gather herself. Had she done the deed, or had she killed the wrong man? Regardless, her only goal now was to escape the scene without being spotted.

Part of Rachel's exacting preparations for the shooting had included laying out and rehearsing exactly what should be done in the aftermath. Once her body was finally under control, she set about executing that plan down to the smallest detail. First she dropped the .22 in the dirt beside the stool. Next she stripped off the excess clothing—the ball cap, the hooded jacket, and the sweats, along with the latex gloves. All those went back into the beach bag. Finally, wearing the red sweater and with the white-and-yellow bag dangling casually from her shoulder, she slipped out of the sheltering hedge and into a scene of utter chaos.

Across the street, a wrecked minivan lay on its side. The van's head-lights still glowed, and a concerned crowd milled around the damaged vehicle. Evidently people were still trapped inside, and efforts were under way to help them escape the wreckage. Closer at hand, a sedan of some kind had come to rest, its front tires stuck against the curb, its headlights still glowing. Passersby who had abandoned their own vehicles stood in the middle of the street, blocking the way for people who simply wanted to drive past. As horns honked and more first responders arrived to the tune of blaring sirens, Rachel decided it was past time to leave.

With the oversize Skechers feeling like clown shoes on her feet, she turned her back on the carnage and walked away. Half a mile from the uproar of the accident, she ambled into the parking lot, slid into the driver's seat of her SEL, and drove off. Rather than heading west-bound and back toward what she knew would soon be a massive traffic jam, she headed east, toward Scottsdale. By the time she merged onto the northbound 101, her hands had finally steadied. Twenty minutes later she uttered a sigh of relief as she turned in to her own driveway. She was home. She was safe.

On the front porch, the candy dish was completely empty. Unlocking the front door, Rachel let herself inside. The house was dark, and every-thing was as it should be—at least until she walked into the family room. Halfway through the unlit room, Rich spoke to her out of the darkness. "Where have you been?" he demanded.

Rachel's jangled nerves were already strung to the breaking point, and she leaped as though she'd been shot.

"You scared me to death!" she exclaimed, switching on the nearest lamp. "Why are you sitting here in the dark?"

"You haven't answered my question," he insisted.

Just as Rachel had been unprepared for her hands to tremble uncon-trollably when it came time to shoot, she was equally unprepared to answer Rich's question. She made a show of putting down the bag and taking a seat while she crafted a suitable answer.

"I was out walking with my friends," she replied finally, sinking into a chair. "There's a group of us who like to do an evening mall crawl over at Metrocenter."

"Sure you do," Rich sneered. "You must think I'm really stupid."

With that he got up and lumbered out of the room. Rachel remained where she was, sitting there with her whole body shaking, rather than just her hands.

If Rich had suddenly decided to emerge from his self-imposed exile, what the hell was she going to do now? She sat still for a very long time, considering that question before realizing that no matter what, she had to go on with her plans exactly as she'd laid them out. She went into the bedroom, stripped off the clothing she'd worn that evening, and took a lengthy shower. Then, after putting all the clothing in the washer, she switched on the TV in the master bedroom. The nine-o'clock news on the local Fox affiliate was just coming on, and the newscast led with the story she wanted to see.

"Phoenix PD is on the scene of a deadly multi-vehicle incident on Lincoln Drive east of the 51," the female newscaster reported, all the while smiling into the camera. "Emergency vehicles are at the scene, and Lincoln is closed in both directions from North Thirty-second Street to North Forty-sixth. Drivers are advised to avoid the area. This is a developing story. We'll pass along more details as they become available."

The segment wasn't much, but it was better than nothing. The word "deadly" meant just that—someone was dead. She was sure she had shot the driver, but maybe the archbishop had died as well. Rachel watched the entire thirty-minute show, but no more details were forthcoming. None. When ten o'clock came around, she switched over to another channel. Still no luck. She stayed up long enough for the laundry to come out of the dryer so she could have it folded and packed for an early-morning trip to Goodwill.

At midnight she finally went to bed, feeling like a failure. If Archbishop Gillespie had been murdered, wouldn't someone have leaked that information by now? And if he wasn't dead, that meant David's death was still unavenged, *and* Rich had suddenly emerged from his stupor.

So all was lost. Or was it? Rachel Higgins wasn't someone to give up that easily. She might have lost that first battle, but she sure as hell hadn't lost the war. After tossing and turning for what seemed like hours, she fell asleep at last, but only after making up her mind that when the new day dawned, she would devise another plan.

|CHAPTER 19|

Ali was dozing in her easy chair with the iPad on her lap and Bella next to her thigh when her cell phone startled her awake. She reached for the phone, expecting to find her husband on the line. Instead Sister Anselm's name appeared in the caller ID, and the time stamp told her it was 10:00 p.m.

Ali was surprised. It was her understanding that inside St. Bernadette's Convent in Jerome it was always lights-out no later than nine. Knowing that Sister Anselm was well into her eighties, Ali couldn't help but feel a sense of alarm.

"Hello," she said uncertainly into the phone. "Is everything all right?"

"No, it's not," Sister Anselm replied, "not at all."

"What's wrong?"

"I just got off the phone with Archbishop Gillespie's secretary, Father Daniel McCray, down in Phoenix. Earlier this evening there was an attempted carjacking outside the archbishop's residence. The archbishop's driver, Father Andrew, was killed in the incident. Archbishop Gillespie has been transported to St. Gregory's Hospital, where he is currently undergoing surgery. Several other vehicles were caught up in the incident. I believe at least one other person is hospitalized at this point, although I don't have any word on that person's condition."

At the mention of Archbishop Gillespie's name, Ali sat bolt upright. Her sudden movement must have disturbed Bella's repose. With a reproving look over her shoulder, the dog abandoned her perch and went to curl up on a dog bed in front of the fire.

"A carjacking?" Ali repeated.

"That's what Father Daniel said. According to him, police officers are still on the scene investigating. Sister Cecelia and I are packed and ready to head out as soon as she finishes making a pot of coffee. I plan to be on the scene the moment Archbishop Gillespie comes out of the OR. I'm expecting St. Gregory's to be a little more accommodating about the presence of a patient advocate than the Mayo Clinic was when he was hospitalized there."

For years Sister Anselm had been a special emissary for the archbishop, serving as a patient advocate for people who for one reason or another needed help negotiating the lines of communication between patients and their health-care providers. Earlier in the year, when Archbishop Gillespie had been hospitalized with a nearly fatal case of pneumonia, Ali knew that either Sister Anselm or her recently assigned assistant, Sister Cecelia Groppa, had been in constant attendance at his bedside. At the time it had seemed only right that he should benefit from a ministry he'd generously provided to so many others.

"How fast were they going?" Ali asked. "With seat belts and air bags, it takes a lot of speed to turn a car accident into a fatality."

"Father Andrew didn't die as a result of the wreck," Sister Anselm said grimly. "He was shot in the head at point-blank range."

Ali took a startled breath. It was a moment before she could speak again. "How awful," she murmured. "Was the archbishop shot, too?"

"By the time I finish with him, he's going to wish he *had* been," Sister Anselm declared with a degree of anger that took Ali by surprise. "He's never liked wearing a seat belt and does so only under duress. The worst of his injuries are a direct result of being tossed around in the backseat, where he went airborne and smashed his head into the dome light. He's being treated for a concussion and a possible brain bleed. In addition, he has a broken shoulder and several broken ribs. There may be internal injuries as well. Believe me, in the near future that stubborn old coot and I will be having a long heart-to-heart discussion about the mandatory use of seat belts."

Ali had done a brief stint as a cop, and some of her police-academy training instantly surfaced. "Has Father Andrew's family been notified?" she asked.

"Yes, Father Daniel was able to provide the detectives with Mr. O'Toole's contact information."

Ali was still trying to straighten out the details in her head. "You said it was an attempted carjacking?"

"Yes, of all the ridiculous things!" Sister Anselm sniffed. "Father Daniel has complained about that old Town Car for years, saying they needed to get rid of it in favor of something newer."

Sister Anselm, with no knowledge of the threats that had been coming the archbishop's way, might have accepted the official determination that what had happened was a simple carjacking. Ali didn't believe a word of it. Francis Gillespie might have wanted to keep the situation under wraps, but now that someone had actually tried to murder him, it was time to set the record straight.

"This was no carjacking, Sister Anselm," Ali stated flatly.

"It wasn't?" Sister Anselm asked, her voice faint. "What makes you think that?"

"And if Father Andrew is dead," Ali continued, "it's only because he's collateral damage. The real target has to have been Archbishop Gillespie."

Ali heard her friend's sharp intake of breath. "I don't understand," Sister Anselm murmured.

"Archbishop Gillespie has been receiving anonymous death threats for months now," Ali replied. "They've been dropped into collection plates all over the archdiocese."

"You can't be serious," Sister Anselm objected. "I've never heard word one about any of this."

"That's because the archbishop went to great lengths to make sure no one else knew about them. He didn't want people worrying. Over the weekend he contacted B. and me, hoping that High Noon could help figure out who's behind all this."

"I really will wring his neck!" Sister Anselm exclaimed. "How dare he not tell me about this? But if someone's been sending him threats, why would he turn to High Noon for help instead of to Phoenix PD?"

"According to the archbishop, he did go to the cops, only to be told that a public person being targeted anonymously like this doesn't qualify as a credible threat."

"I guess it's credible now," Sister Anselm muttered. "So have you made any progress?"

"We've given copies of the notes to Frigg, Stu Ramey's AI, so she could do handwriting analysis. She tells us that whoever wrote them is most likely female, probably somewhere in her fifties or sixties."

"What about DNA?" Sister Anselm asked.

"None," Ali answered. "Since the envelopes weren't sealed, there's no DNA present, and there are no usable fingerprints, either."

"In other words, whoever is behind this is being very careful."

"Exactly."

"So if someone tried to assassinate the archbishop and failed," Sister Anselm said quietly, "what are the chances that they'll try again?"

Ali's thoughts had been running along that same line. "I'd say the chances of that are very high indeed."

"All right, then," Sister Anselm said. "I recently replaced the battery in my Taser. If some bad guy shows up at the hospital thinking the archbishop is a helpless old man, he'll be in for a big surprise."

Despite the dire circumstances, Ali couldn't help but smile. "Will Sister Cecelia be there with you?"

"No, she won't," Sister Anselm answered. "We were notified this evening that late this afternoon there was a major accident on I-10 just west of Willcox. An SUV loaded with migrants was trying to outrun Border Patrol. A high-speed chase ended in a rollover crash with three dead and seven or eight people with life-threatening injuries. Most of the injured were airlifted to hospitals in and around Tucson. The original plan was for Sister Cecelia and me to head for Tucson early tomorrow morning. As things stand now, we'll be leaving shortly. Sister Cecelia will drop me off at St. Gregory's and go on to Tucson by herself."

"Is there any word on the archbishop's condition?"

"Father Daniel told me he was in critical condition when they loaded him into the ambulance. That's all I know so far. I'll learn more once I get to the hospital."

"You'll keep me apprised?"

"Of course," Sister Anselm replied. "You told me about the death threats, didn't you? I guess that makes us even. But Sister Cecelia just came in. She says coffee's done and the car is packed. We're ready to go."

"Travel safely," Ali told her.

Suspecting that B. was probably too preoccupied to talk, she sent him a text:

Call when you can. It's about
Archbishop Gillespie.

After that, Ali began scrolling through Phoenix-based news sites looking for additional details. There weren't many to be had. She gleaned that
the local authorities were treating the shooting incident on Lincoln Drive
as a "carjacking gone bad." Several other vehicles had been involved in
the incident. Three of the four passengers in a passing minivan had been
treated for minor injuries and released at the scene, while a fourth had
been transported with serious but non-life-threatening injuries.

Ali was still reading that first article when her iPad lit up with a flash
briefing from Frigg. The AI was clearly still on the job and had plucked
news of the attack on Archbishop Gillespie out of the ether. She had
supplied several links, not only to the article Ali was currently reading
but also to six more besides.

Ali had clicked on the second link, one she hadn't previously read,
when the AI's voice boomed through the speaker on Ali's iPad.

"Changes in your respiration and heartbeat told me when you fell
asleep earlier," Frigg announced. "Would you like me to resend the
dossiers that were already in the queue at the time you fell asleep as well
as the ones we have accumulated since then?"

Working with Frigg often felt like an invasion of privacy. It was
disturbing to know that while Ali was reading away in the presumed
privacy of her own library, Frigg was surreptitiously monitoring her vital
signs. The AI seemed to see all and know all, but in this case maybe that
was a small price to pay.

"Please," Ali responded. "I have a feeling it's going to be a busy day.
Having you keep track of what I have and haven't read will be a big help.
Hold the dossiers for the time being, and let's see what else you can find
out about the archbishop."

"Very well," Frigg replied, "sending now."

Ali clicked on the first linked-to article, an updated version of the one
she'd first seen, and began reading:

A carjacking gone wrong is thought to be the cause of a
multi-vehicle crash on East Lincoln Drive that left one vic-

tim dead and two hospitalized, one with what are thought to be life-threatening injuries and the other reportedly in good condition.

The incident occurred at around 7:00 p.m. on October 31, just outside the official residence of Francis Gillespie, the archbishop of the Phoenix Archdiocese of the Catholic Church. The sole fatality is thought to be the driver of a Lincoln Town Car.

According to sources close to the investigation, speaking without authorization, the driver died as a result of a single bullet wound to the head. His name is being withheld pending notification of next of kin.

One of the injured, thought to be Archbishop Gillespie himself, was a passenger in the Town Car. He was transported to St. Gregory's Hospital, where he is expected to undergo emergency surgery.

According to witnesses on the scene, the Town Car emerged from the gated driveway to the archbishop's residence at a high rate of speed and drove straight into traffic, smashing into two separate vehicles along the way.

Four slightly injured passengers in a minivan were treated and released. A passenger in the second vehicle involved was transported with what are considered to be non-life-threatening injuries.

Detective Kyle Lasko with the Major Crimes Unit of Phoenix PD and the lead investigator on the case, said that witnesses reported that a man wearing what appeared to be a high-necked hoodie and a ball cap was in the area shortly after the incident. That individual is considered to be a person of interest in the case. K-9 units were brought in to search for him, but he has yet to be apprehended.

Anyone with information regarding this case is asked to call Phoenix PD's non-emergency line at 602-555-1212. Otherwise please contact Phoenix Crime Stoppers, where it's possible to leave information and still remain anonymous.

Ali paused long enough to make a note of the detective's name. She had no intention of going through the non-emergency number. She wanted to speak directly to the lead detective. Someone needed to let him know that this was anything but a random carjacking. Archbishop Gillespie had been the actual target in the attack, and if he was hospitalized with life-threatening injuries, his assassin had very nearly succeeded in taking him out.

|CHAPTER 20|

Ali was about to start reading again when her phone rang. This time it really was B. on the line.

"Hey, what's up?" B. asked. "Your text made it sound urgent."

"It *is* urgent," she replied grimly. "Someone tried to murder Archbishop Gillespie tonight. His driver—presumably Father Andrew—died of a single gunshot to the head. The archbishop has been transported to St. Gregory's with life-threatening injuries and is currently in surgery. From what I'm seeing online, the cops are treating it as a carjacking."

"Whoa," B. said. "Is he going to be all right?"

"Who knows? Sister Anselm is on her way to Phoenix right now. I'm sure she'll be there when he comes out of surgery. I'm equally sure she'll let us know how he is. Now that the cops are releasing his name, it'll turn into a media free-for-all."

"When did this happen? Where and when?"

Over the next several minutes, Ali brought B. up to speed on everything that had occurred.

"Sister Anselm and the archbishop have been friends for a long time," B. observed. "She must be really broken up about this."

"She is," Ali replied, "but she's also pissed as hell. Francis Gillespie evidently wasn't wearing his seat belt at the time. Otherwise his injuries would have been minor."

"Did you tell her about the threats?"

"Absolutely," Ali said. "Under the circumstances I didn't have a choice.

If whoever did this turns up at the hospital intent on taking another crack at him, Sister Anselm needs to know what she's up against." Ali paused. "All right, that's it on my end. What about yours?"

B. sighed. "There've been a whole slew of weather delays," he said. "I'm finally in the car and on my way to the hotel. I'm dead on my feet, but I'll only have time to shower and change before heading over to A&D."

"Any progress on finding the trojan?"

"Nope, none at all," B. answered. "So far our team hasn't found anything out of the ordinary. I'm still concerned that Dieter will jump the shark without giving us a chance to know one way or the other."

"Sounds like you're between a rock and a hard place."

"Doesn't it just," he agreed. "But we're pulling up to the hotel. I'm going in now to prepare for battle, and you're probably on your way to bed."

"Soon," Ali replied.

"Okay, then," B. said. "Call me when you're up and about in the morning."

Ali turned back to her iPad just as Frigg sent another new article, and the headline said it all:

ARCHBISHOP GILLESPIE AMONG INJURED AFTER SUSPECTED CARJACKING INCIDENT

Ali didn't need to read the article to imagine what was happening both outside and inside the lobby at St. Gregory's. Now that Francis Gillespie's name had been made public, the hospital grounds would turn into a media circus. Hospitals weren't great when it came to crowd control, and that made it much more likely that someone with bad intentions might be able to slip past security—all the more reason for Sister Anselm not to be standing guard on her own.

Ali clicked over to Frigg's audio connection. "No need to monitor my vitals," Ali told the AI. "I'm going to bed now. I'll let you know when I'm ready for you to resend all that unread material. In the meantime please tell Stu that due to Archbishop Gillespie's current situation, I'll be heading down to Phoenix first thing in the morning rather than coming into the office."

"I will. Good night, Ms. Reynolds," Frigg replied. "Sleep well."

|CHAPTER 21|

Rachel had gone to bed late. Nonetheless, her eyes popped open at six. Worried Rich might hear the TV if she turned it on, she opted for Internet news instead, and local news outlets were all over the story. She settled in to read the first one that appeared in her search engine, one from the online version of the local newspaper. The headline told the story, putting Francis Gillespie's name front and center.

ARCHBISHOP FRANCIS GILLESPIE SERIOUSLY INJURED IN FAILED CARJACKING INCIDENT

For a moment Rachel could barely breathe, and she certainly couldn't read any further. It was true. She had failed. Francis Gillespie was injured, but he wasn't dead. The sense of failure that washed over her in that moment was almost more than she could bear. Finally, steeling herself, she went back to finish the article.

> One person was killed and two people seriously injured, including Francis Gillespie, archbishop of the Phoenix Archdiocese, in what is being called a failed carjacking attempt, which occurred outside the archbishop's residence on East Lincoln Drive on Tuesday evening.
>
> Early this morning Isabella Maldonado, spokeswoman for Phoenix PD, identified the dead man as Father Andrew

O'Toole, who was reportedly driving the archbishop's Lincoln Town Car at the time of the incident. Father O'Toole is said to have died as a result of a single gunshot to the head.

Witnesses on the scene reported that the Town Car sped out of a driveway directly into the path of oncoming traffic, striking two other vehicles before smashing into a sound barrier wall. Four occupants were traveling eastbound in a Dodge minivan at the time it was struck. Three of those were treated and released. A fourth was transported to a hospital with what were termed serious but non-life-threatening injuries. A passenger in a westbound Hyundai sedan was also treated and released.

Archbishop Gillespie was transported by ambulance to St. Gregory's Hospital in what was reported to be critical condition. At this writing he is said to be undergoing surgery.

At least one witness at the scene mentioned catching a glimpse of an unidentified male standing near the driver's side of the Town Car shortly before it careened into traffic, but so far efforts to locate that individual have been unsuccessful.

Unable to read any further, Rachel closed her computer. She had murdered the wrong person—killed someone who wasn't the archbishop. That was so wrong! Gillespie had been her real target. No one else was supposed to have been harmed, to say nothing of killed. It didn't take long for Rachel to rationalize her way around the problem. After all, if Father O'Toole was part of the Catholic Church, that meant he was almost as responsible for what had happened to David as the archbishop was.

The only bit of good news Rachel gleaned from the article was the fact that her disguise seemed to have worked. The cops were looking for a man who'd been seen near the site of the shooting incident. No one had reported seeing a woman there. Unfortunately, her real problem was much closer to home. She still hadn't recovered from the fact that Rich had been sitting up waiting for her when she got back to the house— waiting and asking questions about where she'd been and what she'd been doing.

Rachel remembered reading a book once that was written by a woman whose husband had been a POW for five years during the Vietnam War.

The whole time he was in captivity, she had prayed for his safe return, but once he came home, their lives were anything but perfect. He'd expected everything to be the same as it was before he'd left, but once he returned, things had changed. His wife had changed. She'd grown used to getting along without him—to making her own decisions, both large and small, and to living life on her own terms. In the end they hadn't been able to work things out and had divorced.

Maybe this was a similar situation. Rachel and Rich had been prisoners of their individual versions of grief for years now, but if Rich thought he could emerge from his emotional cocoon and suddenly reclaim his place as head of their household—

No, Rachel decided at once, *that is* not *going to happen.*

She got dressed. Since she intended to go back to Lincoln Drive, she didn't bother with makeup. She would go there looking the same as she always did.

The night before, by the time the load of clothing and the canvas bag were washed and dried, it had been too late to put them into the trunk, so Rachel brought them with her when she left her room. Much to her dismay, Rich was waiting for her, seated at the kitchen table and staring into a half-empty coffee cup.

"Do you want a divorce?" he asked without looking up.

"A divorce?" she repeated lamely.

"Obviously you're having an affair."

"An affair? Are you kidding?" she replied. "I'm definitely not having an affair."

"So what's in the bag?"

"In case it's any of your business, it's some clothing I'm dropping off at Goodwill. Why the third degree? After all these years, why are you suddenly so interested in what I'm doing?"

"Because you're coming and going at odd hours with no explanation."

Rachel decided her best bet was to fight back. "Since when do I owe you an explanation?" she demanded, cutting him off. "You spend all your time out in the garage with your nose stuck in your damned birdhouses. Just because you're living the life of a hermit, that doesn't mean I have to. I have friends—people I can walk with and grab coffee with. As soon as David died, you gave up on living, but I have news for you, Mr. Higgins. You may have given up, but I didn't. While you've been locked away in the garage, I've learned to live life on my own. You may be dead to the outside world, but I'm not. I'm still alive."

With that she turned and strode out the front door. By the time she got to the driveway, her hands were shaking again. Once she managed to get the car door unlocked and climb inside, it was all she could do to start the engine. She managed to back out of the driveway safely, but she drove only a few blocks before she found herself hyperventilating so badly that she had to pull over and wait for the spell to pass.

Why now? she wondered. *Why did Rich have to break out of his stupor now? And if he knows or suspects what I've done, what will he do about it—go to the cops?*

If he did, if he pointed out she had no alibi and that his .22 had suddenly gone missing and might possibly be the murder weapon—what would law enforcement do then? They would put her in jail—for the rest of her life. Wasn't that what a first-degree murder conviction was worth these days—life without parole?

For some reason that thought brought with it enough fury to jolt Rachel back to the present. If she was off in prison somewhere—say, locked up in the state penitentiary down in Florence—Rich would be sitting pretty. Yes, his retirement benefits had been lower than expected, but they would stretch a lot further if he didn't have to split them with a wife or even an ex-wife. In a divorce their assets, pension included, would have to be divided down the middle. With her in jail, he'd have his pension all to himself, along with the equity from their house.

How fair was that, especially since everything she'd done had been to avenge their son's death? Rich might not have known she was doing it and might not have wanted her to do it, but she'd done it for him as much as for herself. And each piece of her plan had been based on the premise that the situation with Rich would continue the way it had been for years, with Rich exhibiting virtually no interest in anything outside the confines of his workshop, and most especially in his wife.

Rachel pulled in to the Sunrise Diner, a small family-owned café on Bell. She wasn't hungry—in fact, she wasn't the least bit interested in food. She wanted a chance to see the morning news, preferably on the local Fox affiliate that didn't switch over to national programming like the other stations did. As expected, this morning's top story focused on the fatality incident outside the archbishop's residence.

When her usual waitress came to take Rachel's order, the woman nodded toward the TV screen and shook her head. "It's awful for something like this to happen right here in Phoenix," she said. "They're saying the archbishop is out of surgery now, but he may not make it. What'll you have?"

"Scrambled eggs, toast, and coffee," Rachel said aloud. *And a clear shot at the TV screen.*

She had been so caught up in her initial sense of failure that it hadn't occurred to her that there was still a chance Francis Gillespie might die. In fact, at that very minute the two local anchors—one male and one female—were speculating about the archbishop's ability to survive any kind of surgical procedure at his age.

Rachel understood they weren't wrong to wonder. Her own father had died at age eighty-five after undergoing what should have been routine gallbladder surgery. So maybe Gillespie wouldn't make it. In that case, if Rachel did go to jail, at least it wouldn't be for nothing. And if he didn't die? What would she do then? Figure out a way to try again.

When Rachel left the diner almost an hour later, she'd seen everything the local news had to say. Archbishop Gillespie was in St. Gregory's Hospital in Phoenix, where crowds of well-wishers were staging a vigil outside the building; the other person who'd been hospitalized in the incident was reported to be in good condition and was expected to be released sometime later that morning. Phoenix PD had yet to apprehend the unidentified suspect who'd fired the shot that killed Father Andrew O'Toole. Funeral services for the dead priest had yet to be announced.

Rachel drove from the diner straight to a Goodwill store. She had deliberately chosen one that she'd never visited before, a location on Indian School on the far side of I-17. The store wasn't open yet, but the drop-off area was available. She handed the white-and-yellow bag out the window to an attendant and drove away without uttering a word.

Next, hoping to glean more up-to-date information than what was on the broadcast news, she drove to St. Gregory's and spent the better part of an hour mingling with the people holding the vigil. While there, she did her best to mirror their shock and dismay, but she wasn't sure she succeeded.

At last it was time for her daily walk. She had decided that for today it would be best if she followed her customary route along Lincoln, starting from her usual spot in the office park.

As she approached the driveway to the archbishop's residence, she saw that a barrier of crime-scene tape had been strung across the almost invisible opening that led into the hedge. That no doubt meant that the cops had found the gun, but would anyone notice the DNA? And if they did, how long did it take to process DNA evidence these days? And if the cops went to question Jack Stoneman or happened to take him into custody, would he have some kind of solid alibi that would stand up in court? From the collection of tequila bottles she'd seen littering the clearing, she suspected he was most likely a heavy drinker. Would he be able to account for his activities on the night of the shooting? Rachel had far too many questions and not enough answers.

At the gatepost to the archbishop's driveway, well-wishers and mourners had created a small memorial, leaving behind a mound of loose flowers and bouquets in glass vases. A dozen or so lit prayer candles were also on display. The well-dressed man with his two standard poodles stood silently in front of the memorial, his straw hat in hand and his head bowed in prayer.

Sensing Rachel's presence, he looked up at her. "Shocking," he murmured as she joined him, "simply shocking!"

"Yes, it is," she agreed. "Whoever would have thought something like this could happen, right here in the neighborhood?"

"Somebody said the cops are looking for that homeless guy, the one who's usually here begging."

"Jack didn't show up today?" Rachel asked.

"That's his name, Jack?" he asked. "Nope, he's nowhere to be seen. I always thought the guy was harmless, but maybe not."

The news that the cops were actually looking for Jack Stoneman left Rachel almost giddy with relief, but she did her best not to show it.

"I always thought he was harmless, too," she replied.

The man and his two dogs walked away then, leaving Rachel to revel in this small bit of good news. Her strategy had worked. The cops really were looking for her chosen fall guy. Now, if Archbishop Gillespie would just hurry up and die, she would have succeeded after all.

There was that show on TV about how to get away with murder. *I should get in touch with their script writers,* she thought. *Maybe I could teach them a thing or two.*

|CHAPTER 22|

By eight the next morning, Ali was up and out, heading for Phoenix with an overnight bag in case Sister Anselm's need for backup made it necessary for Ali to stay over. Her clothing and makeup were in a Rollaboard, her Taser was in her purse, and her Glock was concealed in her new specially designed sports bra, one that kept her weapon invisible under her upper arm while leaving it readily accessible when needed. For Ali's money it was a big improvement over her old and now-discarded small-of-back holster.

There was still a lot of rush-hour traffic heading into the city, and the drive from her house to St. Gregory's took close to two and a half hours door-to-door. Even so she arrived shortly after ten thirty. On her way into the parking garage, she saw a crowd of people gathered in the hospital's front courtyard. Some of them were there to show their support for the archbishop, but Ali saw enough media vans and cameras to know that reporters were out in force, too, hoping to gather the latest information on Gillespie's condition. Avoiding the group completely, Ali drove into the garage, where she had to go all the way to the top floor before finding an open slot.

An underground tunnel connected the parking structure to the hospital entrance itself. With her purse slung over her shoulder, Ali approached the sliding glass doors, where signage complete with an x'ed-out hand-gun announced St. Gregory's to be a gun-free zone. A quick glance inside revealed no sign of security personnel or metal detectors. Obviously the folks at St. Gregory's believed in voluntary compliance.

Good luck with that, Ali told herself. *The people who might come gunning for Archbishop Gillespie won't give a rat's ass about that sign, and neither will I.*

She didn't bother stopping by the reception desk to check on the archbishop's location. A text from Sister Anselm had arrived just as she drove into the garage, saying the archbishop was still in the ICU, and Ali knew exactly where that was without needing directions.

When she walked into the waiting room, the clergyman sitting with his arms folded, facing the door, was someone she recognized—Father Michael, a former Navy SEAL and now a retired priest, living in Dallas. Several years earlier Father Mike had arrived in the nick of time when B. and Ali, among others, were under attack by a drug-cartel matriarch and her crew. He'd shown up on the scene in a venerable Isuzu Trooper loaded with much-needed firepower and ammunition.

Father Mike stood up, crossed the waiting-room floor, and gathered Ali into a bear hug. The embrace told Ali that she wasn't the only hospital visitor carrying a concealed weapon. Father Mike was also in possession of a handgun, and Ali knew full well that he knew how to use it.

"What are you doing here?" she asked pulling away.

"Sister Anselm called me late last night," he replied. "There was an early-morning flight leaving Dallas for Phoenix, and you'd better believe I was on it."

"I'm glad you're here," Ali told him, "but where's Sister Anselm?"

"She's in with the doctors right now, but what's going on, Ali? According to her, what happened wasn't your basic carjacking, but she wouldn't say much more. What can you tell me?"

With no one else in the waiting room right then, Ali was able to bring him up to speed about the collection-plate threats and about local law enforcement's general lack of interest.

"Have you spoken to the cops about this since last night's incident?"

"Not yet," she answered. "Phoenix PD is on my list, but I wanted to stop by here first."

"Tell you what," Father Mike said. "You go do what you need to do. As long as I'm here, you don't have to be. Once you're back, the three of us—Sister Anselm, you, and I—will put our heads together and figure out what needs to be done."

Within minutes Ali was back in her car and headed toward the

Phoenix PD headquarters building on West Washington. Before going inside, she locked all her weaponry in the gun safe inside her glove box, because she didn't want to have to spend ten minutes explaining who she was and why she was carrying.

The desk sergeant in Major Crimes did his best to keep Ali from seeing Detective Kyle Lasko in person, claiming the man was busy. It was only when Ali insisted forcefully that she had information concerning the Father O'Toole homicide that a tall man dressed in a somewhat rumpled suit emerged from a warren of cubicles and sauntered toward her.

"Ms. Reynolds?" he inquired, offering his hand. He was probably in his late forties and had the look of a seasoned detective.

"Yes," she said, taking his hand, "but you can call me Ali."

"I'm Detective Lasko. I understand this is about my carjacking case?"

"I'm here because I don't believe it *is* a carjacking case."

Lasko gave her an appraising look. "All right, then," he said at last. "You'd better come this way."

|CHAPTER 23|

Detective Kyle Lasko knew from the start that this would be a long day. He had been next up in the rotation when the carjacking call came in the night before. From the moment he arrived on the scene and discovered that Francis Gillespie, the archbishop of the Phoenix Archdiocese, had been involved, he understood this case would be a hot mess as far as media participation was concerned.

Kyle grew up attending parochial schools and still regarded himself as a Catholic, although now that he was divorced and remarried, he attended Mass on Christmas and Easter and stayed away the rest of the time. He had never met Archbishop Gillespie in person. What he knew about the man came mostly from news coverage of his very public stance on the issue of pedophile priests, which was something that placed Gillespie pretty high on Kyle Lasko's short list of good guys.

The attempted carjacking had occurred around 7:00 p.m. Once Kyle arrived at the crime scene, he stayed for the next several hours, overseeing the investigation. He'd spent a good deal of that time with a guy named Sid White. Sid had arrived at the wreckage within moments of the incident, so soon in fact that he was the one who'd shut off the Town Car's engine after the vehicle crashed into the wall. He was also the first witness to report that Father Andrew O'Toole had been the victim of a shooting as opposed to the victim of a motor-vehicle accident. Hours after the event, White was still in shock over seeing brain matter splattered all over the victim's headrest. Kyle was sympathetic. It had taken a long time for him to recover after seeing his first gunshot victim, a guy who'd committed suicide by putting a gun to his head and pulling the trigger.

Once victims and car wreckage were hauled away and the crowd dispersed, Kyle had driven up the long driveway to the archbishop's stately residence where he'd interviewed Father Daniel McCray, the archbishop's private secretary. Kyle's first impression was and continued to be that Father Andrew had been the intended victim. As a consequence he'd turned to Father McCray, asking for anything and everything the priest knew about the victim.

When that interview ended, Kyle walked away with contact information for Father O'Toole's next of kin—his aging parents, Lester and Barbara O'Toole, who lived in Altoona, Pennsylvania. Kyle was grateful the couple didn't live nearby. That spared him having to make the dreaded next-of-kin notification in person. He returned to Phoenix PD and contacted Altoona PD, asking them to send an officer to perform that duty. Within half an hour of the notification, Lester O'Toole was on the phone with Kyle, begging for information, while his wife sobbed in the background. Other than the fact that his son had been shot to death in the course of an apparent carjacking, Kyle could say next to nothing.

When Kyle finally left the department, he decided to swing by St. Gregory's Hospital to check on the status of Archbishop Gillespie. In the ICU waiting room, he found a guard dog of a nun named Sister Anselm running the show. It didn't help that she was a virtual clone of Sister Aurelia, Kyle's nightmarish grade-school principal. Sister Anselm more or less ordered Kyle out of the waiting room, telling him in no uncertain terms that the archbishop was still in surgery and that no information concerning his condition was being released to anyone, including detectives from Phoenix PD.

He had left the hospital with his tail between his legs and driven home to Mesa. After not nearly enough sleep, he returned to the office, where in bleary-eyed fashion he was making a start on the murder book. The good news was that the CSIs had located what was thought to be the murder weapon in a clearing in a hedge near the crime scene. The weapon was currently being examined in the lab in hopes of obtaining trace evidence, although how long it would take to get fingerprint or DNA evidence from that was anybody's guess. Kyle also paged through the reports from the various uniformed officers in attendance to see which of the people who'd given preliminary statements were worthy of being tracked down for more detailed interviews. In Kyle's opinion the on-scene interview he'd done with Sidney White was sufficient.

When he was told that someone named Ali Reynolds was out in the lobby wishing to speak to him about the carjacking, Kyle wasn't thrilled to be interrupted, but if the woman in question really did know something about his shooting incident, he would make time to talk to her.

Out in the lobby, he was met with a good-looking woman, a natural-or-not blonde in her early sixties, who introduced herself as Ali Reynolds. Since the cubicles offered no privacy, Kyle escorted her into an interview room.

"So you don't think what happened last night was a carjacking?" he asked.

"It wasn't," she answered definitively. "Father Andrew wasn't the intended target. Archbishop Gillespie was."

Kyle was taken aback. "You're serious about this?" he asked. "You think the shooting was actually an attempt to assassinate the archbishop?"

"I do," she replied. Opening her purse, she brought out a stack of three-by-five cards and handed them over. "Francis Gillespie has been receiving threatening notes—anonymous threatening notes—for months now. My husband, B. Simpson, and I run a cybersecurity company called High Noon Enterprises. B. and the archbishop have been friends for years. When the archbishop brought his concerns here to Phoenix PD, he was given the brush-off and told that the threats weren't credible. I believe that what happened last night proves otherwise."

Kyle shuffled through the cards one by one. They were threatening, all right. "Where did these come from?"

"They were dropped off in collection plates in churches all over the archdiocese during the course of the last several months."

"So most likely they've been handled by far too many people for us to obtain usable DNA samples or fingerprints," Kyle offered.

Ali nodded. "That's our assessment as well, but we sent copies of the cards to a handwriting analyst, who tells us that the author is most likely female and probably not young—fifty or so and up."

He shuffled through the cards once more. "Do you mind if I copy these?"

"Not at all," Ali told him. "Help yourself."

Kyle took the cards with him and cornered one of the clerks into making copies. While that was going on, he placed a quick call to Records, where he found absolutely nothing with Archbishop Gillespie's name on it. If he'd brought his concerns about the threats to someone at Phoenix PD, no one on this end had bothered generating a report.

Once back in the interview room, Kyle handed Ali several sheets of paper. "Those are copies of the cards," he said. "Under the circumstances I think it's best that I keep the originals."

With that he resumed his seat. "I may be missing something," he said, "but I've checked with Records and have been unable to locate any kind of official police report related to threats against Archbishop Gillespie. Did he happen to mention anyone in particular that he might have spoken to here at Phoenix PD?"

"No, just that he'd brought the matter to someone's attention. It might have been an unofficial inquiry. My understanding is he wanted to get to the bottom of this without creating a hue and cry."

"Exactly when did you and your husband become involved?"

"Archbishop Gillespie dropped by our home in Sedona on Sunday evening. We were having a party, so he didn't come inside, but he definitely had something on his mind and asked us if we'd come discuss it with him at our earliest convenience. We made a special trip into town the next day, Monday, and had dinner with him at his residence. That's when he gave us the cards."

"You said you asked a handwriting expert to analyze the cards. Would it be possible for me to speak to that person?"

A look of apprehension flitted across Ali Reynolds's face. "You'll probably want to call in your own experts," she said quickly. "Ours is just the friend of a friend, and handwriting analysis is more of a hobby for her than it is a profession. I doubt that anything she said could be relied on in a court of law."

"But it might be reliable enough to use as a starting point in an investigation."

Ali nodded, but she didn't volunteer an introduction.

"So," Kyle said, leaning back in his chair. "Besides your handwriting expert, have you and your husband made any other progress in the case?"

"We asked Archbishop Gillespie if he had any enemies. He cited an older brother who is currently confined to a nursing home in Wisconsin."

"Archbishop Gillespie is what—eighty-five?"

"Eighty-six," Ali supplied. "His brother is five years older than that."

Detective Lasko favored Ali with a sardonic grin. "At ninety-one he's not likely to pose much of a credible threat either."

"We also asked about the men Archbishop Gillespie aced out of competition when he was appointed to his current position," Ali continued. "Those, too, are no longer a consideration through either death or infirmity."

"So who else would there be?"

"The only controversial aspect of Francis Gillespie's term as archbishop has been his unbending, no-holds-barred stance against pedophile priests, several of whom have been turned over to law enforcement during his term in office. We're wondering if a female related to one of those priests—a mother, a sister, or an aunt—might be responsible for the threats."

"That's a possibility, I suppose, and we'll look into it," Kyle said. "But I still believe that it's likely that the man who's dead, Father O'Toole, was the intended victim."

Ali didn't want him to veer off topic. "I just happen to have a list of those disgraced priests here on my iPad," Ali began. "If you'd like me to text it to you . . ."

"That won't be necessary, Ms. Reynolds," he said dismissively. "We're fully capable of accessing that information on our own should it be needed." Then, with a glance at his watch, he added, "If that's all, I have an appointment with the ME to view the autopsy. Should your investigation turn up anything germane to our investigation, I'd be more than happy to hear from you."

The expression on Ali Reynolds's face hardened. If by sharing information she had hoped to be given some in return, that wouldn't be the case.

"So that's it, then?" she asked. "You don't think the threats against the archbishop are credible either?"

"Look," Kyle replied patiently, "I appreciate your coming by with this information, and we'll check into it, but beyond that, I need to point out that this is an active police investigation, and no further information is available at this time."

Clearly Ali Reynolds didn't take well to being told no. "I believe I can recognize a brush-off when I hear one," she told him. "I'll be going, but don't think you've heard the end of this. Archbishop Gillespie asked us to look into the threats against him, and that's exactly what we're going to do."

Kyle was put off by her sudden change in attitude. "Please be aware that interfering with an active police investigation is against the law—a felony, in fact."

"You can't have it both ways, Detective Lasko," she told him icily. "You just told me that you don't think the threats are in any way related to what happened to Father O'Toole, so you go right on working your case, and we'll work ours. Fair enough?"

"I suppose it is," Kyle replied.

With that, Ali Reynolds rose and flounced over to the door of the interview room, where she was forced to wait until he clicked it open before exiting. Kyle watched as she stalked off down the corridor. He hadn't quite caught the name of Ali Reynolds's husband, but whoever he was, the poor guy had Kyle's sincere sympathy. The woman was a handful.

His phone rang then with a call from the desk sergeant. "The big boss wants to see you," he said.

Kyle knew that the words "big boss" didn't apply to the captain in charge of Major Crimes.

"Chief Adolfo wants to see me?" he asked

"He does indeed," came the reply. "On the double."

Kyle made his way to the chief's office feeling the same way he'd felt when he was summoned before the dreaded Sister Aurelia for the sin of having broken a school window with an errant baseball hit.

"How's it going?" Chief Adolfo asked.

"So-so," Kyle answered. "It's still early days."

"Just so you know," the chief said, "Archbishop Gillespie is a friend of mine, so this is personal for me. I want the case solved sooner than later."

Kyle was stunned. If the chief knew the archbishop, was he the one who'd decided that the threats weren't serious enough to investigate? Was he why there was no sign that a report had been generated in Records? No wonder the chief wanted it solved in a hurry. This might well be his fault.

"Yes, sir," Kyle responded.

"Now, come on," the chief continued. "I've scheduled a press confer-ence this morning, and we're both due there any minute."

Kyle dialed the ME's office on the way. Obviously the autopsy was going to have to wait.

|CHAPTER 24|

Ali was still seething when she got to her car, and the text from B. that came in moments later didn't improve her state of mind. There were no words in the text, only the pile-of-crap emoji that was her grandson's favorite. In this case a picture was worth a thousand words. Clearly B. wasn't in a place where he could talk or even text properly, so Ali called Stu in Sedona.

"I got a text from B., and it looks bad," she said. "What's going on?"

"Dieter Gunther blinked," Stu replied.

"You mean he paid the ransom?"

"Before B.'s plane even landed," Stu replied, barely containing his own frustration. "The thing is, as far as we can tell, there was never anything wrong and the whole ransomware thing was a sham from the start. But now that A&D is out of pocket for the cash, Dieter is busy blaming us, saying we'll have to prove there wasn't a trojan in the first place. In my experience it's pretty damned hard to prove or disprove the existence of nothing."

Ali had been privy only to B.'s side of the conversation with Dieter, but what she'd heard hadn't endeared the man to her. And the fact that he'd raised so much hell and then gone against B.'s advice absolutely infuriated her.

"Do you think he'll try coming after High Noon, expecting to be reimbursed for a big chunk of the ransom money?"

"I wouldn't put it past him," Stu replied. "In the meantime Frigg's still working all those background checks, but what's going on down in Phoenix? How's the archbishop?"

Ali didn't feel like telling him how things really were. "I'm not sure," she said. "I'm on my way to the hospital right now, and I'll let you know what I find out."

"Be sure to tell the archbishop that we're all rooting for him."

"I will," Ali said.

Once the call ended, Ali started the car, but before putting it in gear she sent Frigg a text requesting an audio connection. When Frigg's voice came on the line, it was, as per usual, unfailingly polite.

"Good morning, Ms. Reynolds. I hope you had a good night's rest."

"I did, thank you."

"I'm still accumulating information on people connected to Archbishop Francis Gillespie. Would you like me to send it to you immediately?"

"No, I'm driving right now and not ready to look at it. I'll let you know when you should send, but as far as the dossiers you're creating on current and former A&D employees—the ones who merit further scrutiny . . ."

"There are currently two hundred eighty-six individuals in that category."

"Does the name Dieter Gunther happen to be among them?"

"Yes, it is," Frigg answered immediately.

"Good," Ali said. "So how about doing me a favor? I'd like you to move his in-depth examination to the head of the line. Now that he's gone against High Noon's advice and paid the ransom, I think he deserves some additional attention."

"As do I," Frigg replied. "As far as Mr. Gunther is concerned, I believe you and I are on the same page—if that's the proper terminology."

With Stu's help, Frigg's ability to use English idioms was slowly but surely improving.

"It is, and we are," Ali agreed. "Please feel free to copy me on whatever you happen to uncover about him."

"Of course, Ms. Reynolds. I will be happy to comply."

Ali was back in the garage at St. Gregory's by the time the call with Frigg ended. Once again she used the tunnel to gain access to the hospital without having to go through the crowd out front. Upstairs in the ICU waiting room, Ali found Sister Anselm sitting alone. Although her face was lined with a combination of weariness and worry, the nun smiled gratefully as Ali entered.

"Thank you for coming."

"How are things with the archbishop?"

"At least he's alive," Sister Anselm replied. "He could have died. He's been on blood thinners for years. If the ER people hadn't done a CT scan, found the brain bleed, and rushed him into surgery, he might be long gone by now."

"Is he going to be all right?"

Sister Anselm shrugged her shoulders. "It's too soon to tell. They drained the blood and repaired the damage as best they could. Right now they're keeping him sedated as a preventive measure. After these kinds of injuries, there's always a chance of seizures. I'm not sure I would have agreed with the decision to go ahead and work on his arm at the same time, but they felt that at his age there was less risk in performing both surgeries under the same dose of anesthesia rather than forcing him to undergo two separate recoveries."

"What about his arm?" Ali asked.

Sister Anselm nodded. "Compound fracture of the left humerus. They've got that screwed back together, and the broken ribs are taped. The brain bleed was the real issue."

"Father Mike is in with him?"

"Yes."

"And you've been up all night?"

"Yes."

"Caregivers need rest, too," Ali said. "It's high time you got some."

Ali knew there was a small room with a cot in it where doctors and nurses as well as visiting clergy were allowed to nap. She expected Sister Anselm to put up more of a fight, but she didn't.

"You're probably right," she agreed, stiffly getting to her feet. "I'll do that, but call me at once if there's any change."

Ali watched as the aging nun walked as far as the nurses' station and collected a small bag before making her way to the elevator. She seemed so frail and beaten down right then that Ali couldn't help but wonder if Sister Anselm wasn't more at risk than Archbishop Gillespie.

Several family groups flowed in and out of the waiting room while Ali settled in with her iPad and began calling up and reading through the material Frigg had sent her. There was a good deal of coverage on the class-action suit initiated by Father Needham's victims against the archdiocese. The name that surfaced most often in various articles was that of a guy named Gavin James, who seemed to be the designated spokesperson for all the plaintiffs. According to information supplied by Frigg, Gavin was now an attorney with offices on Central right here in Phoenix. Not only had Frigg included his physical address, there was a phone number as well.

Ali had her phone in hand and was about to dial the number when a breaking-news notification flashed across the screen of a muted TV set attached to the far wall of the waiting room: UPCOMING PRESS CONFERENCE FROM PHOENIX PD. Since the shooting incident on Lincoln Drive was the number-one story of the day, Ali was pretty sure that would be the topic.

The television remote was right there on the table in front of her. "Does anyone mind if I turn up the volume?" she asked.

When none of the other visitors voiced an objection, Ali turned up the volume just as Chief of Police Luis Adolfo stepped to a microphone-lined podium.

"As most of you know, there was a serious shooting incident on East Lincoln Drive last night around seven, leaving one victim deceased. Two other victims were sent to area hospitals, one with life-threatening injuries. Father Andrew O'Toole, driving a Lincoln Town Car owned by the archdiocese, was pronounced dead at the scene, from a single gunshot wound to the head. The Town Car subsequently collided with two other vehicles, a Hyundai Sonata and a Dodge minivan. Francis Gillespie, the archbishop of the Phoenix Archdiocese who was a passenger in the Town Car, was seriously injured. He was transported to St. Gregory's Hospital here in Phoenix, where he underwent emergency surgery. He is now listed in guarded but stable condition.

"When Father O'Toole was hit by gunfire, the vehicle he was driving went out of control and plunged into oncoming traffic. Other victims include a passenger from the Hyundai who was treated for minor injuries at the scene and released. Three of the four passengers in the minivan were treated at the scene as well. The fourth, Helena Thomas, of Mesa, was transported to Good Samaritan Hospital where she is currently listed in good condition and is expected to be released later today. Funeral arrangements for Father O'Toole are pending.

"I have been informed that the Archdiocese of Phoenix has posted a ten-thousand-dollar reward for information leading to the arrest and conviction of the person or persons responsible for Father O'Toole's death. At this time, and because this is a high-profile case, I would like to introduce the lead investigator, Detective Kyle Lasko of our Major Crimes Unit, who is looking for some assistance from the public."

The detective Ali had met earlier stepped to the bank of microphones set up to accommodate Chief Adolfo. Since the chief was a good six inches shorter than Lasko, the detective had to lean over to talk into them. He wasn't comfortable speaking in public, and it showed.

"Thank you, Chief Adolfo," he said. Then, glaring into the collection of cameras, he added a gruff, "Good morning. As the chief indicated, the shooting that occurred last night is currently Phoenix PD's highest priority. We're still not sure if this was a simple carjacking attempt or something else. There's a chance that Father O'Toole or perhaps even Archbishop Gillespie was the actual target for this deadly assault.

"It has been reported that a male dressed in dark clothing and wearing a ball cap appeared at the crime scene. He was there at the time of the shooting but disappeared in the confusion that followed. This individual is not considered to be a suspect at the moment, merely a person of interest. Because he was so close to the action, however, he may be our best eyewitness as to what occurred.

"If you have any information regarding the identity or whereabouts of this person, please call the non-emergency number at Phoenix PD. If you prefer to remain anonymous, you can also contact the Crime Stoppers tip line.

"As for the person of interest? I'd like to address him directly. Sir, if you are watching this broadcast, please contact me at any of the phone numbers currently displayed on your screen at your earliest convenience to tell us what you know. Your assistance in this matter would be greatly appreciated. Thank you."

At that point a media-relations officer stepped forward to handle any additional questions, but Ali was no longer listening. She knew that the inquiries reporters shouted in the direction of the podium would be mostly unanswerable. No one, including Media Relations, was allowed to discuss details of an active investigation. The questions were designed to exhibit the reporters' perceptions of what was going on rather than addressing what was really going on. Besides, Ali Reynolds already had the answer she needed.

Her earlier talk with Detective Lasko had succeeded in moving the dial ever so slightly. His statement had at least allowed for the possibility that the attack was more complex than a simple carjacking, and he'd hinted at the possibility that one or both of the priests might have been deliberately targeted. With copies of Archbishop Gillespie's collection of three-by-five threats still in Ali's purse, that was the best she could hope for.

|CHAPTER 25|

That morning Jack Stoneman rose later than usual with something more serious than his customary hangover. If anyone asked, he often claimed that he lived in a homeless shelter. That wasn't entirely true. He did have shelter in that he at least had a roof over his head—a tin one at that. Pulling on his clothing, he was dismayed to discover that the pocket where he usually kept his previous day's take was now totally empty. A glance around the tumbledown RV told him that the fifth of tequila he'd bought the day before was also nowhere to be seen.

Neither outcome was especially surprising. Jack drank way too much way too often, and blackouts weren't unusual occurrences. The probability was that he himself had spent the money and downed the tequila. There was also a chance that he'd been rolled. He checked under the bright green insert in his shoe to make sure that his brand-new monthly transit pass was still there. If he *had* been rolled, at least whoever did it hadn't gotten that.

Jack's landlord, Jimmy, was an old widower who supplemented his social security by RV ranching—renting out space in two aging RVs to people who would otherwise be homeless. He kept the decrepit vehicles parked in the backyard of a house located in a crumbling neighborhood blasted day and night by noise from planes taking off and landing at Sky Harbor.

It was the kind of neighborhood where nobody questioned the fact that Jimmy's backyard was surrounded by an eight-foot-tall block wall topped with a layer of razor wire. If his neighbors noticed the parade of panhandler types who came and went through a wooden gate that opened into his yard off the back alley, they didn't blink an eye or bother turning anyone in. They generally had their own businesses to attend to and didn't want people looking too closely at their affairs either.

After his wife died, Jimmy had discovered he was lonely. Wanting company as much as hoping to augment his meager retirement income, he'd bought the two run-down RVs, paying less than nothing for them, because they were falling apart and were no longer fit to travel the open highways, let alone spend nights in reputable RV parks. Jimmy had bought them for a song because he didn't care if some of the appliances no longer worked. What did work were the toilets, which he managed to hook up to his sewer connection.

With water and electrical service added into the mix, Jimmy parked the two RVs side by side and created a canvas-covered shade structure between them, stocking the small makeshift patio with a collection of cast-off yard furniture. Once his lowbrow RV park was ready for business, Jimmy went looking for customers. He charged ten bucks a night, payable in cash. For an extra five bucks, anyone who wanted a shower was welcome to use the primitive shower stall he'd built inside a lean-to garage converted from a long-ago carport. For another fiver, his tenants could wash a load of laundry in the garage-based washing machine next to the shower. Clothes had to be hung out on a line, but in Phoenix air-drying was hardly a problem.

Jimmy's accommodations were the kind that Roger Miller would have described as your basic "no phone, no pool, no pets." Tenants were expected to provide their own bedding. No sheets, blankets, or pillows were included in the deal. Jimmy limited the number of tenants to six—three per RV—and he vetted them carefully. Troublemakers who couldn't sit around on the make-do patio furniture drinking, smoking, and talking far into the night without raising too much hell found themselves out on the street again in short order.

In other words, Jimmy's place was a shelter of sorts without all the do-gooder rules and regulations. As far as Jack was concerned, it was a whole lot better than rolling out a sleeping bag in a public park or under a freeway overpass. He had lived at Jimmy's ranch ever since his release from prison. He'd been there for the better part of three years now, with the exception of a few weeks in the dead of summer each year when he hitchhiked north to cooler climes and camped out on the Mogollon Rim. For five bucks a night, Jimmy was good enough to hold Jack's place while he was gone.

During two of the three years Jack had been fortunate enough to live there, he'd shared his RV with a gay couple, longtime partners, one of whom was blind. Tom Mather's blindness was compliments of a high-school football injury that had resulted in two detached retinas. George Wooten, his supposedly sighted companion, was usually blind drunk, but somehow the two of them managed to make things work. In fact, Jack had gifted George with his old pair of shoes after that nice latte lady had given him his new Skechers. Tom and George occupied the RV's only bedroom, while Jack, usually the last to arrive home at night, made do on the fraying remains of a pull-out sofa in what passed for a living room.

That morning he walked three blocks into eye-piercing sunshine to reach a church-sponsored soup kitchen on Washington that handed out low-cost breakfasts for a buck apiece. To that end Jack had been forced to withdraw some walking-around money from inside the springs of the sofa, the not-so-subtle hiding place that functioned as his make-do piggy bank.

Jack's tardy arrival at the soup kitchen meant there were still a few scrambled eggs available when he got there, but the ham and hash browns were long gone. After breakfast he continued his daily commute, hobbling west on Van Buren far enough to catch a bus over to Central.

The damage to his right leg, compliments of Desert Storm, was permanent and entitled him to a small disability pension. That combined with what he made from panhandling was enough to pay his rent and buy food and booze. It also allowed him the luxury of a monthly transit pass to commute from the RV ranch to the driveway on Lincoln. Some of his panhandling pals made fun of him for focusing on that seemingly empty stretch of Lincoln rather than choosing a busy intersection where he could set up shop on the median next to a left-turn lane. What they didn't understand and what he never mentioned was the food.

Early almost every afternoon, Father Andrew, the priest who served as the cook for the huge house behind the oleander hedge, would stop by and drop off a bag of leftovers from meals at the residence. Often there was more than enough for Jack to share with his two roommates. Occasionally, after some big do, there would be enough to go around so everyone at the RV ranch could enjoy a feast outside on the patio. And on those days when there were no actual leftovers, Father Andrew would show up anyway, bringing along a couple of sandwiches. So even when traffic with cash donations was scarce, the food made it worth Jack's while to stay put at that location.

His bus stop on Lincoln was across from an office park some distance beyond his actual destination. That morning, after exiting the bus, he was limping toward the opening in the hedge when he noticed a flurry of decidedly unusual activity ahead of him. As he approached, several different vehicles pulled into the drive, stayed for a few seconds, and then left again almost immediately. When he arrived at the place where he usually ducked into the oleanders, Jack was dismayed to find his entryway blocked by a barrier of yellow crime-scene tape that had been strung from branch to branch. His hidden shelter was now a crime scene? How could that be?

Rather than stepping inside, Jack kept on walking. He approached the driveway just as another car pulled in and stopped without bothering to come within touching distance of the pillar-posted intercom. Instead a woman hopped out of the passenger side of the car and deposited a small spray of flowers on a pile that was already close to a yard deep. There were vases all around the pile and several burning candles as well. After depositing the flowers, the woman immediately returned to her car and took off.

What the hell is going on? Jack wondered as her car turned right on Lincoln. This kind of spontaneous display usually meant that someone was dead, and the absence of teddy bears meant that whoever had died most likely wasn't a kid. The very existence of the memorial probably meant there would be lots more in-and-out traffic on the driveway today, but Jack decided to play it safe and not hang around long enough to take advantage of it. Instead he continued walking as far as the nearest bus stop, where twenty minutes later he caught the next bus traveling back the way he'd come.

By the time he ordinarily would have been setting up shop on Lincoln, he was back on Washington stepping inside the dim interior of a neighborhood dive, his customary hangout. The Sneak Joint was a dingy bar that smelled of beer and piss, not necessarily in that order. Generally speaking, Jack bought his beverage of choice—cheap tequila—by the pint or by the fifth, depending on the funds available, at a nearby liquor store, reserving patronizing the bar for days when his take was either especially good or especially bad. For the former he went to celebrate. For the latter he went to drown his sorrows. This was one of those sorrow-drowning visits.

It was late morning on a weekday—too early for the lunch crowd. Besides Jack and the bartender, the only other people inside were four of the most serious drinkers, who were already ensconced at their usual stools along the scarred, Formica-topped bar. Weekday mornings meant there were no sports shows available to speak of, so the TV mounted over the bar was tuned to a local channel, which appeared to be showing some kind of empty-headed cooking demonstration.

Jack settled in, ordered his first boilermaker, and was sipping on it when a red-lettered ticker appeared at the bottom of the screen announcing an upcoming Phoenix PD press conference.

"What's happening?" he asked the barkeep.

"Big shooting up on Lincoln last night," the bartender explained. "It's been all over the news. Somebody shot a priest and put two other people in the hospital. One of those happens to be the archbishop of the Phoenix Archdiocese. No word yet on whether or not he's going to make it."

Somebody shot a priest? a dismayed Jack wondered. *Which priest?*

A sudden fit of trembling assailed his hands. He had to set his glass down on the bar to keep from slopping booze everywhere. The crime-scene tape blocking his bolt-hole into the oleanders might well have something to do with whatever had happened. That meant cops would be all over his clearing, and the last thing Jack Stoneman needed was any kind of dealings with cops.

This would not be Jack's first rodeo as far as law enforcement was concerned. Years earlier at a house party when he and his then-wife, Julie, were both hopped up on meth, he'd stumbled into a bedroom in time to find Julie and her new boyfriend in bed together and getting it on. Jack might have had a game leg, but his arms were strong enough—even stronger with a load of meth in his system. He'd dragged the guy out of bed and hurled him face-first against the wall, leaving a skull-size hole in the Sheetrock and breaking the boyfriend's neck. The boyfriend died on the spot while Jack went after Julie next, chasing her stark naked and screaming through the house and out into the street.

In other words, it had been a bad scene, especially when he subsequently went to war with the cops who'd shown up to arrest him and break up the party. The incident had brought about the end of Jack's marriage. His public defender advised him to accept a deal in which he'd plead guilty to one count of second-degree murder in exchange for dropping all six counts of aggravated assault. He was given a fifteen-year maximum sentence and paroled on good behavior after six. By the time he was released, Julie had divorced him and moved on. While in prison Jack had managed to wean himself off meth and now limited his intake to booze. Drinking tequila maybe wasn't good for your liver in the long run, but if you didn't drive drunk or get into fights, it was far less likely to land you in prison than either meth or crack was.

Once the promised TV press conference finally got under way, Jack listened to every word with rapt attention. When a photo of the dead priest appeared on-screen, Jack was stunned to see that Father Andrew O'Toole was *his* Father Andrew—the friend who'd always brought him leftovers. Who would murder someone like that? And why?

For a while Jack sat there mulling over those thoughts. By the time he turned his attention back to the press conference, the police chief had disappeared. In his place was a guy in a gray suit and a purple tie, someone Jack assumed to be one of the detectives on the case, who was on the air asking for the public's assistance in locating someone thought to have been at the scene at the time of the shooting—a "male dressed in dark clothing and wearing a ball cap."

Someone had seen a guy wearing a ball cap in the vicinity of his bolthole at the time of the shooting? Jack and his cap had been a constant presence on that part of Lincoln Drive for months now. Naturally people would assume he was the one they were looking for. But the chief had said the shooting happened at 7:00 p.m. That bit of timing was a big problem for Jack Stoneman, because he hadn't the foggiest idea where he'd been the night before at 7:00.

After getting off the bus, he remembered going into the liquor store and running into a couple of guys he knew on his way out. They had all hung around together for a while, leaning on the hood of a car in the parking lot and sharing a hit or two of his tequila. It had still been light when things started turning hazy on him. He didn't remember drinking that much, but maybe he had. Or maybe his newfound drinking buddies had hit him up with a dose of scopolamine, better known on the streets as devil's breath, so they could relieve Jack of his pocket change and whatever was left of the tequila.

As far as Jack knew, he hadn't been anywhere near Lincoln Drive at 7:00 p.m., but if even *he* couldn't remember anything about the night before, how could he prove he hadn't been at the crime scene?

Sipping his drink, he tried to remember the detective's exact words—that the guy they were looking for, someone wearing a ball cap, was a person of interest in the case. The cop had distinctly said "person of interest" rather than "suspect," but that was small comfort. The people who knew Jack from Lincoln Drive, the people he saw on a daily basis—like the latte lady and the guy with the poodles and the professional dog walker—once they heard the words "ball cap," they would all go straight to the cops and tell them what they knew.

Almost subconsciously, Jack peeled off his Desert Storm cap and stuffed it into his back pocket.

So did any of his Lincoln Drive acquaintances know where he lived? Jack didn't remember ever telling anyone, not even Father Andrew, about the RV ranch, but one of them might have noticed him coming and going by bus. If the cops asked the bus drivers, it wouldn't take long for them to find their way to the neighborhood—to the liquor store and the bar and the soup kitchen—and to people who knew that Jack was one of Jimmy's long-term tenants. And once the cops figured out that their ball-cap guy was an ex-con with a second-degree-murder conviction, it would be a short trip from person of interest to prime suspect.

The bartender came by and eyed Jack's empty glass. "Ready for another?" he asked.

"Sure," Jack replied. "Why the hell not?"

When the refill came, he sat for a long time, staring into the glass as though hoping that somewhere in the depths he would find the answer to where he'd been and what he'd done the night before. If he'd somehow made his way from the liquor store back to Lincoln Drive, surely he'd have some dim memory of it. And how the hell would he have laid hands on a gun? He didn't own a gun and never had. The last time he'd touched a firearm of any kind had been during his deployment to the

Middle East, and why the hell would he target someone who'd been his friend? None of it made any sense at all.

With the archbishop involved, this would be a high-profile case. Several important realities of criminal life had been drummed into Jack's head while he was in prison. One said that everybody was innocent and that crooked, tunnel-vision cops could usually manage to dig up enough evidence to make everything they found somehow coincide with whatever scenario they had in mind.

Jack sat there hunched over his glass, trying to analyze his situation. *What exactly do the cops know?* he wondered. The crime-scene tape told him that the CSI folks had most likely ventured inside the clearing. What would they have discovered there? His stool, the cooler, empty tequila bottles, and fast-food containers. The bottles and containers would have his DNA on them for sure. As for the stool and the cooler? His fingerprints and his alone would be on both of those.

Because of the homicide conviction, Jack realized that his fingerprints and DNA profile would both be in the system. Once the cops had a match, there'd be no need for them to check with bus drivers. They'd know exactly where he lived. After all, Jack's parole officer was the guy who'd steered him to Jimmy's RV ranch in the first place.

So what was Jack's best move at this point? Go on the run? If he tried that, he would end up looking even more guilty. Besides, where would he go? To Mexico maybe? Not with every cop in the country on the lookout for him.

Despairing, Jack shook his head. What he needed—the only thing that could possibly save him—was an alibi. And with the blackout . . .

As he downed the last of his drink, it seemed as though that final jolt of tequila gave him the answer he was looking for. He might have been drunk out of his gourd and operating in a blackout at the time, but by God he'd managed to find his way home. And just because he was too drunk to remember what had gone on, that didn't mean everybody at the RV ranch had been in the same condition. The residents of Jimmy's RV ranch might not have been the most reliable of witnesses, but they were the only possible witnesses Jack had.

———

Back at the RV ranch, he was dismayed to discover that no one was home—not his roommates, not the occupants of the other RV, not even

Jimmy. Since Jack usually wasn't home at that time of day, he had no idea what the others did in his absence. He was standing there in the middle of the RV's tiny living room wondering what to do next when a hard knock hammered the door, shaking the whole flimsy structure. Jack recognized it for what it was—a cop knock. Crooks and former crooks recognize those whenever they hear them.

"Police, Mr. Stoneman," someone announced from outside. "I'd like to have a word with you about a shooting incident that took place last night."

So they had found him. That hadn't taken long. And was it one cop outside the door asking to talk, Jack wondered, or was it a whole slew of them? And if he opened the door and went outside, would they be standing there with guns drawn and trained on him in case he stepped out of line? If some itchy-fingered raw recruit pulled the trigger, it wouldn't much matter if Jack was considered a suspect or merely a person of interest. Either way he'd be just as dead.

He glanced around the shabby room one last time. This had been his home for more than three years. Tattered and grungy as it was, it beat the hell out of the bolted-down furnishings in some eight-by-ten jail cell. As he stepped to the door, he felt a real sense of loss.

"Coming out," he called back.

Expecting a SWAT team, Jack was surprised when he stepped outside to find only a single cop standing in front of the door—the same guy he'd seen on TV at the bar two boilermakers earlier. What was his name again?

"What seems to be the problem?" Jack asked as casually as he could manage, standing there swaying in his doorway.

The man flashed a badge. "I'm Detective Kyle Lasko with the Major Crimes Unit of Phoenix PD," he said. "I'm investigating a homicide, and I'm hoping you can help us."

Jack had come outside expecting to encounter both an arrest warrant and a pair of handcuffs, but neither materialized.

"Who's dead?" Jack already knew the answer to his question, but he decided to play dumb.

"The victim is a Catholic priest, Father Andrew O'Toole, who was shot to death on East Lincoln Drive early last evening outside the residence of Archbishop Francis Gillespie," Detective Lasko replied. "I've been given to understand that you spend a good deal of time in that general area, and I'm hoping you might be able to provide information that will be helpful to our investigation."

Jack almost laughed aloud at that. No way could his secluded clearing in the oleander hedge be considered the "general area" of the homicide. It was the exact spot. He'd been there. He'd seen the crime-scene tape. He'd seen the remaining bits of broken glass and metal left by the collisions that had resulted from the shooting and subsequent car crashes. He knew that, and Detective Lasko knew that, so there didn't seem to be much sense in playing dumb any longer.

"Father Andrew was a friend of mine," Jack found himself blurting. "He always gave me food. He was a good guy. Why would anyone want to hurt him?"

"Does that mean you'd be willing to help us?"

"I guess," Jack allowed. "What do you need?"

"I'd like to take you over to police headquarters and talk with you in one of our interview rooms so I can record our conversation."

"You're not placing me under arrest?"

"No, I just want to ask you a few questions, although it would probably be a good idea for us to run a GSR test on your hands and clothing which would help eliminate you as a suspect."

"Fine with me," Jack replied.

"My car's out in the alley," Detective Lasko said. "You'll have to ride in the backseat, but I'll give you a ride there and bring you home when we're done. You're not carrying any weapons, are you?"

"No, sir."

"Do you mind if I pat you down?"

"Help yourself."

Detective Lasko did so and came up empty. "Shall we?" he said.

"By all means," Jack replied. "Let's get this done."

|CHAPTER 26|

Ali Reynolds and Jack Stoneman weren't the only viewers hanging on every word of the Phoenix PD press conference. Rachel Higgins was, too.

When she arrived home that morning, she was grateful to see that Rich's Escalade wasn't in the driveway. These days he seldom went anywhere other than the cabinet shop in Cave Creek to pick up lumber scraps or else to Home Depot to gather supplies. She didn't want to have to talk to him, and she sure as hell didn't want another session of the third degree with him asking questions and her not answering.

She switched on the TV in advance of what she thought would be the noon news and ended up seeing the entire Phoenix PD press conference. From her point of view, most of it was excellent news. They were looking for the guy wearing a ball cap—too bad for Jack Stoneman. There wasn't a single mention of a silver-haired woman limping along the sidewalk in oversize shoes and carrying a white-and-yellow bag about the time all hell was breaking loose out on the street. Witnesses had spotted a "him," not a "her."

That was all to the good, but the part of the press conference that stuck with her most was where the detective had asked for help in iden-tifying the ball-cap guy. She knew Jack Stoneman's name. She was pretty sure if the cops knew that, they'd be able to find him, but was it up to her to tell them? And if so, how?

Could one of those anonymous tip lines really be trusted to keep her anonymous? And if Rachel tried using a pay phone—if there were even any of those left—the cops would still be aware of who had called. Rachel watched enough reality TV to know that there were security cameras everywhere these days, to say nothing of facial-recognition software. No, calling in a phone tip was out of the question.

As for dropping off a note at a TV station or at one of Phoenix PD's precincts? Those were both nonstarters for the same reason—security surveillance. Rachel had felt safe dropping her notes for Archbishop Gillespie into collection plates because there weren't usually security cameras inside or outside houses of worship, but cop shops would be a different story.

In the end Rachel decided that her best bet was to put her faith in the U.S. Postal Service. If she got her note written and in the mail today before 5:00 p.m., chances were Detective Lasko would have it in hand sometime the next day.

As soon as Rachel reached that conclusion, she acted on it, retrieving the packet containing the rest of her three-by-five cards from the dresser drawer in her bedroom and her box of latex gloves from the cabinet under the kitchen sink. On the bottom shelf of a cabinet in the family room, she found her box of leftover Christmas cards and located an unused envelope. Since she no longer sent Christmas cards to anyone, having an orphaned card or two wasn't a problem. Then, seated at the kitchen table and with her hands sheathed in latex, she pulled a note card out of the packet and went to work.

This time, rather than employing her penmanship skills, she printed out her message in all caps:

THE MAN YOU'RE LOOKING FOR IS NAMED JACK STONEMAN.

Once the note was written, she stuffed it into the envelope. She had to use her computer to track down the street address for Phoenix PD. After addressing the envelope to Detective Kyle Lasko, she attached a self-adhesive stamp and finished the job by sealing the envelope shut with the help of a damp sponge from the kitchen sink.

Rachel had just finished stuffing the sealed envelope into a Ziploc bag and placing it in her purse when Rich's Escalade pulled in to the driveway. She managed to shed her gloves and disappear all evidence of what she'd been doing before the garage door opened. Fortunately, once the noon news was over, she had turned off the TV set. Rachel fully expected Rich to unload whatever supplies he'd picked up onto his workbench and then stay in the garage with his birdhouses, but he didn't. He came into the house through the kitchen door instead.

"You were up and out early," he observed, studying her keenly as he removed a soda from the fridge and popped the lid.

"I had places to go and people to see," she told him. "Unlike you, I don't have to spend every minute of every day in the garage."

"Have you given any thought to what I asked you last night?"

"About what?" she demanded. "About getting a divorce, you mean? Of course I haven't thought about it. On the amount of money we have coming in, we can't afford a divorce, and you know it."

"I won't live under the same roof with a wife who's whoring around on me."

Whoring around? Rachel thought. *What about living under the same roof with a killer?* That's what she wanted to say, but she didn't.

"Who is he?" Rich asked. "The guy who runs that pawnshop you like so much over on West Thomas? Or is this someone you meet up with on Sunday mornings when you're supposedly going to Mass at all those churches? Or maybe the two of you get together in the mornings when you're supposedly out walking. I know for damned sure you weren't anywhere near Metrocenter last night."

Rachel was utterly astonished. Rich knew everything—where she went, what she did. How was that even possible? It took every bit of self-possession she could muster to keep from flailing at him with both fists.

"We are not having this conversation right now," she told him evenly. Picking up her car keys and purse, she headed for the door.

"You're just going to turn your back and walk out on me?" he demanded.

"I'm going to mail a letter," she replied over her shoulder. "By the way, you're on your own for dinner, and don't bother waiting up. I'm not at all sure when I'll be back."

Beyond furious, Rachel managed to maintain her dignity long enough to climb into the car and start the engine, but that was it. Trembling with outrage, she sat in the driveway in her idling SEL for several minutes, trying to calm herself and attempting to get her head around the scope of the problem. Somehow Rich knew every single place she went. That meant he knew about her frequent stops on Lincoln Drive. And if he knew about those, how soon before he'd be able to string the whole story together?

Eventually Rachel's head cleared enough for her to determine her next step. She immediately backed out onto the street and drove straight to Chet's Automotive Repair, a small one-man garage on Bell. Years earlier, when budgetary issues had decreed that using car dealerships for necessary repairs and upkeep was no longer feasible, Rachel's good fortune had led her to Chet's garage, and it had become her standby as far as automobile maintenance was concerned. Maybe she'd slightly exaggerated their family's dire financial plight to Chet, but she knew for a fact that when she came in with a repair problem, he generally shaved 10 to 20 percent off the top.

"Good morning, Ms. Higgins," he said, approaching her open car window.

There was no need for her to mention to him that she was upset. Her tearful face made the case for her.

"What seems to be the problem?" Chet asked.

"It's my husband," she said. "We're having marital troubles, and I think he might have put something on my car so he can keep track of where I've been and what I've been doing."

Chet paused long enough to wipe grease off his hands with a towel. "Sorry to hear that, ma'am," he said. "Let me take a look and see what I can find."

He inspected the car in a purposeful manner, checking behind the bumpers and under the fenders. As he examined the third wheel well—the one on the SEL's passenger side—he removed a small item from its hiding place and brought it back to the driver's window, where he showed it to Rachel. The small object, encased in black plastic, fit easily inside the palm of Chet's massive hand.

"This is your bad boy," he told her with a grin. "If I'm not mistaken, it's top of the line, with real-time GPS tracking and route-playback capability added into the bargain. It has a built-in battery that's good for three weeks at a time without recharging and a powerful magnet that attaches to the body of the vehicle."

"What should I do with it?" she asked. "Run over it? Throw it away?"

"If I were you and if I really didn't want the guy to know what I was up to, I'd head over to the nearest truck stop, clap this onto the fender of one of those big rigs, and let your husband chase after an eighteen-wheeler while you go on about your business."

"Where would you suggest I find eighteen-wheelers?"

"There's a new truck stop off I-17 just north of the 101," Chet told her. "That would be a good place to start. Just be sure you don't get caught messing around with someone's rig. Truckers don't take kindly to that sort of thing."

"I'll be careful," Rachel said. "Thank you."

As Rachel drove off, she could barely contain her anger. So Rich could afford to spend money on high-tech tracking gadgets without her knowing it while every expenditure she made was examined under a fiscal microscope. He'd been taking money out of their accounts to spy on her, but for how long? He had mentioned something about her going to churches. Did that mean he had records of all of her church visits—of where she'd gone and when she'd been there? If Rich turned that data over to the cops, Rachel was done for. The only possible piece of good news was the fact that he seemed focused on the idea that she was having an affair. With any kind of luck, Rich wouldn't make the connection between his supposedly straying wife and what had happened on Lincoln Drive the night before, but if he did, all bets were off. Unfortunately, Rich was a black-and-white sort of guy—someone with no shades of gray. If he figured out what she'd done, there was no question he would turn her in. In other words, one way or the other Rich would have to be dealt with.

As advertised, the truck stop that Chet had mentioned was shiny and new, as was the Denny's outlet located inside it. Once in the restaurant, Rachel made her way to a booth by a window and ordered a cup of coffee while she surveyed the lay of the land. She knew that the gasoline and diesel pumps outside were busy, but they were located on the far side of the building and away from her line of sight. On this side of the building at the edge of the property sat a long row of trucks, parked side by side. They seemed to be settled in for some kind of extended stay. Maybe the drivers were making mandatory rest stops. What she needed was to locate a vehicle that was heading back to the highway, and her best bet for finding one of those would be at the parking lot's nearest exit, where several trucks were lined up and waiting to merge onto the freeway access road.

It wasn't until she was paying her restaurant bill at the counter that she remembered the sealed envelope still buried in her purse, waiting to be mailed.

"Where's the nearest post office?" she asked the hostess.

"There's a regular post office located in Sun City on the far side of I-17, but that's a long way from here," the woman told her. "If you just want to mail something, you can drop it off at the cash wrap out in the lobby. The mailman picks up from there every afternoon around three thirty. And if you need a stamp, they'll sell you one of those, too."

The lobby was crowded and busy. Rachel made her way to the self-serve beverage counter, where, although she had no intention of drinking another cup of coffee, she poured one into a paper cup before going to pay for it. At the counter two overworked clerks were busily ringing up fuel sales as well as food items and touristy gewgaws. No one paid the least bit of attention to Rachel as she placed her coffee on the counter and used a paper napkin to remove the envelope from her purse. When it came time for her to pay, she shoved the envelope toward the clerk with the back knuckle of her pinkie finger. Cops might be able to identify suspects using fingerprints, but knuckle prints would most likely be tougher.

"Can you mail this for me?" she asked when the clerk finally glanced in her direction.

"Sure thing," the clerk said, picking up the envelope and dropping it into a basket on a shelf behind her. "Anything else?"

"Nope, thanks," Rachel said. "That's all I needed—some coffee and getting that in the mail."

Out in the parking lot, she made straight for the nearest exit, where not one but three trucks were waiting to turn onto the access road. With Rich's tracker in one hand and the coffee container in the other, Rachel paused on the edge of the curb cutout long enough to catch the eye of the first truck's driver. He nodded in acknowledgment and motioned for her to cross. Directly in front of the truck's rumbling engine, Rachel faked a lurch to the right and made a production of tumbling to the pavement, spilling her coffee on the way. By the time the driver leaped from his vehicle to come to her aid, she had the tracker securely attached to the inside surface of his front bumper.

"Lady?" the panicked driver said, coming toward her with his hand outstretched. "Are you all right? Are you hurt? What happened? I was scared to death I had hit you."

As the driver helped Rachel to her feet, drivers from the other two rigs stepped forward to offer assistance. She thanked them all, assuring them she was fine.

"So sorry," she said. "I didn't mean to scare you. I tripped over a loose piece of gravel and went sliding."

"That coffee's still steaming. Did you get burned?"

In actual fact Rachel had made sure that during her faked fall none of the coffee had landed on her.

"I'm fine, really," she assured them. "Thank you again."

With that she continued on her way, walking north along the sidewalk next to the access road. Only when all three trucks had merged into traffic and driven out of sight did she turn around and go back to her parked Mercedes. Once inside, she switched on the radio and located an all-news channel, where there were still no updates on Archbishop Gillespie's condition. Funeral arrangements for the dead priest, Father Andrew O'Toole, remained pending.

With that thought in mind, Rachel steered the Mercedes out of the parking lot and headed under the freeway to the southbound entrance onto I-17. She knew exactly where she was going now—to her favorite pawnshop, One and Done, on West Thomas Road.

Rich wasn't completely wrong about Dan Morgan, the guy who ran the place. Rachel wasn't exactly having an affair with him, but a good deal of back-and-forth flirting went on whenever the two of them had any dealings.

Rachel hoped that if she played her cards right, she'd be able to trade her engagement ring and wedding band for an untraceable handgun. If Archbishop Gillespie somehow pulled through and ultimately survived, that part of the job still had to be completed. This time she'd make sure it was.

As for Rich? What would happen to him remained to be seen.

|CHAPTER 27|

By early afternoon the waiting room outside the ICU was thronged with people, including numerous members of the clergy. Sister Anselm, looking surprisingly refreshed after a two-hour nap, was back in Archbishop Gillespie's room when a call from Stu came in on Ali's phone.

"Hang on while I step out into the corridor," Ali told him. "What's going on?"

"I was right. B. spent most of the day locked in meetings with Dieter, who, as expected, was in a rage, demanding that we cough up half the ransom he paid out, even though he did so against our advice. Unfortunately for him, Frigg seems to have found a silver lining."

"She did?"

"We don't believe the trojan ever existed, and we now have reason to believe that Dieter Gunther himself was behind the whole plot. Apparently he's in a serious financial bind due to mounting gambling debts. The money for the ransom came from company funds. I believe he intended to use the ransom to bail himself out of the hole. I just sent B. an encrypted e-mail with everything our brilliant Frigg found on the guy."

If Frigg had somehow gotten the goods on Dieter Gunther, she wasn't the only brilliant one in the group. Ali herself had suggested taking a closer look at the man, and Frigg had sussed out all the damning details. Unfortunately, exactly how the AI had managed that extraordinary feat was also cause for concern.

"How problematic are Frigg's actions in all this?" Ali asked.

"We should be in the clear," Stu replied. "Dieter was adamant about no police involvement. At the moment this is still an internal A&D issue, and I'm hoping B. can keep it that way."

"You've all done excellent work on this," Ali said. "Thank you. Anything else I should know about?"

"One more thing before you go," Stu replied. "A snail-mail letter from Archbishop Gillespie arrived today. It's addressed to B. and marked urgent. With the archbishop in the hospital and B. out of the country, Shirley wanted to know what we should do about it."

"Open it," Ali said at once.

"Okay, hang on."

She listened to the sounds of rustling paper as Stu slit open the envelope and unfolded whatever was inside it. Ali waited for a long moment while he examined the contents.

"Well," she prodded at last, "what's in it?"

"It appears to be a listing of Archbishop Gillespie's social media accounts, along with all relevant passwords. Having those gives us complete access to examine every one of them."

Ali closed her eyes. Over pepperoni pizza with Francis Gillespie only two nights earlier, she and B. had suggested the author of the threats might be lurking among the archbishop's social media followers. Right this instant that possibility seemed even more likely.

"I suggest you pass that information along to Frigg and let her take a look at it," Ali said decisively. "Since she's done such a bang-up job scoping out what the deal is with Dieter, maybe she can do the same thing for Archbishop Gillespie."

Ali ended the call and went back inside, where she found Sister Anselm standing in the doorway to Archbishop Gillespie's room, speaking to the people gathered there.

"The archbishop is awake and talking," she said. "He has asked me to make the following announcement: According to his doctors, his condition has been upgraded from critical to serious but stable. Soon he'll be moved out of the ICU and into a regular room. He's grateful for all the thoughts and prayers, and he sends his sincerest sympathies to Father Andrew O'Toole's family and friends. Father Andrew's death is a terrible loss to everyone who knew and loved him."

Sighs of genuine relief passed through the room, and Ali wasn't the least bit surprised that one of Archbishop Gillespie's first concerns would be for someone other than himself.

Father Daniel raised his hand. "Do we have permission to pass his statement as well as his health update along to the public?"

Sister Anselm nodded. "Yes, you do," she answered.

Father Daniel immediately exited the room, followed by most of the priests, leaving behind Sister Anselm and Father Mike.

"With the death threats still active, is moving him to a regular room a good idea?" Father Mike was asking.

That was Ali's concern as well.

"It's not my call, but he won't be there alone," Sister Anselm answered grimly. "Not as long as you and I are there, but that's not the only problem. Now he's gotten it into his head that he wants to officiate at Father Andrew's funeral."

"Officiate at the funeral?" Father Mike echoed. "You can't be serious."

"I am, and evidently he is, too," Sister Anselm replied.

"But a funeral like that will be a full-out public event," Father Mike objected. "If whoever's after the archbishop is looking for another opportunity, he'll be a far easier target there than in a hospital room."

"Tell me about it," Sister Anselm snapped. "Now I need to go call that Detective Lasko. He asked to be notified as soon as the archbishop regained consciousness and was well enough to speak, which seems to be the case at the moment, even if what he's spouting doesn't make a lick of sense."

|CHAPTER 28|

For Jack Stoneman, being confined to that Phoenix PD interview room was exactly what Yogi Berra would have called "déjà vu all over again." Someone had swabbed both his hands for gunshot residue, and someone else had taken away his clothing—shoes included—so they, too, could be examined. Back in an orange jumpsuit and wearing a pair of plastic jail scuffs on his feet, Jack felt overcome by a sense of hopelessness as he answered Detective Lasko's endless questions.

"How long have you been panhandling around Archbishop Gillespie's residence?"

"Two and a half years, give or take."

"How well do you know Archbishop Gillespie?" Lasko asked.

"I don't know him at all—never met the man."

"What about Father O'Toole? How well did you know him?"

"We were friends, more or less," Jack allowed. "Shortly after I started working there, he started bringing me food. I may not have taken home as much cash as I would've from a busy intersection, but I never went away hungry."

"So you were friends?"

"Not friends so much, more like acquaintances."

"When's the last time you saw Father O'Toole?"

"That would be yesterday afternoon around four, just before I went to catch the bus to go home. He brought a couple of sandwiches that were left over from lunch. I ate them on the bus."

"Was there anything unusual about him at the time? Did he seem upset or worried about anything?"

"Not that I remember."

"What about the other people you saw that day—anyone out of the ordinary?"

"Same old, same old," Jack replied.

"Like who?"

"Like the people I see there all the time—a guy with two poodles, a woman who walks a bunch of dogs, and the lady who brings me lattes."

"And everyone acted completely normal?"

"Completely."

"And you caught your bus around four?"

"Ten after," Jack replied. "Takes me until five fifteen or so to get home. The bus stop is about four blocks from where I live."

"What did you do after you got off the bus?"

Jack knew this was where it would all go south. "I stopped off at a liquor store and bought a bottle of tequila—a fifth. We had a couple of shots."

"We who?"

"I met up with some buds in the parking lot."

"What happened after that?"

"I have no idea."

"What do you mean?"

Jack shrugged. "Once we started drinking, the whole night from then on is a blank."

"As in you blacked out?"

"I guess," Jack muttered. "Either that or they slipped me something. When I woke up this morning, my tequila was gone and so was all the money I brought in yesterday."

"You're saying they rolled you?" Lasko asked.

"Seems like," Jack replied.

There was a tap on the door to the interview room, and a woman stuck her head inside. "A word, Detective Lasko?"

The detective rose and stepped out of the room, leaving Jack sitting and stewing in his own juices. He had just admitted to the cop that he knew the dead victim and had zero alibi for the time the shooting happened. He was toast now, for sure.

A moment later the detective popped back into the room. "I have to go out for a while," he said. "If you don't mind, we'll finish up when I get back. In the meantime do you need anything—a sandwich, a soda?"

"No," Jack answered. "Don't need nothin'. I'm good."

"All right, then," Detective Lasko said. "I'll be back as soon as I can."

He departed. The door closed, leaving a despairing Jack alone. He knew exactly how all this worked. Cops often walked off in the middle of interviews and then watched through two-way mirrors to see and hear whatever the suspect did next.

Jack Stoneman steeled himself to do absolutely nothing. He sat perfectly still, doing his best to keep his legs from twitching. He tried not to shift around in his chair. While his body might have been still, his mind was working a mile a minute, thinking about the relative size of this interview room compared to a prison cell.

In truth they weren't all that different.

|CHAPTER 29|

Archbishop Gillespie lay on his back in his hospital bed with his eyes closed and his rosary resting in his hands, letting tears dribble onto the pillow beneath him. He had awakened in the hospital without any idea of how he'd gotten there. Sister Anselm—his dear friend Sister Anselm—was the one who'd delivered the appalling news that Father Andrew was dead of a bullet wound to the head.

"It's my fault," the archbishop had told her. "That bullet was meant for me. I should be dead, not Father Andrew."

Sister Anselm wasn't in an especially sympathetic frame of mind. "You probably wouldn't have been hurt at all if you'd been wearing your seat belt," she admonished him.

That was the last thing he actually remembered—getting into the backseat of the Town Car and not fastening his belt. "You're never going to give me a break on that, are you?" he said.

"Not on your life!" she replied.

"Am I going to live?"

"You are for now," she answered. "The doctors have upgraded you from critical to serious but stable, and they'll be moving you to a regular room sometime later today. But it was close, Francis, very close."

Only in private did Sister Anselm ever use his given name. "You developed a brain bleed from hitting your head on the dome light. If the doctors hadn't performed emergency surgery to repair the damage, you might have died. It's a miracle you're not partially paralyzed. The whole city has been praying for you, by the way. There's been a round-the-clock prayer vigil in the courtyard in front of the hospital lobby and all kinds of media attention as well."

"If my condition has been upgraded, do the people outside know?"

"I'll see to it," Sister Anselm said.

"Tell me what happened."

"You don't remember?"

"The last thing I remember was getting into the car."

She told him, including as much detail as the investigating officers had been willing to share with her.

"Father Andrew died instantly?"

"Yes. Someone called Father Daniel to come down from the residence and administer last rites."

"What about Father Andrew's family?"

"They've been notified. His father and mother are flying in from Pennsylvania today. Father Daniel has arranged for someone to pick them up from the airport. They'll be staying at the residence along with several additional guests. Father Daniel and I have arranged for a Sister of Providence to come in and handle cooking duties for the time being."

"What about funeral arrangements?" the archbishop asked.

"There's nothing definite so far," Sister Anselm answered. "I believe the family is hoping to schedule the funeral for Friday, but that's going to depend on how long it takes the medical examiner to release the body."

"Please let the family know that Father Andrew's services should be held at the cathedral, and I'd like to officiate if at all possible."

"Officiate?" a frowning Sister Anselm repeated through lips that had tightened into a thin, stiff line. "You'll need to discuss that with your physicians. In the meantime Father Daniel will go downstairs to update the people gathered there, press included, letting them know about your progress. I believe I'll join him."

Sister Anselm stalked out in a huff. Francis Gillespie remained where he was, alone with only the steady beat of the machines at his bedside for company. Left to himself in that humming silence, he could only pray, grieve, and weep, because he held himself entirely responsible for what had happened.

This was all his fault. Father Daniel had known about the threats, but not Father Andrew. It was sheer pride on Francis's part that Father

Andrew hadn't been told. Francis had been so intent on doing what he saw as his priestly duty as far as the church was concerned and on saving his potential killer's soul that he'd failed to warn his good friend that danger possibly lurked just outside the walls of their residence, not that telling Father Andrew would have done any good. And now he was dead at the hands of a killer who was not only going to hell but who was also walking free.

"Excuse me, Archbishop Gillespie," a voice said. "Would it be possible for me to speak to you for a moment?"

Brushing away his tears, Francis turned toward the unfamiliar voice. The speaker was a tall man in his late forties wearing a suit and tie. "I'm Detective Kyle Lasko with Phoenix PD," he announced, flashing a badge. "I'm the lead investigator looking into the death of Father O'Toole. If you're up to it, I'd like to ask you a few questions, but first let me say I'm sorry for your loss."

"Thank you," Francis murmured. "Father Andrew's death is a terrible blow to all who knew him and to me especially. As for your questions, I don't know how much help I can be. I really don't remember anything beyond getting into the car to go to Peoria."

"What can you tell me about Father O'Toole?"

"He was originally from Pennsylvania and had been at the residence the past ten years, where he functioned as our man-of-all-work. He looked after the place, was in charge of the kitchen, managed the house-keepers, oversaw the work of the gardening crew, and handled any necessary repairs. And whenever I went out in public, he was in charge of driving."

"Did he have any enemies?"

"Not as far as I know."

"Does the name Jack Stoneman ring a bell?"

Archbishop Gillespie had to think about that one for a moment. "I don't believe so," he said at last. "Who's he?"

"Mr. Stoneman was the neighborhood panhandler who liked to station himself at the end of your driveway."

"Oh, him," Francis said at once. "Yes, I'm familiar with Jack, although I don't believe anyone ever mentioned a last name. He was a constant presence outside the residence, always wearing that Desert Storm cap of his. According to Father Andrew, Jack was a veteran with PTSD as well as a severe drinking problem. Father Andrew tried to look after him. He wouldn't give him money for fear Jack would spend it on booze. Instead Father Andrew made sure Jack never went away hungry."

"So there was no ill will between the two of them—between Father O'Toole and Jack?"

"Not so far as I know, but why are you asking about him?"

"Because we have witnesses who tentatively place him at the crime scene at the time the shooting took place, and I was wondering if the two of them had had some kind of disagreement."

"No," Francis said at once. "This makes no sense. I can't imagine Jack would be involved in any way. Father Andrew is dead, may he rest in peace, but believe me, I was the killer's primary target. The bullet that hit Father Andrew was really intended for me."

"Because of the threatening notes?" Detective Lasko asked.

"You know about those?"

"Yes, a friend of yours, Ali Reynolds, came by Phoenix PD this morning and showed them to me. She claimed you'd reported them to the department and were told that they were most likely harmless. I looked through departmental records, but I wasn't able to find any kind of official report."

"There wouldn't be," Francis said. "I was trying to keep from making a big fuss about it. Luis and I discussed the situation during a private conversation at a prayer breakfast we both attended down at the civic center."

"Luis?" Detective Lasko asked after a moment's hesitation. "You mean Luis Adolfo—as in Chief of Police Luis Adolfo?"

"Yes, he's the one," Francis answered. "We were seated side by side at the head table. He told me not to worry, that they didn't sound like credible threats. I think he was wrong about that."

Detective Lasko heaved a resigned sigh—the sigh of someone who'd just learned that his life had become infinitely more complicated. Francis understood that having the chief of police involved in his case probably wasn't doing the poor detective any favors.

"When I realized that going to the authorities about the situation had been a nonstarter," Francis continued, "I turned to some of my friends—B. Simpson, Ali Reynolds, and their company, High Noon Enterprises—to see if they could be of any assistance."

Detective Lasko nodded. "As I said, I spoke to Ms. Reynolds about this at some length earlier today. She and her people have evidently consulted with a handwriting expert who believes the writer of the notes to be a female in her fifties or sixties. Is it possible that the threats are related to some kind of romantic entanglement?"

Francis attempted a hoot of laughter, but a stab of pain from his broken ribs brought him up short.

"My dear man," he said at last. "I became a priest in my early twenties. I've been celibate all my life, and I have no reason to believe that Father Andrew ever violated his vows either."

"And you have no idea about the identity of any person or persons who might be targeting you?"

"None whatsoever."

Sister Anselm returned to the room. "Time's up," she announced brusquely. "Ten minutes is the limit."

Detective Lasko closed his small notebook, put away his pen, and left the room.

"I think you should rest now, but next up will be Father Mike," Sister Anselm said. "He was here earlier, while you were asleep. Now that you're awake, he's been champing at the bit to see you."

"Father Mike?" Francis repeated. "As in Father Mike from Dallas?"

"Who else?"

"How on earth did he get here?"

"How do you think? Someone was trying to kill you, so I called him. Under the circumstances can you imagine anyone better to have in your corner?"

Archbishop Gillespie looked at his longtime friend and smiled. "No," he said at last. "Between you and Father Mike, I think I'm in pretty good hands."

|CHAPTER 30|

Detective Lasko stood in the hospital elevator mulling over the latest complication in his already challenging, high-profile case. So Chief Adolfo and Archbishop Gillespie were pals. How long would it be before the chief disregarded the chain of command a second time and came to Kyle asking for updates and issuing marching orders?

That's when his phone rang. The face showing on the screen belonged to Emmy—short for Emmeline Vasquez—a savvy tech from the crime lab who happened to be one of Detective Lasko's favorites and the same person who'd been in charge of Jack Stoneman's GSR test.

"Hey, Emmy," he said, "what have you got for me? Good news, I hope?"

"I'm not sure if it's good news," she said. "I ran the GSRs. Nothing on Mr. Stoneman's hands or clothing, including his shoes."

"So he's probably not our guy, then."

"Hard to tell. I just sent you two photos. You might want to take a look at them and call me back."

"I'm in an elevator. I'll be a minute."

He stepped off the elevator on the lobby level. Outside, he tried to dodge the crowd, but one sharp-eyed reporter came racing after him, shouting questions.

"Hey, Detective Lasko, do you have any suspects?"

"You know the rules," Kyle growled back at him. "No comment."

Once safely inside his vehicle, he opened his phone and downloaded the photos in Emmy's texts. Peering at the two images, all he could make out were collections of small circles. Puzzled, he dialed Emmy right back.

"Okay," he said, "I give up. What am I looking at?"

"The one on the left is a photo of a footprint cast taken from the crime scene last night. The one on the right is a close-up of the sole of the right shoe Jack Stoneman was wearing when you brought him in today. As I said, both photos are of the right shoe."

"They look the same," Kyle said.

"That's because they *are* the same," Emmy replied. "Carbon copies."

"Then it would seem that Mr. Jack Stoneman has some serious explaining to do," he said.

"It certainly does," Emmy agreed.

"Okay, thanks," Kyle said. "I'm on my way back to the department right now."

As he ended the call, another came in, this one from a blocked number. He and Emmy were friends as well as colleagues. She had called him from her cell phone. Calls from inside the department showed up as blocked calls rather than displaying a number, so he picked up.

"Detective Kyle Lasko here," he said.

"Please hold for Chief of Police Adolfo," a woman's voice told him.

That hadn't taken long. Waiting for the call to be put through, Kyle held his breath. A moment later the chief's voice rumbled through the phone.

"Good afternoon, Detective Lasko," Chief Adolfo said heartily. "I hear you're making progress."

So the chief knew about the crime-scene photo situation before he did. That figured.

"I hope so, sir," Kyle said.

"Good work and glad to hear it," the chief continued. "Let's get this thing done. The sooner the better. Please keep me posted on any new developments."

"Yes, sir," a pained Detective Lasko agreed. "I most certainly will."

|CHAPTER 31|

With the waiting room full of priests, Ali took herself down to the cafeteria, where she toyed with her food, worrying about the idea of Archbishop Gillespie going out in public to perform a funeral service while his potential killer was still on the loose. Detective Lasko might be convinced he had his man. Ali was not. Needing to feel as though she were doing something useful, she dialed up Frigg's audio connection.

"Good afternoon, Ms. Reynolds, I hope you're having a pleasant and productive day."

Ali always felt a bit silly thanking a computer program for her polite small talk, but she did so all the same.

"How can I help you?" Frigg asked.

"I'm still working the Archbishop Gillespie case, and I need you to resend one of the last texts you sent me, the one about the attorney with an office on Central Avenue."

"Very well," Frigg said. "Sending Gavin James's address. Do you also require his phone number?"

"No, just the address is fine," Ali said as her phone jangled an announcement for the arriving text. "I think I'm going to do a surprise drop-in visit on him this afternoon rather than call for an appointment."

When Ali viewed the text, knowing that it would vanish the moment she ended the call, she memorized the address in the 3800 block of North Central. The location was barely two grids north of St. Gregory's, less than a ten-minute drive. Once there, she pulled in to the underground parking garage for a medium high-rise and slipped her Porsche Cayenne into one of the visitor slots. In the lobby she scanned the directory until she located the office of Anderson, James and Hill on the topmost floor. Penthouse office suites didn't come cheap, so obviously Gavin James was doing all right for himself.

When Ali presented her High Noon business card, the receptionist wasn't pleased to have someone show up without an appointment while still expecting to be admitted to the inner sanctum.

"May I ask what this is about?" she wanted to know.

"I'm actually here on behalf of Archbishop Francis Gillespie."

Merely dropping the name made all the difference. The receptionist whispered into her headset. A moment later a second woman appeared, and the receptionist handed over Ali's business card.

"This is Mr. James's secretary," she explained. "She'll escort you to his office."

Ali followed her guide past a collection of very plush offices, stopping only when they arrived at a top-drawer corner suite. She was ushered into an office with a breathtaking view of Camelback Mountain where a handsome forty-something man was hurriedly rising from a massive glass-topped desk while shrugging his way into the jacket of what was clearly an Italian-made designer suit.

He stepped forward to greet her with an expression of genuine concern on his face. "This is about Archbishop Gillespie?" he asked.

Ali nodded.

"I heard about what happened. How's he doing?"

"Better, it would seem," Ali replied without going into any more detail.

James turned back to his secretary, still lingering in the doorway. "When's my next appointment?" he asked.

"Forty-five minutes."

"All right," he said. "I'm sure we'll be done by then." Still examining Ali's card, he motioned her into a visitor's chair. "I take it from your business card that you're not an actual police officer?"

"No, I'm not," Ali admitted. "My husband, B. Simpson, and I run a cybersecurity firm called High Noon Enterprises. Archbishop Gillespie came to visit us this past Sunday asking for our assistance."

"What kind of assistance?"

"For months now he's been receiving anonymous threats, all of them delivered by way of messages dropped into collection plates at churches throughout the archdiocese. He came to us hoping we could identify the source and prevent anything bad from happening."

"But now something bad has happened," Gavin James put in.

"Exactly," Ali agreed. "Father O'Toole's shooting last night may or may not be related to those previous threats, but my suspicion is that although he's the one who's dead, he wasn't the actual target."

"You think it was the archbishop?"

Ali nodded. "In the course of our investigation, we've come to suspect that the threatening notes may be related to the archdiocese's difficulties with pedophile priests from years ago, and since you played such an important role in one of those cases, I was hoping you could help us."

Gavin resumed his seat behind the desk and studied Ali gravely for a moment before he spoke again. "What do you need?"

"What we're looking for is in-depth background information," Ali told him. "Most of what we have now is what was reported in the media at the time. In my experience the whole story seldom makes it anywhere near the nightly news."

"That's true," he agreed with a smile. "For instance, are you aware that it was Archbishop Gillespie himself who encouraged us to go after Father Needham in the first place?"

Ali managed to keep her jaw from dropping. "I had no idea," she replied.

"Would you care to know how that happened?"

"I certainly would," she said. "It would also be helpful to know how you came to be the designated spokesman for all of Needham's victims."

"That's easy," Gavin said. "I was in my last year of law school at the time. I'd been on debate teams in both high school and college, and when all this happened, the other guys more or less nominated me to be the face in front of the cameras. That was an education in and of itself. So where should I start?"

"At the beginning?" Ali suggested.

"What do you know about St. Francis High?" Gavin asked.

"Not much," Ali replied, "other than that it's a church-sponsored private high school."

"Correct," Gavin agreed. "It came into being in the 1930s as St. Francis Academy, founded by an old guy named William Ford. Despite having only a fourth-grade education, he had managed to accumulate a fortune in the stock market during the Roaring Twenties and was smart enough to cash in before the big crash. While everybody else was broke, he started accumulating real-estate holdings in and around what's now downtown Scottsdale.

"Initially the school was located on Ford's cattle ranch. At the time it was well outside of town, and students earned their keep by working as ranch hands. Once development engulfed the property, Ford sold most of it off, retaining only the parcel where the school was located. Originally St. Francis was for boys only. The school went coed in the 1980s, and it's considered to be one of the top prep schools in the country."

Ali felt as though she were being given a sales pitch for a scholarship donation, but she simply nodded and kept listening.

"The original building on the new campus opened in 1953. Ford loved swimming. For a long time, St. Francis was the first and only high school in the area with an Olympic-size pool. We had football and basketball teams, yes, but at St. Francis being on the swim team was a very big deal—the 'in' thing. My father was swim-team captain his senior year, and so was I when I was a senior."

"Which brings us to Father Paul Needham," Ali put in.

James Gavin's face darkened. "Yes," he said with a sigh. "When he singled me out for attention and eventually abuse, I thought I was the only one it had ever happened to, and I never told anyone, not even my folks. By 2003 I was twenty-four and in my last year of law school. It was the fiftieth anniversary of the new campus, so the alumni association hosted a huge all-class reunion. It was a multi-day party. Some of my old teammates attended, and we ended up putting together an unofficial gathering of former swim-team members. It was during that off-the-books party, with plenty of booze flowing, that the truth finally started leaking out."

"No one had said anything until then?" Ali asked.

"Nope," Gavin said. "It was a conspiracy of silence. We all had to be pretty much falling-down drunk before people started speaking up. We were too ashamed. I understand those dynamics a little better now than I did then. Sexual-abuse victims, especially male victims in same-sex situations, are somehow deemed to be complicit in whatever happens to them. They're often held in the same kind of contempt as their abusers.

"Over the years Needham had a reputation for choosing kids who weren't necessarily the best athletes to be team captains. Everybody acted as though it was a good thing that he was giving second-tier kids a chance to shine. That was certainly true in my case, by the way. I might've been captain of the team, but I was by far the least talented swimmer."

"In other words, being appointed captain came with a dark side," Ali suggested.

Gavin nodded. "It was part of Needham's grooming process. He did it to me and to plenty of others as well, but until that all-class reunion none of us had guts enough to step forward and blow the whistle. The gathering didn't end until the wee hours of the morning, but it was like we had taken the weight off a pressure cooker. Years of pent-up steam had come pouring out. Although we were all hammered at the time, none of us were so far gone that we forgot what had been said."

"That's when you decided to fight back?"

Gavin nodded. "We called ourselves the STS, Swim Team Survivors. Too much booze might have been what *started* us talking, but we didn't need booze to *keep* talking. Gradually we worked our way down the line, talking to people who'd been on teams that had come before and after ours. As we moved back in time, guess what we discovered? The abuse started only after Father Needham came on board as swim coach and ceased once he was gone."

"When did you decide to go to the cops about it?" Ali asked.

"I doubt any of us would have done so if my father hadn't died."

"Your father?" Ali asked with a puzzled frown.

"My folks were always big-time supporters of the church, and they were both very involved with activities inside the archdiocese. My mother served on all kinds of committees. So did my father, but to a lesser extent. When he died, I think Archbishop Gillespie came to the funeral less to honor my father's passing and more to provide moral support for my mother.

"It was during the reception afterward that I screwed up my courage and actually talked to him about it—not straight out, exactly. I asked him if he'd heard any complaints about Father Needham. He said he hadn't, but then he looked me straight in the eye and asked me if I had. I couldn't very well talk about it, not right there in my mother's living room with the place full of her friends and relations. All I could do was nod. He looked at me again with those piercing blue eyes of his, like he was seeing right through me, and I'll never forget what he said. 'Why don't you call my secretary and make an appointment to stop by my office so we can talk about this?'"

"And you did?"

"Yes, the very next week. I told him my story, and I let him know that there were plenty of other victims out there who'd suffered the same way I had. When I finished, he sat there at his desk with his hands crossed for the longest time, not saying a word. I couldn't tell if he was thinking or praying. Finally he said, 'This is a very serious matter. . . .' He sort of left the sentence hanging there, and I thought he was going to finish it by telling me to shut up and go away. But he didn't. 'What you've told me constitutes egregious criminal behavior. The church can atone for its sins later. For now what you and the other boys involved deserve is justice. You must go to the police.'"

Ali had always liked Francis Gillespie, but hearing that story through Gavin James's point of view sent her respect for the man soaring. He was a straight shooter and always had been.

"It took time," Gavin continued. "Some of the victims didn't want to be outed in public. Two of them were already sick and dying."

"Of AIDS?" Ali asked.

Gavin gave her a searching look and then nodded. "Of AIDS," he agreed. "In the end fourteen of us agreed to go to the cops. We made an appointment and showed up at the county attorney's office as a group, and we stayed as a group, sticking together like glue throughout the criminal proceedings along with the civil ones that followed."

"Did Archbishop Gillespie advise you on the civil side of the equation?"

Gavin shook his head. "He didn't have to," he replied, "because he already had in that initial conversation. I'm sure he played a pivotal role in the fact that the archdiocese settled our civil claim out of court. And there you have it—the whole story, but there must be something else you want rather than just hashing over all that ancient history."

"I'm here because of the threatening notes," Ali explained. "Our handwriting analyst has determined that they appear to have been written by a female, a woman most likely in her fifties or sixties. I'm wondering if, in all the court proceedings, you might have encountered someone associated with your group or outside it who harbored ill will against the archbishop."

Gavin shook his head. "You can count all of us out on that score—along with our family members. Archbishop Gillespie is a hero who made a huge difference in our lives. My share of that out-of-court settlement meant that I was able to pay off my student loans and pay cash for my first house. It put me way ahead of the game. It did the same thing for several others. For the guys who were sick, it helped them manage what would have been impossible medical expenses."

"Were there any affected victims who didn't come forward?" Ali asked.

"I suppose that's possible," Gavin agreed. "There were lots of swim-team members over the years, and I didn't know every one of them personally, so there might well have been other victims who didn't join in."

"Would there be any way to track them all down?" Ali asked.

Gavin thought about that for a time before he spoke again. "As a result of my involvement, I ended up accumulating a complete set of *The Clarion*, St. Francis High School's yearbooks, covering the years Paul Needham was at the school. If you'd like, I could probably give you a listing of each swim-team member during that time. Would that help?"

"Immeasurably," Ali replied. Glancing at her watch, she saw that her forty-five minutes were over and then some. "I'd best be going," she added, getting to her feet. "You have my contact information on the card. If you could send that information along to me, I'd be most grateful."

"Will you be seeing the archbishop?" Gavin asked.

Ali nodded. "I'm headed back to the hospital now."

"Please tell him I said hello and that I'm wishing him the best."

"I'll do that," Ali assured him.

She had silenced her phone once she headed into Gavin James's office. She'd had several notification buzzes while they were talking, but she waited until she was back in her car in the garage before she looked at the screen. One had been a missed call from B. The other, also from B., was a two-word text—CALL ME!

She did. "What's going on?" she asked.

"If Frigg were a person, I'd be waltzing her around a maypole right about now," he declared.

"Why? What's happened?"

"She saved our bacon. First she uncovered Dieter's gambling debts. The bank had called his notes, and he was about to go bust."

"I know about that," Ali said aloud. "Stu told me earlier."

"It turns out his gambling debts were just the tip of the iceberg. A&D is a family-held partnership, with Dieter at the helm and Albert semiretired. Frigg's research uncovered the fact that Dieter has been hatching a secret buyout deal with one of their major competitors."

"Was Albert aware of the pending sale?" Ali asked.

"Not until I told him," B. replied. "As managing partner, Dieter was able to pay the ransomware demand out of company funds without having to answer to anyone else—with the money going to pay off his personal debts. Now that Albert knows what's going on, the jig is up and all bets are off. As long as the ransomware money is immediately returned to company coffers, Albert is willing to cover Dieter's gambling shortfall long enough to get the bank off his back."

"How will Albert get repaid?" Ali asked.

"Believe me," B. said, "one way or the other he'll get his money if he has to take it out of Dieter's hide."

"What about the proposed sale?" Ali asked. "Will that still go through?"

"I doubt it, not once Dieter's mismanagement comes to light—as it's bound to if the other company does any kind of due diligence. What's good for us is that Albert is officially coming out of retirement. From now on he'll be running the show at A&D. The other company's cybersecurity business is handled by one of our biggest competitors. For right now, as far as Albert Gunther is concerned, High Noon is golden."

"So A&D's cybersecurity business will stay with us?" Ali asked.

"And so will our reputation."

"What a relief!" she breathed.

"What's going on with you?" B. asked, abruptly changing the subject.

For the next several minutes, Ali brought him up to date. The eighthour time difference meant it was close to midnight in Zurich, and B. was ready to hit the hay.

"Good work today," Ali told him before hanging up. "Now, get some rest. It sounds like you really earned it."

|CHAPTER 32|

J ack had concentrated so hard on not pacing or twitching in the interview room that he'd actually fallen fast asleep, with his head resting on his arms the way kids at school used to do when they came back in from lunch and teachers made them put their heads on their desks. He awakened abruptly and sat up when the door opened. The clock on the wall said 2:05, so more than an hour had passed since Detective Lasko had left the room.

The moment Jack saw the grim expression on the cop's face, he knew that things had changed—for the worse. Lasko was carrying a clear plastic bag with the word EVIDENCE stamped on it in bright red letters. Inside were Jack's new Skechers.

Without a word of greeting, the detective slammed the bag down on the table in front of Jack before sitting across from him. Pulling a small printed card from his pocket, the detective began reading Jack his rights.

A Miranda warning? Jack thought. *What the hell?*

"What's going on?" he asked when the caution ended.

"Why don't we take another crack at your telling me what you were doing last night?" Lasko growled. "That blackout bullshit isn't going to cut it."

Clearly Lasko's previous kid-gloves treatment was a thing of the past.

"What's changed?" Jack asked.

Lasko held up the bag with the shoes in it and shook it in Jack's face. "This is what changed. The soles on these match the casts we took of footprints found in your clearing near the crime scene last night—the same clearing where we found the murder weapon."

"So what?" Jack asked, trying to maintain a bit of bravado. "That's where I hang out every day. Why wouldn't my shoe prints be there?"

"But those are the only ones we found there, Jack. Nobody else but you was in that clearing last night."

"Like I already told you," Jack insisted, "I wasn't there. I caught the bus home the way I always do, bought some booze, and drank it. That's it. If you don't believe me, talk to my roommates. They'll tell you where I was."

"We already tried that," Lasko said. "I dispatched a pair of detectives to interview the people you live with as soon as I left here. They talked to a pair of guys named George Wooten and Tom Mather. Sound familiar?"

Jack nodded. "Sure," he said. "They're my roommates."

"According to them, you stumbled into the RV drunk as a skunk at three o'clock in the morning. So maybe you did end up blacking out eventually, but I'm guessing that happened a lot later than you told us the first time around. You didn't black out until after you got back from shooting the priest, so help yourself out here, Jack. Tell me what really happened. Did Father Andrew cut you off and tell you no more freebies? Did cutting into your panhandling proceeds make you mad? Is that why you went gunning for him?"

"I'm telling you I didn't do that. Father Andrew was my friend."

"Did you argue?"

"No."

"By the way, the crime lab has located traces of DNA on one of the cartridges inside the murder weapon. Once we're able to profile it, chances are it will lead right back to you."

Jack's head was swimming. "I need to take a leak," he said.

"Fine," Lasko replied. "Be my guest."

Lasko escorted Jack down the hall to a single-stall restroom and then stationed himself against a wall next to the door to wait. Jack did need to pee, but not all that badly. What he really needed was to clear his head and think. Finished at the urinal, he washed his face with cold water and then stared at his bleary-eyed reflection in the mirror. Was it possible he really had done this? If so, why? He'd had no beef with Father Andrew, none at all. And he had no access to a gun either, so how could his DNA be found on a murder weapon? Unless someone had put it there—unless someone was framing him, but that made no sense either.

For several long minutes, Jack couldn't bring himself to leave the restroom. It seemed likely that these were the last few breaths he would take as a free man. If he stopped talking and asked for a lawyer, Lasko would immediately place him under arrest. After that he'd have a court-appointed attorney, one who would probably be worse than useless. And even if he ended up with a court-appointed lawyer who managed to get the court to grant bail, Jack had no money to post it. No one he knew, with the possible exception of Jimmy, maybe, had any money at all. In other words, he would be stuck in the Maricopa County Jail until the case went to court, which could just as well be forever away. No matter how you sliced it, Jack Stoneman was toast.

|CHAPTER 33|

Rachel was happy. She had trotted out her womanly wiles with Dan Morgan, the owner of One and Done, and they had worked like a charm.

"I've finally gotten ahold of the paperwork for a protection order," she had told him. "I'll be filing it first thing next week."

For months now, she had been crying on Dan's shoulder, telling him what a tightwad her abusive husband was. At least the tightwad part was true.

"In situations like yours, getting a restraining order is often the most dangerous time," Dan advised her sympathetically. "If things are going to go bad, that's when it happens. Is there a chance he'll get violent?"

Rachel sighed and did her best to look as though she was trying to hold back tears. That worked, too.

"Do you have a weapon?"

Rachel shook her head. In exchange for her engagement ring, she left the pawnshop forty-five minutes later with a replacement for Rich's revolver—an off-the-books loaded Ruger LCP in her purse. Dan was nothing if not full-service. He just happened to have a drawerful of ammunition in his back room, which included a box of the .380 ammo the little Ruger called for.

"Have you ever done any shooting?" he asked as he loaded cartridges into the clip, showing her how in the process.

Not since last night, she thought. "Not lately," she said. "Years ago I did some target practice with a twenty-two."

"Firing an LCP is a lot different from firing one of those," he told her, handing her the loaded weapon. "For one thing, this has a laser sight. All you have to do is point and shoot, but you need to be close to the target. If I were you, I'd head for the nearest shooting range and practice, in which case you'll need to pick up some more ammunition."

"Thank you so much," she said, giving him a brushing peck on the cheek as she left. "I owe you big time!"

Twice during the day, wanting an update on the archbishop's condition, she had used her burner phone in an attempt to log onto his homepage, only to be told it couldn't be found. On the drive back home, she tuned into a local all-news channel on the radio. That was where she heard the unwelcome news that not only was Francis Gillespie still alive, but also his condition had been upgraded from critical to serious but stable. In other words, he would most likely live, but wasn't that what she had expected? Wasn't that why she was driving around with a loaded pistol in her purse? Her first attempt had failed, but the next one wouldn't. And she had to make that happen before Rich, now emerged from his birdhouse stagnation, could turn her in to the cops. With that in mind, she headed for the hospital.

As she drove, it suddenly occurred to her that she wasn't at all affected by the death of the other priest, Father O'Toole. Shouldn't she be sorry about that? Had her preoccupation with David's death finally sent her completely around the bend? Maybe she really was nuts. In that case, if the cops arrested her, maybe she could opt for an insanity plea. *Maybe I'll end up in a mental institution,* she told herself. *That way I won't have to go to prison, and Rich can make those damned birdhouses to his heart's content.*

|CHAPTER 34|

Back at St. Gregory's Hospital, Ali discovered that the crowd waiting outside the entrance had thinned considerably. Almost all the media vans and cameras had disappeared from the scene. If Francis Gillespie wasn't on the verge of death, then the newsies had more urgent stories to attend to. There was still a small assembly of the faithful waiting there, including a number of priests and habit-wearing nuns. Several of those folks were obviously elderly, and someone in the hospital hierarchy had seen fit to send out a collection of folding chairs so they wouldn't have to stand.

When Ali showed up at the reception desk and inquired after the location of Francis Gillespie's room, she was told that information was unavailable. Seeing Sister Anselm's handiwork as the cause of that security precaution, Ali texted the nun and was directed to Room 514, where she found Father Mike stationed in a chair next to the door.

"She's inside," he said.

Peeking in through the doorway, Ali saw the archbishop asleep in his bed, with Sister Anselm half dozing on a visitor's chair next to him. Catching sight of Ali, the nun put her finger to her lips, signaling for silence, and then motioned for Ali to stay where she was.

"They just gave him more pain meds for his shoulder," Sister Anselm said, joining Ali in the hall. "Are you able to stay for a while?"

"Of course," Ali said. "That's why I'm here."

"With him asleep now, Father Mike has offered to drive me over to the residence. Father Daniel has invited Father Mike and me to stay there. I'll shower and come right back. Father Mike is hoping to get some sleep. He's been up since I called him last night."

"Sure," Ali said. "Whatever you need."

"You're prepared for any eventuality?" Sister Anselm asked.

Ali recognized that in a purportedly gun-free zone this kind of conversation probably called for a certain amount of subtlety. "Would I be here if I weren't?" she replied. "You and Father Mike go ahead and do what you need to do. I'll see to Archbishop Gillespie's safety."

"Good," Sister Anselm said. "Now, come with me. The staff here is well aware of the existence of an ongoing threat, so they're limiting visitors to authorized people only. Let me introduce you to the charge nurse so she knows you have my stamp of approval. Father Daniel advised me that a priest from Prescott, Father Winston, is on his way and has asked to be part of the archbishop's security detail."

"We don't have his ETA, but he's ex-military," Father Mike explained. "I think he'll make a great addition to the squad."

Once Sister Anselm and Father Mike took their leave, Ali settled into the visitor chair, a complex recliner sort of thing that could be folded down into a makeshift bed for overnight stays. The TV set, on but muted, was tuned to some afternoon game show. Wanting up-to-the-minute news, Ali turned on her iPad, only to discover that the battery was down in the red zone. Locating a usable electrical outlet in the room was a challenging and surprisingly noisy process, but the archbishop didn't stir.

Once logged in, she quickly found a news site with an article on Father Andrew's shooting that had been updated only five minutes earlier.

SUSPECT IN CUSTODY IN DEADLY PRIEST SHOOTING ON LINCOLN DRIVE

Phoenix PD reports that a suspect has been taken into custody in regard to the shooting death of Father Andrew O'Toole on East Lincoln Drive last evening. Archbishop Francis Gillespie of the Phoenix Archdiocese was injured in the incident and remains hospitalized at this time.

Because the suspect hasn't been charged, he has not been

named, but sources close to the investigation not authorized to speak publicly suggest that he may be the panhandler who was often seen begging in close proximity to the archbishop's residence.

At the time of the shooting, Father Andrew O'Toole, age 56, was at the wheel of a Lincoln Town Car with the archbishop traveling as a passenger. Once the shooting occurred, the vehicle plunged into traffic, colliding with a number of additional vehicles and injuring several occupants. . . .

Scanning the remainder of the article, Ali could see that it was a verbatim rehash of what had been published earlier. Only the first two paragraphs contained any new information. Was solving a high-profile case really so easy that the first person named as a possible suspect could be placed under arrest in what, in terms of homicide investigations, was little more than the blink of an eye?

―――――

Sometime later, Archbishop Gillespie awoke. "Where's Sister Anselm?" he asked.

"She'll be back," Ali answered. "Father Mike took her to the residence so she could shower. By the way, according to the news, Phoenix PD has made an arrest."

"Who?" the archbishop asked.

"The name hasn't been released, but it's evidently your friendly neighborhood panhandler."

The archbishop shook his head. "That's not right," he said. "Father Andrew and that guy—I believe his name is Jack Stoneman—had a good relationship, a cordial relationship. You know as well as I do that what happened had nothing to do with Father Andrew and everything to do with me. I never spoke to Jack directly, but I remember Father Andrew telling me that the man didn't own a vehicle—that he traveled from place to place strictly by bus. How could he possibly have commuted all over the archdiocese, especially on Sunday mornings, to deposit threatening notes in the collection plates?"

"So you don't think this is over?" Ali asked.

"I do not."

"That makes it four to one—you, Sister Anselm, Father Mike, and me against Detective Lasko. Make that five to one. I understand someone named Father Winston is coming down from Prescott to give us a hand in keeping an eye on you."

"Did you know that Father Winston was the one who brought me that first note way back last summer?"

"I had no idea."

Archbishop Gillespie lapsed into silence. For a time Ali thought he had fallen back asleep.

"Do you think the killer will try again?" he asked at last.

"Maybe," Ali hedged. "There's really no way to tell."

"I think he will," the archbishop asserted quietly. "The cops have the wrong man, Ali. Please promise me that you'll keep looking for whoever sent those notes. With Father Andrew gone and that woman from Mesa injured, I can't stand the idea of anyone else being hurt or killed."

"I promise," Ali said at once. "We'll keep looking."

Just then someone tapped on the doorframe. Ali looked up to see an unfamiliar priest standing there.

"May I come in?" he asked.

"Of course, Father Winston," Archbishop Gillespie said. "Come in. Ali, this is Father Winston. Father Winston, this is my friend Ali Reynolds."

Father Winston, a handsome man in his late forties, held out a friendly hand bolstered by a warm smile. "Yes," he said. "I believe someone named Father Mike mentioned that you're another member of the security detail."

Shaking his hand, Ali smiled back. "Guilty as charged," she said.

Aware that the only guest chair in the room was the one she was using, Ali vacated it and headed for the door. "Why don't I step outside and give you two a chance to visit?" she suggested.

She had barely settled into the chair recently occupied by Father Mike when her phone rang with a Phoenix area code but no caller ID. "Hello."

"Ms. Reynolds?"

"Yes."

"Gavin James here. My last appointment of the day canceled, so I came home to sort out the names I told you about. I happen to have the applicable yearbook pages right here, complete with team photos. I've scanned them and can text them to you or send them by e-mail. Which do you prefer?"

"Either one," Ali said. "Suit yourself."

"Will do," he said.

When the text notifications started coming in, Ali used the larger screen on her iPad rather than her phone to view them, counting alerts as they arrived—nineteen in all. Nineteen years! That was how long Father Needham had been at the school, victimizing young boys year after year. The very idea left Ali feeling sick to her stomach.

When she began to open the texts, the photos were mostly worthless. A lack of contrast allowed for only hazy, ghostly images of adolescent boys smiling or grinning into the camera. The photos might have been mostly useless, but that wasn't the case for the captions beneath each picture. Those were crystal clear, and they listed not only the boys in the photos but also the names of ones who hadn't been present for the various photo sessions.

Ali scrolled through the texts one at a time, realizing as she did so that she was most likely looking at a comprehensive catalog of Father Needham's victims. Did that mean that the author of Archbishop Gillespie's threatening notes was hiding somewhere in the family tree of one of these young men?

She counted the number of boys on each team. It varied from year to year. Once it was as low as ten and once as high as fifteen. Most of the time, however, the number held steady at twelve. In the entire nineteen years, the total number of boys came to 225. That was far fewer than the three thousand–plus A&D employees Frigg had been tasked with doing background checks on the night before.

After only a moment's thought, Ali dialed up Frigg's audio connection.

"Good afternoon, Ms. Reynolds, I hope you're having a successful day."

"I am, thank you," Ali said, "but you could make it a lot more successful."

"How can I be of service?"

"I'm going to send you a series of swim-team photos covering the nineteen years Father Paul M. Needham was the swim coach at St. Francis High. What I need is background checks on each of these boys, including information about where they currently reside and what they're doing for a living. I'm especially interested in knowing if any of them have female relatives who fall into the same age bracket as whoever authored the handwritten notes I asked you to analyze yesterday."

"Very well," Frigg said. "I'll get right on it. In the meantime I've accumulated a good deal more material on the people you expressed an interest in earlier. Would you like me to start sending them along as well?"

The elevator door opened, and Sister Anselm came into view. "Not just now," Ali told Frigg. "I'm coming back home this evening, and I'll read them once I'm there and can do so in peace and quiet. In addition, a detective from Phoenix PD took someone into custody in connection with Father O'Toole's death. I'd like to see any additional information you're able to pull together, but there's no big rush on that either."

Ali ended the call and turned her full attention on Sister Anselm. "No Father Mike?"

Sister Anselm shook her head. "Father Daniel brought me back. Father Mike is sleeping—at least I hope he's sleeping."

It occurred to Ali that Sister Anselm probably should have been sleeping, too, but she knew better than to say so.

"I take it you've heard about Father Andrew's funeral?" the nun asked.

"What about it?"

"With the approval of Father Andrew's family, the funeral is now set for eleven on Friday morning at the Cathedral of the Holy Mother, with Archbishop Gillespie himself officiating—in a wheelchair if necessary."

"How's that even possible?" Ali asked. "He's barely out of the ICU."

"Tell me about it," Sister Anselm returned darkly. "I tried explaining to him that it's doubtful his doctors will be willing to release him that soon, but he's adamant. What am I going to do with that man?"

Ali had no ready answer for that question. Between the stubborn archbishop and his equally stubborn patient advocate, this had the potential of turning into an epic battle.

"I'm sure he feels responsible for what happened to Father Andrew and wants to do whatever he can to comfort the family."

"I suppose you're siding with him now?" Sister Anselm sniffed.

"Not siding with him," Ali replied. "I'm just suggesting why he might be so insistent."

Shaking her head, Sister Anselm stomped off into the archbishop's room. A few minutes later, while Ali was still sending texts of the swim-team photos to Frigg, Father Winston emerged.

"Here I am, reporting for sentry duty," he said, giving Ali a grin and a mock salute. "By the way," he added, "there was a news flash just now. The man they took into custody has been arrested and is currently being booked into the Maricopa County Jail. That's good news, isn't it?"

It could be, Ali thought, *but only if they've arrested the right man.*

"Maybe," she said aloud, "but for right now let's keep acting as though whoever wants Archbishop Gillespie dead is still on the loose. It's way too early to let down our guard."

|CHAPTER 35|

At four o'clock Jack Stoneman had had enough. "I want a lawyer," he said, and that was the end of the interview. No matter what the cop said, no matter how much physical evidence they supposedly had, he was sure he hadn't shot Father Andrew. Unfortunately, he had no way of proving it.

As jail personnel walked him through the booking process, Jack realized that every door that closed behind him sent his old life receding into the background. His days of living free were ending. He was being sent up for something he hadn't done, and he was pretty sure he wouldn't get out of the situation alive. He'd end up dying of old age in prison.

But if he was innocent—if he hadn't fired the shot that killed Father Andrew—the only thing that made sense was that Jack was being framed. Back in the joint, how many times had he heard guys claiming a frame job? Dozens, he supposed, but that was then and this was now. Those were other people's lives. This was his. So who was doing it—and why?

The guys he'd been drinking with, the ones who'd stolen his booze and his money? Not likely. He didn't know their names or where they lived, but they were dumb as stumps. They didn't know about his private panhandling preserve on Lincoln Drive. Somebody at Jimmy's RV ranch, then? The people he lived with? Nope, none of them knew about his preferred panhandling spot either. That was a secret he guarded the way a starving dog would protect a juicy bone. Who else was there? No one—except, of course, the cops themselves.

Since this was clearly a high-profile case, there had to be major pressure on Detective Lasko to come up with a fast solution, and that's what he was doing. All the crime lab had to do was install a bit of transferred evidence here and there—like inside the gun, for example—and they were good to go. Evidently the gunshot-residue tests hadn't turned out the way they'd anticipated, because when the detective came back from his extended break, he hadn't mentioned the GSR again. Instead he'd been totally focused on the shoes. What was the big deal with the shoes?

As the last door slammed behind him, Jack settled into all-too-familiar surroundings. He was lost. This would be his home from now until his case eventually came to trial.

As for whoever was framing him? Obviously that's who was winning.

|CHAPTER 36|

Ali had popped into the archbishop's room long enough to say good-bye and was on her way to the elevator when her phone rang with Cami's face showing up in caller ID.

"Hello?"

"Oh, Ali," Cami Lee gasped. "Thank goodness you answered! Where are you?"

Cami was generally calm, cool, and collected, so the near panic in her voice was unusual.

"About to step into the elevator at St. Gregory's to head home. Why?"

"I'm so relieved. I'm at the office. Something bad just came in over Stu's police scanner."

The fact that Stu kept a police scanner up and running in the computer lab was one of his many peculiarities, but it had come in handy on more than one occasion.

"What's up?"

"A southbound fuel truck lost its brakes coming down the grade on I-17 just north of Black Canyon City. It crossed over the median and into oncoming traffic, where it crashed into several northbound vehicles before catching fire. Evidently there are multiple fatalities, including the truck driver. The situation is chaotic, and the freeway is currently closed to traffic in both directions. No word on when it's projected to reopen. I was worried that you might have been caught up in the wreckage. The highway patrol is advising people to use alternate routes."

"What alternate routes?" Ali asked.

The only possibilities would have entailed going miles and hours out of the way, either east on the 60 and then north through Payson or northwest through Wickenburg and Prescott. Either way, if freeway traffic from I-17, eighteen-wheelers included, was being rerouted onto mostly two-lane roads, this was going to be a bumper-to-bumper nightmare.

"Thanks for checking on me, Cami. I was on my way home, but it's already been a grueling day. Getting caught up in that kind of traffic-disaster mess would have done me in."

The Arizona Biltmore, Ali's favorite hotel in the Phoenix area, was due east and a little north of the hospital, so she called there from the parking garage to make a reservation. Once inside her room, she turned on the TV. Naturally every local station was doing wall-to-wall coverage of the I-17 disaster, where not only was the truck still engulfed in flames but it had also ignited a fast-moving brushfire that was now burning out of control. Authorities were in the process of trying to evacuate passengers from dozens of stalled vehicles. Although they'd managed to avoid injury in the initial wreck, they were now in jeopardy due to the fire.

After seeing the carnage, Ali sent Cami a heartfelt thank-you, letting her know that she was safely settled into the Biltmore for the night rather than stuck in a gigantic traffic jam between Phoenix and home.

In the quiet of her room, Ali began scrolling through the dossiers Frigg had prepared. The AI had tagged each one with a threat level, and the low-level ones merited little more than a cursory scan. Relatives of the pedophile priests themselves were easy to dismiss, since all four sets of parental units were already deceased. There were a few elderly aunties in existence, but none of them measured up as possible assassins. Frigg had also accounted for a number of nieces, but most of them lived well outside the Phoenix area and were easily discounted as possible suspects.

Ali was discouraged and close to giving up when her phone rang.

"Hey, Stu," she said, seeing his face in caller ID. "What's up?"

"Frigg is sending you something hot," he said tersely. "Take a look at it so she can disappear it immediately."

The urgency in his voice was unmistakable. The moment the text alert came in, Ali opened the message. It contained what appeared to be two separate photos, both of them containing nothing but small, tan-colored circles. Mystified, Ali stared at them for a long time before they disappeared.

"What was that?" she asked.

"It's evidence from the Father O'Toole homicide investigation," Stu replied.

No wonder Stu was upset. Frigg had done it again. Somehow she'd managed to hack into active files from the Phoenix PD. Whatever those circles meant, no one from High Noon should have been able to see them.

"These are shoe imprints from two separate pairs of Skechers walking shoes," Stu explained. "One is a photo of a cast taken at the crime scene. The other is from a pair worn by the guy they've placed under arrest, a homeless Desert Storm veteran named Jack Stoneman."

Ali might have known Jack Stoneman's name from Archbishop Gillespie, but she was also quite sure that the suspect still hadn't been arraigned. That meant his name would not yet have been released to the public, and High Noon shouldn't have been able to access that either.

"What's the issue?" Ali asked.

"The issue is that although in the photos the shoes appear to be exactly the same, they're not. They're both Skechers walking shoes, size ten, but they appear to be of two different pairs, most likely from two separate batches," Stu replied.

"I don't understand," Ali began.

"When Stoneman was brought in for his interview, his shoes were collected for a GSR test. Someone in the crime lab made the connection between the shoes he was wearing and the shoe imprints found at the crime scene. I'm sure the cops think they have their shooter. Unfortunately, the soles on Stoneman's shoes don't match the ones they made casts of at the crime scene."

"How do you know that?" Ali asked.

"Because of Frigg," Stu answered simply. "She says there's a tenth-of-an-inch variation between the location of the circles on the crime-scene shoes and the ones belonging to Jack Stoneman."

"One-tenth of an inch?" Ali repeated.

"That's right," Stu replied, "one-tenth, and the difference would be almost invisible to the naked eye. I'm sure the cops are in a huge hurry to close the case right now. Once somebody gets around to doing more than eyeballing the sole prints, they'll figure it out, too, but for right now I believe they've got the wrong guy in custody."

"While the real killer is still running around loose," Ali breathed, "and still gunning for Archbishop Gillespie."

"Exactly," Stu said. "Now take a look at the next photo."

A new photo appeared on Ali's screen. What she saw appeared to be a small clearing in a patch of greenery made up of long, narrow leaves. In the foreground was a yellow kitchen stool with a torn seat and a cooler of some kind. The whole area was littered with trash.

"What's this?" Ali asked.

"According to the interview transcript, this is the clearing where Jack Stoneman hangs out during the day and where he stores his panhandling goods overnight. It's located inside the oleander hedge that surrounds the archbishop's residence, near the entrance. According to crime-scene photos, the patch of dirt in the foreground is where the CSIs made their footprint casts."

Ali took a moment to assess that information. "If the soles don't match, does that mean someone is deliberately trying to frame Jack Stoneman for murder?"

"That's how it looks to me," Stu agreed, "but here's the problem: Since we shouldn't have any of this information—including the suspect's name—there's not a hell of a lot any of us can do about it. We can't go to the cops or even report the discrepancy to Stoneman's defense attorney without having to reveal our sources."

"Source," Ali corrected, because she understood that they had only one of those—Frigg—and the AI's way of doing things was definitely not according to Hoyle.

"Does Stoneman even have a defense attorney at this point?" she asked.

"Not as far as we can tell."

"All right, then, Stu. Thanks for the call. You've given me plenty to think about."

Ali sat there without moving for a long time after the call ended. Frigg was a powerful tool, but one with unlimited access to things that should have been off-limits. Dieter Gunther's insistence on no law-enforcement involvement was the only thing that had enabled B. to unleash Frigg on solving the A&D ransomware issue, but here things were different.

Cops were already involved in Father Andrew's homicide, and Stu was right. Ali couldn't simply drop by Detective Lasko's office at Phoenix PD and lay out this new set of suspicions. After all, she wasn't supposed to know there were *any* shoe prints at all, much less two different sets. Besides, Lasko had already told her to butt out. And she couldn't warn Jack Stoneman about this either, especially since she wasn't supposed to know the suspect's name. And even if she had the name and went to the Maricopa County Jail to warn him, all conversations between visitors and jailed suspects were routinely recorded.

There was an exception to that rule. Visits between defense attorneys and accused suspects were held in private and not recorded, but as far as Ali could tell, Stoneman had yet to be assigned a public defender. And once that happened, would Stoneman's new attorney of record be willing to give Ali Reynolds the time of day? Not only did she need Jack Stoneman's name from a standard media source, she also needed to get the information about the shoe-print evidence in front of his defense attorney in a way that wouldn't turn around and bite High Noon Enterprises in the butt. Finally she called Stu back.

"Ask Frigg and her eight hundred CPUs to scan the media for any source that publicly names Jack Stoneman as the suspect in Father Andrew's case. As soon as she has one, let me know."

While she waited, Ali got up and paced the floor, resisting the temptation to awaken B. in his hotel room in Zurich to ask his advice. Fortunately, Stu called her back less than fifteen minutes later.

"Check your e-mail," he said. "I'm sending a link."

She did so and found an article posted on the *Arizona Sun* Web site:

SUSPECTED PRIEST KILLER
ID'D AS HOMELESS VETERAN

Sources close to the investigation into the shooting death of Father Andrew O'Toole have revealed that the suspect taken into custody in connection with the homicide is one Jack Edmund Stoneman, age forty-eight, a homeless Desert Storm veteran and ex-con currently living in Phoenix.

In recent months he has been known to panhandle on a

regular basis outside the residence of Francis Gillespie, the archbishop of the Phoenix Catholic Archdiocese. The priest who was murdered, Father O'Toole, is believed to have been personally acquainted with Mr. Stoneman, and his death may have been the result of a dispute between the two men.

Mr. Stoneman, originally from Fayetteville, North Carolina, served in the U.S. Army for two years and deployed to Iraq during Desert Storm. After being honorably discharged, he moved to Phoenix, where he worked briefly as a firefighter for Phoenix FD before being terminated due to problems related to drugs and alcohol.

On October 15, 2007, Mr. Stoneman, while under the influence of drugs, was involved in an altercation involving his wife, Julie, and her alleged lover, Gary Harmody. Harmody died as a result of injuries sustained in the incident, and Julie Stoneman was also injured. When officers arrived on the scene, Stoneman attacked them as well.

He was arrested and charged with second-degree murder and six counts of aggravated assault. After a plea bargain, he served six years of a fifteen-year sentence before being released on good behavior three years ago.

There was more to the article than that, but that was where Ali quit reading, because in a moment of divine inspiration she had realized exactly what she needed to do. First she did a quick check on the Internet, then picked up the phone and asked for her car to be brought around. She left her room five minutes later, heading for St. Gregory's Hospital in search of Archbishop Francis Gillespie and redemption.

|CHAPTER 37|

Once Rachel had the Ruger in her possession, the last thing she wanted to do was go home, not when there was a good chance Rich would be waiting for her, ready to bombard her with all kinds of questions and accusations. She switched on the radio as she headed back eastbound on Osborn, but suddenly the only story to be heard was something about a huge truck fire on I-17 north of Black Canyon City that had the freeway closed for miles in both directions. Much to her frustration, there was no news at all about the shooting or about Archbishop Gillespie.

Hungry for information, she headed for St. Gregory's. All along, the media had been reporting on the crowd of people gathered outside the hospital's entrance, devoutly praying for the archbishop's full recovery. If there was information to be found, that's where it would be. In case there were cameras still on the scene, and wanting to keep her features as inconspicuous as possible, Rachel donned her cataract sunglasses before stepping out of her Mercedes. They didn't do much to provide a disguise, so she would simply have to avoid visible surveillance and television cameras.

To Rachel's intense relief, when she arrived, the crowd at the hospital had thinned considerably from what she'd seen on TV earlier, and the media presence had evaporated. There were no film crews on the scene at all. Most of the civilians in the crowd were no longer present. Because of their collars, priests were easy to sort out. Nuns were a bit more challenging. Some of them wore old-fashioned habits, but Rachel suspected that a few of the women dressed in ordinary street clothes but clutching rosaries in their hands were nuns of one stripe or another.

Rachel slipped onto a folding chair next to one occupied by a priest. "Any word?" she whispered.

The priest nodded. "A spokesman came out a while ago and announced that his situation has been upgraded from serious but stable to good."

Dismayed by the news, Rachel breathed what she hoped sounded like a heartfelt sigh. "What a relief!"

"Father O'Toole's parents were here earlier. His father told me that Archbishop Gillespie is hoping to be well enough to officiate at the funeral on Friday."

That was jaw-dropping news, and Rachel could barely believe her good fortune. With nothing showing on social media, she had lost all hope of being able to anticipate the archbishop's movements, but now someone was gifting her with information about her target's next public appearance.

"How wonderful!" Rachel exclaimed. "I hope he's well enough to do it. I'm sure Father O'Toole's parents are suffering terribly. Having the archbishop himself conduct their son's funeral will be such a blessing. Will the funeral be private or open to the public?"

"Open, as far as I know," the priest replied. "Since it's going to be held at the Cathedral of the Holy Mother, I can't imagine that it would be kept private."

"Have they said what time?" she asked.

"My understanding is that it's scheduled for eleven a.m."

Rachel wanted to leap up and dance a jig, but she forced herself to remain where she was. She bowed her head, closed her eyes, and folded her hands. Then, for the first time in many years, she really did pray:

Thank you for giving me exactly what I needed, and may thy will be done, on earth as it is in heaven.

She stayed for another hour after that, afraid that a hurried departure might attract too much attention. When she finally left the hospital, she was downright giddy. Once she knew for certain where and when the funeral would be held, she'd make sure she and her Ruger were in attendance. She no longer really cared that much about getting caught. All she wanted now was to get the job done.

|CHAPTER 38|

On the fifth floor of St. Gregory's, the ever-faithful Father Mike, stationed outside Room 514, motioned Ali inside to where Sister Anselm was seated in the chair next to Archbishop Gillespie's bed. From the unhappy looks on both their faces, Ali deduced that she was interrupting a serious discussion.

"Sorry," she said, "don't mind me. I can come back later."

"Not to worry," the archbishop told her. "We're having a bit of a squabble."

"It's more of a knock-down-drag-out," Sister Anselm grumbled. "He's stubborn as the day is long. No doctor in his right mind is going to let him out of the hospital in time for him to officiate at a funeral on Friday morning."

"And no doctor in his right mind is going to stop me," Archbishop Gillespie declared. "Either they release me or I walk or roll on my own recognizance. Father Andrew was my friend, and I owe his family my being there to honor his passing. Now, what can we do for you, Ali?"

The battle lines were definitely drawn, and Ali didn't relish stepping into the crossfire.

"I need a word with the archbishop in private, if you don't mind."

Over the years of her friendship with Sister Anselm, Ali had often witnessed the nun's piercing-eyed glare that usually sent recipients scurrying for cover. This was the first time that daunting look had been aimed at Ali.

"Very well," Sister Anselm said stiffly. "I'll take myself elsewhere." With that she marched out of the room, closing the door behind her. Only the door's soft-closing hinge prevented her from slamming it.

"This sounds serious," Archbishop Gillespie said as Ali took the chair Sister Anselm had just vacated. "What's going on?"

"I need a favor."

"What kind of favor?"

"Will you hear my confession?"

The archbishop seemed taken aback. "I suppose," he answered with a frown. "But confession is a serious business, Ali, and I must ask, have you ever been baptized? That's a requirement, you know."

"When I was a baby," Ali answered. "My parents are Lutheran, but because they owned a restaurant while I was growing up, we seldom went to church on Sundays. Now that the folks are retired, they go every week."

This was a strange admission on Ali's part, but considering she was there to make her confession, it seemed as though some further explanation was necessary.

Archbishop Gillespie studied her face. "You're quite serious about this, aren't you?"

"Quite," Ali agreed.

"Very well," he said. "I think we can bend a few rules here. Do you know how to begin?"

"I think so." Ali folded her hands and bowed her head. "Forgive me, Father, for I have sinned."

"How long has it been since your last confession?"

"My whole life," Ali responded. "Over time I've broken one or more of the Ten Commandments. I've told some white lies and suffered from bouts of envy, but right now I have a thorny issue, because I've actually broken the law. When Father Andrew died in that shooting, I believed that his death was a mistake and that you were the real target."

Frowning, as if wondering where this was going, Francis Gillespie nodded in puzzled agreement.

Ali went on. "The cops have arrested a homeless man named Jack Stoneman in conjunction with the homicide, and now, with him in custody, law enforcement believes the situation is under control."

Ali paused for a moment, grateful that due to the last article she'd read online, she could now account for knowing the suspect's name without anyone pointing an accusing finger in Frigg's direction.

"Through the use of hacking technology," she continued, "I've come into possession of some illegally obtained evidence suggesting that Mr. Stoneman is being deliberately framed by someone else—most likely the same person who's been targeting you. As it stands, I have no way of bringing that evidence to bear on Jack Stoneman's behalf without implicating myself and placing others in legal jeopardy."

B. and the archbishop were unlikely but good friends, just as Ali and Sister Anselm were good friends. Ali had no doubt that Archbishop Gillespie had been clued in about the existence of Frigg and her astonishing, if illicit, capabilities.

Ali waited a moment to see if the archbishop would say something. When he didn't, she went on.

"The evidence in question has to do with shoe prints. The CSI team took several castings from the crime scene. When Mr. Stoneman was arrested, the shoes he was wearing were taken into evidence. When soles of those were compared to the castings, they appeared to be the same. However, our independent analysis found a slight variation in pattern location, which suggests the possibility that two different pairs of shoes are involved. I'd like to go to the jail and discuss this with Mr. Stoneman, but I can't because I'm not supposed to know about it. Conversations between defendants and their attorneys are confidential, but conversations between prisoners and anyone else are recorded. Any on-the-record mention of the shoe situation would put too many people in jeopardy."

She paused and looked at the archbishop, awaiting some kind of input. He appeared to be listening intently, but again he said nothing.

"As you requested," Ali resumed, "we've been looking into the threatening notes you've received over the last several months. Earlier today I spoke to a guy named Gavin James. I'm not sure if you remember—"

"I remember Gavin very well," the archbishop observed. "As I recall, he's an exceptionally sharp young man and a practicing attorney, too."

"From what he said, I believe he thinks the world of you," Ali added. "I talked to him about the threats and have a feeling that if there was anything he could do to help, he would. As it happens, I suspect that Mr. Stoneman has yet to be assigned a public defender. If someone could prevail on Mr. James to offer to defend Jack Stoneman on a pro bono basis, and if I could accompany him on an attorney-client visit to the jail, perhaps I could steer the conversation in the direction of the shoe-print issue. That way I could at least alert the defense team to the fact that there's a possible problem with the state's main piece of evidence."

Finished with what she had to say, Ali fell silent. For a long moment, neither of them spoke. Finally Archbishop Gillespie reached out and patted Ali on the shoulder. "God has forgiven you your sins, my child," he said with a smile. "As a penance say three Our Fathers, then go and sin no more."

Ali took that as a signal that the confession was over. She was a little disappointed. It was fine to be forgiven, but what she'd really wanted was the archbishop's advice. She started to rise, but he motioned her back into the chair.

"It has come to my attention that someone has been arrested in regard to Father Andrew's murder," Archbishop Gillespie said as Ali resumed her place in the visitor's chair. "It's such a high-profile case that I'm concerned about a possible rush to judgment. I'm acquainted with a successful attorney here in town, a fellow by the name of Gavin James. I believe I'll ask him if he'd be willing to look into the case and perhaps offer to serve as the suspected killer's defense attorney."

It took a moment for Ali to realize what the archbishop was doing—discussing the situation in a manner that in no way broke the seal of her confession.

"Is it your belief that Father Andrew's death is somehow related to the handwritten threats I asked you and B. to investigate?"

"It is," she replied. "It's also my belief that while the cops concentrate their efforts on Jack Stoneman, whoever is after you is still out there and you are still in danger."

"In that case, when I speak to Gavin, I'll ask if it would be possible for him to take you along as an associate when he goes to visit his new client. Would you be willing to do so?"

"Absolutely," Ali said.

"You wouldn't happen to have Mr. James's phone number on you, do you?"

The number Gavin had used to call her earlier from home was still in her iPhone. "Yes, I do," Ali said as she jotted it down on a scrap of paper and handed it over.

"Thank you," he told her. "I'm sure Gavin will be in touch."

"You're pretty cagey, you know," she added.

The archbishop beamed at her. "So I've been told," he said.

Out in the corridor, a still-fuming Sister Anselm stood with her arms crossed and a frown embedded in her forehead. "What was that all about?" she wanted to know.

"A strategy session on the threatening notes," Ali answered, fully aware that as the words came out of her mouth, she'd just told another white lie. "But take it from me," she added. "King Solomon and his idea of threatening to chop that baby in half has nothing on Archbishop Francis Gillespie."

|CHAPTER 39|

Like a kid heading home with a bad report card, Rachel still wasn't quite ready to face the music. Stalling, she made two small detours along the way. First she stopped by the Cathedral of the Holy Mother to check out the lay of the land. One year they had taken David there for midnight Mass on Christmas Eve, but she hadn't set foot inside the place since.

The parking lot wasn't completely deserted. There was a meeting of some kind going on in the social hall. She parked a row or so back from the other vehicles. Trying the doors and finding them unlocked, she let herself in and discovered she wasn't alone. Somewhere inside the vast cathedral, an organist was playing. Rachel had intended to be alone, and the unexpected sound of music gave her a sudden chill.

Aware that someone might be observing her actions, she crossed herself before making her way down the center aisle to the front of the church, where she slipped into the second row of pews and dropped onto the kneeler. She remained there for a time, inhaling the combined fragrances of incense and burning candles and thinking about how things would play out on Friday during Andrew O'Toole's funeral. That was how she regarded the deceased now—as Andrew O'Toole. She refused to apply the honorific "Father" to his name. After all, he was a priest, wasn't he? That meant he, too, was partially responsible for David's death. They all were.

Dan had warned her the major problem with the Ruger would be distance and that she would need to be close to her target. Unfortunately, the cathedral was huge. A seat even as close as the first row might put Archbishop Gillespie out of range. During the service the first two, or maybe even the first three, sets of pews would be reserved for grieving friends or family. Trying to hit a target from four rows back would be impossible.

Remaining on her knees, seemingly in prayer, Rachel tried to come to terms with this latest challenge. If she couldn't sit in one of the front rows, where else should she sit? At last the answer came to her.

With the archbishop in attendance, processions at both the beginning and end of the service were almost mandatory. In that case all she'd need to do was grab a place next to the center aisle. No doubt she'd have to arrive early to score one of those.

Back in her churchgoing days, Rachel had always resented the people who arrived early and parked themselves on the aisle, forcing everyone else to climb over them, but on Friday morning, with any kind of luck, she would be one of those obnoxious aisle sitters.

She left the church a few minutes later. She glanced around the narthex as she went back outside and studied the underside of the front portico. She spotted at least one security camera at each entrance, but she'd taught herself how to duck her head and avoid them whenever possible.

On the way home, she delayed once more, stopping off at a wine bar on Shea. Twin Vines was a place she'd frequented long ago, when she was still hanging out with friends on a regular basis, but it was long enough ago that no one inside recognized her. She took a seat at the bar and ordered a glass of cabernet and a burger. The television over the bar was still airing nonstop coverage of the huge accident on I-17 that had left six people dead. The fire had been extinguished, but the freeway remained closed in both directions. Traffic wasn't Rachel's problem. Going home was.

By now Rich had probably figured out that she'd ditched the tracking device, which was most likely stuck somewhere in that northbound traffic nightmare. So what would Rich do about it? Maybe not much. Since he seemed to be under the impression that she was carrying on a passionate affair, he would probably continue railing at her about that. Of course, the whole idea of her being caught up in an affair was laughable. Rachel had zero time for anything so meaningless. She had far more important matters on her plate.

Finally, with her burger eaten and wineglass empty, she went home. As soon as she saw lights in the living room, she realized it would be bad, but she had no inkling how bad.

"I know you ditched the tracker. Where have you been, and what the hell have you been up to?" Rich growled at her before she barely got through the entry.

Rachel stopped short in the archway leading to the living room, dismayed to see her empty hatbox lying on the carpet with all its treasured contents scattered across the glass coffee table.

"Where's my damned .22?" Rich continued without bothering to wait for her reply. "And why the hell would you need a gun?"

He was seated on the sofa. Dropping into a nearby armchair, Rachel placed her purse on the floor between the arms of both the chair and the couch in hopes it would be both out of sight and out of mind. Rich's missing .22 wasn't in her purse, but Rachel's newly purchased Ruger was, and she didn't want him to find it.

"You had no business going through my room," she said accusingly.

"Why not?" he shot back. "You're my wife, and I live here, don't I? This is my house. Come to think of it, I'm the one who paid for it."

She hadn't been a wife to Rich for a very long time. She was more like his personal housekeeper and laundress. Drawing a steadying breath, Rachel decided that rather than sit there and take it, she could go on the offensive. And after years of dodging the issue, maybe it was finally time to get the truth about David's death out in the open.

"Did you look at the yearbook?" she asked.

"Yes, I looked at it," Rich grumbled. "We paid good money for that yearbook back in the day. Why on earth did David have to deface it the way he did?"

"You mean defacing as in blacking out Father Needham's photos?"

"Of course that's what I mean."

"And you have no idea why he might have done such a thing?"

"I know Father Needham ended up in prison after that abuse scandal, but—"

"You never looked at David's autopsy report," Rachel said with a sneer. "You couldn't be bothered."

"I didn't need to look at it. I already knew what it said. David was an addict. He died of an accidental overdose."

Rachel was astonished that even having seen the photo evidence, Rich remained firmly grounded in denial. "Haven't you ever wondered why our beautiful son turned to drugs in the first place?" she demanded. "What if his death wasn't accidental? What if it was deliberate?"

"Are you saying you think David committed suicide?"

"That's what I've come to believe. If that's the case, would you have any idea why?"

"He didn't commit suicide," Rich insisted. "It was an accidental overdose. If he'd wanted to commit suicide, he would have left a note."

"He didn't leave a note because he couldn't face admitting to us that he was HIV-positive," Rachel said, spitting out the damning words as if they were daggers. "He preferred taking himself out with an overdose rather than dying of AIDS, and I don't blame him a bit."

"AIDS," Rich repeated numbly, as though he couldn't quite make sense of the word. "Are you saying our son was gay?"

"I don't know if David was gay or not, and it wouldn't have mattered to me either way. Once he said that college wasn't for him, you ran him out of the house. After that we were never close again, but where do you suppose he might have picked up that AIDS virus in the first place?"

"How should I know?"

"Paul Needham went to prison for molesting the boys on his swim teams. David was on the swim team. Oh, and for the record, what do you think took Needham out once he ended up in prison?"

"I heard he died of natural causes."

"Screw natural causes! That damned priest died of AIDS," Rachel stormed, "and before he did, he gave it to our son. Yes, David died of an overdose, but he overdosed because he knew AIDS was in his future, all because of what that low-down swine of a pedophile did to him."

Rich's face blanched. He looked stricken, as though Rachel had just landed a powerful blow to his gut—as though everything she'd told him just now had come at him out of nowhere. Without another word he pushed his bulky frame off the couch and stumbled from the room.

Bingo, Rachel thought, watching him go. *It took long enough, but at least I finally got your attention.*

|CHAPTER 40|

Less than half an hour after Ali returned to her hotel room, Gavin James gave her a call.

"I take it you heard from Archbishop Gillespie," she observed.

"I certainly did," Gavin said, "and I'm more than happy to be of assistance. I've called the jail and was able to speak directly with Jack Stoneman. I happen to have a little pull in that regard. He's overjoyed to have me as his defense attorney. The last time he had a public defender, and things didn't turn out too well for him. He ended up serving six years of a fifteen-year sentence.

"According to Archbishop Gillespie, Father O'Toole was one of Jack Stoneman's chief benefactors and someone he never would have targeted. The archbishop is bound and determined to prove that he himself, rather than Father Andrew, was the intended victim of the attack. He's also concerned that Jack Stoneman is being railroaded."

"That's my concern as well," Ali told him, "and I continue to believe that the archbishop remains in danger."

"Given that," Gavin said, "have you had any success in locating the author of those threatening notes?"

"Not so far," Ali replied.

"You mentioned that the notes had been dropped into collection plates at churches located throughout the area. I asked Mr. Stoneman if he owned a vehicle or had access to one. He doesn't. Not only that, his driver's license expired years ago. If he'd had anything to do with the notes, he would have needed an accomplice to provide transportation."

"For the moment," Ali suggested, "let's assume that Stoneman didn't author the notes. It seems likely to me that the source of the notes and the person who shot Father Andrew are one and the same. Since the killer was lying in wait at the end of the driveway, she was most likely familiar with daily comings and goings at the residence."

"You think our killer is female?"

"Handwriting analysis suggests that the author of the threatening notes is female. That leads me to suspect our killer is, too."

"I see," Gavin said.

"In addition," Ali continued, "as far as I know, no one has spent more time hanging around that area than Jack Stoneman. I believe it's possible he might have seen something without even realizing it."

"Wait," Gavin said. "You're suggesting that Stoneman might be a witness rather than a perpetrator?"

"Exactly."

"That's an interesting supposition, and one that bears looking into. Unmasking another suspect would certainly be the easiest way to create reasonable doubt and exonerate my client. But here's the thing: I have a midmorning meeting that will last until noon, so I won't be able to stop by the jail to meet with him until early afternoon. The archbishop was most insistent that you accompany me to that initial meeting. I told him that would be highly irregular, due to concerns about attorney-client privilege. He suggested that perhaps, for the time being, it might be a good idea if I offered to serve as your attorney as well. That way our interactions would also be accorded privilege."

"That archbishop is one cagey old guy, isn't he?" Ali observed.

Gavin laughed aloud. "He certainly is, but based on that understanding, would you be available to join me for that meeting, attending it as one of my associates?"

It occurred to Ali just then that maybe she really did need a defense attorney. After all, good intentions or not, she had clearly set herself on a course of interfering with an active homicide investigation. Maybe Archbishop Gillespie was far wiser than even she suspected.

"Absolutely," she said aloud.

"Would you like me to text you the address of the jail?"

"Don't bother," she replied. "I'll find it on my own. I'll meet you there at two sharp tomorrow afternoon."

It was 6:00 a.m. in Zurich, and she decided it was still too early to call B. Instead, thinking he might call her once he awakened, she put the phone and its charger on the nightstand and went to bed.

Considering all that had happened the last couple of days, it came as no surprise that she dozed off within a matter of minutes and slept like a baby.

|CHAPTER 41|

Long after Rich retreated to his bedroom, Rachel stayed in the living room. One by one she gathered up her treasures and returned them to her hatbox. These precious few things, including the damning yearbook, were the only mementos she still had of her son.

The last thing she picked up was the Disneyland snapshot. Staring at the photo, she recalled that whole day as if it were yesterday. They'd started with breakfast at the hotel, where David had been thrilled with his Mickey Mouse–shaped pancakes. Yes, there'd been crowds. Yes, they'd had to wait in long lines for the most popular rides, but none of that had mattered. She'd still had her precious David back then, and she and Rich were still in love, or at least they seemed to be. It was a day that Rachel now wished could have gone on forever.

For the first time since March, since the day Tonya had delivered the banker's box to her doorstep, a series of wrenching sobs escaped Rachel's lips as she grieved for all the things that had once been and would never be again—her son, her marriage, her life. In the end, rather than returning the photo to the hatbox, she carefully slipped it into her purse, right next to the Ruger. For tonight at least, that seemed like the best place to keep it.

Once she'd returned the hatbox to its accustomed place on her closet shelf, Rachel went back to the living room. The TV was still blaring behind Rich's closed door. She could hear muffled sounds of gunshots and sirens as some police drama or other played out in his room, but she doubted the racket bothered him. The man could sleep through anything.

Sitting there in her familiar living room, the enormity of what Rachel was about to do finally hit home. She'd done nothing in the preceding weeks and months but plot the archbishop's death. She'd gone to great lengths to frame Jack Stoneman for the crime, even sending that anonymous tipster letter to the detective. Although her letter couldn't possibly have arrived, according to the latest news the cops had already placed Jack under arrest. With a shock Rachel realized that framing Jack was no longer of any concern to her, because she had stopped caring about getting away with the crime. That no longer mattered to her—only succeeding did.

Out of force of habit, she tried logging on to the archbishop's social media accounts. The feeds were back online, but only in minimal fashion. Each one now carried the same message: "Due to a medical emergency, all posting is currently suspended."

Had it not been for that chance encounter with the priest outside the hospital entrance, Rachel would have had no way of knowing that Archbishop Gillespie planned to officiate at Andrew O'Toole's funeral. What would he do after that? What if the archbishop disappeared from public life in the same way he'd abandoned his social media? If that happened, how would she find him? In fact, his appearance at the funeral might well be Rachel's last opportunity to finish the job, and this time there would be no possibility of escape. That meant there were only two choices left—Rachel could die in a hail of bullets in a shoot-out with cops or spend the rest of her life in prison. Which would it be?

For the first time ever, she understood how David must have felt when he found himself staring ahead into a bleak future where the eventual outcome would most likely mean a slow, agonizing death from AIDS. No wonder he'd opted for what must have seemed the faster and seemingly less painful solution of an opioid overdose. And here was David's mother at a similar crossroads. Given a choice between the two—death or prison—Rachel would choose door number one. Either she would commit suicide by cop or she would turn the Ruger on herself. Those were her options.

So Friday would be it—her deadline, as it were, her last day on earth. Once Rachel was gone, the house would still be here. Rich would still be here. . . . Thinking about Rich stopped her cold. He had barely survived the death of their son. How would he endure the ensuing scandal once he realized his late wife had turned into a stone-cold killer? And how would he ever manage on his own without her there to take care of things? Rich had no idea how to run the washer and dryer or even the dishwasher. He never bothered cleaning up in the kitchen or vacuuming the living room. As for his buying groceries? Never.

And just like that, at one o'clock in the morning, Rachel decided that Rich had to go, not because he would be crushed by the aftermath of her death but because he posed a real liability to her endgame.

He'd been following her movements for who knows how long? Now that he knew the truth about David's death, what would happen if, between now and the funeral on Friday, he somehow made the connection between her daily stops on Lincoln Drive and what had happened there on Tuesday night? What if he decided to go to the cops and blow the whistle? If he turned her in, David's death would go unavenged. No, Rachel simply couldn't let that happen. And so, with no further premeditation on her part, she set about doing what had to be done.

She took the loaded weapon from her purse and carried it down the hallway to her room. Once in the master, she undressed before donning her nightgown and robe along with a pair of bedroom slippers. Only after removing her makeup did she head for Rich's room with the deadly Ruger nestled in the right-hand pocket of her robe.

She made no effort to conceal her fingerprints. They landed wherever they landed. Only two people lived in the house. When homicide investigators finally turned up, they would know exactly what had happened and who had done what to whom. She paused for a moment in front of Rich's closed door before reaching for the knob and turning it. As she pushed the door open, it creaked a little on its hinges, but Rich always slept with his ceiling fan turned on high. Between the noisy whirring of blades and the blaring TV, the tiny creak of the door barely registered.

Rachel didn't bother switching on a light. The glowing television screen gave her all the illumination she needed. After pausing for a moment, she walked over to the window and closed the blinds, then she pulled the drapes and blackout curtains shut as well. In case any of her neighbors happened to be out and about when it all went down, Rachel didn't want them to catch a glimpse of a sudden flash from inside the room.

For as long as Rachel and Rich had been married, he'd preferred to sleep on the left-hand side of the bed. She stood over him for a time, looking down at him. He lay on his back as he always did, snoring a blue streak. Since he often watched TV in bed, the remote was within easy reach on his bedside table, and a mound of discarded pillows lay on the floor where he'd shoved away all the extras when it came time to go to sleep.

Rachel used the remote to raise the volume on the TV even higher, although since a noisy commercial was on at the moment, turning up the volume was hardly necessary. Everything Rachel Higgins knew about becoming a successful killer had been learned either by scouring the Internet or by watching true-crime programs on TV. Some people insisted that shooters could use pillows to help muffle the sound of gunfire. Others said the presence of a pillow made no acoustical difference whatsoever. Just in case it might work, she picked up one of the discarded pillows.

Unlike her demeanor outside the archbishop's residence, this time Rachel was implacable and utterly resolute. Standing at Rich's bedside, the hand that held the pistol didn't tremble, not in the slightest. She draped the discarded pillow over both the hand holding the gun and the weapon itself. Then, pressing the barrel of the gun to Rich's forehead, she pulled the trigger. Despite the pillow, the sound was still much louder than she expected—loud enough that she was sure the neighbors must have heard it.

There was no need to turn on a light to examine the damage. She knew that Rich was dead. Dropping the pillow over his face, she stepped away from the bed, used the remote to turn the volume back down to a normal level, and left the room, closing the door behind her. Surprised by her total sense of calm, she slipped the pistol back into her pocket. Only later would she realize that she had accomplished her exit in a fashion that came straight from a CSI textbook. Killers known to their victims tend to cover bodies and/or faces so they don't have to witness the damage they've done. That was exactly why she'd left the pillow on Rich's face. She had shot him dead, and she didn't want to see it.

With no sign of tears or hysterics, Rachel returned to the living room, where without turning on any lights she peered outside through the blinds over the front windows. Up and down the street, porch lights flipped on as alarmed neighbors spilled out of houses and into the street. Rachel waited long enough to allow more time for a crowd to gather. When several folks showed up on the sidewalk at the far end of her driveway, Rachel left the Ruger on the entryway table and hurried outside to join them.

"What was that?" she demanded breathlessly of her exceedingly nosy next-door neighbor, Margaret Bendixen, who stood at the end of her own driveway clutching her obnoxious and perpetually shivering Chihuahua, Chico. "It sounded like a gunshot to me."

"To me, too," Margaret agreed, "but Ed says it was probably nothing but a backfire."

"Could anyone tell where it came from?" Rachel asked.

"Ed's out there talking to people, but so far no one seems to know," Margaret replied.

"Has anyone called the cops?" Rachel inquired. She was surprised that her voice sounded completely normal—alarmed and anxious, true, but normal nevertheless.

"I dialed 911 first thing," Margaret replied. "Someone's bound to be on their way. I don't understand why it's taking so long."

"I don't either," Rachel returned, "but since it's cold out here, and since I'm not exactly dressed to be out in public, I'm going back inside. I just hope no one's been hurt."

With that, Rachel took herself back into the house, where she could unobtrusively keep tabs on what was happening out on the street through her darkened living-room windows. A squad car turned up a few minutes later. A pair of cops hopped out and then walked around the neighborhood, seemingly questioning concerned onlookers. They were there for half an hour or so. Then, having found nothing, and to Rachel's immense relief, they got back into their squad car, turned off the flashing lights, and drove away.

As for Rachel? At a little past two, and still too wound up to sleep, she seated herself at the kitchen table and used one of her remaining three-by-five cards to set forth the broad outline of a to-do list for what was destined to be her last full day on earth, starting with the word "Birdhouses." Yes, that part of Rich's life had to be dealt with, and they would be.

Next on the list was "Spa." Rachel wanted to go out in style, so a spa visit was definitely in order. It was years since she'd had a full-meal-deal spa treatment, complete with a haircut, facial, mani-pedi, and massage. In addition to a splurge at a spa, she wanted a new outfit to wear on Friday. So the next word up was "Shopping."

What will all of that cost? Rachel wondered.

She had her single Rich-approved credit card in her purse, but that was seldom used, since he'd declared it was only for emergencies. She worried that if a bunch of unexpected charges began appearing on the balance, the bank's fraud department might shut the card off entirely. Not only that, there was always the possibility that in the unlikely event the cops did manage to identify her between now and the funeral, they might be able to follow her by tracking her credit-card purchases. No, rather than relying on the card, she'd need to go to the bank and actually cash a check so she'd have real money in hand. Therefore "Bank" was the next thing on the list.

At the end of the day, she wanted to treat herself to a nice dinner and maybe even indulge in a glass or two of expensive wine. One thing was certain: She had no intention of spending Thursday night in a house where Rich lay dead in his bedroom. No, in the morning, once she turned the A/C in the house as low as it would go and drove away, she'd be leaving behind the place she'd called home for the past thirty-plus years. But, just in case, she wanted her final departure to be as normal as possible, so as not to arouse any suspicions.

After adding "Room Reservations" and "Dinner Reservations" to her list, Rachel rose from the table, went down the hall, and packed a small overnight bag, filling it with a few necessities—underwear and cosmetics mostly, along with one of the wigs she'd purchased months earlier and never worn. Once the bag was zipped shut, she rolled it into the entry-way so that it would be ready to go in the morning. Then she returned to the kitchen table one final time. With her to-do list handled, she sat down to write out what Rachel regarded as her last will and testament.

It wouldn't be a real one, of course. Those had to be signed in front of witnesses in order to be valid. As far as she knew, the official ones she and Rich had drawn up in the aftermath of David's death were still in effect. Each had left everything to the other. In the event they both died at the same time, the remainder of their combined estate would go to Rich's younger brother, Les, assuming he was still alive. The last time

Rachel had seen Les and Molly Higgins in the flesh was when they'd flown in to Phoenix for David's funeral. Once they went back home to New England, they might just as well have dropped off the earth. At this point, however, where the remainder of their estate went was of no concern to Rachel. Since she couldn't leave it to David, she didn't give a damn where it went.

No, the will she intended to leave behind was of another sort entirely, and once again it was written out on three-by-five cards:

> *I, Rachel Irene Higgins, being of sound mind and body, do attest and proclaim the following:*

Rachel paused for a moment and studied the words she'd written. She was of sound body, but was she really of sound mind? Could someone who wasn't crazy calmly shoot her husband and then sit down at a kitchen table to write out a to-do list and a confession? So maybe she was wrong about being of sound mind, but someone else would have to sort all that out later. It wouldn't be up to her to decide.

> *I alone am solely responsible for the events that have occurred in recent days, as well as the one that will occur on Friday. My husband, Rich, is in no way to be held accountable for any of my actions, all of which have been done and will be done entirely of my own volition.*
>
> *My husband and I entrusted our beloved son, David, to the care and teachings of the Catholic Church by having him attend St. Francis High School in Scottsdale. While there, he suffered incalculable abuse at the hands of a convicted pedophile named Paul M. Needham. What happened to our son damaged him in such a way that he never recovered. Unable to deal with what had been done to him, he took his own life.*
>
> *As for Jack Stoneman? I had planned on using him to cover my tracks, but that was when I still intended to get away with doing what I must do. That is no longer the case. I'm under no illusions that escaping the consequences of my intended actions is remotely possible.*
>
> *I want the world to know that I hold Archbishop Francis Gillespie entirely responsible for my son's awful outcome. It was the archbishop's lack of judgment, as well as lack of oversight, that allowed the cancer of sexual abuse to flourish at St. Francis, damaging my son and many others.*

It is far too late to help my son. He is gone forever, but I am willing to give up my life to guarantee that the archbishop never allows a similar travesty to be visited on some other innocent child.

Yes, my husband is dead at my hands. He betrayed our son by not being willing to stand beside me and fight for justice for David. Father O'Toole should not have died the other night. The bullet that killed him was intended for Archbishop Gillespie.

I regret none of my actions. I will go to my death with my head held high and vengeance in my heart. And if God has mercy on my soul, no one will be more surprised than I am.

When she finished writing those final words, Rachel signed her full name with a flourish. Then, her work done, she put down her pen. Arranging the cards in a neat stack, she slipped them into her purse, right next to the Ruger. She didn't bother with a clear plastic bag. Concealing her fingerprints was no longer necessary. When she finally made her way back down the hall, she didn't bother pausing at Rich's door or even glancing in that direction. She simply went into her own room, stripped off her robe, and fell into bed.

She expected a restless night. Instead she surprised herself by immediately sinking into a deep and dreamless sleep. Now that she'd made up her mind, there was nothing left to worry about and no reason to toss and turn. She would do what she'd decided to do, and nothing was going to stop her.

|CHAPTER 42|

When Ali opened her eyes at eight the next morning, a text from B. was waiting for her:

On the train to Munich where I'm
due at a meeting which won't
start until I arrive. Call when you
wake up.

Up now. I'll call but only AFTER
I have some coffee.

While liquid burbled though the room's coffeemaker, Ali switched on the local news. The big story of the day remained the carnage on I-17 from the day before. A seventh victim had died overnight. Three more remained hospitalized in burn units in three separate Phoenix hospitals. The one mention of Archbishop Gillespie was that his condition was now listed as good and that it was expected he would be released sometime during the course of the day.

With coffee in hand, Ali dialed B.'s number. "Hello, sleepyhead," he said. "I've been up for hours."

"I'm sure you have," she replied, "but here's some mixed news. A moment ago I saw a segment on Archbishop Gillespie on TV. His condition has been upgraded to good, and he's expected to be released later today. The problem is, based on what he said last night, he plans to officiate at Father Andrew's funeral tomorrow morning."

"Officiate, really?" B. asked. "Will he be up to making that kind of public appearance?"

"Believe me," Ali said, "Francis Gillespie is prepared to move heaven and earth in order to make it happen."

"He may be up to it, but if whoever's after him is still on the loose, this doesn't sound like a great idea," B. said. "In the hospital he's had three guardian angels—Father Mike, Sister Anselm, and you. Out in public he'll be a lot more vulnerable."

"You know that, and so do I. But when Sister Anselm tried to talk him out of participating, it turned into the clash of the titans."

"Get him a Kevlar vest, then," B. advised. "If he's bound and determined to turn himself into a target, the least we can do is make taking him out as difficult as possible."

"I'll see what I can do," Ali said.

For several minutes Ali brought B. up to date, telling him about the freeway inferno that had kept her in Phoenix overnight. When she told him about the nonmatching soles on the two pairs of Skechers, B. was suitably impressed, but his response mirrored Ali's—he was glad Frigg had noticed the issue but sorry she'd done so by illegally accessing confidential internal communications at Phoenix PD. And he was grateful that Archbishop Gillespie and Ali had managed to create a situation where Frigg's information could be passed along to Stoneman's defense attorney without betraying the source.

"That's what's up on my end," Ali finished. "How about yours?"

"The A&D situation is well in hand. Dieter's been effectively sidelined, and Albert is back at the helm."

"A good day for High Noon all around, then," Ali said.

An incoming call from Sister Anselm arrived, forcing Ali to end one call and switch over to the next.

"What's the news?" Ali asked. "Is he being released?"

"This is a Catholic hospital, and he's the archbishop, so he's leaving come hell or high water," Sister Anselm observed with more than a hint of sarcasm. "Father Daniel is out renting a van equipped with a wheelchair ramp. Given the damage to his shoulder, using the walker is out of the question."

"And he's still up for the funeral tomorrow?"

"Absolutely."

"All right, then," Ali said, "I'll need his shirt size."

"His shirt size?" Sister Anselm echoed. She sounded mystified.

"I'm heading out to buy him a Kevlar vest, and you're going to make sure he wears it to the church tomorrow."

"You can count on it," Sister Anselm muttered. "Hang on. I'll go check his closet." She came back on the line a moment later. "The one Father Daniel brought over is a size eighteen, but he's lost a lot of weight in the last few months. I wouldn't be surprised if this one isn't too big for him."

"Okay," Ali said. "I'll keep that in mind."

She ordered breakfast from room service and then checked in with the office, where in the aftermath of the averted A&D crisis everyone was breathing sighs of relief. Next she touched base with Frigg.

"Good morning, Ms. Reynolds. I hope you had a restful night."

"I did," Ali responded. "I have some free time this morning. Do you have any swim-team dossiers for me to look at?"

"I do," Frigg replied. "Two hundred twenty-six in number. Of those, thirty-two no longer have any familial connections to the Phoenix Metropolitan Area. None of the remaining ones have raised any red flags, but I'll be happy to send them along for you to examine. In the meantime we're also delving into Archbishop Gillespie's social-media history."

"All right, then," Ali said. "Go ahead and start sending. I have an appointment early this afternoon, but I'll scan through as many as I can to see if anything jumps out at me."

Fortified by breakfast and with a cup of coffee at hand, Ali dove in to read that daunting collection of dossiers. Frigg had helpfully organized the list in terms of threat assessment, working from highest to lowest. Families who'd suffered the most serious losses, those in which their swim-team member was already deceased—six in number—had bubbled to the top. Two of Father Needham's swim-team athletes had died of AIDS, one in a DUI-related car crash, one of an opioid overdose, one of melanoma, and one of a heart attack.

Ali scanned through as many of those as possible, but by 10:00 a.m., when the doors opened at Phoenix Peace Officer Outfitters, she was on hand to purchase not one but two Kevlar vests, a size 2X for Archbishop Gillespie and a large for Sister Anselm. Ali was reasonably sure that Father Mike wouldn't have shown up without bringing along his own, and Ali's was in the back of her Cayenne.

Ali made it to the hospital around eleven. By then Archbishop Gillespie was dressed but still in his hospital room, anxiously awaiting the doctor's arrival with his dismissal orders.

"What's this?" he asked, peering inside once she handed him the bag.

"It's a required costume component for tomorrow's funeral."

"A bulletproof vest?" he asked, pulling it out. "Surely I don't need one of these."

"Bullet-resistant, rather than bulletproof," Ali corrected, "but that's exactly what it is. I bought one for you and one for Sister Anselm, since I'm pretty sure that as far as the funeral is concerned, the two of you will be joined at the hip."

"And you think whoever is after me will try again tomorrow?" Archbishop Gillespie asked.

"I do."

A grim-faced Sister Anselm, standing next to the door with her arms folded across her chest, added her two cents to the mix. "No vest, no funeral," she decreed, "and that's final!"

"All right, all right, I'll wear it!" Archbishop Gillespie agreed, throwing up his one good arm in mock despair. "My life was always much simpler without so many women in it."

"It might have been simpler," Sister Anselm muttered, "but that doesn't necessarily mean it was better. As long as you're wearing yours, I suppose I'll have to knuckle under and wear mine as well."

Ali had expected an argument from Sister Anselm, but that didn't happen. "Come on out to the waiting room and try it on," Ali said. "If it doesn't fit, I can exchange it for another size."

"You're coming to the funeral, too, aren't you?" Sister Anselm asked as she shrugged her way into the vest.

"I'm coming, all right," Ali said. "When I left the house, I had no idea I'd be staying over for a funeral, so I'm going to need to go back to Sedona later today to pick up more appropriate funeral attire."

"I'm in the same boat," Sister Anselm complained. "I usually wear civilian clothing, but there'll be lots of clergy present tomorrow, and I'll blend in better if I'm wearing a habit. Since you're going that way, would you mind stopping by the convent, picking mine up, and bringing it back down tomorrow morning? I can call Sister Sarah. She'll have it all laid out and ready for you."

"Sure," Ali said. "I'll probably stop by the office for a time while I'm there, and Jerome isn't that far out of my way."

The archbishop's attending physician arrived just then, as did Father Daniel. As the waiting room filled with people, Ali took herself out of the mix. With almost two hours to go before her meeting with Gavin James at the jail, she found a quiet place in the hospital lobby and settled in to read more dossiers. Ali was always surprised that investigative work involved far more reading than it did anything else.

|CHAPTER 43|

By seven fifteen on Thursday morning—the day Rachel Higgins thought of as her end-of-days day—she was out in the garage banging away, using the business end of a sledgehammer to smash every last one of Rich's damned birdhouses—finished and unfinished—to splintered pieces. She had learned there were people out in the world who bought and sold crime-scene memorabilia, and she didn't want one of those contemptible folks selling Rich's handiwork to some other macabre nutcase.

Before leaving the house, Rachel made one final foray into Rich's room. The TV was still on, and she left it that way. Without glancing at the still figure lying on the bed, she went straight to the dresser, where he always emptied his pockets. There she relieved his wallet of the two hundred-dollar bills he customarily carried, along with a stack of smaller denominations. There was no sense in leaving the money there for some sticky-fingered crime-scene investigator to find and slip into his or her own pocket. Why not spend it instead?

A few minutes later, on her way out the door, Rachel revised her packing decision. After unplugging her laptop and turning off her phone, she retrieved an extra rolling bag from the closet and shoved her electronic devices into that. If the cops somehow did manage to figure out who she was and what she was up to, she didn't want them to be able to trace her by following her devices. With the single exception of her burner phone, all her electronics would be dropped into the Arizona Canal sometime later on tonight, where they would disappear into watery darkness, never to be seen again. As an afterthought she used a paring knife from the kitchen to slice several long rents in the top of the bag, thus ensuring that once it hit the water, it would sink rather than float.

She drove away from the house right at nine o'clock in the morning without so much as a backward glance. She had lived on Menadota Drive for more than three decades, but her time there was over now. She was done.

At the Sunrise Diner, she splurged on a pecan waffle with extra whipped cream and a side of crisp bacon. This was a day to treat herself, and a luscious pecan waffle was just the ticket. She had picked up a newspaper on the way inside. She sat there reading it for a while after breakfast, stalling for time and waiting for the bank to open at ten. When she left, she dropped two of Rich's twenties on the table, leaving behind a more-than-generous tip. Why not? After today Rachel wouldn't need the money.

From the diner she drove to the bank, where she wrote a check to cash in the amount of thirty-five hundred dollars. Had she been asked, Rachel had planned to explain to the teller that she was buying her husband a new computer as a surprise, but the disinterested teller simply counted out the bills without bothering to ask. With the money stowed in her purse, Rachel went straight to Nordstrom's and blew a thousand of it on a stylish black pantsuit that showed off her figure, which, due to all the walking she'd been doing, was better than it had been in years.

Rachel's last stop in the store was in the shoe department, where she giddily picked up a pair of low-heeled Tory Burches that had an eye-popping price tag of three hundred bucks. It had been years since she'd been able to go on a shopping spree like this without having to worry about Rich pitching a fit later when the bill came due.

No, this was a day of indulgence, and indulge she would.

She had always wanted to stay at the Phoenician Resort, so that's where she went next. It turned out that checking in with cash was more of a hassle than she'd expected. In the end she had reluctantly handed over her credit card, deciding that it probably wasn't that big of a risk, since having one pending charge probably wouldn't be enough to set off any alarms on the account. Once she'd deposited her goods in the room, she headed over to the spa, where she'd booked herself in for the works—manicure, pedicure, shampoo, cut, facial, and full-body massage.

Clad in a luxurious robe and sipping a glass of complimentary champagne, Rachel sat in the spa's anteroom waiting for an attendant to lead her to the massage room. This was the calm before the storm, but it was the perfect way for her to spend what was most likely her last day.

Death-row prisoners only got to choose their last meal. Rachel had been able to choose much more than that, and by this time tomorrow David's death would finally be avenged.

|CHAPTER 44|

"Rich Higgins didn't put his garbage cans out this morning," Margaret Bendixen remarked to her husband, Ed, that day as they ate their noon meal of grilled cheese sandwiches accompanied by bowls of tomato soup.

Ed, done with his morning's worth of Fox News, was peering at the paper-and-ink edition of the *Wall Street Journal*.

"Maybe they didn't have very much trash this week and he decided not to bother," Ed suggested, lowering the paper far enough to look across the table at his wife.

"He always puts the trash out," Margaret insisted.

Ed wasn't having any of it. "Maybe they've taken a trip and are out of town for a day or two."

Margaret didn't reply to that. They had a doggie door in the house, but Chico was so tiny, she didn't allow him outside without her being there to supervise in case a marauding hawk or eagle tried to snatch him out of the yard. She'd been outside for his first morning walk much earlier that day and had heard Rich banging around in the garage. That wasn't at all surprising. That's where he spent most of his time. The problem was, since then, there had been radio silence from next door.

"I haven't heard a peep out of him since early this morning," Margaret continued, "and his missing garbage day is really unusual. We're none of us spring chickens, you know. Maybe Rich has fallen and hurt himself. Or maybe he's had a stroke and can't call for help."

Ed rattled the newspaper in irritation. "Oh, for Pete's sake, Maggie," he said. "Just because the guy gave you one of his fancy birdhouses once doesn't make you Rich Higgins's keeper. Believe me, he's fine."

"But what if he's not?" Margaret persisted. "I think we should call 911 and ask someone to do a welfare check."

"Don't be silly. Asking for a welfare check because somebody didn't put their damned garbage out in the morning?" Ed demanded derisively. "The cops will end up thinking you're nuttier than a fruitcake. They might even haul you off to the funny farm."

"But what if—" she began.

"There's no what if," Ed said, cutting her off. "If you're so bound and determined to see whether something is wrong with the man, why don't you go over there, ring his doorbell, and ask him to his face? But don't be surprised if he tells you to mind your own damned business. I sure as hell would."

With that, Ed folded up his paper, pushed himself back from the table, and stalked off into the family room. A moment later Fox News was once again blasting away.

After he left, Margaret cleared up the lunch things and loaded them into the dishwasher before sitting down with her final cup of coffee for the day. In the fifty-five years she and Ed had been married, this wasn't the first time he'd implied that she was a busybody. Maybe she was, but sometimes that's what was needed—people who weren't so caught up in their own little worlds that they actually paid attention to what was going on around them.

Finally, shortly after three, Margaret slipped her cell phone into her jacket pocket and clipped Chico's leash to his collar. Then she stuck her head into the family room. "Chico and I are going for a walk," she announced.

"Have fun," Ed replied with a dismissive wave of his hand.

Chico liked going for walks, but he objected when, instead of heading down the sidewalk on their usual route, they turned in at the very next driveway. With Rich's car there, Margaret assumed he probably was, too. With the dog tugging on the leash, Margaret stood for a time with her ear plastered to the garage door. Hearing nothing, she finally pounded on it.

"Hey, Rich!" she called out. "Are you in there? Are you all right?"

She listened for a moment. When there was no response, she tried again with the same result. Dragging a reluctant Chico behind her, she headed for the front door. When she pressed the button, the doorbell rang deep inside the house, but no one came to the door. Rich had told her that they had long ago given up having a landline phone, but he hadn't bothered giving Margaret his cell number, so there was no way for her to call.

She tried the doorknob. It was locked. That was hardly a surprise. Most people tended to keep their front doors locked these days, but what about the ones at the rear of the house? With a six-foot-tall block wall surrounding their backyard, Margaret and Ed often went to bed without bothering to lock the slider on the patio. Maybe Rich and Rachel Higgins didn't lock theirs either.

Chico was still raising objections to what he regarded as an unwarranted change in itinerary when Margaret went around to the side of the house where a latched gate led into the Higgins's backyard. Because they had a pool, it was a state-mandated self-closing one that took both hands to operate. Struggling with the leash, Margaret had to stand on tiptoes to make it work, but eventually she managed.

Since her own house was a mirror image of the one next door, Margaret knew just where the slider was. With the reluctant Chico having to be tugged along, she headed for the back patio. On the way she pressed her face to a bedroom window, trying to see inside, but she couldn't see past the blinds. The slider wasn't locked. When she opened it, she waited for a moment, expecting an alarm to sound. None did.

"Rich?" Margaret called through the narrow opening. "Is anybody here? Anyone home?"

From somewhere inside she heard a rumble of voices, but no one responded to her summons. After securing Chico to the arm of a wooden deck chair, Margaret eased the door open the rest of the way and stepped inside. She was immediately surprised by how cold the interior of the house was. Someone must have mistakenly turned on the A/C as opposed to the furnace.

Why would someone turn on the A/C at this time of year? Margaret wondered.

Remembering Ed's admonition about minding her own business, she sidled through the house. If the cops happened to show up, the worst they could charge her with was trespassing. She certainly wasn't guilty of breaking and entering.

The interior of the house was neat as a pin. There was nothing out of place and no sign of a struggle. Still calling out for Rich, Margaret made her way down the hall, where she realized that the voices were coming from a television in the second bedroom. Since the door was closed, she knocked, but again there was no response.

When she pushed it open, other than the light from the flickering television screen, the room was bathed in darkness. As soon as she switched on an overhead fixture, she was appalled by the mess. Piles of clothes were scattered everywhere—on the floor, on the chairs. At first glance it reminded Margaret of the way her son's room used to look back when Jed was in high school and before he'd morphed into the world's most persnickety neatnik.

Turning away from the mess on the floor, Margaret allowed herself to take in the rest of the room, and that's when she saw someone lying on the bed—a motionless figure completely covered by a flowered bedspread over the length of the body and with a pillow perched on top, over the face.

"Rich," Margaret called nervously as she edged her way into the room. "Is that you? Are you all right?"

Gingerly, Margaret picked a path through the debris on the floor. Once at the bed, she reached out and tried to shake the person awake, but the still figure was stiff to the touch. With a growing sense of dread, she pulled back the covers. Rich was there, all right. His eyes were wide open and staring sightlessly at the ceiling, and in the middle of his forehead was a star-shaped hole.

Horrified, Margaret stumbled backward and dropped heavily into a nearby easy chair. Had it been one step farther away, she would have plummeted clear to the floor. Barely able to breathe and unsure if her legs would hold her, Margaret stayed in the chair long enough to wrestle her cell phone out of her pocket. Once she did, it took three tries for her to dial the simple three-digit number.

"Nine-one-one," a calm voice said. "What is your emergency?"

"Come quick," Margaret gasped. "My neighbor's been murdered. He's dead."

"Is he breathing?"

The fact that the operator wasn't really listening got Margaret's back up. "No, he's not breathing!" she shouted into the phone. "I already told you, he's dead—cold, stiff, and dead."

"What is your name, please?"

"Margaret Bendixen."

"All right, Margaret. Units are on their way. Please stay on the line."

But Margaret didn't heed that last instruction. Instead she hung up and dialed Ed.

"You've gotta come quick," she wailed into the phone once her husband answered.

"Where? What's wrong, hon? Are you all right?"

"I'm not all right," she sobbed. "I'm next door—in Rich's bedroom. He's dead, Ed, and Chico's tied to a chair out back on the patio. I've called 911. The cops are on their way. You've gotta come fetch Chico before they get here."

"Rich is dead? Are you sure? How?"

"There's what looks like a bullet hole in his head. Maybe he committed suicide. Rachel isn't here. Somebody needs to call her and let her know so she doesn't come home and find him like this."

"Hang on, Maggie," Ed said. "I'll be right there."

By the time Ed showed up, clutching Chico to his chest, Margaret had her wits about her. She had known for years that Rich Higgins was left-handed. There were pillows on the floor on the left-hand side of the bed—pillows but no weapon. This wasn't a suicide.

"Come on," Ed urged, reaching for his wife's hand. "We need to get out of here right now."

"I think Rachel shot him," Margaret managed, "and that's what woke us up in the middle of the night. What we heard wasn't a backfire, it was a gunshot. It was Rachel shooting Rich in the head!"

"We still shouldn't be here. How did you get inside?"

"The slider was unlocked. I let myself into the house because I was worried," Margaret told him, wiping away tears. "It turns out I was right to be worried."

"Because he didn't take out the trash."

"Exactly."

The wail of an arriving squad car blasted into the room. "Come on," Ed said again, helping Margaret to her feet. "We'd better go outside to talk to them. They're not going to be happy we were here first. They'll probably think we're the ones who did it."

|CHAPTER 45|

At the Maricopa County Jail, Ali once again locked her Glock and her Taser in the glove box gun safe before exiting the Cayenne. She found Gavin James waiting for her inside the front lobby.

"Ready to do this?" he asked.

"I am."

"All the same, whether I'm your attorney or not," Gavin told her, "the less you say inside, the better."

After checking in and being issued visitor passes, they were led to an interview room, where Jack Stoneman was already seated and waiting.

Gavin paused in the doorway and looked up at an overhead light that no doubt concealed video recording equipment. "This is an attorney consultation," he said aloud, "so this interview is not being recorded, correct?"

"Correct, sir," the guard replied.

"All right, then."

As Ali and Gavin stepped inside, Jack, dressed in jailhouse orange and cuffed to the table, looked up at them.

"I'm Gavin James, and this is Ali Reynolds," Gavin said by way of introductions. "Ms. Reynolds has been doing some work for Archbishop Gillespie on a related manner, and he thought her presence might be helpful."

"Thank you both for coming," Jack said, "but I don't understand why Archbishop Gillespie would ask you to take my case—"

"The archbishop is a friend of mine," Gavin explained. "He's concerned that you might not be getting a fair shake and has asked me to intercede on your behalf, because he doesn't want the tragedy of Father O'Toole's death to cause undue hardship to anyone else."

"But why would he do that when I don't even know him?" Jack wondered aloud.

"Because he's a good man," Gavin answered, "one who truly believes that people are innocent until proven guilty."

As Ali took her seat, she examined the man seated across the table from them. Jack Stoneman looked decidedly ill. His coloring was pallid, his eyes bloodshot. His trembling hands caused the metal cuffs on his wrists to clatter against the tabletop.

"Are you unwell, Mr. Stoneman?" Gavin asked.

"I could use some hair of the dog," he said, "but don't worry. I'll be okay."

"All right, then," Gavin said, getting down to business. "What can you tell us about what happened on Lincoln Drive the night before last?"

"That's the whole problem," Jack said. "I can't tell you a damned thing. I don't remember being there that night."

"But you were there earlier in the day?"

"Just like always. I've got me a sweet panhandling gig all staked out right next to the driveway that leads in and out of the archbishop's place."

"That's your usual spot?"

He nodded. "It has been for quite a while."

"So going back to Tuesday evening," Gavin urged. "What exactly do you remember?"

"I left about the regular time—in the middle of the afternoon. Just before I left, Father Andrew brought me some sandwiches. I ate them on the bus."

"Where did you go then?"

"I headed home, but I stopped off to have a couple of drinks along the way and didn't get home until much later."

"Where exactly do you live?" Gavin asked.

"Off Washington in a shared RV parked in some old guy's backyard."

"So you stopped off for a drink."

"I stopped off to buy a bottle, not a drink," Jack specified. "At the liquor store, I ran into a couple of guys I know. We ended up having some drinks in the parking lot, and that's the last I remember."

"Do these guys have names?"

"One's called Monkey Wrench—he's a mechanic, I think, or used to be. The other one's called Willy. They're just guys from the neighborhood. I don't know their last names, but you can bet that the next time I see them, I'll beat the crap out of them."

"Why?"

"Because they rolled me, that's why. I'm guessing they slipped me something that knocked me out. They stole my booze and all the money I had in my pocket. My roommates told the cops that I came home at three in the morning, but I don't have any idea how I managed to get there. The last thing I remember, it wasn't even dark."

"So it was still light when you left the liquor store?"

Jack nodded. "Definitely," he said.

"Then what?"

"The next thing I knew, it was morning and I was back home with a hell of a hangover. I went to the church just down the street for breakfast, the way I usually do, and then caught the bus over to Lincoln Drive. I got there and saw the crime-scene tape. That's when I knew something bad had happened, so I turned around and came home."

"Why?"

"Why do you think?" Jack echoed. "Because I'm an ex-con. I've done time for second-degree homicide, and I'm still on parole. The last thing I needed was to be caught up in a police investigation. On my way home, I stopped off at a bar, and that's when I saw some guy on the news talking about what happened. He said the cops in the Lincoln Drive case were looking for a guy wearing a ball cap."

"Do you wear a ball cap?"

Jack nodded. "I used to."

"Where is it?"

"I threw it away in the dumpster outside the bar."

"Why?"

"Because I was afraid they'd come looking for me, and it turns out they did."

"How do you get back and forth from your home to your panhandling post?"

"I take a bus—a couple of buses, actually."

"You don't own a vehicle?"

"Naw, I have a transit pass. Anyhow, there's this little clearing in a hedge next to my panhandling spot. That's where I store the stuff I don't want to carry each way on the bus. CSIs working the crime scene musta found my prints in the clearing. Since I'm in the system, the lead detective came looking for me right quick."

"That would be Detective Kyle Lasko?" Gavin inquired.

"Yes," Jack said. "He asked me to come down to police headquarters with him to give a statement. He said they only needed to talk to me—that I was a person of interest rather than a suspect. They took my clothes—shirt, pants, shoes, everything—so they could test them for GSR."

"GSR as in gunshot residue?" Gavin asked.

Jack nodded. "Lasko left me alone in the interview room for a while. When he finally came back, everything changed. All of a sudden, instead of being a person of interest I was now the prime suspect—make that the *only* suspect. He read me my rights and was all over me for the rest of the afternoon, hammering away, trying to get me to confess, which I didn't. The interview didn't stop until I finally asked for an attorney. I thought I'd get a public defender. I didn't expect someone like you."

"You mentioned that Detective Lasko's demeanor changed when he came back. In what way?"

"Like I said, they'd already done the GSR test. I figured that once they didn't find anything with that, I'd be good to go. But when he came back, he wasn't interested in my clothes. All he wanted to talk about was my shoes."

"What shoes?" Gavin asked.

"My new ones," Jack answered. "Lasko was all excited because he said they'd found shoe prints in the clearing with soles just like the ones I was wearing when they brought me in. I tried to tell him that of course my footprints would be there. That's where I hang out. Who else's do you think would be there?"

"You said the shoes were new?" Ali asked.

"Yes, this nice lady, one of my regulars—I call her the latte lady—gave them to me the day before all this happened."

"What kind of shoes?"

"Skechers fresh out the box," Jack answered. "It had been years since I'd had a new pair of shoes. Now they're probably locked up in an evidence room, and I'll never see them again."

"Tell us about the latte lady," Ali said quietly. "Who's she?"

Gavin shot her a warning look but said nothing.

Jack shrugged. "She's just this nice lady who comes by almost every day. A lot of the time when she's out for a morning walk, she'll bring me stuff—drinks from Starbucks mostly."

"What kind of drinks?"

"Usually an iced latte," Jack replied. "The one the other day tasted like pumpkin."

Gavin looked as though he wanted to tell Ali to stifle, but once again he didn't.

"What does this latte lady look like?" Ali asked.

Jack shrugged again. "She's Anglo," Jack replied, "definitely an Anglo, and probably somewhere in her sixties."

"What color hair?" Ali asked.

"Beats me," Jack replied. "I've never seen her hair. She's a cancer patient—breast cancer, most likely, since she's always wearing one of those pink scarf things around her head."

Having accomplished what she'd set out to do, Ali sat back in her chair, zipped her lips, and left the rest of the talking to Gavin. She had managed to raise the issue of the shoe-print evidence, and that had been the whole point.

Gavin didn't speak to her again until after they ended the interview, turned in their visitor's badges, signed out, and were back in the parking lot.

"Okay," he said. "What's the big deal with the shoes?"

"There's a good possibility that there's more than one pair of Skechers."

"You think there is or you know there is?" he asked.

"It's just a hunch," she said. "Call it women's intuition if you will, but think about it. One morning this very generous latte lady who happens to be in her sixties stops by to give Jack Stoneman a brand-new pair of shoes for no reason at all. The very next day, those same shoes become a key piece of evidence linking him to a homicide investigation—a homicide that Jack claims he didn't commit and has no knowledge of. Isn't that shoe evidence just a little too convenient, especially given the fact that our handwriting expert tells us that the person sending threatening notes to Archbishop Gillespie is probably a female in her fifties or sixties?"

Gavin studied Ali's face for a long moment. "You don't say," he said eventually.

"I do say," Ali insisted.

"All right, then," he said.

As Ali walked back to the Cayenne, a text came in from Sister Anselm.

Our impatient patient is at home
at the residence. Don't worry.
Father Mike and I will be here
with him.

Ali glanced at her watch. By then it was close to three. A moment later she texted back.

Okay. On my way home.

With that, Ali turned the Cayenne toward northbound I-17 and home. If she had any kind of luck, there wouldn't be any fuel-truck wrecks or brushfires along the way.

|CHAPTER 46|

I t was coming up on midafternoon on Thursday, and Detective Kyle Lasko was not having a good day. Yesterday, on the first full day of a homicide investigation, he should have been out tracking down witnesses and people who'd given preliminary statements to the uniformed officers at the crime scene. Instead he'd wasted the better part of his day trying to wrest a confession from his prime suspect, the drunken bum Jack Stoneman. After spending hours in the box, Stoneman had finally lawyered up, leaving Kyle with nothing. In other words, it had been a total waste of time.

He'd spent today dragging his weary ass all over the Valley of the Sun conducting interviews. Although everyone had been on East Lincoln Drive at the same time and at the same location on the night of the murder, they came from different corners of the Phoenix area, stretching from Fountain Hills on the east to Sun City on the west. Fortunately for Kyle, even though he worked for Phoenix PD, he was able to take his city-owned vehicle home to Mesa overnight. That way he'd been able to start his interview chores from home rather than having to go into the city to check one out.

Before he ever left the house, the morning had kicked off with a mixed-bag phone call from Captain Anthony Robard, the guy in charge of Major Crimes.

"I've got some good news and some bad news," Captain Robard said. "Which do you want first?"

"Good news, please," Kyle replied.

"We just heard from the crime lab. They got a complete profile off the cartridge in the murder weapon."

"And?"

"Our shooter is none other than Jack Stoneman."

"What's the bad news?"

"I just got off the phone with the county attorney. He says DNA and footprints aren't enough—too circumstantial. Without a confession he wants more—something that puts Stoneman at the scene of the crime when the shooting took place."

"In other words, he wants me to pull an eyewitness out of my hat?"

"Something like that," Robard agreed.

Kyle sighed again. "All right, then," he said. "I'll be doing witness interviews today. With seventeen people on the list, it's going to take most of the day. Stoneman travels by bus, so I've got people checking security video on transit vehicles and neighborhood-surveillance videos as well. Stoneman claims he left the archbishop's residence at around four o'clock in the afternoon. I want to know how and when he came back."

"Sounds like you've got things handled, then," Captain Robard said, "but just so you know, Chief Adolfo is all over my ass on this one, texting me practically minute by minute to see if we're making progress."

This wasn't news as far as Kyle Lasko was concerned. "Got it," he said.

His first stop was on East Peso Place in Fountain Hills with a couple named Wayne and Connie Carlson. Their Hyundai Sonata, with Wayne at the wheel, had been the first vehicle struck by the speeding Town Car when it roared into traffic. Wayne answered the door sporting a pair of shiners. Kyle held up his badge.

"This about the other night?" Wayne asked, and Kyle nodded. "Come in, then, and don't worry about the black eyes. The air bag got me, but without it things would have been a lot worse. Have a seat. My wife's in the shower. I'll let her know you're here."

When Wayne returned to the room with his wife in tow, her face was in much rougher shape than her husband's, due primarily, Kyle supposed, to the difference in their heights. He was more than six feet tall. With Connie almost a foot shorter, her face had taken the full brunt of the exploding air bag.

"Sorry about the way I look," Connie apologized self-consciously. "I didn't bother trying to put on makeup. It really doesn't help much. Wayne says you're here about what happened the other night."

"That's right," Kyle agreed. "I know you gave statements to the uniformed officers at the scene, but if you don't mind, I'd like to go over it again while I record what you have to say."

"Feel free," Connie said quickly. "We want that guy caught."

It took a few seconds of juggling before Kyle got his iPad set up. Once it was, Connie looked at him expectantly. "What do you want to know?" she asked.

"Tell me everything you can remember about that night."

"We have some friends who just moved into an assisted-living place over on Seventh Avenue," Connie answered. "We were on our way to see them when the crash happened. We were driving along, minding our own business, when wham, this other car comes barreling out of nowhere and slams right into us. They hit the back end of our car and sent us spinning. When the air bags deflated, we were up against the curb, facing the wrong way, with Wayne yelling, 'Are you all right? Are you all right?'"

"The car came to rest on which side of the street?"

"Westbound, but we were facing the other way, the way we'd just come."

"What happened then? What did you see?"

"I didn't see the shooter, if that's what you're asking," Connie replied, "but I did see a woman. Our headlights were still on, and I was pissed that she just walked past us like that, as though nothing had happened, and she didn't have a care in the world. In all that chaos, most people would have had the common decency to at least stop and offer to help."

A *woman*, Kyle thought. So who was this unconcerned female passerby? An accomplice, maybe? Since she showed up as soon as the air bags deflated, she was, at the very least, a possible witness.

"Can you describe her for me?"

"An older woman, Anglo, I think," Connie answered. "I'd say she was a little taller than I am—five-five or so—with blond hair. I remember she was wearing pants—like jeans, maybe—and a long-sleeved sweater or jacket. It could have been red or maybe purple. Under the streetlamps it was hard to tell. And she was carrying a light-colored bag of some kind—

not a purse. This looked more like a beach bag or maybe one of those grocery store totes but without a name."

A beach bag? Kyle wondered. *Why would someone be carrying a beach bag around in Phoenix in November?*

Kyle turned his attention to Wayne. "What about you? Did you see her?"

"Nope," he answered. "I was too busy getting out of the car so I could come help Connie. By the time I got around to her side, I didn't see anyone else."

When the interview ended, Kyle stayed focused on the woman Connie had described. She was a potential witness, and Kyle was determined to find her. The presence of that beach bag was something that stood out. Back in the car, he dialed into headquarters and asked that the guys canvassing for surveillance video to be on the lookout for someone with a light-colored beach bag and a red or purple sweater.

And now, much later in the day, that tiny possible lead was still all Kyle had managed to turn up. The four people in the overturned minivan, all of whom lived in Venture Out, an RV resort in Mesa, had been too traumatized by the wreck itself to have seen much beyond what was happening inside their own vehicle. None of the four had seen the shooter, nor had they spotted a woman of any kind at the scene, let alone one carrying a beach bag.

The information that the shooter had been wearing a ball cap had come from surveillance video off a camera situated in the gatepost at the archbishop's residence, which had captured the whole incident. Unfortunately, none of the people Kyle talked to that day—two witnesses from Apache Junction, one from Tempe, and two from Chandler—had caught a glimpse of him, nor did anyone other than Connie report having seen the woman and her bag.

The next guy on Kyle's list, number thirteen of the seventeen, was one Humberto Martinez, who lived in Glendale on the far side of Phoenix proper. Back in his vehicle, Kyle was headed west on State Route 60 when a call came in. "Please hold for Chief Adolfo," he was told.

Kyle felt a clutch in his gut. Another call from the chief was not a good sign.

"How the hell did a retired news anchor named Ali Reynolds, who evidently regards herself as some kind of half-assed private investigator, get mixed up in your homicide?" the chief blustered at Kyle once he came on the line.

"She's a friend of Archbishop Gillespie's," Kyle answered. "I interviewed her briefly yesterday. Before any of this happened, the archbishop had asked her and her husband to investigate some threats the archbishop has been receiving—"

"I know all about those threats," the chief interrupted, "and since I've been following your investigation, I know you already interviewed her. But here's what I really want to know: Why the hell did she turn up at the jail a little while ago, accompanied by Jack Stoneman's defense attorney, and why the hell was she allowed to speak with your suspect inside an interview room with no recording equipment running? Can you answer me that?"

Kyle was dumbfounded. "Ali Reynolds has been in touch with Stoneman's public defender?"

"Who said anything about a public defender?" Chief Adolfo grumbled in return. "I'm telling you Gavin James is a big-shot attorney here in town, and apparently he's handling this case pro bono. So what's going on here, Lasko? Did you leak information to this Reynolds woman?"

"I didn't tell her anything out of line," Kyle said, "but I'll get to the bottom of this."

"You'd better," Chief Adolfo shot back, "and that's an order!"

Kyle Lasko was furious. He had told Ali Reynolds plain as day to back off and stay out of his investigation, yet here she was seriously undermining his case. It was time to read her the riot act! Once off the phone with the chief, Kyle scrolled through his recent-calls list and located Ali's number.

"Detective Lasko here," he said when she answered. "Just who the hell do you think you are?"

Her reply wasn't the least bit ruffled. "I'm someone charged with keeping Archbishop Gillespie safe. You happen to believe that you've got the right guy locked up, but I respectfully disagree."

"Respectfully my ass," he growled back. "A little while ago, you showed up at the jail accompanied by Jack Stoneman's attorney."

"News must travel pretty fast around your department," she observed.

"You bet it does, especially if Chief Adolfo is involved. May I remind you, Ms. Reynolds, that interfering with a homicide investigation is a felony. So here's the deal: If you so much as step near this case again, you can expect to be arrested and charged. Do I make myself clear?"

"Abundantly," Ali told him.

With that off his chest, Kyle ended the call and kept on driving despite the overwhelming feeling that this interview, too, would most likely be a wasted effort.

Humberto Martinez lived in a working-class neighborhood off Fifty-seventh Avenue on West Myrtle. Arriving there, Kyle was dismayed to learn that Humberto was at work as a groundskeeper at Camelback Golf Club on the near east side of the city. Rather than wait for him to come home, Kyle headed back the way he had come, burning up his steel-belted radials rather than shoe leather.

After stating his case to the pro in the golf shop, Kyle was issued a cart and directed to a tastefully camouflaged equipment shed off to the side of the course between the ninth green and the tenth tee box. He found Humberto inside the shed, enjoying a short afternoon break at a grungy picnic table.

"This about the other night?" Humberto asked.

Kyle nodded. "What can you tell me?"

"It was after work, and I had stopped off for a beer on my way home," Humberto answered. "I was headed for the 51, driving west on Lincoln, when suddenly all hell broke loose, and there were cars flying in every direction. Luckily, I managed to stop my pickup without hitting anybody or getting hit myself. I jumped out and went running to see what I could do. A couple of people were trapped in a minivan, and I helped them get out and stayed with them until the EMTs arrived. Someone told me that the driver of the Town Car was already dead. I thought he died in the wreck. I didn't find out until later on the news that somebody'd shot him."

"I know there was a lot of uproar at the scene, but did anything strike you as odd or out of place?" Kyle asked.

"Only the woman," Humberto replied.

"What woman?" Kyle wanted to know.

"This woman was strolling along on the sidewalk just as pretty as you please, walking past all that mess like nothing had happened. Most people would have offered to help or else turned into a looky-loo, but not her. She just kept on walking. It was like multi-car wrecks happen every day and aren't worth a second glance."

"Can you describe her?"

"Older woman, I'd say—an Anglo with short, light-colored hair."

"Silver? Blond?"

"Couldn't tell."

"How was she dressed?"

Humberto shrugged. "Like she was out for a walk is all. Long pants and a sweater of some kind."

"What color sweater?"

"Couldn't tell you," Humberto said. "I'm color-blind."

"Which direction was she going?"

"She was walking east on the north side of Lincoln."

"Anything else?"

"She was carrying a bag of some kind."

"Like from a grocery store?"

"No, most of those have the store's name on them. This was a light-colored bag with no logo," Humberto answered. "It struck me as odd."

Me, too, Kyle thought. All his instincts had shifted into high gear. Somehow or other this unconcerned passerby with her light-colored bag had to be involved in all this. He just didn't know how.

"Thank you, Mr. Martinez," Kyle said. "You've been a big help."

He took the cart back to the pro shop and then got on the phone with the desk sergeant at Major Crimes. So far his video-surveillance canvassers had come up empty.

"Tell them to keep looking," Kyle directed.

"Any idea when you'll be back?" the desk sergeant asked.

Kyle glanced at his watch. It was after four, and traffic was getting worse all over the valley. "Beats the hell out of me," he muttered. "I headed out this morning with a list of seventeen witnesses needing to be interviewed, and I just crossed off number thirteen. My next stop is in Peoria. You can expect me when you see me coming, and not a moment before."

|CHAPTER 47|

A li was stuck in a parking lot otherwise known as I-17 when Kyle Lasko's irate call came in. He was well within his rights to light into her and threaten her with arrest, since she really was interfering with his investigation. As far as she was concerned, however, she was doing it with good reason. He believed Jack Stoneman to be guilty. Ali believed otherwise.

As complicated as things had become on the ground, Ali had ignored the barrage of incoming alerts from Frigg. Now though, driving north, she reached out to the AI.

"Good afternoon, Ms. Reynolds," Frigg said. "I hope you are well."

"I am," Ali replied. "Sorry to go AWOL on you."

There was a momentary pause.

"AWOL," Frigg repeated as if reading a definition verbatim from a dictionary. "To be absent, often without notice or permission, from one's duty station or post. There must be some sort of misunderstanding," the AI added. "There is no need for you to report your whereabouts to me."

"I just meant that I shouldn't have gone dark for so long without being in touch."

"Gone dark," Frigg repeated.

Despite Stu's determined efforts on that score, there remained some idioms Frigg had yet to untangle.

"Never mind," Ali interrupted before Frigg could launch into yet another Merriam-Webster recitation. "I've been busy and couldn't pay attention. Has anything new turned up?"

"We've made a thorough study of Archbishop Gillespie's social-media interactions," Frigg replied. "The most interesting one came through in March of this year as a comment on the archbishop's blog from someone named Susannah."

"A threat of some kind?" Ali asked quickly. "What did it say?"

"The comment read, 'How dare you call yourself a shepherd?'" Frigg responded.

"That doesn't strike me as especially threatening," Ali observed.

"What's interesting is the sender's IP address," Frigg replied. "That leads back to a physical address belonging to the parents of one of the boys on Father Needham's swim team, Richard and Rachel Higgins. Their son, David, died of a drug overdose in 2010 at age twenty-six."

"So young," Ali murmured.

She had made the remark to herself rather than to Frigg, but the AI responded anyway. "Unintentional injuries account for 39.7 percent of the deaths in males ages twenty to forty-four. Suicide is listed as the cause of death in 13.9 percent of the cases."

"So where does David Higgins's death fall in that listing?" Ali asked. "Suicide or accidental?"

"The medical examiner lists his overdose as accidental."

"And what if anything do we know about the parents?"

"David's father, Richard, went to work for the Central Arizona Project shortly after graduating from Arizona State University. He retired from there a year or so after David's death. The mother, Rachel, also graduated from Arizona State and taught briefly. Since then, other than volunteering, she hasn't worked outside the home. They purchased their current house in the mid-eighties and have lived there up to the present. Neither of them has any criminal history, not even so much as a parking ticket."

Clearly Frigg had been working to put together a dossier on the Higgins household. "If the mother's name is Rachel, who's Susannah?" Ali asked.

"I'm guessing that would be a reference to Rachel's maternal grandmother, Susannah Perkins Anderson," Frigg replied. "Since Susannah died in 1992, I doubt she was personally responsible for the comment on Archbishop Gillespie's blog. Someone else used her name as a pseudonym."

"But one or both of the parents might be carrying some kind of grudge against Archbishop Gillespie," Ali said. "Keep looking, and let me know what you find."

Ali had Frigg put the lineup of dossiers on an audio feed so she could listen as she drove. In Cottonwood she whipped right past the High Noon campus and drove directly to Jerome, where she collected Sister Anselm's habit from Sister Sarah. Back in Cottonwood she stopped by the office to catch up on whatever paperwork she'd missed by being absent for two full days. It was after hours by then. Stu was in the computer lab doing the evening shift. Everyone else had gone home. She was at her desk in her office with the iPad situated at her elbow and still listening to dossiers in the background when a howler came in from Frigg.

"There are unsubstantiated reports of a fatal shooting incident on Menadota Drive in Phoenix earlier today. The victim is said to be male, and a BOLO has been issued for a female believed to be missing from the residence. The address has not yet been made public, but it's the same one as the IP address from that comment on the archbishop's blog."

"Richard and Rachel Higgins?" Ali asked faintly.

"Correct. I am sending you a copy of Rachel Higgins's driver's license. The signature line doesn't provide much of a sample, but I believe elements there are a match to the handwriting in the threatening notes sent to Archbishop Gillespie."

Ali looked up to find Stu Ramey standing in her doorway. "You know?" she asked.

"I'm copied on all howlers," he replied, while Frigg's voice, coming through the phone's speaker, continued in the background.

". . . no word yet on when the shooting occurred, but if Rachel Higgins is the perpetrator targeting the archbishop, then it would seem her behavior has escalated in the past twenty-four hours. Based on these developments, I am now raising the archbishop's threat level to 9.3 on a scale of 1 to 10."

Ali stared at the image of Rachel Higgins's driver's license. There was nothing out of the ordinary about the face of an older woman smiling confidently into the camera lens at the Department of Licensing—nothing that hinted she might be a cold-blooded killer. She looked to be completely harmless, like someone who'd be able to walk into Father

Andrew's funeral service the next morning without arousing the slightest suspicion.

"Then this is most likely Jack Stoneman's latte lady," Ali concluded, "the woman who gave him the Skechers. Frigg, are you of the opinion that another attempt on Archbishop Gillespie's life may occur at Father Andrew's funeral?"

"In my experience, frustrated killers often operate in an absence of logic," Frigg replied. "The fact that Rachel Higgins is sure to be caught may no longer be of any consequence to her. In fact, at this point she might prefer what's sometimes referred to as 'suicide by cop.'"

As those words sank in, Ali searched for her best course of action. What had once seemed like a vague potential threat was now an all-too-real one. Clearly law enforcement needed to be brought into the picture, but how could Ali do that without spilling the beans about Frigg? The AI's knowledge of confidential police information about the shooting was out of bounds, as was her being in possession of Rachel's driver's license information, which Frigg had no doubt hacked from the Department of Licensing.

So what was Ali supposed to do now? Call Detective Lasko back and let him know she knew about the Menadota Drive homicide and suggest that it might be related to Father Andrew's? Hardly, especially since, once again, Frigg was the sole source of that unauthorized information. Not only that, Lasko had already threatened to arrest Ali for interfering with his case, and this would be a giant step in that direction. No, calling Lasko at this point was absolutely out of the question.

And then there was the issue of Father Andrew's funeral. The Cathedral of the Holy Mother was huge. It probably held close to a thousand people. In a crowd that large, what were the chances the archbishop's defenders would be able to protect him from a most likely deranged and clearly deadly woman, who on the surface appeared to be perfectly harmless? Letting the funeral go forward as planned risked putting any number of innocent lives in jeopardy. On the other hand, it seemed equally unlikely that Archbishop Gillespie could be persuaded to call it off.

"What do you suggest?" Frigg asked.

Lost in thought, Ali struggled for a moment before responding. "One way or another, Rachel Higgins needs to be found and neutralized before the funeral and before she launches another attack on Archbishop

Gillespie. We should go to the cops with what we know, but we can't, not without putting Frigg at risk."

Much to Ali's surprise, Stu was the one who spoke up and laid out a strategy. "First we need a different photo of Rachel Higgins," he said decisively, "one that doesn't come from the Department of Licensing. Can you locate one of those, Frigg?"

"Certainly," the AI replied. "One moment, please."

Seconds later another photo appeared on the screen of Ali's phone. It featured a much younger Rachel helping fit a wig on someone the caption described as a recently diagnosed cancer patient.

"In searching for images of her, I found this on Facebook," Frigg replied. "It's from a volunteer organization called Phoenix Survivors' Boutique. They operate a number of shops where cancer survivors can purchase low-cost intimate apparel as well as wigs and scarves. Rachel Higgins served as a volunteer at the Shea Boulevard branch for a number of years."

Stu plucked Ali's phone off the desk and studied the photo closely. "She's younger here, but this will work," he said finally. "Facial features change over time, but facial rec is based on underlying bone structure, and that doesn't change, at least in theory."

Ali looked on in wonder at this new take-charge version of Stuart Ramey.

"Does the Cathedral of the Holy Mother have surveillance video?" he asked.

"Yes," Frigg replied, "but it's an outdated system with very limited resolution capability."

"Would it support facial-recognition software?"

"That would require a complete system upgrade," Frigg told him, "as well as a mainframe computer."

"What about Wi-Fi, Frigg?" Stu asked. "Does the cathedral have that?"

"One moment," Frigg said before adding, "Yes, Stuart, Wi-Fi is available."

Stu turned to Ali. "How many people do we have on our team?"

The question left Ali somewhat mystified. "On the archbishop's team?" she asked.

Stu nodded impatiently.

"Let's see, there's me, Sister Anselm, Father Mike, Father Winston, and most likely Father Daniel as well. Why?"

"Archbishop Gillespie's safety is a High Noon problem, right?"

"That's correct," Ali agreed.

"We have several new iPads still in their original containers," Stu continued. "I'll charge them up tonight, bring them online, and install a modified facial-rec app based only on Rachel's features."

"Which means we'll be looking for only one face in the crowd rather than trying to identify all of them?" Ali asked.

Stu nodded. "Correct," he said, "that's much simpler. I could install the program on people's cell phones, too, but I'd need to have access to all of them in order to do it. Tomorrow morning, with Lance here to mind the store, Cami and I will bring the iPads down to Phoenix in time for the funeral. At the cathedral we'll have as many people as we have iPads circulating through the crowd with their cameras turned on, looking for Rachel Higgins. I'm not sure what we'll do once we find her. That's up to you."

Ali was impressed. "That's nothing short of brilliant," she said. "We'll need enough people to cover all the entrances and have others mingling in the crowd. How many iPads do we have?"

"I'll check."

A quick inventory revealed there were seven iPads available.

"All right, then," Ali said. "By the way, when you come to Phoenix, both you and Cami need to wear your Kevlar vests under your street clothes."

"What about weapons?" Stu asked.

"We'll be limited to Tasers only," she said after a moment. "The inside of the cathedral is all hard surfaces. We can't risk having a ricochet take out innocent bystanders."

"I'll have my Taser," Stu said with a grin. "Cami doesn't need one. With her Krav Maga training, she's a deadly weapon all by herself, and she comes with one added benefit."

"What's that?"

"She doesn't ricochet."

|CHAPTER 48|

It turned out to be an afternoon and evening Margaret Bendixen would never forget. The first officer who arrived on the scene hurried into the Higginses' house and came back out a few minutes later.

"I've called for detectives and the ME," he told them. "Ma'am, if you wouldn't mind having a seat in the rear of my patrol car here, someone will get back to you."

Margaret climbed in, taking Chico with her. When Ed tried to join them, the cop put a restraining hand on his shoulder. "Where do you live, sir?"

"Right there," Ed said, pointing.

"Why don't you go have a seat on your porch, then," the officer said. "I'm sure one of the detectives will want to have a word with you as well."

In the end it was far more than a word. Margaret and Ed Bendixen were transported in separate vehicles to Phoenix PD's headquarters. Chico went along for the ride because Margaret absolutely refused to be separated from him. Once at Phoenix PD, they were led into adjoining interview rooms, where they spent the next several hours being interrogated by homicide investigators.

Detective Horner, the guy interviewing Margaret, was especially interested in the fact that she was the person who'd made the 911 call that had summoned officers the night before. For some reason, since she'd found Rich Higgins's body as well, the detective seemed to think that established her as his prime suspect. Over time she was able to make some headway in getting him to see that Rich's missing wife was also someone they should be investigating.

It was ten o'clock at night and hours after dinnertime when Margaret and Chico finally emerged from the interview room. In the waiting room, they found Ed dozing in a chair with a bag of now-cold Kentucky Fried Chicken sitting on the floor beside him. He startled awake when Margaret touched his shoulder.

"Are you done?" he asked anxiously.

She nodded. "Chico needs to go for a walk."

"I'll take him," Ed said, reaching for the leash. "In case you're hungry, I brought some food."

Margaret almost burst into tears again, this time out of sheer gratitude.

"Thank you," she murmured. "Thank you so much."

"They told me that someone would take us home when you were done," Ed told her. "Do you want to eat here or at home?"

"At home, please," Margaret said. "I'd much rather eat at home."

They left Phoenix PD headquarters in the back of an unmarked car driven by the detective who had interviewed Ed. He sat behind the driver, holding the bag of Kentucky Fried while Margaret, clutching Chico to her breast, snuggled next to him.

For a long time, neither of them spoke. Margaret was the one who finally broke the extended silence. "This afternoon on the phone, you called me 'hon,'" she murmured at last. "You haven't called me that in years."

Ed placed an arm around her shoulders and pulled her close. "Why wouldn't I?" he asked. "From the sound of your voice, I was afraid you were hurt or maybe even dying. You've been my hon for a very long time, and I didn't want to lose you."

|CHAPTER 49|

Shortly after 7:00 p.m., Kyle Lasko was down to his very last witness. Aaron Miller lived in a modest duplex located in one of Sun City's original neighborhoods. Within minutes Kyle learned that Miller wasn't home. A next-door neighbor informed him that Aaron's sister had died unexpectedly back home in Minnesota, and he'd flown out of town that very afternoon in order to attend her funeral.

Feeling frustrated and dejected, Kyle put his car in reverse, backed out of the driveway, and headed home to Mesa. He had already put in a long day, and there was no point in stopping by the department. At the moment, with nothing happening in his case and no progress to report, he was in no mood to risk running into Chief Adolfo.

Kyle had just merged onto the 101 headed eastbound when his evening got that much worse. His phone rang. "Hey, Detective Lasko," a familiar voice said when he answered. "It's Emmy, from the crime lab."

"With good news, I hope?"

"Sorry," she said. "That would be a no."

"Why? What's wrong?"

"I just ran a computerized comparison of the shoe prints from the crime scene with the shoes Stoneman was wearing at the time of his arrest. They're not the same."

"What do you mean they're not the same?"

"They're slightly out of sync," Emmy reported. "They're size-ten Skechers, but they're not the same shoes."

"What are you saying?"

"They're very similar, with circles on the soles. Unfortunately, the circles on Stoneman's shoes and the circles in the crime-scene photos don't line up the same way. We're definitely looking at two separate pairs of shoes."

"Crap," Kyle said. "So Stoneman may not be our guy?"

"Think about it," Emmy replied. "No GSR and the wrong shoes. We found DNA, but only on a single cartridge located inside the weapon. There was none at all on the outside."

"You're saying the DNA might have been planted," Kyle concluded.

"It's certainly a possibility," the lab tech returned.

Kyle paused a moment before he answered. "Thanks, Emmy," he said finally. "Better to know this sooner than later."

Hanging up, he immediately called the jail and spoke to the deputy in charge. "I've got a guy named Jack Stoneman in your lockup," he said. "There's a better than fifty-fifty chance he's not our guy. I need to talk to him, but he's lawyered up. See if you can find a phone number, preferably a cell, for his attorney of record."

Five minutes later, with the number in hand, Kyle Lasko phoned Gavin James. "My name's Detective Kyle Lasko with Phoenix PD," he said when the man answered. "I understand you're Jack Stoneman's attorney of record."

"That's correct," Gavin replied.

"I need you to contact your client," Kyle said before the attorney could comment further. "It has come to my attention that there are problems with some of our evidence—specifically with the shoes Mr. Stoneman was wearing at the time of his arrest. We originally thought they matched prints taken from the crime scene. We've now learned that the prints come from a different pair of shoes. Based on that I believe someone may be trying to set your client up."

"As in frame him?"

"Yes," Kyle replied. "I'm on my way to the jail right now. I need to speak to Mr. Stoneman to find out how he came to be in possession of the shoes he was wearing, and I can't speak to him without your presence."

"How soon will you be at the jail?"

"Twenty minutes, give or take."

"Fair enough," the attorney answered. "I'll meet you there."

When Kyle arrived at the jail, the interview rooms were exceptionally busy. "What's going on?"

"Shooting up in North Phoenix," the deputy told him. "Some poor guy got shot to death in his bed, and his wife has gone missing."

Kyle shook his head, grateful this new case had been handed off to someone else while he dealt with this one.

It turned out that Gavin James had arrived faster than Kyle had. Both he and his client were already waiting in an interview room. Not bothering with any niceties, Kyle turned on the recording equipment and cut straight to the chase. "Mr. Stoneman, where did you get the pair of Skechers you were wearing at the time of your arrest?"

"My Skechers?" Stoneman repeated, looking questioningly at his attorney without answering.

"Tell him about the latte lady," Gavin urged.

"What latte lady?" Kyle asked.

"When I'm up on Lincoln Drive, this nice lady stops by most days and gives me stuff," Stoneman answered. "Often it's a latte, but the other day she gave me a latte and a pair of shoes. It's the first time I've had new shoes in years."

"What does this lady look like?"

"She's older," Stoneman answered with a shrug. "I'd say somewhere in her sixties or maybe seventies. She's most likely a cancer patient, because she usually wears one of those bright pink scarves when she's out walking. But she's friendly, like she really cares about people."

"Do you know her name or where she lives?"

"No idea. I only see her when she walks by."

"Is this woman an Anglo?" Kyle asked. "Or Hispanic, maybe?"

"Anglo for sure."

"How old?"

"Like I said, it's hard to tell with women—fifties, sixties, or seventies. I'm not good at guessing women's ages."

"What color hair?"

"No idea," Stoneman answered. "I've never seen her hair—only her scarves."

"Did she happen to be carrying a bag when you saw her?"

"A bag?" Jack shook his head. "Not that I remember."

"What about those lattes she brought you?" Lasko asked. "Where do they come from?"

"Most of the time they're from Starbucks," Stoneman responded at once. "That's what the cups generally say, but I don't have any idea which one she uses."

"What kind of latte?"

"I think the one she brought me the other day is called pumpkin something—pumpkin pie or maybe pumpkin spice—in honor of Halloween. Come to think of it, she brought me the same flavor two days in a row—the day before Halloween and Halloween itself."

"Does she stop by at any special time?"

"Usually sometime around noon, a little before or a little after."

Kyle Lasko digested that information for a moment or so. "All right, Mr. Stoneman. I believe that the evidence we have now is insufficient for us to hold you any longer. You're free to go. Sorry for the inconvenience. Once you've been released and your property, other than the shoes, has been returned, I'll have an officer drive you back to your residence."

"That won't be necessary, Detective Lasko," Gavin assured him. "I'll be glad to give my client a ride home."

Kyle stood up and held the door open while a dazed and disbelieving Jack Stoneman stepped through it into the corridor.

"One more thing," Kyle said as he passed.

"What's that?"

"Would it be possible for you to stop by the department tomorrow morning and do a composite sketch of your latte lady?"

"Sure thing," Jack agreed at once. "I'll be glad to, but isn't tomorrow morning Father Andrew's funeral?"

Kyle nodded.

"Eleven a.m.," Gavin put in. "Why?"

"Father Andrew was always kind to me," Jack explained. "I'd like to attend his funeral and show my respects, but I'll be glad to come by the department after that."

"I can send someone to pick you up," Detective Lasko offered.

"Don't bother," Jack said. "As long as they return my bus pass, I can get wherever I need to go."

Kyle didn't walk back to his car when he left the jail—he sprinted, calling home as he ran. "It's going to be a late night," he told his wife,

Michelle, when she answered. "I just picked up a hot lead, so don't wait up."

Because of the earlier shooting, by the time Kyle made it back to Major Crimes, pickings were pretty thin, but he grabbed the people who were available, gave them a list of all the Starbucks locations in Phoenix proper, and sent them out canvassing, looking for customers who had purchased pumpkin-flavored lattes late in the morning hours of October 30 and October 31. Night-shift clerks most likely wouldn't have any firsthand knowledge, but they might be able to access relevant cash-register records and surveillance-video footage.

It was Kyle Lasko's fondest hope that somewhere out in latte land he'd find the woman who'd brought Jack Stoneman all those flavored iced drinks. If someone had tried to frame Stoneman for the murder of Father Andrew O'Toole, Kyle Lasko was pretty sure the so-called latte lady had something to do with it.

|CHAPTER 50|

Following an afternoon of incredibly luxurious spa treatments, Rachel finally returned to her room. She watched TV for a time, checking the local channels for any updates on the Lincoln Drive incident. The only mention was a brief announcement about Father O'Toole's upcoming funeral, at which Archbishop Francis Gillespie was expected to officiate. Smiling in satisfaction, Rachel switched off the television and got ready to go to dinner.

While at the spa, she'd had her makeup professionally applied, so all she needed to do was slip into her newly purchased duds—the stylish pantsuit along with that pair of Tory Burch heels. Once she topped her new outfit off with the wig she'd brought along, Rachel's transformation was complete.

Examining the results in the mirror, she was surprised. She looked like her old self—like the Rachel she'd been long ago, before David's untimely death had robbed her life of all meaning. Now her search for vengeance had given her back a sense of purpose, and in a way it had given her back her looks as well. Not only did she *look* younger, she *felt* younger.

She called for her car and then walked out to the valet stand to collect it. Years before, she and Rich had celebrated their twenty-fifth wedding anniversary at Vincent on Camelback, and she'd decided earlier in the day that was the restaurant where she would dine tonight.

Just after five thirty, she eased into the almost empty parking lot and handed her car keys over to the valet. Inside, she was greeted by a smiling woman at the hostess station.

"Do you have a reservation this evening?"

"No, I don't," Rachel said. "I was hoping maybe you could squeeze me in. My husband and I came here for an anniversary dinner years ago, and I've never forgotten it. My husband passed away recently. I came here on a whim, hoping to have a private remembrance of him."

The smile on the hostess's face vanished. "I'm so sorry for your loss," she murmured. "We're pretty full tonight, but let me see what I can do."

As the hostess walked away, Rachel marveled at how easy it had become to tell plausible lies. What would the hostess think if she knew exactly how recently Rich had passed away?

The woman returned a few minutes later with a sympathetic smile on her face. "I believe we'll be able to accommodate you. This way, please."

The hostess led Rachel to a quiet corner table that had been swiftly reset from a table for two to a table for one. The waiter arrived the moment the hostess departed. After he delivered her vodka tonic, she took her time studying the menu before choosing the duck tamale appetizer, followed by spinach salad. She settled on the lobster with pesto pasta as her entrée. For dessert she chose a raspberry soufflé.

Throughout Rachel's suitably delicious and sumptuous meal, the waiter hovered discreetly in the background, making small talk and doing his best to ensure she felt at ease. Clearly the hostess had passed on the word that this wasn't exactly a celebratory meal. When the server brought her check, it turned out the soufflé had been on the house. Rachel paid the bill from her roll of cash and gave both the waiter and the valet ridiculously large tips.

After exiting the restaurant parking lot, Rachel turned left and then left again onto North Fortieth, where she immediately pulled into a driveway and parked in the first available spot. Hauling the bag of electronics out of the trunk, she left the parking lot, crossed the street without benefit of a crosswalk, and then walked north to the bridge across the Arizona Canal. She strolled onto the bridge itself, dragging the loaded Rollaboard behind her. Then, during a brief break in traffic in both directions, she dropped the bag into the water. As she watched it sink out of sight, Rachel smiled, knowing that electronics and water don't exactly mix.

With her mission accomplished, Rachel hurried back to the car, noticing as she did so that her new shoes weren't as comfortable as she'd hoped they'd be. Back in her room, she undressed, slipped on the hotel robe, and laid out her clothing for the next morning. A little before nine, she switched on the TV in time for the early news. The lead-in promo was all about officers from Phoenix PD investigating the homicide of a man who had apparently been shot to death in his bed at a home in North Phoenix.

Rachel was utterly stunned. Before the newscast itself had even started, she already knew that someone must have discovered Rich's body. This was a disaster. She hadn't expected his body to be found so soon. By now the cops probably knew that Rachel herself was among the missing and might even have issued an APB for her and for her vehicle.

When she checked into the hotel, she'd had to show her ID in addition to using her Visa. Both were in her own name. If the cops were actively looking for her, what were the odds they'd find her before she had a chance to go to the funeral and do what needed to be done? Obviously she had to revise her plans. If the cops were looking for her Mercedes, maybe the best place for it to be was out of sight in the parking lot at the Phoenician, far from the prying eyes of passing patrol officers and traffic cameras.

She had planned on driving to the funeral in the morning, but now the playing field had changed. She would need to be up and out of the hotel bright and early, before anyone at the front desk saw a local news report and realized she was staying there. As for driving herself to Father O'Toole's funeral? That was no longer an option. She would have to find some other means of getting there.

Rachel sat for a long time trying to calm herself and searching for a feasible alternative. Eventually one came to mind, one that would send the cops looking in the wrong direction. She got up at once, dressed, packed her things, and then called down to the front desk.

"My father has been involved in a serious traffic accident down in Tucson and is currently undergoing surgery," Rachel told the clerk. "I won't be able to spend the night after all. Please close out my account and have my car brought around."

"I'm so sorry to hear that," the clerk said. "Will you need a copy of your folio, or should I e-mail it to you?"

Paying the bill would be someone else's problem. "Go ahead and e-mail it," Rachel said. "That will be fine."

At the valet stand, just to underscore her intentions, she asked the attendant for directions for the fastest route to Tucson. He obliged, of course, but Rachel barely listened. She already knew exactly where she was going.

Not daring to show her face at the front desk of another hotel, she would spend the night sleeping in her car, and the best place to abandon a vehicle would be in one of the several parking structures at Sky Harbor, where it might be days before someone would find it.

En route to the airport, she stopped off at a Safeway. Inside, she went straight to the front of the store, where from a display of Cardinals gear she picked out three oversize sweatshirts, several scarves, and two plush blankets. She left the store after paying for all the merchandise in cash.

If this stuff was good enough to keep football fans warm at nighttime games, they would be good enough keep her toasty that night.

At the airport Rachel circled the Terminal Three garage until she found a vacant spot between two hulking vehicles—a Chevrolet Suburban on one side and a Dodge Ram pickup truck on the other. Once she was parked, she donned her several layers of clothing and wrapped herself in blankets. Then, after leaning her seat back as far as it would go, Rachel closed her eyes and willed herself to sleep.

She would have to be up and out early in the morning, and she'd need to be on her toes.

|CHAPTER 51|

Kyle Lasko was at the computer in his cubicle trying to make some headway on reports when a call came in from one of his surveillance guys that changed everything.

"Hey, boss," Bill Wagner told him. "Are you sitting down?"

"I am. What's up?"

"We got a line on the lady with the beach bag. Surveillance video caught her exiting and entering a vehicle—an older-model Mercedes SEL—located in the parking lot of an office complex on Lincoln, half a mile away from our crime scene. She arrived at six thirty and left at seven forty-eight."

"Timeline fits perfectly," Kyle said. "Did you get a license?"

"Not from the parking lot, but we got it off a traffic camera a ways east of there at Camelback and Fortieth. The plate leads back to Rachel and Richard Higgins on Menadota Drive in Phoenix. There's a problem with that, however."

"What kind of problem?"

"There was a shooting at the Higgins residence earlier today—a homicide. The dead vic is Richard Higgins. His wife, Rachel, is MIA. She could be the doer, or she could be a second victim. Jury is still out on that."

"Who's lead?" Kyle asked.

"That would be Detective Horner."

"Got it," Kyle said. "I'll give him a call."

Seconds later Kyle was on the phone with Mason Horner. "I think our two homicides just crossed paths," Kyle told the other detective. "Someone driving a Mercedes SEL registered to Rachel and Richard Higgins was observed at the scene of a shooting on Lincoln Drive on Tuesday night."

"The one involving the archbishop?"

"That's the one."

"Holy moly," Horner said. "I'm here at the Higgins residence waiting for a search warrant. Care to join me?"

"Give me the address," Kyle answered. "I'll be there, Johnny-on-the-spot."

And he was. The exterior of the house on Menadota Drive was the usual crime-scene circus—lights, camera, action. Kyle found Detective Horner sitting quietly in his vehicle, smoking an illicit cigarette.

"What's going on?" Kyle asked as he slipped into the passenger seat.

"Victim's name is Richard Higgins. The ME's already come and gone. Next-door neighbor found the guy shot dead in his bed with a pillow covering his head. The neighbor was worried because the guy hadn't put his garbage cans out this morning."

"No sign of a struggle inside the home?"

"Nope, and no defensive wounds either. I think the poor guy was sound asleep when she plugged him."

Kyle noted the automatic assumption that the wife was the doer, but he didn't comment on that. "How long ago did it happen?" he asked.

"Probably sometime overnight last night, maybe right around one when 911 fielded a shots-fired call from Menadota Drive. Uniforms investigated but couldn't find the source. By the time first responders arrived today, rigor was already going away, so he died more than twelve hours earlier."

"Decomp?" Kyle asked.

"Mixed bag," Horner said. "Somebody tried to slow decomposition by turning the thermostat down to sixty-five degrees."

"And you're pretty sure the shooter is the wife?"

"Who else?" Horner replied. "And that's why we're not touching anything inside that house without a warrant in hand."

The paperwork arrived twenty minutes later. Walking into the house, Kyle was struck by how neat and clean it was. Nothing was out of place. Nothing was disturbed. It wasn't until they reached the room where the body had been found that things were different. Unlike the rest of the house, the dead man's bedroom was in shambles. Dirty clothes and trash littered the floor, and the air was thick with the odor of unwashed bedding.

Kyle sniffed the musty air and found only the barest trace of the distinctive odor of decaying flesh. Whoever had committed this crime had planned ahead.

Over the years Kyle Lasko and Mason Horner had teamed up on other cases, and they worked well together. They did a joint survey of the house with a CSI following their progress, photographing and inventorying each piece of evidence along the way.

As for the house? The place was clearly divided into two parts—one belonging to the wife and the other to their victim. On the basis of cleanliness alone, it seemed likely that Rachel laid claim to most of the common living spaces—the family room, kitchen, and living room. All those, along with the master bedroom, were neat as a pin. Empty spaces on the shelves in Rachel's closet suggested that pieces of luggage were missing, and the absence of toiletries on the bathroom countertop indicated she had packed up her goods and taken off.

Richard's room, on the other hand, was a mess, not due to any kind of struggle but because the man had most likely been a slob. Dirty clothes spilled out of an overflowing hamper and littered the floor. Both the tub and the basin in his bathroom were caked with grime, and the toilet was filthy enough to make Kyle gag. The toilet-paper holder was empty. A half-used roll sat on the floor next to an overflowing trash can.

"Whoever looked after the rest of the house never came in here," he muttered over his shoulder to Mason.

There had been one notable exception to the room's general air of slovenliness—an old-fashioned rolltop desk parked in a corner under a window and next to the sliding mirrored closet doors. Under the distinctive tambour, they found an older-model Toshiba laptop with most of the letters worn off the keyboard, along with a ledger-style checkbook. Their search warrant included electronic devices, but since the computer was password-protected, examining that would have to wait for another day and for someone with more tech skills than either of the homicide cops possessed.

The desk itself had three drawers. The shallow long one over the kneehole contained the usual items—pens, pencils, paper clips, stamps. The medium-size drawer to the right of that held Post-it notes, boxes of envelopes, and stationery, but in the bottom file-folder-size drawer they found a treasure trove of materials. Obviously Richard had been a fanatic when it came to keeping track of the family finances.

The file folder labeled "Bank of America" contained records for the couple's joint checking account. Another folder held monthly statements for his-and-her Visa cards, both with zero balances according to the latest statement. Richard evidently hadn't liked paying interest on carry-over balances. Their Verizon bill listed charges and calls for two phones. When Mason tried dialing the first number, a phone rang in the pocket of a pair of jeans on the floor beside the bed. When he dialed the second one, it went straight to voice mail.

The last bedroom they entered was the master. Compared to the dead man's slovenly digs, this was night and day. The bed was made. The drawers were neatly arranged. The counter in the bathroom was completely empty, and the basin and shower were both pristinely clean.

It wasn't until they started searching the closet and located a hatbox that they finally hit pay dirt.

"Well, well, well," Detective Horner said as he lifted a hatbox down from a shelf in the closet and removed the lid. "What have we here?"

The topmost item was a copy of St. Francis High School's 2001 *Clarion*. When Horner opened it, the pages fell open, seemingly on their own, to the one featuring the swim team where the face of the coach had been completely blacked out.

Wordlessly, Detective Horner passed the open book to Kyle. He studied the photo first and then read the caption at the bottom. David Higgins was front and center as the captain. And the name of the blacked-out coach in the back row was Father Paul Needham. Seeing the name was enough to make the hair on the back of Kyle's neck stand on end.

"What do you think that's all about?" Horner asked.

"I believe we've just found the reason Rachel Higgins is after Archbishop Gillespie," Kyle said.

"You think she's the Lincoln Drive shooter?"

"I certainly do," said Kyle. "This also means that I owe someone named Ali Reynolds a serious apology."

Their examination of the hatbox alone took the better part of an hour.

By the time they finished sorting through the various items as well as printouts of Rachel Higgins's many Internet searches, Detective Horner, too, was reasonably sure that their suspect had a grudge against the Catholic Church in general and Archbishop Gillespie in particular, but they had no idea what she'd had against her husband.

The last place the detectives searched was the garage. There on the workbench, they found countless pieces of wood that had been smashed beyond all recognition.

"What the hell are these?" Kyle asked.

"Used to be birdhouses is my guess," Mason answered. "The neighbor told me Richard Higgins loved making birdhouses."

"Looks like Rachel didn't love them as much as he did," Kyle observed.

At midnight, finally finished with their search and while a CSI reinstalled crime-scene tape, the two detectives stood on the front porch with Horner smoking another cigarette while they took stock of where they were. The BOLO on Rachel Higgins had already been kicked over to an all-points bulletin, but Kyle and Mason knew that in this day and age the most effective way to follow someone's movements would be by tracking their devices. Unfortunately, just like searching the dead man's computer, that took technical skill beyond their capability and warrants beyond the scope of what they'd used to search the house itself. Hoping to divide and conquer, they returned to their respective desks at Phoenix PD where Mason went after the financial institutions while Kyle worked on the cell-phone provider.

They both knew that middle-of-the-night warrants were not easy to come by, but even with warrants in hand, getting the folks at overnight call centers to respond to their requests for information was iffy at best. The cell-phone provider came through first. Unfortunately, the last time Rachel's phone had pinged had been around 8:46 a.m. on Thursday, from a cell phone tower less than half a mile from Menadota Drive, most likely while Rachel was still at home. After that the phone had been turned off.

Visa finally came through around three in the morning, noting that a large-purchase transaction from the Phoenician Resort had been posted around 9:00 the previous evening. Less than thirty minutes later Kyle and Mason were displaying their respective badges in the spacious lobby of the Phoenician.

"I remember her well," a helpful desk clerk told them. "Ms. Higgins called down to the desk late in the evening—sometime around nine, I think. She said she wouldn't be able to stay the night because her father had been injured in an accident somewhere in or around Tucson and that he'd been airlifted to Banner Medical Center, where he was undergoing surgery. She said she needed to check out and asked me to call for her car. She said she didn't need a paper copy of the bill—that I should just e-mail her a copy of the folio."

"What about the valet?" Kyle asked.

"The people who were working then are off duty now," the clerk continued, "but I can get the head guy on the phone if you'd like."

They did. When the parking crew chief answered, Mason put his phone on speaker. "Sure I remember her," he said in answer to Mason's question. "Before she drove off, she asked me about the best way to get to Tucson."

"What say we check with the hospital?" Mason asked when the call ended and they were walking back through the lobby toward their cars. Kyle heard only Mason's side of the conversation, but it was enough to tell him that no such patient had turned up at Banner Medical Center the previous afternoon or evening.

"So she was trying to send us down a two-hundred-mile rabbit hole," Kyle concluded as Mason ended the call. "I wonder if the guys at the airport have gotten around to checking their parking lots."

They hadn't. "I've got the APB right here in front of me," the captain in charge told Kyle, "but we've been busy as hell tonight, and we're also shorthanded. Once the day-shift guys come on duty, we'll have someone grab the Segway and do a survey. If you need it sooner than that, you'll have to come do it yourself."

"Thanks," Kyle said, silencing a more sarcastic, *Thanks a lot!* After he ended the phone call, he turned to Mason.

"I don't know about you, but I'm beat," he added. "It's four a.m. I've been up and working nonstop since eight o'clock yesterday morning. What say we call it a night and tackle this again after we both get some shut-eye?"

"Sounds good to me," Horner replied. "Let's call it a day."

|CHAPTER 52|

Originally Ali had planned to stay at home in Sedona on Thursday night. When news of the Menadota Drive shooting surfaced, though, things changed. She gathered her clothing and headed back to Phoenix, having been invited by Archbishop Gillespie to stay at the residence rather than in a hotel.

On the way down, she worried that she'd be arriving too late, but as she approached the manor-style residence, rows of windows on both stories were brightly lit, and the vehicle directly in front of hers in the porte cochere was a racing-red Ferrari Portofino. It was new enough that a temporary license plate was still attached to the back window.

As Ali stepped out of the car, Sister Anselm came to greet her. "For a moment there, I thought I'd taken a wrong turn and wound up at one of Agatha Christie's famous house parties," Ali said, gesturing toward the Ferrari.

"Gavin James is here," Sister Anselm explained, helping with the luggage. "He's waiting to talk to you."

The last bag out of the car was the one from Sister Sarah containing Sister Anselm's habit.

"If Gavin is here, does that mean something's wrong?" Ali asked.

"Not at all," Sister Anselm said. "We're gathered in the drawing room, where Sister Anne has laid out some refreshments."

Gavin rose to his feet to greet Ali as she entered the room. "So glad to see you," he said. "I wanted to give you the good news in person. Jack Stoneman has been released from custody."

"Really?" Ali asked in astonishment. "How did that happen?"

"It turns out that discrepancy you were worried about—the thing with the shoe-print evidence—was on the money. Detective Lasko let Jack go due to lack of evidence, but they kept his shoes on the suspicion that they might have been used in an attempt to frame Jack. The poor guy had to walk out of the building in a pair of jailhouse scuffs. Not to worry, though. I took him shopping before I dropped him off at home. Got him a pair of Skechers to replace the ones in the evidence room and a dressier pair of shoes along with some slightly more suitable clothing—a new shirt and a new pair of pants—for him to wear to Father Andrew's funeral tomorrow. I told him I'll come by in the morning to take him to the cathedral."

"That was very kind of you," Ali said.

Gavin grinned back at her. "Let's just say I owe a huge debt of gratitude to Archbishop Gillespie."

Ali glanced around the room. The members of her proposed posse were all there—Fathers McCray, Winston, and Mike, along with Sister Anselm, but the archbishop himself was nowhere in sight.

"Speaking of whom," Ali began. "Where's the patient?"

"Believe it or not," Sister Anselm replied, "he admitted he might have overdone things today and went to bed early. He has a nine a.m. appointment at the cathedral tomorrow so Father Howard can hear his confession."

"Is his going to confession a good idea?" Ali asked.

"Whether it is or isn't, good luck trying to talk him out of it," Sister Anselm harrumphed. "But Father Mike has agreed to drive him there, so at least he'll be in good hands. Father Mike will also be in charge of the archbishop's wheelchair during the service."

"Well, then," Ali said, "there've been a few developments on our end, and with the archbishop out of earshot I need to bring you all up to date."

She did, clueing them in on what had happened on Menadota Drive and the very real likelihood that Rachel Higgins was the archbishop's would-be assassin. She went on to explain the iPad-based facial-recognition protocol they would be using at the funeral and ended up handing out Tasers. In addition, she had brought along B.'s Kevlar vest. Since Father Winston looked to be the closest fit, she gave that one to him.

Later Ali went upstairs to a guest room that was far more spartan than her room at the Biltmore had been the night before. She was undressed and about to climb into bed when a text came in from Detective Lasko.

I need to speak to you. Please
give me a call.

"Oh, no you don't," Ali said into her phone, replying aloud to his request rather than texting back or phoning him. "You're probably going to tell me to stand down, and I don't need to hear it."

|CHAPTER 53|

Despite Rachel's hopes she barely slept—she was too cold, miserable, and uncomfortable. She'd turned on the engine occasionally overnight, both to get warm and to recharge her burner phone. In the course of those wakeful hours, she compulsively checked the online news.

As far as Rachel was concerned, the news from Phoenix PD concerning what they termed "the incident on Menadota Drive" was devastating. The male homicide victim had been identified, but that information was being withheld pending notification of next of kin. Just because the information wasn't being released to the media didn't mean the cops were sitting on it. By now every law-enforcement officer in the Valley was probably looking for her, and if they had found her hatbox and looked through what was inside, what were the chances she'd be able to get anywhere near the Cathedral of the Holy Mother, much less gain entrance to the sanctuary?

By the time morning came and traffic picked up inside the garage, Rachel had concocted a plan. This was a Catholic funeral honoring a priest. Who would be there? Nuns and priests, most likely, lots of them. Maybe with a little help from a costume shop, Rachel would be able to blend in.

According to the Internet, there were only three year-round costume shops operating in the Phoenix Metropolitan Area, and the closest one of those was near Metrocenter. At 7:00 a.m., still chilled to the bone, Rachel unloaded her luggage from the trunk. With her bulky cataract sunglasses covering much of her face, she strolled into the terminal.

Fortunately, there were a few restaurants operating outside the security lines, and she was able to grab some breakfast before taking a cab to the costume shop. The cabdriver, sullen and reeking of too many cigarettes, exchanged barely a word with her during the half-hour drive, and that was fine. He cheered up when she offered him fifty bucks to wait for her while she picked out a costume.

She was there at nine thirty when the shop's doors opened for the day, and a smiling clerk stepped forward to greet her.

"We're having an after-Halloween costume party at lunch today at my assisted-living place," Rachel said, spinning out a string of lies with practiced ease. "I've decided to go as Sister Mary Frances, who was my third-grade teacher. Can you help me? Would you happen to have any nun habits in stock?"

They did, of course, and Rachel returned to her waiting cab half an hour later carrying a bag that contained what she felt would be a fool-proof disguise. Not wanting to use the same cab she'd taken from the airport to go to the funeral, she asked to be driven to the mall itself.

Once inside the mall, she located the nearest restroom and used that to change into her new duds. Fortunately, the rented habit came complete with prodigious pockets. She stuffed the Ruger, her three-by-five confession cards, the Disneyland snapshot, and the rest of her cash into one of those. Then, dressed as a nun, she divested herself of everything else by strolling through the mall, dragging an almost empty Rollaboard behind her, and dropping bits and pieces of her remaining possessions—purse, clothing, and cosmetics—into trash cans along the way.

Rachel had called for a cab the moment she finished changing her clothes, but it turned out that getting a cab at the shopping mall was a lot more challenging than catching one from the airport. She soon realized she should have kept the cab she'd used to get from the costume shop to the mall. As time went by and hers still didn't show up, she became more and more frantic. It took three more increasingly hostile calls before the cab finally arrived. When it did so, it was already 11:10, and the mall was a good twenty minutes away from where she needed to be.

"Sorry," the driver apologized as she climbed into the backseat.

Sorry didn't cover it, not nearly. "Just hurry," she said. "The funeral's already started."

|CHAPTER 54|

As Father Mike rolled Archbishop Gillespie's wheelchair into the nave of the Cathedral of the Holy Mother at ten to nine, Francis breathed a deep sigh. Entering this holy place always made him feel as though he was coming home.

The cathedral was built during the sixties by an architect whose guiding principle had been simplicity rather than ostentation. The building was constructed with an east-west orientation. The main entrance faced the afternoon sun, while behind the altar six narrow but soaring floor-to-ceiling stained-glass windows captured the morning rays. Today those windows colored the entire sanctuary with glowing slices of jewel-shaded sunlight. One of those splashed across Father Andrew's casket, already laid in its place of honor at the head of the center aisle.

Banks of flowers were arrayed on either side of the casket. Father Andrew had always loved flowers, and Archbishop Gillespie knew he would have been pleased by the massive floral display.

"The temporary ramp they put in yesterday is over there on the left," Father Mike was saying, pointing. "The procession will turn left at the casket, and then we'll make our way up onto the dais."

Francis Gillespie was well aware of the effort installing that ramp must have taken. Someone, Father Daniel most likely, must have moved heaven and earth to make it happen.

"The confessional is right back there," Father Mike told Francis, pointing off to the right side of the vestibule. "Father Howard is probably already there." Archbishop Gillespie knew full well where the confessional was, but he allowed himself to be bossed around.

Although the Cathedral of the Holy Mother was the archbishop's home church, the priest in charge on a day-to-day basis was Father John Howard. He was also Francis's usual confessor. At breakfast Ali had told Archbishop Gillespie what had gone on the day before. He now knew that a woman named Rachel Higgins was most likely the person who'd murdered not only Father Andrew but also her own husband. There could be little doubt that she was intent on murdering Francis Gillespie as well.

Considering everything Ali had told him about what had happened to the Higgins family, Francis could hardly blame the poor deranged creature for what she'd done. Once confession was over and he'd said the required Hail Marys, he planned to spend whatever time remained between then and the service in solitary prayer.

Having been exposed to Ali's very real concerns that Rachel might come for him today, Francis realized that this period of quiet counted as the calm before the storm. Confession would put Francis Gillespie's spiritual affairs in order. After that it would be time for the archbishop to turn to his favorite Bible verse of all time, Psalm 46:10: "Be still and know that I am God." Shielded by that, he would face whatever came his way with a joyful heart.

Father Mike wheeled the chair over to the door of the confessional and helped the archbishop enter.

"I'll be right outside whenever you're ready," Father Mike said.

"If you don't mind," Archbishop Gillespie said, "I'd like you to leave me here until it's time for the procession to start. If you'll bring my vestments, I'll put them on inside the confessional."

"You want me to leave you here?" Father Mike asked. "Alone and in the dark?"

"Yes," the archbishop said. "Sometimes being alone in the dark is the only way to find the light."

|CHAPTER 55|

Cami and Stu showed up at the residence at ten past eight, moments after Father Mike and the archbishop had departed. Once again Ali was impressed by the way Stu took charge of the gathering in the drawing room, explaining to the impromptu posse how the iPads had been set so that once the camera on each iPad was activated, it would run continuously until the device ran out of battery power. He showed them how the iPads should be held to provide the widest possible angle for the camera lenses. Finally he produced a paper showing the layout of the cathedral's entrances and interior, pointing out where each person would be stationed in order to provide maximum coverage.

"All right," Father Winston said when Stu finished. "What happens if we find her?"

"The screen on the affected iPad will go full red. When that happens, Frigg will be notified, and she'll send texts to everyone, letting us know and directing everyone to the target's location inside the church. The idea is to surround the suspect and isolate her in such a way as to mitigate any potential damage."

"And the Tasers?" Father Winston asked.

"You have to be within fifteen feet of the target before one of those works," Cami explained. "Hitting her with the darts will disable her long enough to disarm her, and that's the whole point. She obviously has a lethal weapon and isn't afraid to use it."

"I always thought churches were supposed to be gun-free zones," Father McCray observed sadly.

"Trust me," Cami said. "If Rachel Higgins shows up today, the cathedral won't be a gun-free zone for anybody. That's why the rest of us are using Tasers. We can't run the risk of setting off a barrage of gunfire inside the church. If innocent bystanders end up being zapped by Tasers in the melee, at least they won't be dead. Questions?"

With no further comments, and with no objections either, it was up to Stu to end the pre-encounter briefing. "All right, then," he said. "I suspect that people are going to start showing up at the cathedral early. The doors open at ten. I want you all inside and at your designated stations ten minutes before that. Got it?"

"Got it," Father Winston said. "We'll be there."

|CHAPTER 56|

When Kyle Lasko reached for his ringing cell phone at eight o'clock on Friday morning, he hadn't had nearly enough sleep. He was frustrated that despite an exhausting overnight effort the search for Rachel Higgins had come up empty. On less than three hours of sleep, he now had to contend with a phone call from Captain Robard.

"Lasko here," he mumbled into the phone.

"I know you and Horner both worked until all hours, but we just got word that Rachel Higgins's SEL is on the third floor of the Terminal Three parking garage at Sky Harbor Airport."

That snapped Kyle wide awake. "I'll be right there," he said.

He was, and so was Detective Horner. Without a search warrant covering the vehicle, the best they could do to begin with was inspect it from outside.

"Looks to me like she slept in the car," Mason said.

Kyle nodded. "We can check with TSA to see if she cleared security and flew out somewhere, but my guess is she didn't."

And she hadn't, but determining that for sure took them the better part of two hours. "What now?" Mason asked.

"If Rachel's still gunning for Archbishop Gillespie, she'll be at Father O'Toole's funeral," Kyle told him, "and we'd better be there, too."

"Should we call in SWAT?" Mason asked. "Bring in an army of uniforms and make a show of force?"

Kyle Lasko knew about Chief Adolfo's involvement in the case. Mason Horner did not. Kyle worried that a visible police presence might very well set Rachel off. With a church full of mourners in possible danger and with the likelihood that the chief would be among them, that wasn't a risk Kyle was willing to take.

Ali hadn't bothered responding to his earlier text, but as he and Detective Horner left the TSA command post, Kyle sent her a second, more urgent message.

> We've posted an APB on Rachel
> Higgins. She's likely the Lincoln
> Drive shooter. Call me. Now.

Ali called back almost immediately. "If you're expecting me to stand down," she said, "you can forget it."

"Rachel's given us the slip," he told her, deciding in that moment that it was time to treat this woman as a capable ally instead of the opposition. "I'm guessing she's on her way to the funeral. What do you have going?"

"We've got facial rec on Rachel Higgins running at all entrances. My people are carrying Tasers only. No handguns—way too many chances for collateral damage."

Considering his concerns about potentially turning the Cathedral of the Holy Mother into a shooting gallery, Ali's plan made sense.

"Good call," Kyle said. "If you can bring her down, you'll need sworn officers on hand to place her under arrest. I'll be there, and so will Detective Mason Horner, the lead detective on the Richard Higgins case."

"Rachel shot him?" Ali asked.

"That's the theory," Kyle replied, "but at the moment it's too thin to prosecute. We'll need to locate the weapon she used to kill her husband. Chances are," he added, "she probably still has it."

"All right," Ali said after a pause. "My people are on the job. See you when you get here. I'll be stationed on the left-hand side of the main entrance."

"Okay, on our way."

|CHAPTER 57|

Archbishop Francis Gillespie sat in the quiet gloom of the confessional and prayed without ceasing. He paid no attention to the hushed conversations as mourners gathered to honor Father Andrew. Had he focused on the people out in the cathedral's vestibule, he might have been derailed into wondering whether Rachel Higgins was already outside waiting for him. No, thinking that way might have disrupted his concentration. His original intent had been to save the soul of whoever was targeting him. That seemed unlikely now.

After chapel that morning and before going to breakfast, he'd asked Father Mike to wheel him into his study. There, seated at his desk for possibly the last time, he had used the Montblanc pen from Cardinal Moser to write a letter. With his arm in a sling and his body encased in a layer of body armor that felt like a straitjacket, that wasn't easy, but once it was written, he sealed the letter in an envelope and dropped it on Father Daniel's desk on the way out.

During breakfast Ali had brought everyone up to speed. There hadn't yet been any public announcements about the murder of Richard Higgins, but somehow Ali had access to details of the investigation that had not yet been released. How, the archbishop wondered, did she know that not only was Rachel Higgins the prime suspect in her husband's murder but also that she was most likely the person responsible for taking Father Andrew's life?

The archbishop regarded the fate of Richard and Rachel's son, David, as his own personal failure. Despite Francis's wholehearted effort to wipe the archdiocese clean of pedophilia, Father Needham had continued to practice his evil almost in plain sight. And it was the terrible loss of Rachel's beloved and tormented son that had driven her to this madness, because madness it was.

Despite High Noon's best efforts, she might well succeed, so if these were Francis's last few hours on earth, he would spend them in the best possible way—praying, forgiving, and asking forgiveness.

The archbishop had a long list. He started with the Higgins family and prayed for all of them—for Richard, Rachel, and David. For David especially, he prayed that the young man's death had indeed been accidental rather than deliberate. Next he prayed for all the other St. Francis boys who'd been abused by Father Needham and for the boys damaged by other predatory priests, both in his archdiocese and elsewhere, and he prayed for their families as well.

Next Francis prayed for all the people who had come to aid him in his time of need—the EMTs, doctors, and nurses who'd cared for him after the shooting, and for the people at High Noon who'd taken the threats against his life so very seriously. He went so far as to include a word of thankfulness to the Almighty for High Noon's strange but obviously very effective associate, an AI named Frigg.

Francis prayed for the immortal soul of Father Andrew and asked that Father Daniel might be comforted in his grief. He gave thanks for his long-lasting friendship with Sister Anselm and for the presence of her new partner, Sister Cecelia, who would, he hoped, be there to take over when it was time for Sister Anselm to lay down her own burdens.

At last, done with his church family, Francis turned his prayerful attention to his own family—giving thanks for his father and mother, his brothers and sisters, and for his niece, Marcella, whose occasional letters had continued to give him a window into his brother's life despite the decades of estrangement between them.

Finished at last, Francis was in the process of praying for the courage to face whatever dangers this day might hold when there was a light tap on the door of the confessional.

"It's time," Father Mike said from outside. "I'm here with your vestments, and I'll help you into them."

By the time the archbishop was properly dressed, it was 10:55, only five minutes before the procession was due to start. Francis knew that five minutes of small talk were probably all he could manage. Father Mike, already wearing a set of borrowed vestments, helped Archbishop Gillespie don his own.

"I'll be seated next to you on the dais," Father Mike said as he opened the door to face the crowd. "If you need anything, let me know."

Archbishop Gillespie had conducted countless funeral Masses over his lifetime, but this one was far too close to his heart. Father Andrew's mother, Barbara, had selected the music. As the congregation sang "Loved One, Farewell," Father Mike slipped the archbishop into his spot in the processional and wheeled him down the center aisle.

The acoustics in the cathedral were perfect. As the words "Friend of our happy days; brother of prayer and praise" rose to fill the sanctuary, Archbishop Gillespie felt a hard lump form in his throat. Yes, he and Father Andrew had indeed been friends in prayer and praise, but now was not the time for Francis to succumb to his own private grief. His job today was to comfort others. As Father Mike rolled him up the makeshift ramp, Francis pulled it together, and when it came time for him to speak, he was ready. His voice didn't waver as he greeted the congregation and introduced Father Andrew's good friend Father Daniel to deliver the first reading.

It occurred to Archbishop Gillespie then that if the facial-recognition surveillance team hadn't located Rachel Higgins by now, maybe she wasn't coming.

|CHAPTER 58|

As the procession left the vestibule and started down the center aisle, Ali breathed a sigh of relief. Of course it was possible Rachel had managed to slip through their facial-rec screening, but she doubted it. Everyone on the team had been on high alert. As for Archbishop Gillespie? She'd caught a glimpse of him as Father Mike rolled him into his place of honor. He sat with his hands on his knees, his face solemn but composed. He didn't look like someone worried about an assassin's bullet.

She had spoken briefly to Detectives Lasko and Horner when they arrived, shortly before the service started. Once she'd pointed out each member of her security team, the two detectives had opted to enter the sanctuary, where they took seats in separate pews, one a third of the way down the aisle and the other at the two-thirds point. Strategically, that made sense. If an attack were forthcoming, front or back, one of them would be close to the action.

Nothing in the two officers' understated arrival had announced a police presence, but Ali was grateful to have sworn officers on the scene. If all hell broke loose, she was confident that High Noon's people could bring Rachel Higgins down, but having cops available to take her into custody would be best for all concerned. And if it turned out Tasers weren't enough to do the job, it would be better for High Noon to have law-enforcement bullets ricocheting off the cathedral walls rather than civilian ones.

The vast church was full but not overflowing. After the second scriptural reading, Archbishop Gillespie delivered a poignant homily. Then, as the congregation sang chorus after chorus of "Amazing Grace," Father Howard stepped forward to serve Communion.

Engrossed in the Mass, Ali was surprised when the iPad in her arms suddenly lit up. Startled, she looked around. A latecomer to the funeral, a nun, had quietly entered the church behind Ali and had just walked past. With the center aisle clogged by communicants, the newcomer made a beeline for the aisle that ran along the wall on the left-hand side of the sanctuary.

Ali's first thought was that maybe this was some glitch in the facial-rec software. Then it dawned on her—the woman who was dressed as a nun wasn't. She was Rachel Higgins. As other members of the team received their notifications from Frigg and turned to look in Ali's direction, she, too, hurried toward the side aisle, pointing as she went and reaching for her Taser.

|CHAPTER 59|

Sitting quietly on the dais during the Eucharist, Archbishop Gillespie was the first to see the latecomer dart into the sanctuary. He understood at once that she was an impostor. No real nun would have entered the cathedral without pausing to genuflect and cross herself. No, the new arrival had to be Rachel Higgins herself, masquerading as a nun.

Prior to setting foot on the dais, Father Mike had told the archbishop if he needed to leave for any reason, all he had to do was say so. Wanting to face the threat head-on and confine it to as small an area as possible, Francis touched Father Mike's knee and nodded in the direction of the wheelchair ramp.

"Are you ill?" Father Mike whispered as he hurried to comply.

"I need to leave," Archbishop Gillespie replied urgently. "Use the side aisle, please."

The side aisle was crowded, too, with people returning to their pews after receiving Communion. "Sorry, coming through," the archbishop said, motioning them out of the way.

As members of Ali's team hurried in that direction from other parts of the sanctuary, members of the congregation seemed to tumble to the idea that something was amiss. Although the organ kept on playing, the singing faltered and "Amazing Grace" came to a ragged halt. By the time the archbishop was face-to-face with the make-believe nun, the organ music had faded away as well.

There was no gun visible in the woman's hands. It might have been concealed in a pocket, but that was a good thing. Had someone seen the weapon and sounded the alarm, there would likely have been a wholesale stampede toward the door.

As his wheelchair came to a stop, Francis paused long enough to say a silent prayer of thanksgiving that Rachel hadn't come out shooting—at least not yet. And if this was indeed his time to die, he wasn't going to be a coward about it.

"Rachel Higgins, I presume," he said firmly. "I'm Archbishop Gillespie. I believe you wished to see me."

In a cathedral blessed with perfect acoustics, the archbishop's booming voice reverberated throughout the space. Beyond Rachel stood Ali, Taser in hand.

"Let her be, Ali," Archbishop Gillespie ordered. "Rachel came here with something to say. Let's hear what it is."

"You killed my son," she snarled.

"I did not kill your son, but I'm certainly responsible for his death. For that I am very sorry," he said. "David was one of Father Needham's unfortunate victims, and that happened on my watch. As soon as I became aware of the situation, I put a stop to it."

"But not soon enough," Rachel shot back. "The damage was already done. David died of a drug overdose, but what really killed him was the abuse perpetrated against him, and you're the one who should have prevented it. The Catholic Church should have prevented it."

That's when the gun appeared, as she extricated it from the folds of her habit. Alarmed people in nearby pews scrambled to distance themselves from danger, but Archbishop Gillespie held his ground.

"I'm very sorry for your loss," he said, "but you're right. I failed your son—failed your whole family—and that failure did incalculable damage. But killing me won't bring your David back, and it won't bring your husband back either. If you decide to splatter this holy place with my blood, you may kill me, but you won't harm the Catholic Church. It will still be standing, long after I'm dead and gone and long after you've been hauled away to prison. So shoot me if you must, but please aim carefully. You've already taken one innocent life—please don't take any others. I'm so sorry for what's happened to you and your family, Rachel, but don't make it worse."

For a long moment, it was as though the people inside the cathedral were all holding their breath. No one moved. No one spoke. And then, without another word, Rachel surrendered the weapon to the archbishop and raised her hands. It was over.

By then Detective Lasko had shouldered his way past Ali. Holding a pair of cuffs, he wrenched Rachel's arms down behind her back and cuffed her wrists together.

"Rachel Higgins," he said, "I'm placing you under arrest for the murders of Father Andrew O'Toole and Richard Higgins."

Rachel stood there for a moment with her head bowed. As Detective Lasko prepared to lead her away, she raised it again and gave the archbishop a piercing look.

"At least you said you're sorry," she murmured. "Those are words I never thought I'd hear."

"I *am* sorry, my child," he said. "And I'll be praying for your immortal soul."

"Don't bother," she hissed back at him. "I'm not afraid of going to hell. I've been living there for years."

"Yes," the archbishop said quietly, "but if you ever ask for forgiveness, it shall be granted."

With that, Detective Lasko, joined by someone the archbishop didn't recognize—another cop, most likely—stationed themselves on either side of her, took hold of her arms, and escorted her back up the aisle the same way she had come.

"Thank you, Father," Archbishop Gillespie whispered aloud. "Thank you for your many blessings."

|CHAPTER 60|

Having just witnessed what had to have been a miracle, Ali eased her Taser back into her purse. For the longest time, no one in the congregation moved or uttered a word. It was as if they'd all been frozen in place—some in their pews and some still standing in the aisle awaiting Communion. Then Archbishop Gillespie broke the silence.

"Please take me back to the dais, Father Mike," he said. "I would like to take Communion today along with everyone else."

Then, to Ali's astonishment, Father Howard picked up exactly where he'd left off, almost as though nothing had happened. The organ started up again, and soon the congregation returned to singing "Amazing Grace," more softly than before, but she had the sense that as the familiar words came from the singers' mouths, they did so with a whole new meaning.

After receiving his own Communion, the archbishop closed the service by reciting the Lord's Prayer, joined by every person in the Cathedral of the Holy Mother. For Ali in particular, and most likely for everyone else who heard them, those words resonated more powerfully than ever before. Everyone there had been within a matter of feet from what could have turned into a mass shooting, and yet they'd all walked away unscathed. Was it the calming words of Archbishop Gillespie that had saved them, or was it something else? Someone else?

The recessional was a song Ali had never heard before—"When I Come to the End of the Road"—and it seemed entirely appropriate, not only for Father Andrew O'Toole but also for Rachel Higgins. She hadn't died today, but in every way that mattered, her life was over. There would probably be years of court proceedings before her fate was ultimately determined, but for now she no longer posed a danger to anyone other than herself.

Since Father O'Toole was returning to Pennsylvania for burial in the family plot, the casket, along with all the masses of flowers, remained in the church when everyone left. Ali glanced back in that direction as she departed and saw a single multicolored ray from the stained-glass windows crowning the top of the polished wood casket, almost as though it were bestowing a final blessing. For some reason that, too, seemed oddly appropriate.

There was a public gathering in the cathedral's social hall. After that a much smaller group headed back to the archbishop's residence, where, in the main dining room, Sister Anne had produced a sumptuous buffet luncheon.

Approaching Archbishop Gillespie's head table, Ali was surprised to see Jack Stoneman—a clean-shaven, neatly dressed Jack Stoneman—sitting there chatting with the archbishop while Gavin James looked on from the sidelines.

"I'm so sorry about Father O'Toole," she heard Jack say. "I'll be forever grateful for his kindness, and I can't thank you enough for bringing Mr. James on board."

"You're most welcome," the archbishop said. "I'm glad I could be of help, but I believe I had some outside help on that score," he added, giving Ali a wink that neither Jack nor Gavin could see.

Sister Anselm, now in civilian clothing, was back to fussing. "You mustn't overdo," she warned her patient. "Officiating at the funeral was one thing, but playing host to a whole group like this . . ."

"I can manage, Sister Anselm," he told her. "If being at that funeral this morning didn't kill me, I'm a lot tougher than you give me credit for."

Ali could see that Sister Anselm didn't appreciate what came dangerously close to being a reprimand. When she walked off to stand by herself for a while, Ali went to join her.

"He is tough," Ali noted. "Rachel Higgins came to that funeral determined to kill him, and he talked her down."

"That may well be," Sister Anselm retorted, not the least bit mollified, "but that doesn't change the fact that he's my patient and he's still just a matter of hours out of the ICU."

Ali had been concerned that Detectives Lasko and Horner might turn up at the residence, asking too many questions about how exactly the folks from High Noon had known as much as they knew, but the investigators must have had other fish to fry, and they didn't make an appearance. For the time being, it looked as though Frigg's assistance in solving the case would go unnoticed, and that was all to the good.

Toward the end of the early-afternoon luncheon, Father Daniel entered the room looking distressed and holding an envelope. He went straight to Archbishop Gillespie, and the two men huddled together for some time, speaking back and forth in urgent but hushed tones. Finally the archbishop pulled away and tapped on his glass with a spoon, silencing the general conversation.

"I left Father Daniel a message earlier today, which he will forward to the proper authorities in due time," Archbishop Gillespie announced. "For now it's not fair to leave him carrying the burden of that message all on his own. The letter tenders my resignation as archbishop of the Phoenix Archdiocese."

Audible gasps erupted around the room. Ali looked quickly in Sister Anselm's direction and saw that her friend's face had suddenly gone paler than usual.

"I was brought on board to deal with some very specific problems here in the archdiocese," the archbishop continued. "Some of those had already come to light by the time I arrived. Others, like the one with Father Needham, didn't surface until later. Father O'Toole's unfortunate death and what happened today are the final culmination of that shameful story. And now that it's over, I need to put it behind me as well.

"I've had a good run. I loved working here with Father Daniel and Father Andrew. And I've loved working with the nuns and priests who are always on hand doing the Lord's work. But I'm old. I no longer have the kind of stamina it takes to do this job. And now, after years of mending the church's fences, I have some fence mending of my own to do.

"Some of you know that I have an older brother named Anthony from whom I've been estranged for decades. He's in ill health and confined to an assisted-living facility in Green Bay, Wisconsin. Once I turn in my miter, that's the first place I'm going—to Green Bay to see if there's any way to put the quarrel between my brother and me to rest while there's still time.

"After that there's a monastery near Santa Fe that takes in broken-down priests like me and puts us out to pasture. So with that, and before Sister Anselm pitches a complete fit, I'm going to ask Father Mike here to wheel me back to my quarters so I can have a lie-down. She's right, you know, I'm not as young as I used to be, and for that matter, Sister Anselm, neither are you."

For the first time in a long time, it appeared as though Archbishop Francis Gillespie had had the last word.

Ali had been invited to spend a second night, but she declined. Instead, at three o'clock, once again in full afternoon traffic made worse by its being Friday, she headed home, first up the 51 to the 101 before eventually merging onto I-17. As she inched along, she found herself looking around at the bright blue sky above the desert scenery, and it was as though, for the first time in months, she was seeing it—as though the dark clouds left behind by Alex Munsey's death had finally lifted. Maybe the challenges of the last few days had been enough to drag her out of the doldrums.

Somewhere north of Cordes Junction, she called B.

"So it's over, then," he marveled when she finished telling him the story. "The killer's in jail, and nobody else got hurt."

"That's how it looks," Ali replied. "I can't help but feel sorry for Rachel, though. She lost everything, yet all it took for her to hand over her weapon was for someone to finally get around to saying he was sorry."

"Didn't the cops wonder how it was that you were always one step ahead of them?"

"They might have wondered," Ali allowed, "but they didn't ask."

"Sounds like a job well done," B. said. "So I guess you can hang up your Wonder Woman costume for the time being."

They both laughed at that, but then B. fell quiet. "I'm going to miss Archbishop Gillespie," he said finally. "From the moment I met the man, I felt like he was my rock. Now, after everything we did—and especially after what you did—to save him, with him retiring, it sounds as though we're going to lose him anyway."

"You must not have read the fine print," Ali said.

"What fine print?" a puzzled B. asked.

"It's all part of the grand bargain," Ali replied. "If you let yourself care about someone, it's always with the understanding that someday, one way or another, you're going to lose them. I felt the same way when Leland Brooks went back to the UK, and I know I'll feel that way again when Sister Anselm finally retires. That's how life works."

B. paused again. "So you're saying better to have loved and lost?" he asked.

"Absolutely," Ali told him. "One hundred percent."